A Small World

Derek Jordan

ISBN: 978-0-9847775-5-6

Published by Jordan Marked Publishing
340 S Lemon Ave #6271
Walnut, California 91789

Author contact: djordan77@comcast.net

Also by Derek Jordan

Next of Kin

Drought (short story)

A Small World 2: Seek and Destroy coming soon.

Acknowledgements

To God, Nalani, Jaci, Rudy, Speedy, Maribel, Anson, friends, the rest of my family, and supporters.

A Small World

Second Edition

1-Waterbury

Burton Street was dark, but a little illumination from the flickering streetlight shone on the interior in Big Chris's 1991 Honda Civic, making the haze of weed smoke visible. Claude coughed harshly, spat phlegm out the window, and toted the blunt once more before handing it to Rocks. Claude rode shotgun while Rocks sat in the backseat. The seventeen-year-olds waited for their prey. Claude pulled out his .22 from the big pocket of his fatigue shorts and examined it. He vowed to get back at Twalique Bennings for orchestrating their ass whipping a month ago. Twalique and six of his boys jumped them. Rocks caught the worst end of it. Both of their faces looked like they were beaten up by professional prizefighters.

Now they were hell bent on revenge.

"That motherfucker can't dodge us forever," Rocks growled from the back seat.

"He gonna feel it as soon as he step out," Claude said. "And what the fuck is you so quiet for? You ain't scared, are you?" Big Chris sat stoned face behind the wheel.

"Ain't no shook ones over here. This is how I get when I know something is about to go down," Big Chris stated while his quiet demeanor began to reveal itself. Claude noticed his involuntary leg pouncing.

"Alright man, you do look like you kind of shook. You shaking like a motherfucker. I just hope you saving your energy for the road after we buck that nigga," Claude said sinisterly while checking the safety of the gun.

"You know me C," Big Chris said flatly, trying his hardest to conceal his fear.

"A yo, you do seem a little scared."

"Nah, I'm straight bro," Big Chris said to Rocks. Big Chris heart pounded. The weed enhanced his fear. Paranoia and anxiety spread throughout his body like a disease. Claude and Rocks knew that he wasn't cut out to cause mayhem, but they didn't give a fuck. He was the only one with a car.

"Fuck all that shit. We just gonna pop this nigga and bounce. Whip this motherfucker quick out this hood and drive like you got some goddamn sense once we hit the main road," Claude instructed sternly.

"How many fucking times you gonna tell us? We know the drill. You talking to some young thoroughbreds. We got this," Rocks said

convincingly while he patted Big Chris on the shoulder a little harder than he had to.

"You in the back seat. Big Chris the driver, so where the fuck does that leave you? A nigga that's just watching the action."

"Don't even go there C. I just wanted us to catch Twalique slipping and all of us stomp him out. You the one that thought we should shoot him."

"Who in they right mind going to fuck with us after we blow this nigga top off?"

"You trying to kill that nigga?" Big Chris asked. Rocks's curiosity also peaked. Plans on killing didn't cross anyone's mind. After Claude bought the gun from Shakes, a known gun dealer, he said he was going to aim for an arm or leg. Aiming for murder wasn't in the plan. Big Chris began to feel the pressure of being a follower.

Claude cracked a subtle, wicked smile.

"Either way, he's going to feel these shells."

Big Chris wondered if Claude was going to actually kill Twalique. He thought about all the times that he brushed his mother off when she warned him that Claude was nothing but bad news and that he didn't need to be hanging with him. Claude and Rocks were arrested numerous times and had no future. They thought small and lived dangerously. Big Chris went to school everyday and was college bound. He wished at that moment that his mother were there to remind him.

Rocks rolled another blunt to kill some more time. Big Chris shook noticeably. It got Rocks's attention. Claude looked at him and regretted putting Big Chris on the task. His fear was a distraction and knew that he needed some reassurance.

"Chris, don't be getting scared on us now nigga. We need you, for real. Ain't nobody going to find out. The only thing you got to do is drive. I'm the one with the gun so you got nothin' to worry about."

"Man, he been fuckin' the shit out that bitch. He been in that motherfucker for damn near a hour. We should just catch up to that nigga…"

Twalique's departure from the ramshackle three family house stopped Rocks in mid sentence. The three teens were camped out three houses down from the target. At first sight of him, Claude took the gun off of safety and gave everyone a nod. Claude focused on him, remembering each and every blow he took from them. Rocks stopped rolling the blunt and put the unfinished remains back in the zip lock. They waited until Twalique was almost at the end of Burton before starting the car. Claude turned down the music to a whisper and took another look at his boys.

Twalique was being watched through weed-ridden eyes by young teens with gold fronts in their mouths, oblivious to the danger that awaited him only one thousand feet away.

"Let's do this," Claude finalized.

Big Chris proceeded slowly down the street. Claude beckoned him to stop the car. As soon as Twalique turned the corner to walk up Bishop Street, Claude got out of the car and moved hastily in his direction. When he got to the corner, Twalique was crossing the street.

Twalique heard footsteps and turned around. Claude stood in the middle of the street with the gun in his hand. Twalique froze.

"Remember me?" Claude asked before pulling the trigger. He aimed for Twalique's upper body, but he ended up shooting him on the lower left side of his torso.

A gunshot and screeching tires ruined the silence of the night. A lone middle-aged woman ran behind a car for cover as Big Chris made the fast getaway. Neighbors turned on the lights in their homes. Dogs barked and a car alarm went off while Twalique bled and grunted face down on the street.

. . .

"Slow the fuck down!" Claude growled as he looked around for cops. He didn't see the woman who ran for cover when she heard the gunshot.

"For real man! I ain't trying to get locked up tonight fucking with your scary ass!" Rocks added impatiently.

There was a stop sign at the top of Bishop. Big Chris stopped at it and took a left on to Pine and rode the street until he hit another stop sign. He hung a left onto Cooke and coasted down the street. While still in motion, the aimless group of teens talked about the shooting in sinister excitement.

"You see how that motherfucker dropped after Claude popped his ass? That nigga got to be dead! Let somebody else fuck with anybody in our set! Niggas is gonna feel it!" Rocks said with pathologic excitement. Big Chris got the car under control, but he didn't engage in any talk about what just happened. Instead, his mind was occupied with worry and regret. He was experiencing dark uncertainty.

"What the fuck is you going this way for? Matter of fact, we got to

ditch this whip," Claude stated, his high wearing off, wishing he hadn't done it.

"Ditch what? We ain't ditching shit! My moms will flip if I come home without this motherfucker!" Big Chris bitched, snapping out of his deep thinking about the ordeal.

"Is you fucking stupid? We hot as fuck right now and so is this whip. Your moms will really flip if she finds out you in Whalley," Claude stated logically.

"You talking that Big Chris is hot shit. We got to get rid of that burner. That's what we need to do," Rocks warned.

"You think I don't know that?" Claude asked defensively.

"Shit nigga, you sitting up there lounging with that shit like you got a permit! Like you never smoked that nigga."

They rode around aimlessly for ten minutes. Claude and Rocks provided their input on what should be done except Big Chris. Claude wiped the gun clean and threw it in the reservoir on Lakewood Road. Just when the teens thought that everything was clear, Rocks wanted to get dropped off. Claude's pager vibrated in his front pocket. He checked it and it revealed an unrecognizable number, but he recognized Tommy's code. Tommy paged Claude's pager again from the same number with 911 being the code.

"Chris, head up Darlene's crib. Something ain't right."

"You could find out what that nigga want when y'all niggas drop me off. We got no fucking business being out here as hot as we are," Rocks said nonchalantly.

"Tommy just paged me on some 911 shit. Something ain't right man," Claude stated, unable to conceal the fear in his voice.

"Chris, take me to the fucking Hill," Rocks said, his patience wearing thin.

"Yo, go to Darlene's house so we could use the phone," Claude blasted, putting Big Chris in the middle of Claude and Rock's verbal war.

"Claude, you bugging the fuck out..."

"We on Chase Ave nigga! It's hot as fuck on that side of town we just left! If we go there right now, we fucked!"

The teens rode cautiously to Bucks Hill projects to use Darlene's phone. Claude didn't know if Twalique was dead or alive. Rocks and Big Chris pondered the same thing, but they knew that they weren't the ones who pulled the trigger. That was their way of thinking. They didn't think *about conspiracy or being an accessory to a shooting.*

A few minutes later, the teens pulled into the parking space next to Darlene's blue 1996 Ford Escort. The inaudible tension among the teens increased. Big Chris killed the engine. The minacious talk died as each teen experienced their self-inflicted anxiety.

"We should've just pounded the motherfucker out, fucked his bitch, and went home," Rocks said sarcastically.

"And we riding around this bitch like we didn't just shoot that nigga," Big Chris said, finally mustering enough courage to tell Claude what he really felt.

Claude had a twisted look on his face. He looked at his peers incredulously. He knew they were riding dirty, but God only knew what kind of news Tommy had once he made the phone call.

"Alright man, I feel what y'all saying, but y'all don't feel what the fuck I'm kicking. I just shot that nigga. Tommy just paged me 911. What the fuck? I ain't trying to hear shit else right now."

They were worried. Claude suspected that someone knew something. After the last page, Rocks and Big Chris knew that they had to find out the 411, so they both knew that Claude had to make that phone call.

Claude got out of the car and headed to Darlene's apartment. He didn't know whether or not her mother was home, in bed, working, or awake, but he didn't give a shit, even though it was two thirty in the morning. When he tapped on the door, Darlene's bedroom light came on. She looked out the window. Claude stood at the front door looking up at the window, gesturing for her to come downstairs. He paced within the small confines of the walkway while he waited impatiently for Darlene to open the door.

"Damn, what took you so long? I got to use your phone," Claude said, attempting to hide his desperation.

Darlene wore her pink robe and wore a scarf to maintain her jet-black mane. She had a fatigued look on her face, still not recognizing the emotion that lay beneath her man's voice.

"Damn boy, you know my mother doesn't work this week. Do you know what time it is? Why are you here so late? She's gonna trip if she knows you're here C," Darlene said.

"Listen, I don't got time to explain. I just need to use your phone and I'm out.

She started to sense her man's tone.

"Claude, what's going on?"

"I can't get into that right now. Where's your phone?"

"Keep your voice down. I don't want to hear my mother's mouth if she wakes up," she said, handing Claude the phone.

Darlene looked on with fearful suspicion when he dialed the number. His high was gone and his first instinct kicked in; somebody knew something. Tommy picked up on the first ring.

"Yo, what up?"

He gripped the phone tight, absorbing the expected news while Darlene looked on. Claude trembled noticeably.

"What? When did you find out all this?" The cops were on to them. Twalique mentioned his name to the cops when he was being carried on the stretcher. The cops knew what vehicle they drove. After Claude shot Twalique, Big Chris almost hit a woman in her mid fifties. She stayed out there with him until the ambulance and cops arrived. She gave a detailed description of the car. Twalique couldn't make out the car description, but he knew the shooter.

After Claude spoke with Tommy, he dropped the phone. He felt that his days in society were numbered.

"Baby, talk to me! What happened?"

"I got to get the fuck outta here," Claude said with delirium as he damn near tripped over the phone wire to race out the door. "Listen, if the cops come by here, you never saw me! I can't explain this shit now, so bare with me, I'm out!"

They kissed briefly, but Darlene didn't want to let him go. She felt as if that would be the last time she would kiss him in a while; she held on to every minute of the brief passion.

After Claude broke the embrace, Darlene watched him walk out of her door. She was lost for words. She feared the worst for her boyfriend. She ran to the door and watched him get into the passenger seat of the Honda. She wondered what he did. She saw Big Chris and Rocks and gave them a menacing stare. She tried hard to lead Claude astray from the two bad influences, but she didn't know that he was more devious than all of them.

. . .

"We got to get the fuck out of here! Them motherfuckers is on to us."

"Start this shit nigga,"Rocks demanded loudly from the back seat. "We should have laid low man."

"It didn't make a difference Rocks. The cops knew about this whip almost as soon as I shot him."

Big Chris drove carefully down North Main St, the occupants in the car keeping a watchful eye for police.

"Aw shit," Big Chris blurted.

"Fuck you mean?" Rocks questioned.

"The motherfucking gas light is on!"

"You got enough gas to get us home?"

"Listen to yourself Rocks. We can't go home. I don't trust that thirty miles to the gallon shit. We'll put five beans in this bitch. That should get us to New York. Then we could fill it up. We going to have to risk it. Even if we ditch the whip, our names is buzzin' on their radios. Go to the gas station down the street," Claude instructed impatiently.

After Big Chris paid the gas station attendant, he took long strides back to the pump. When the pump read three dollars, two officers driving a squad car made their way to the gas station; they recognized the description of the car immediately. Big Chris froze for a few seconds before it dawned on him that the two cops in the cruiser were headed towards them.

"Fuck," Claude exclaimed.

The police turned the sirens on. Big Chris ran back into the car, put the car in second gear, and took a sharp left out of the gas station. He headed in the direction of Lakewood Rd, unable to make the Honda move like he wanted it to.

"This bitch can't go faster?! Hurry up," Rocks stated loudly.

When they made their way up Lakewood Rd, another cop cruiser traveled the opposite direction, heading straight towards the group. The cop trailing them clipped them from behind. None of the men wore seat belts. Big Chris lost control of the car and crashed into a telephone pole on Mass Ave. Big Chris went through the windshield headfirst; his body rolled on the hood of the car. The impact of the collision killed him instantly. The officers came out of their cruisers with their guns drawn and apprehended the teens. The car was totaled. Claude made it out of the car accident with a medium-sized cut on his cheek. When Big Chris went through the windshield, Claude caught the tail end of a shard of glass. Rocks didn't have a scratch. As the cops led them to the cruiser, the two teens stole a glance at the grotesque sight of Big Chris's lifeless, open-eyed, mangled body.

...

The sound of the correctional officer's voice announcing

rec took Claude out of his zone. He had no idea how much time went by since he picked up the ten year old photo. He looked at the picture again and noticed how young they all looked. They were posted up against Big Chris Honda Civic. The picture was taken three days before the shooting. In the picture, Claude wore braids and had a small, frail frame. He wore a black tank top and baggy blue jean shorts. Rocks, tall and wiry, had on a "Boss" t-shirt and his hair cut in a high fade. Big Chris, medium sized and burly, rocked an Afro with an oversized t-shirt. His leaned on his car with his arms crossed. Claude continued to gaze at the photo, wondering where all the years went since his first day of incarceration.

Claude Porter could never get used to the horrid smell of prison despite being incarcerated since 2000. Even though he was in a level two facility, the smell seemed to only get worse. There were one hundred twenty people who lived in the dorm and one would think that there was a better system in place to minimize the funky body odor, especially in the dead heat of summer. He transferred from a level four facility shortly after being approved for parole. He had lived the last thirteen years in prison cells rooming with one cellmate. Bunking with multiple people was a difficult task for him.

Getting used to living out in society would be another challenge for him. Convicted of attempted murder and invading responsibility, the mandatory minimum of sixteen years was a gift given to him by the judge because of the Alford Doctrine; he didn't admit any guilt, but acknowledged the state had enough evidence to convict him. He had two other drug cases pending and one was dropped due to a technicality. His youth played a major role in his sentencing, not to mention Twalique's survival. He would have had more time if he hadn't rid himself of the gun.

He had taken good care of his body, adding twenty-five pounds of muscle to his former frail frame. He was beefed up, bullnecked, and virile. He walked around the prison with a strong silence, his face tight and belligerent. He was medium height. His brown skin was clear with the exception of the scar on his left cheek, a scar that left a reminder of the day Big Chris went through the windshield. He displayed perfectly boxed teeth. He had a Spaniard style mustache and goatee that was always trimmed to perfection.

As he finished the last set of his decline push-ups, William "Tech" Freeman, a dark-skinned, tall cat from Bridgeport, walked in his dorm with a sullen look on his face while Claude paraded a huge smile. He gave him a look indicating that Tech had something for him.

"I think you owe me something playa. I heard Floyd Mayweather popped shotted the fuck out of Manny Pacquiao," Claude said in his deep, husky voice. Without hesitation, Tech handed him four packs of Oodles of Noodles for the boxing bet he lost.

"I like Pacman though. He just couldn't touch Floyd," Tech said.

"Niggas told me Mayweather schooled that motherfucker. He made him frustrated and all that shit," Claude said as he adjusted his hair clippers.

"You won't be having any more wins," Tech said with confidence as he left Claude's dorm to go to his own. Claude laughed and proceeded to cut his hair.

Later on that evening, Claude stood silent as he waited in the chow line. He noticed Mercer giving out small proportions of mashed potatoes. Mercer became annoyed when he spotted Claude. He told Claude that he would give him extra portions of food for one week if Pacquiao beat Mayweather. Mercer, just like Tech, lost the bet. Unlike Tech, Mercer was a sore loser. He went on rampages placing bets. If he won a bet, which was a rare occasion, he'd be the first one in someone's face. If he lost, he'd catch a case of amnesia. Claude could care less about Mercer being watched by CO Walker. Mercer had no commissary to gamble with, so he had to give Claude extra food at chow time. Mercer initiated the deal.

Mercer sweated underneath his brown prison gear when Claude stood in line and paraded a sly smirk.

"I can't keep doing this shit. These rednecks are watching nigga," Mercer said discreetly. C.O. Walker eyed him suspiciously.

"Fuck that. You were the one who put that extra food shit on the table. Not my fault that you have no commissary."

"That's fucked up Claude. You trying to make a nigga lose his job."

Claude felt no empathy for him. He didn't even like him, but would have paid Mercer any type of debt if he lost. C.O. Walker's sudden appearance made Claude fall back. His six foot six frame towered over Mercer's short, round body.

"Hey fucker, if you want to give more food to these fucking rodents, don't come out later for rec, fuck stick! And if I catch you doing it again, it's gonna be a Class A for your fat ass," C.O. Walker yelled.

That was one of the tools in a guard's circle of power. Tickets were the silent factors for guards going home every night in one piece. Without the use of tickets, more guards would be attacked. If one had a parole hearing in the near future, a ticket could ruin a welcome home party. If someone were doing life, a ticket would be used for toilet paper. Guards secretly distanced themselves from lifers.

"This includes you Porter. Go sit the fuck down!"

"Yes sir." Claude was being facetious.

C.O. Walker eyed the bulky black man for a moment and walked away. Claude knew he had to be careful.

As Claude walked his way to the table where he normally ate, Flip looked at him proudly as he made room for him to sit down.

"That's exactly what those cocksuckers want. They want niggas to say something back so they could get a reaction an' shit," Flip stated. He had a half-inch knife scar on his face. Unlike Claude, Flip was self-conscious about his scar. Flip's scar was bigger and morbid. After being sliced in the face in his youth, he became increasingly indignant as he got older.

Terrance "Flip" Riggs, a medium sized, light skinned and solidly built man was from the west coast. He flew out to New York to help his cousin Nick move some weight. Six months after arriving in Queens, Flip and Nick was parked at a red light when some masked gunman drove by and opened fire on the two dealers. A bullet entered the left side of Nick's head and exited out of the middle of his cranium. Flip was shot twice. He was hit on the upper left thigh and underneath his left armpit. While he bled and gasped, he was able to make out the voice of one of the masked men while they searched the car. It was Big Foot; there was no doubt about it. He had just bought Nick and Flip two rounds of drinks at the bar. Because of Nick's loose lips and flamboyant style, he leaked the amount of money he had in the car, which was over thirty thousand dollars cash.

Once the men found what they were looking for, they didn't bother to see if Flip was still alive. They moved hastily to the car, got in it, and sped off. Flip knew that they were set-up and followed.

He packed his shit and moved to Connecticut after his recovery. He set up shop in Bridgeport. He arrived there with thirty-five grand. He rented in apartment and bought a crasher. Needing to flip something, he rode the streets, meeting one person that led to another person that had the purest grade. Once he identified the right people, business boomed. Three months after his arrival in Bridgeport, he stacked enough greenbacks to head back west.

Victor, Flip's connect, called him and asked to meet him in Westport for a transaction so he wouldn't have to be alone in case the deal went south. Flip was confident that the meeting meant more money, so he figured he could postpone his scheduled trip back west to make a few extra grand.

The men were in the master stateroom of the large, Viking convertible yacht when the DEA invaded it and pinned them on the floor along with Mike, the yacht's owner. A CI said that there had been shady activity surrounding the yacht for months. Flip was scheduled to leave Connecticut that night.

After a year of negotiating with the district attorney, Flip's lawyer got him an eight-year deal. Considering the circumstances and the consequences if the case went to trial, eight years wasn't that bad. That was the best deal his attorney was able to muster. Victor, on the other hand, felt that his case should be heard in trial. He was offered twelve and a half, but he declined. After going against his lawyer's advice, Victor's choice was granted. In the outcome, he received a thirty-five year sentence. Flip was finishing off his sentence. If Victor weren't so stupid, he would have been finishing off a single digit sentence. He had no prison record at the time of his arrest. Flip was on the waiting list for a halfway house. Claude and Flip met eight years ago when Flip came to Cheshire CI.

"Oh, no doubt," Claude stated as he scooped a spoonful of mashed potatoes in his mouth. "They ain't gonna get that reaction shit outta me. I haven't slept on a soft mattress in ten years. I'm trying to go home."

J-Rock, born James Sharif, dropped the remaining juice into the mouth of his dark, gaunt face, slammed the empty juice box on the table, and continued to undo one of the thick corn rows in his hair. He was a dark, short, slender man with sharp features. His eyes looked like black dots. He was dangerous. Finishing out a bid for drug distribution, he would have been out on the streets sooner if he didn't get packed in from a work release program for a dirty urine.

"That shit could only go so far though. Those fucking pigs could catch a nigga venting to himself about his girl leaving, taken the baby and all that shit. Some niggas got to spend dimes in this bitch listening to nothin' but bad news coming from mothafuckers they thought they could count on," J-Rock exclaimed.

Power, an overweight forty six year old light skin recidivist, shook his head while he stroked his long goatee.

"You can't be fallen victim to that type of shit. That means they would always win if everybody had that mentality. You got to think about shit like that young blood. They use your personal outside shortcomings against you. You can't let them get to you. You can't give those pigs any type of leverage," Power emphasized.

J-Rock shook his head in disgust. He didn't like Power and didn't feel like hearing him out. His input wasn't needed. He decided to nip it in the bud.

"Mind your fuckin' business bro. Save all your Elijah Muhammad shit for the new jacks."

The table fell silent. Claude was one of the few that knew J-Rock didn't care for Power. He didn't want them getting out of hand. He didn't want them bringing unnecessary attention to their table.

"Come on man, just chill," Flip stated as if he read Claude's mind.

Power gave J-Rock a stare that could've meant murder in the streets. "Naw, it's cool. If the nigga got a problem, I want him to get it the fuck off his chest." Power took off his glasses.

"I already got it off."

Everyone at the table looked around nervously, hoping the two men arguing didn't catch the attention of the passing guards. Luckily, they didn't, but the reckless eyeballing between the two men ignited more tension that would have escalated if the situation didn't have an intervention.

"Settle this some other time. Not here, not now," Claude said casually.

The conversation went smoothly after Claude's intervention. Flip took up the bulk of the chow time by telling Cali war stories. It eased the tension between J-Rock and Power. They held on to their glare, but Power decided to be the man and drop the issue. He knew it wouldn't be long before someone ended up killing him.

Later on during the evening, Claude stretched out across his bunk, ignoring the stench of bowel movements. As he began to wonder about the outside world, his introductory thoughts on it came to a halt by hearing Bronson's voice.

"You scared to go home," Bronson, a tall, yellowed toned, crooked eyed cat from New Haven asked while he climbed to the top of the bed.

He was definitely afraid to go home. When he made parole, he got excited. The more he started to anticipate his release, the more anxious he became. He had been to every prison in Connecticut after sentencing, starting with Manson Youth Institution, with the exception of a few level two facilities in his fifteen-year bid. He knew that he had to start living a normal life once he was released; moreover, he knew that he had to prepare for a battle with society. He knew he was going get a low paying job. He lacked a supportive family. The only person he had was his sister, and she had her own issues. He would be paroling to her house and he knew she was on the struggling end. His mother had been in Niantic since 1995 for killing her boyfriend out of self-defense. She was eligible for parole in 2017. Other than his mother and sister, most of his other relatives were either incarcerated, dead, or caught up in their own madness.

"Believe me C, I didn't want to talk about that shit either," Bronson added as he noticed Claude's quiet demeanor when he asked the question about his release. Bronson knew his freedom walked all over his mind. He had been around the system twice and could definitely tell if someone had a nearby release date. Claude stared at the bottom of Bronson's mattress, realizing that it was a good time to talk about his fear. He hoped that someone would listen.

"I feel you. I probably won't even know how to feel around people who hasn't seen a jail cell. I could see myself not fitting in. There ain't nothin' out there for us. The only jobs for us are the scrap jobs like McDonalds, Burger Kings, and Wendy's. I wouldn't mind doing something that is going to generate residual income. Who the fuck is gonna give a nigga like me a chance with my record? Don't get me wrong; I can't wait to get out of here, but I could wait for the bullshit that is in store for me."

Bronson didn't react to Claude's frustration. Bronson has had the same problems in the past about creating a new life. That was why he chose the streets because it was all he knew. He tried to make the transition and gave up.

"You knew the consequences when you were out there like that. You gotta start from scratch. If you that serious about doing something with your life, you have to get some credentials; some type of expanded identity, "Bronson emphasized.

Claude sat up in his bunk.

"You don't get tired of this shit?"

"I can't get tired of it C. I got to live. I don't have ambitions like that. My first ambition is the streets 'cause that's all I know. If I can't hustle my dollar, I can't make my dollar. I said fuck my dreams a long time ago. Fuck that. I ain't kissing no white man's ass."

Claude leaned over and looked up at Bronson, wondering if he was serious about not chasing his dreams. "So what are you trying to say?"

"You got to do what you know how to do. No matter what job you get, legit or illegal, every job has consequences if the rules are broken."

Claude tucked his head back underneath the bunk and put his hands on the back of his head.

"I know what you're saying, but you can't hustle for the rest of your life. That shit gets old. Even if a nigga doing it, making millions, top dogs, so called untouchable, you can't even get the comfort of taking a shit without a nigga breathing jealousy." He shook his head slowly and quickly cut Bronson off before he interrupted his point and continued. "Niggas be walking around feeling grimy and paranoid an' shit." Claude paused and continued. "Not for the rest of my life. Fuck that. There has to be something else, it has to be. I hustled my entire life and shot somebody, but he still breathing. I'm paying the price. Someone got killed in the process and I spent more than a decade in here, so why do niggas like us got to be condemned for the rest of our lives? If I hustle, it's just gonna make matters worse. I gotta prepare my mind for struggle, you know what I mean?"

"You trying to say you ain't hustling when you get out."

"I don't know. I couldn't tell you," Claude answered truthfully.

Bronson chuckled while he adjusted his tiny commissary fan.

"So why are you on this good boy shit?"

"It's not no good boy shit. Its just plan A or B. Whatever one you want to pick first."

Bronson maneuvered his head over the edge of his bunk.

"Just remember that you may have to do something you don't want to do to be legit. Keep thinking that you could just walk out the game like that. The game always finds you. That shit be finding you when you rock bottom. That's when you realize that everything around you is a hustle. Why stress and you got fiends walking up and down your street with money or some good shit they stole? When I get out, I ma' go see my man so he could front me a brick, or at least a half, if that. Watch Claude. Try that legit shit if you want. You coming home off of a fifteen year stretch. Good jobs ain't trying to invest money into niggas like us, but we save the state money by doing that outside clearance shit. Fuck that. I make my money my own way. I got one more bid left in me." He lay down on his bunk. "Stick to ya guns C, stick to ya guns," Bronson concluded as he made one final adjustment to his fan before nodding off to sleep.

Claude was wide-awake an hour after the lights went out. He began to scan his dorm and wondered how he lived in confined environments for over a decade. The only items that stood out in his cubicle were pictures of Sahara, his niece Destiny, his mother in her Niantic sweat suit, Big Chris' funeral program, and "Aunt" Pearl, Claude and Sahara's surrogate mother who raised them following their mother's incarceration. Pearl died in 2001, which was the last time he caught a ticket. He found out he couldn't attend her funeral because she wasn't a "real" relative. There were no papers indicating that she was his legal guardian. He was so enraged that he cracked the glass of the sally port with his foot. The guards led him out of the unit in handcuffs and spent a few months in Northern.

He had a picture of Darlene, but that picture was shredded when she came to visit him while he was at Manson. She told him she had a boyfriend and that she was pregnant. He was only nineteen years old when he felt his first dose of heartbreak. If he was a seasoned career criminal entering the system for the thirtieth time, he would not have had any expectations of loyalty. He was so high on himself upon his admission to the department of correction that he didn't think Darlene was capable of hanging out with another man.

He stared at his pictures in the dark for the next hour. He stared at Big Chris's funeral program, capturing anything he could in the dark. Where did the time go? He reached for the program and took it off the wall next to his bunk. He held the front of the program that had Big Chris's picture and stared at it, remembering when Tommy sent it to him. He sulked in New

Haven Correctional Center when Big Chris's body was laid to rest. He began to drift. His hand released the program and it fell to the floor.

. . .

"Porter, wake the fuck up and stand against the wall. You too Bronson," C.O. Smith demanded abrasively.

Claude and Bronson were moving too slow for C.O. Smith. They were reluctantly getting off of their bunks.

"Get off your fucking asses!"

The guards on the night shift would do anything to stay awake. C.O. Smith stood on Big Chris' funeral program. Claude was pissed, but kept quiet. They rummaged through everything.

"Take off those jumpsuits. We got a call saying you two fucks may be holding weapons in here," C.O. Zimmerman lied.

"How the fuck could we keep weapons in this bitch? Y'all mothafuckers don't got shit on us! Always fucking wit niggas," Bronson yelled loud enough for the entire dorm to hear.

"Bronson, shut the fuck up before we send your ass up north with the rest of the jail celebrity fucks! Now shut the fuck up before that happens boy," C.O. Zimmerman yelled. The inmates stared at C.O. Zimmerman with uncut venom. Bronson wanted to smack the toothbrush, Adolf Hitler mustache off of the short, Polish stubby guard.

Claude was heated from C.O. Zimmerman's "boy" comment.

"You shut the fuck up pig! That's why your wife is fucking my man. Yeah cracka, I know about that birthmark she got on her ass," Bronson yelled.

Claude beckoned Bronson not to say anything anymore, but he knew it was too late. Bronson broke the switch. A guard who was properly trained would know that one shouldn't bring their personal business to work. People like Bronson preyed on that type of shit. An inmate had all day to think about ways to fuck with their authority. Rumor had it that C.O. Zimmerman's wife was a slut. Bronson wasn't the only one who knew about the birthmark on her ass. The administration in the prison system was grimy. They were the people that put C.O. Zimmerman's business out there. It was three in the morning and every inmate in the dorm heard the commotion.

As soon as Bronson's last word came out of his mouth, C.O. Zimmerman swung and caught Bronson at the tip of his jaw. Bronson quickly brushed it off, displayed a subtle smile, and caught C.O. Zimmerman with a short and sharp right that made Zimmerman's head cock back before falling to the floor. C.O. Smith didn't bother to intervene. He pulled his body alarm. Two other guards touring the dorm joined the chaos.

"Put your jumpsuit back on Porter," C.O. Smith demanded like he just ran a marathon. "Tonight is your lucky night asshole." C.O. Smith joined the rest of the guards who had to escort Bronson away from the area. Two other guards arrived at the scene and helped C.O. Zimmerman off the floor and guided him out of the dormitory.

It was a situation of patience being tested, Claude figured. He would be tested until the day he left. It was too bad he won't be able to vibe with Bronson anymore. He was on his way to Northern.

2-Los Angeles

Aaron Banks's dilapidated low-rise flat had seen better days. The shag carpet was littered with cigarette butts, blunt roaches, and empty bottles of Hennessy Cognac. The food on the dishes in the sink was stuck to them like magnets on a refrigerator. The gnats seemed as if they were guarding them. A gaping hole in the wall came as a result of a domestic violent dispute. The floor model television displayed Sports center in which the men in the slum paid no mind.

Aaron, Flex, Prime, and D-Bone played Spades, killing time before the meeting with the new connect Prime's man, D-Bone, had a connection with, which meant big money. Aaron was in his late twenties and he starved and itched for a come up. He felt less of a man because his twenty-five year old girlfriend was making every end meet. He had no time for games despite the logic Prime told him earlier. He told Aaron the new connect D-Bone had could put more bulges in their pocket.

D-Bone's heartbeat increased as he felt Aaron's eyes penetrate through his person. With a quick glance, D-Bone zoomed in on his large, dark-skinned, six foot four, jail built bulky frame. Aaron had a clean-shaven hostile face that seemed it had a permanent frown on it. He wore his hair in cornrow braids. He was cruel and vicious and didn't care about anyone outside of his circle. He looked at D-Bone as if he stole money from him.

Dennis "D-Bone" Howard, an attractive, thin twenty-four year old, light-skinned, green-eyed drug trafficker, managed Stephanie & Company in Beverly Hills. He wore a tight Affliction shirt and plaid twill denim jeans. He was not built for the game. He conducted his extra curricular activity because of easy money and greed, not because he had to do it to survive. He had a degree in communications and made good money from being the manager at his place of employment. He couldn't wait until Prime took him out of Aaron's ramshackle low rise flat and Aaron's presence.

Oscar "Prime" Pittman met Aaron in 1989. From the first

day that he met him in first grade, Aaron always intimidated Prime, especially after the incident where he stabbed a classmate with a pocketknife. He missed his eye by a hair. Prime was in shock along with the other kids as they watched Aaron standing over the boy. He was in a fetal position on the ground trying desperately to stop the massive bleeding. Aaron was exhibiting behaviors that were abnormal at a young age. The rest of the students were horrified as Aaron rode in the back of the cruiser. At six, Aaron got expelled and went to an alternative school.

Aaron and Prime's separation didn't last long. A month after the incident, Aaron popped up at Prime's house unannounced at eleven thirty at night. Prime's mother, Janet, put some clothes on and took Aaron home. Aaron's mother, who was murdered that same year and a few months after Aaron stabbed a classmate, looked like a walking zombie when she came to the door. She wore a torn t-shirt and panties, showing no decency. Her hair was tied in a ponytail that was bound to fall out. Her hair thinned on one side. Her teeth were stained yellow and decaying. She gave Aaron a nasty stare while he hid behind Prime's mother.

"Boy, if you don't bring your fucking ass in this house!" she snarled at him as she pulled Aaron from the back of Janet's lower body and smacked him in the back of the head repeatedly until he distanced himself from his mother's flurry. She thanked Prime's mother loudly and slammed the door. Janet did not want her son hanging with Aaron because she knew about the stabbing incident.

Aaron's younger cousin Walter "Flex" Banks was a heavyset brown skinned man with a mini-afro. He had cocaine in front of him that he placed in lines. He wore an old, number eight Kobe Bryant jersey over a purple, slightly soiled t-shirt and dingy Southpole jean shorts that extended over his knees. Aaron and Flex came up in the same household. Aaron's grandparents were too old and had lived beyond their child   raising years to keep up with the boys.

As they neared the conclusion of the game, Aaron held out the joker and slammed the card on the table, breaking the short-lived silence that took over the house.

"Game motherfuckers!" Aaron said sternly.

Aaron and Flex sniffed lines of coke off the table, enjoying the fruits of their winnings. Aaron sniffed another line, looked up at Prime and D-Bone through watery eyes, and ran the back of his hand across his nose.

"I think y'all niggas need to learn a new strategy," Aaron said.

"That's the only way y'all niggas could win. Cheatin' ass mothafuckers," Prime stated jokingly.

Prime sat with his hands mounted on top of one another. His triple X shirt was too big for him. He was six feet even and his skin sagged. Prime used to be three hundred pounds. A couple of years of smoking weed and walking made him lose the weight. Aaron would joke and say that he needs to start lifting. His skin sagged. His head was huge and he sported a thin, dark mustache. His yellow complexion was sprinkled with blemishes. His new weight of one hundred and seventy five pounds made him look worse.

"How y'all figure we cheating? Stop playing if y'all don't want to lose no more money," Aaron said as he gathered all the books from each side.

D-Bone didn't feel safe. Prime was the only one that he was comfortable with; however, he didn't know Prime long enough to trust him, but he did trust Prime to keep him safe. He didn't come over to the house to be bullied psychologically; he was there to kill time. He cursed Colin for taking long with what he had to do. He thought they were going to play one round of spades and get down to business. A half an hour to Colin meant an hour and a half.

D-Bone waited for everyone to stop talking.

"Good game. Y'all won. Let's go and take care of that business," D-Bone said nervously.

Aaron looked at D-Bone.

"We move when I say so."

D-Bone looked at Prime as a cue to calm his man.

"Chill. This nigga don't mean no harm. He just 'bout his money. No harm in that." Prime didn't want to challenge Aaron and he picked his words carefully. Aaron understood, but he still had it in him to fuck with him.

Aaron nodded as he began to shuffle the cards. He continued to watch D-Bone. Aaron wanted to make moves, but he wasn't going at D-Bone's request.

The men played three more hands. Aaron got up from the table and went upstairs to get a wave cap. D-Bone went to the bathroom. Flex was looking for his cell phone. He was high on coke. As Prime began to put the cards back into the box, Sonya walked through the door carrying a duffle bag of her personal belongings and a bag of groceries. She had a look of disdain on her face. The place was a mess.

Prime came to her rescue and grabbed both of the bags out of her hands and placed them on the counter.

"Thank you," Sonya responded quietly while she looked at the mess around the kitchen.

"You're welcome," Prime said. He fought the temptation of marveling at her. Aaron was jealous and weary of any man in her presence.

She wore a colorful nursing uniform with a pair of Sketches. Her caramel complexion skin was smooth and flawless. Her hair cascaded to the middle of her back. She was average height for a woman. Her C-cup breasts were firm. Her stomach was flat. She had light brown eyes that slant upwards, enhanced by beautiful dark long eyelashes. She was exhausted from working all afternoon. She waited forty minutes for a cab when her shift ended. Aaron was supposed to pick her up, but the potential deal distracted him. Sonya didn't look upset. She was a kind-hearted person. She spoke with a southern drawl and was thoughtful of others. She loved Aaron, but the love was fading from the mental and physical abuse he inflicted on her. She looked like she could use some sleep. She knew her man well and wasn't planning on putting up with his shit any longer.

Aaron walked into the kitchen, witnessing Prime putting the bag up for Sonya, and leered at Sonya coldly.

"What are you doing home?"

"Because my shift ended...an hour ago," Sonya said sarcastically. She turned around to unload the grocery bag Prime put on the counter. She was putting the groceries up in their rightful places as if Aaron wasn't there.

"I thought you had to do a double."

Sonya exhaled deeply.

"Aaron please. Not right now. I just walked in the door," she said quietly.

Aaron looked at Sonya incredulously. Prime wanted to intervene, but he lacked the heart to do it.

"You come up in here and start that bullshit. Now you don't want to finish what you fucking started.

Sonya didn't respond. She knew that if she retaliated after his last statement, he would muster up the nerve to attack her. She knew Flex and Prime were afraid of Aaron so she would be as good as dead if he decided to go that route.

"Yeah, you know you can't say shit."

Sonya put a carton of orange juice in the refrigerator and noticed someone coming out of the bathroom with a grin on his face.

"Sonya, what's up girl?" D-Bone asked excitedly as he came out the bathroom.

Sonya faked a half smirk to hide her disgust at Aaron. She wished that D-Bone could take a hint. Anything else would add insult to injury. Their past encounter was innocent. His grandmother was her patient at the hospital. D-Bone was thankful for her quality of work.

"Hey D, how are you?" D-Bone was oblivious to Aaron's growing anger. In an instant, he connected the dots. His fear faded because Colin never went anywhere to do business alone. He knew that he had Earl and B-Bum with him and he would see them in a matter of minutes. Sonya glanced at Aaron and knew he was going to question her later about her association with D-Bone. She picked up her purse from the counter and went to the bedroom.

. . .

Sonya Williams was from Dallas, Texas and graduated from the University of Southern California with a degree in nursing. Two years later, she met Aaron while she shopped at Walmart. She always told herself she would never date a drug dealer, but she did. Aaron's features and charm swayed her. He had no job, but the money he brought to the table was consistent. When Aaron was caught in a drug sting and bagged, Sonya supported him during his case until Aaron's lawyer found a loophole. After nine months of sitting in county, Aaron was discharged.

His major supplier got busted a few weeks after Aaron was released. When his pockets became thin, he displaced it on Sonya. A year and a half later, she was at her breaking point.

Sonya lit a candle and took a long bubble bath. She closed her eyes, took a deep breath, and contemplated a move out of California.

. . .

Meanwhile, Aaron, Flex, Prime, and D-Bone camped out in front of Colin's house on Monteith Drive. The house looked conventional and a dark green manicured lawn flanked it. They waited for Colin's arrival. Aaron cracked the window to Sonya's 2010 Chevy Tahoe and exhaled the greenery out into the cool August night while he listened to the mild commotion within the environment. Aaron gave the two white teenagers skateboarding on the sidewalk an intimidating stare. A car almost hit one of them as he desperately tried to avoid hitting the truck. They only saw Aaron and Flex in the front seat with only a glance. The teens did not want to engage themselves in a stare down with the two ruthless men.

"What time is this dude coming?" Flex asked impatiently.

"That's what I'm saying. Trying to get this shit done and over with," Aaron added.

On cue, Colin pulled up in a forest green, 2014 Audi A4. He turned the car off and two other men exited it and walked towards the other group. D-Bone was relieved to see his comrades because he was scared to death of being in Aaron's presence.

Aaron looked at Colin and noticed his size. Colin was the size of a NFL running back. His white wife beater looked as if it stuck to every single cut in his chiseled body. The chain he wore was custom-made with diamonds. The medallion attached to it enhanced it. B-Bum was a skinny, dark-skinned individual with crooked teeth. He wore jean shorts with an official Cleveland Cavalier LeBron James jersey. Earl was an obese man who wore his hair in twists.

"Names aren't important. Let's just handle this shit now so we could be on our way," Colin said curtly. He led the men into the residence.

Colin's Rolex glistened. Aaron looked at it. His motivation grew. He wanted the fast cash, cars, and jewelry.

The living room was simple. It contained two black leather sofas, a fifty-five inch smart Samsung television, and a round glass table. Earl and B-Bum stood in the living room looking like bouncers. Both men stood there with their arms folded.

"Let me see what y'all working with since you in a hurry," Aaron said coolly.

Colin nodded and looked at his henchmen, letting his subordinates know, without words, to watch the strangers.

Let me hurry up and get these bitch ass niggas out of here, Colin thought as he made his way upstairs.

Colin opened a safe and withdrew two kilos. He knew using his grandmother's house as a stash spot was fucked up, but he made good use with it since her admission into a convalescent home. He figured he'd use it before the bank took it over.

He walked down the staircase and what he saw next heightened his senses; the barrel of Aaron's nine. He grabbed Colin by the collar and led him down the rest of the stairs. Colin stole a glance at the bleeding bodies on the carpet and knew silencers cut them down. Without warning, Aaron squeezed the trigger and blew Colin's brains all over the wall.

Prime stood in the middle of the bodies in shock. Murder happened in front of him. He stood with the bodies while Aaron and Flex rummaged and looted the house. Aaron had the duffle draped over his shoulder; he beckoned the followers. Prime ran behind the cousins. He didn't pull the trigger, but he was just as guilty. He pondered his future as the men quietly made their escape.

. . .

"We had to do it. Niggas would have came after us."

Prime wasn't buying in. They were supposed to rob them; murder wasn't in the plan. He was still in a shocked state and declined to say anything. Aaron and Flex had blood and murder on their hands; he didn't think they would have a problem doing it again.

. . .

Sonya was numb and her vagina was sore. Aaron pulled up his pants and buckled them. He forcefully thrusted his dick into Sonya's womb while she slept. Despite Sonya's hard resistance, he overpowered her and forced himself on her petite frame. She gave up on the battle and allowed him to have his way.

"Go clean yourself up. And if I get any word you fucked that nigga D-Bone, he'll be one dead ass nigga," he threatened. He looked at her and felt regret before leaving the house.

Sonya balled up, cried, and continued to ponder her move out of California.

3-Webster CI
Cheshire, CT

The day was hot and humid. Claude didn't mind it. The dorms were funky and the air was paramount. His days were numbered in the penitentiary. He looked forward to new beginnings. The days drew closer to his discharge, but his anxiety increased. His only responsibility in the last fifteen years was waking up, eating, shitting, playing chess, cards, basketball, gambling, reading, and being a burden on taxpayers.

Flip spotted Claude walking and caught up with him.

"Whats the word?"

"Any day now; waiting for my name to be called. You ain't too far from me bro."

Flip smiled. He was nearing his discharge date as well. He just came from using the phone; he was getting his outside shit in order before stepping back onto the streets.

"Yeah, not that far, but Cali is calling me though. Once my parole is up, I'm gone."

"Wouldn't mind stepping out of Connecticut either. I want to see the world. This jail shit is for the birds," Claude said.

Flip looked at Claude and maintained the snarl he normally had on his face.

"I got one more bid left in me. If you come up with something and I'm still in CT, put me on."

Claude laughed.

"I could put you on to a job."

The men laughed and continued their walk. Claude hoped he would never have a taste of the underworld again; that was his plan. Flip didn't have any legal ambition. Flip was a walking time bomb. He planned on doing exactly what brought him to prison.

The men played a few games of chess, traded war stories, and talked about freedom until Flip went back to his bunk.

Claude sat on his bunk. His fear of not succeeding legally kept him up. He knew parole was a lot harder than what people made it out to be, but his plans was to expel all the odds despite lacking credentials. He thought about the first week of his fifteen-year bid. People cracked jokes with him and said he was still shitting McDonalds. He'd been told as a youth he'd be murdered or incarcerated like his mother. He remembered how he felt the day Darlene told him she was pregnant. Now he was at the end of his sentence and was curious about what waited for him beyond prison walls.

While he processed his life, Domino walked smoothly into his vision. Claude wasn't thrilled and was not in any mood to talk to him. Dreaded, brown-skinned, and medium sized, he was from Waterbury. He was a few years older than Claude. He made money back in the day and was in and out of prison since he was fifteen. During Claude's incarceration, Domino had been released and readmitted three times.

The men went into general conversation. They spoke about the streets. Claude knew Domino was hanging on to old glory. He wanted and needed a come-up. Most importantly, Claude was aware of the bad blood between Rocks and Domino. Rocks was the hottest thing since crack and Domino was mad at Rocks's shine. He wanted a piece of the pie and he was only getting the crust. The conversation was tolerable until Domino threw shade at Rocks.

"You about to be home fam. I feel you on that legal path. Just be careful. It ain't the same. I know the hearts of men change, but remember, association breeds similarity."

Claude caught on.

"What are you trying to insinuate bro? I ain't into riddles." Claude felt his anger rising.

Domino shrugged arrogantly.

"I got no problems with you fam. Just giving you some wise words. You haven't been on the streets in years. I just don't want your existence short-lived. Its not the same C."

Claude got up and got in Domino's face. Their noses touched.

"Is that a threat motherfucker?"

Flip was returning Claude's hair clippers. He was in the vicinity and he intervened on time. He pulled Claude away before the spectators chimed in. Domino seized the moment.

"Not a threat, but it is what it is bro."

Domino walked away.

"You know better bro. Don't risk your freedom over these cocksuckers."

Claude didn't dispute his friend. He was right. He could have ruined his chances of discharge, which was exactly what Domino wanted. Flip spoke to Claude until the lights when out. When Flip left, Claude pondered the situation and knew that he would have to keep an eye on Domino. The beef with him and Rocks was bad, but Claude didn't want any part of it. He wanted to walk that legal road.

4-Los Angeles

Sonya sat in the musty break room at her job. She felt the small mouse under her left eye. Aaron beat her up and raped her the night before. All day she tried to figure out a way to leave him. She came close to calling her sister. She wanted a solution. Aaron had treated Sonya like a queen for the last two days because of the abuse he inflicted on her, but she knew that he had caused her too much drama. It may be tomorrow or the day after when he flipped the script. She didn't want anything to do with Aaron after she leaves him, not even a friendship. She harbored no love for him. He was a dud. He didn't appreciate her worth.

The industrial clock ticked. Sonya sighed when she looked at it. It read a quarter past seven. She would have to endure five more hours of serving patients and facing her co-workers with the small mouse underneath her left eye. Trudy Douglas, Sonya's co-worker and friend, walked through the door. She carried a hand full of change so she could get a snack out of the vending machine. A short, top heavy, pudgy, light skinned woman in her mid-twenties, she wore a black weave that cascaded below her shoulders. She had soft eyes with long eyelashes. She was a party chick and lived the nightlife, which explained her absenteeism. Every weekend and on any given work night, she'd bar hop and danced.

Trudy adjusted herself in the seat across the table and looked at her with remorseful eyes.

"When is it going to stop? When he is locked up for murdering you?"

"It's going to stop tonight," Sonya said curtly. She kept the rape quiet.

Trudy looked at her friend again and knew that she was serious. Sonya would normally make excuses or justify the situation.

"Is there anything I could do to help?"

"Maybe, but I can't get into it now. Just leave it like that for now. Let me think it through," Sonya said as she stood up and stretched.

"Are you going to let me know tonight?"

Sonya sighed.

"Trudy, I will let you know, trust me."

Trudy looked disappointed.

"How are you going to just bring something up and just leave it there?"

"I will let you know. I can't give you any details without me knowing them," Sonya said, trying not to sound harsh. She knew she would need Trudy's help.

"What time are you getting off?" Sonya asked her, changing the subject.

"I'm supposed to leave at midnight but I was thinking about leaving around eleven. I gotta pick up my son from my mother's because her and her boyfriend goin' to Vegas for a few days."

Sonya wanted to leave early too. She felt embarrassed. She cursed Aaron for scaring her.

"If I ask to leave at eleven, could you take me home?" Sonya realized that she didn't have an official ride. As usual, Aaron had her vehicle.

"Have I ever said no?" Trudy asked good-naturedly.

Trudy never denied Sonya a ride, but the amount of sick days she took in recent weeks had caused Sonya to walk, catch a cab, or stay at work until Aaron showed up, sometimes a few hours after her shift was over.

The women finished their lunch break and went back to their post. Mrs. Patterson, an elderly patient, said her daughter was killed because of domestic violence. She confronted Sonya about her black eye and gave her advice. The women did their duties and hung out in the nursing station for the rest of the shift.

After clocking out at eleven, Trudy drove her 2015 maroon Camry slowly on Crenshaw, going with the flow of traffic, trying to seek attention from the young, unemployed black men that stood in front of drab storefronts. Sonya leered out the window, eyeballing the cracked sidewalks and the window bars and security gates that front everything from the auto-repair shops to the churches. She began to link Aaron with the sight of Crenshaw. She knew she had to go. The thought of Mrs. Patterson and the message she provided bothered her. Aaron was a dangerous man and he was going to end up killing her.

As Trudy made the left onto Sonya's street, Sonya broke the silence.

"Trudy, listen, I just have to know one thing. You said you wanted to help, right?"

"Sonya, you know I want to help you. Whatever you need me to do, I'm here for you." She parked her car next to Sonya's residence.

"I am doing this behind his back. Aaron is in and out of the house, so there is no set time. I am just going to have to let you know. If I see an opening, I'm on it. I just hope you are available when I need you. Sonya was testing Trudy's loyalty.

Trudy's curiosity grew larger. She wanted to know what she was getting herself into.

"Sonya, you are making me nervous."

"I just need a ride to a hotel, maybe one next to an airport. The main thing is your availability, not that I am trying to tie you up, but I can't afford for you not to be around when I call on you. I am leaving a lot of my shit behind, including my truck. It's paid for so I don't care; I just need to get out of California. It could be tonight."

"I'll be there. All you have to do is call," Trudy said while she lit a cigarette and continued. "Why do you want to go all the way to Texas just to leave a nigga?"

"Dallas is where I'm from. I been in L.A. for years and I'm still not used to this place. If I would've never met him, my perception of L.A. might be a little different."

"Does your mother know about all of this?"

"She doesn't know about our status. Besides, my momma has her own issues with her own boyfriend. I just want to get out of here and away from that psycho."

"So I'm aiding your escape?"

"Pretty much."

"I'm mad at you. You are going to Texas and you're not taking me," Trudy said good-naturedly.

"Girl, you better bring yourself," Sonya said jokingly. The women hugged each other before Sonya stepped out of the car.

When Sonya walked through the door, she walked into a living room teeming with pink, white, and red roses. A little love opened in her heart for him, but disregarded the idea of Aaron changing. It wasn't the first time he beat her and tried to seal things up by buying her forgiveness.

After she showered and slipped into her nightgown, she poured herself a glass of wine. The day wasn't good. After getting settled into the bed, her cell phone rang. It was Trudy.

"Turn to channel nine right now!" Trudy blasted before hanging up.

Sonya tuned in. Mugshots of Colin, Earl, and B-Bum were broadcasted on the television. News reporter Debbie Rinaldi described them being killed by unidentified drug dealers. The forth man didn't have a mugshot; he didn't have a police record. The news reporter described a man in a collage of Facebook photos. Sonya gasped as she described a small portion of D-Bone's life and how a bullet ended it. When the reporter mentioned the Chevy Tahoe, Sonya's jaw dropped and her fear had heightened. If her car was never mentioned, she would have rode it off as a coincidence.

After establishing a time and date with Trudy, she ordered a one-way ticket to Dallas, packed a small bag, and placed her nursing scrubs on top of the bag to throw Aaron off in case he snooped. When Aaron pulled up in the driveway with a Nissan Maxima and not the Tahoe, her suspicions were confirmed. She went underneath the covers and played sleep.

Aaron paced the living room. He was nervous and edgy. The mention of the Tahoe being connected to a drug deal gone wrong spooked him. Police and homicide detectives had the house blocked and sealed. Prime displayed all the subtle signs of a snitch and Aaron made a vow to kill him if he had to.

Running was an option, but he knew he had to play it cool. After the restlessness settled in his head, he got into bed with Sonya and placed his arm around her, but she rejected him. He didn't take it personal; his freedom was in grave danger.

5-Webster CI
Cheshire, CT

Every guard in the prison had it in for everyone since the Bronson incident. Claude, Flip, and J-Rock stayed under the radar. In recent days, prison guards took shots at the trio, especially Claude. Every inmate was on edge.

Claude was set to leave. He gave Flip and J-Rock his belongings. Claude wanted nothing to do with any remembrance of prison. He felt anxious as he waited for his name to be called. Today was the day. Freedom with stipulations was minutes away.

The men shared stories and triumphs; Claude spoke of new beginnings and foreseeable struggle because of his felony. They enjoyed a good laugh and they spoke of Claude's confrontation with Domino.

"I've been removed from these streets for years and I ain't letting no crab ass nigga entice me back into them, but yeah, he dodged a bullet fucking with me."

Flip knew Claude was right. Domino wanted to take him out of his element because he knew Claude's feet was about to hit the street. Flip had a theory.

"That dude don't know your ambition about that legal life. He think you going to dive back in the streets like the rest of us. Your homeboy is a threat to him. You being on the streets with him is double trouble."

Claude understood Flip's point.

"We will keep an eye on him and keep you informed while you do your thing. The nigga seem corny and is hanging onto his glory days," J-Rock added.

Claude dapped them and they went their separate ways. Claude was left alone with his thoughts. He stared at the hard institutional floors. He sat at the end of his bed with his hands folded. He thought about Rocks. He didn't want to take Domino seriously, but he knew he was up to something.

He didn't have a big foundation other than his sister and niece. He was seventeen when he came into the system. Now thirty-two, he knew he would have to start over. While incarcerated, he obtained his GED He took a few business courses and a course relating to resumes and interview strategies. He understood that no matter how many courses he took in prison, he was still labeled a felon.

Living the good and honest way was good and all, but temptation was a real bitch. He knew Waterbury and only Waterbury. The thought of Waterbury alone made him depressed. He wanted to start building his life out of state, but he couldn't leave it due to parole stipulations. He wanted all his expectations to piece together, but time and patience would be needed for his plan to go into effect.

Keys jingling and heavy footsteps took Claude out of his thoughts. C/O Sharper, a medium sized man with spiky, blond hair, walked up to the cubicle.

"Get your stuff."

Claude spoke of some very down to Earth guards who would rather make there jobs easier. That didn't apply to C/O Sharper. He was among the top five for drowning inmates with tickets. Claude anticipated C/O Sharper's sarcasm.

"I don't know why that woman is picking you up knowing your ass will be right back. I don't know what it is with you indigent fucks," C/O Sharper said with a coffee-stained grin.

Claude flashed a grin.

"Since I'm indigent, I love to work in the dirt. Who knows? I may be the gardener your wife hires."

Claude's comment caught C/O Sharper off guard.

"Very funny asshole. Just remember, I'm not the one who has a stain on the record. I make the big bucks. Maybe my wife and I could use a muscular field Negro like yourself to pick the cotton in my garden," C/O Sharper shot back.

Claude smirked at the comeback. He didn't want to push it. The only thing C/O Sharper had to do was push the body alarm.

After receiving his property, Claude walked coolly into the building's lobby and cracked a wide smile as his five-year-old niece Destiny ran happily towards him. The only place she pictured him was in prison because that was where she met him. Sahara used to bring her bundle of joy to see her brother.

Claude had the pleasure of watching his niece grow through visiting rooms.

"Uncle C, Uncle C, I missed you!" Destiny said playfully. She jumped in Claude's arms.

Claude held her while C/O Sharper stood unemotional, hating the moment Claude had been waiting. Sahara walked up to him and hugged him. Destiny had never seen Claude outside the visiting room.

"What's up big boy?" Sahara said playfully.

"Ready to get up out of here." He put Destiny down and picked up his bag. He turned around and gave C/O Sharper a wink. C/O Sharper returned with a wink of his own, discreetly giving Claude the finger. "*He'll be back,*" he thought as he beckoned the guard at the front desk to buzz him back in.

6-Los Angeles

Sonya squirmed around in the bed. When she opened her eyes from what she thought was a dream, she saw Aaron's head moving in her crotch. She felt discomfort because she perceived him as an intruder. She played along and pretended that she was enjoying it, even though it irked the shit out of her. She wondered how she allowed herself to be caught up with a person with kingpin dreams. She couldv'e had her master degree if she kept her guard up. She would have seen the filth beneath his mask. He was a dud with no aspiration.

She made fuck noises and fronted like she was having an orgasm. She wanted him to get off of her. He entered her abruptly and without warning. She opened her eyes and yelped. The feeling was painful. He pumped and pumped like he hated the womb. After five minutes, he came, squeezing every single drop of passion into her. He figured by impregnating her, she would be stuck with him. Unbeknownst to him, she took the birth control shot when she received her annual check-up.

She lay on the bed looking frigid. Her mouth was slightly ajar as she relived the horror he brought down on her the other night. She felt disgusted, angry, and used. Her genital was on fire from his precipitous invasion. Her vagina ached. It was his second unwanted entry in two days.

She maneuvered herself away from him. He caught her drift and rolled on his back. He grabbed his pack of Newports, took one out of the pack, and lit it.

"You like that, huh?" he asked arrogantly.

She felt disgusted.

"Look at you, all dazed an' shit. You could never get enough of this nigga," Aaron boasted, feeling himself. He took another pull of the cigarette.

"Ain't no nigga like me. Ain't none."

The more he spoke, the more she scorned herself for staying with him. She wanted to scream.

"You heard about D-Bone and dem niggas?" He hoped she hadn't come across the news.

She made sure he had her undivided attention. The blank

look on her face gave him no indication that she was suspicious.

"No, I didn't," she lied. She rose from her position and looked at Aaron with the look of grave concern.

"What happened?"

Aaron flicked some more ash in the ashtray. He felt relieved.

"I heard D-Bone and some niggas he ran with got murdered. Him and his homeboys strong armed these weak, scary ass niggas in Compton. Them same weak dudes became strong and came back for 'em, that's all. Just a classic case of a comeback." He paused and took another pull of his cigarette before putting it out and continued. "He was probably your homeboy, but niggas like that get dealt with. Niggas don't got time for snakes." He got out of the bed to start his day; he was thankful that she didn't have a clue to what was going on. Sonya's instinct told her that he was responsible for D-Bone's death and the others and she refused to ignore it.

Aaron heard the sound of the water coming from the shower. He grabbed a CD cover and walked to the corner of the bedroom looking for the jeans he had on last night. When he found them, he fumbled through the front pocket and pulled out a zip lock bag that held an ounce of coke. The coke was tied into little baggies. Aaron took out one of them, opened it, and sprinkled a reasonable amount on the CD cover. He held one nostril and snorted the entire line he laid out. *There's more where this shit came from*, he said to himself. He tied the sandwich bag of coke and stashed it in the corner of the closet. Moments later, he heard Flex walk in the back door.

He walked in the kitchen and saw Flex sitting at the kitchen table.

"We got to find them white boys. If they could stop breathing today, we could start living tomorrow," Flex said.

Flex told Aaron that Jimmy saw a news segment that featured the actual eyewitness. The eyewitness described the Tahoe and how long it was parked outside the residence. It was a good thing he destroyed the Tahoe.

"Yeah, you right 'cause we'll jeopardize everything if them kids got a clean look at us. I don't think they did, but it doesn't pay to leave our guard down, especially since they spotted the vehicle," Aaron said.

"Aaron, could y'all go into the living room for a minute?" Sonya asked. She heard someone walk through the door a few minutes ago and figured Aaron had company. She didn't want anyone to see her wrapped in a towel.

When the men went to the living room, Sonya peeked out into the kitchen. She moved swiftly across the kitchen floor and into the bedroom. She closed the door behind her.

Aaron waited until the door closed.

"It's too much money on the table to gamble. It's either them or we go to jail for life. I don't know how you feel, but I'm ready to terminate those motherfuckers," Flex said smoothly with a pinch of coldness in his tone.

Aaron turned the fan on to the highest level so it could interfere with the clarity of their conversation in case Sonya was eavesdropping.

"They the only two motherfuckers alive that have any type of idea of what happened the other night."

Aaron nodded and continued to ponder about those white boys on Monteith Drive. He searched for alternatives but didn't find any. With those white boys murdered, his conscious would rest.

"I ain't really trying to go up there knowing that there may be cops waiting for the stupid mothafuckers to come back to the scene of the crime. I ain't one of those stupid mothafuckas." Aaron stopped in mid-sentence. He went inside of the bedroom and saw Sonya stretched out on the bed watching her late afternoon talk shows and wearing work clothes. He went into the drawer and pulled out a t-shirt. He walked out the room and back into the living room and continued his conversation.

"We got to catch them around that area. We got to be sure that no one is around. That neighborhood ain't that quiet. We got to do spot checks and spread 'em out to kill suspicion. We pull over and wait a few minutes, then we peel off, go somewhere for ten, fifteen minutes and come back. We do that three times. If we don't see 'em the third time, we gon' have to come back tomorrow. Believe me, they'll slip," Aaron said.

Aaron lit up another Newport. "Did Prime call you?"

"Nope."

Prime hadn't been seen or heard from since the murders. The men's suspicions grew.

"Call that nigga."

Flex made the phone call. Flex let it ring six times before hanging up. They left the house after the failed attempt at contacting Prime.

...

Aaron and Flex drove slowly on Monteith Drive. They drove in front of Colin's former safe house and didn't see anyone in it. There was police tape blocking the driveway, door, and the rest of the property. The men didn't match the normal description of people living in that area, nor did Colin, so they had to be discreet. The neighborhood was aware that black people were shot and murdered.

They drove around for twenty minutes before they arrived at their vantage point.

Hours passed. The men waited patiently, but there was no sign of the eyewitnesses. The men were thinking about calling it a night until the witness rode by the men on a mountain bike. The ruthless thugs looked at each other for confirmation. They pulled out their handguns and made moves. Meanwhile, Sonya was making her moves out of the state.

7-Waterbury

Waterbury was the fifth largest city in Connecticut, but not one of the deadliest. It was a city of diverse ethnic and cultural backgrounds. Also known as "Brass City," Waterbury gained the nickname due to its history of a brass industry; moreover, it was also known for strong communities. Waterbury wasn't a town known for its massive landmarks or boroughs, but for the grimy shit that happened there. Like any other city, Waterbury had some areas that weren't safe for the average tourist. The small inner city contained criminally minded individuals like any other major city in America.

The rain subsided. Sahara drove cautiously on East Main St. Claude rode shotgun while Destiny slept in the backseat. He glanced at his sister and noticed her weight gain. She gained a few pounds, but she still looked good. Her body was still shaped. Her caramel complexion had a youthful look and the blue contacts that she wore made her look exotic. Her shoulder length mane had blond highlighted streaks. At thirty-three, Sahara was introduced to the game by Sapp, Destiny's father. When she was born, she drifted away from the drug game so she could raise her daughter. She now worked as a residential assistant in a group home in Bristol, but she was trying to get into the state. Claude hadn't spoken to her in a little over a month. He recalled their last conversation. She began to talk about Sapp, but the time ran out on the phone.

Claude took in his surroundings while Sahara fought against traffic. He shook his head dejectedly and realized that Waterbury was the same as he left it fifteen years ago, with the exception of the Palace Theatre Sahara just drove by. The Palace Theater was a historical tourist attraction that reopened their doors to the public in 2004. Claude stared at the Renaissance style building like an individual staring at a tall building in New York.

"It's been a long time," Sahara said, watching her brother scan the city from the passenger side window.

"I know. It has definitely been a minute. I never seen that theatre before or these colleges down here, but I did hear about them. My man Stew got a janitor job in one of them. I'm gonna see if they hiring. I need to get on my grind A.S.A.P. But it's only the same story with me. What's good with you?"

Sahara sighed as she stopped for the red light. Claude knew that Sapp was the subject of her problems. He had a feeling he was going to hear it sooner or later. He called her one day a few months ago with the sole purpose of talking to her about parole stipulations, but Sahara steadily talked about Sapp, wasting the entire ten minutes.

"A lot of bullshit Claude. Her father is one sorry ass excuse for a human being. Don't want to help out with shit. I haven't heard from him in months."

Claude listened attentively, wondering why she was so oblivious about what was going on with Sapp. He was definitely a candidate for a hit. He stepped on too many toes. The streets have deemed him intolerable. He robbed, hurt, and snitched. Child support was the least of his worries.

"He running from the streets. I wouldn't expect shit from him any time soon."

She knew Sapp was no angel, but didn't know his life was riding on fumes. She didn't have any desire to be with him, but he was Destiny's father.

She made sure Destiny was asleep. "Has he killed anybody?"

"I wouldn't put it past him."

She looked at her brother and knew he didn't want to be probed. His gaze remained out the passenger side window. His response spoke volumes. She would dig later, she thought. She decided that Sapp wasn't going to be the topic.

The mild summer heat brought out the best of people living in the inner city. A younger generation of drug dealers drove in style through the streets. Young mothers walked their children in strollers with one or two more children behind them. A few young thugs bopped vigorously down the sidewalk on East Farm. The voluptuous women were scattered throughout the street. He almost failed to stop his manhood from rising in the car as a tall, light-skinned, thick female sporting two long braids crossed the street. She wore a Cami and a pair of tight jean shorts. Her hair was cut short. He cursed himself for not asking Sahara to bring an outfit for him to wear home. Claude still had on the gray state property sweats. He didn't want to give off the wrong impression. He saw a few more women, but no one he would bother with. He had the thought of him approaching a woman, but feeling less of a man because he'd be out of her league because of his own sense of detachment. His desire for success increased with that thought. He knew he had to get on his grind.

Sahara's apartment was like an African gift shop. Two giant carved masks and four little masks hugged the living room walls. The wooden coffee table held many other figures of African men and women holding baskets or praying to a higher being. Paintings of African ancestry rested on the walls as well as a huge mask surrounded by two large spears. Claude looked around the living room in astonishment. He looked as if everything around him was foreign. A few hours earlier, he was living in a funky dormitory with over a hundred men. He was now in his sister's apartment enjoying her creativity. He became more impressed when he spotted her collection of books underneath one of her end tables. Reading seemed like an escape route for him when he was incarcerated. He would read until the lights went out. He strained his eyes many nights trying to finish a book.

While Claude played with the remote to the sixty-five inch *Samsung*, Sahara dipped into her bedroom and retrieved four big bags of new clothes.

"Damn Sa, you didn't have to."

" Go in that closet in your room and look at them skinny ass clothes," Sahara said good-naturedly.

"My room? Damn, I thought I was going to be sleeping on the couch. I can't wait to get a job so I could contribute something." He felt uneasy, but he appreciated it.

"Relax. You've been in prison for fifteen years. One day at a time C."

"Just can't wait to get on my grind." He knew Sahara was right, but parole didn't have that concept.

"Good looking, even though you could've brought one of

these outfits up there."

Sahara put her hands on her hips.

"Why, cause of that girl that walked in front of the car?" Sahara asked sarcastically.

He smiled and he fronted. "Nah, it's hot as hell outside."

"Yeah right. Try the rest of your clothes on so you could let me know whether or not they fit. You need to go somewhere?"

"No, I'm straight. You go relax. I'm just happy to be out. I'm gonna hang out here and just chill. Tomorrow is the day I got to go see parole. If it ain't raining, I'll walk. I'm gonna fill out some applications while I'm at it."

Destiny slept until Sahara got her up, dressed, and ready. Claude sat on the sofa the majority of the afternoon thinking and watching TV; he fell asleep. An hour after Sahara and Destiny left, he woke up. Sahara didn't want to wake him up. He figured that Sahara dropped her off at her friend's house to give him some space to unwind. That was part of the reason, but he didn't know the real reason why Sahara took Destiny. He had a surprise arriving later on.

8-Los Angeles

Sonya killed some time by hanging out with Trudy. She held no regret. She felt that she owed Aaron no explanation for her abrupt departure. She wasn't riding with a killer. Despite the black around her eye, she felt good; she felt that Aaron had it in him to kill her. She believed she dodged a bullet.

When Trudy pulled into her apartment complex and parked, her hopes went up in smoke. Prime's Buick was parked four spaces from Trudy. She hoped to the Gods that Aaron wasn't with him. She decided to keep that to herself.

Sonya settled on Trudy's couch. When Trudy went to the bathroom, Sonya walked to the living room window and peeked out of it. Prime's car was still parked outside. She reasoned to herself; Prime secretly wanted her. She would have to use his admiration for her as a tool.

Trudy planned on arriving a few hours late to work so she could drop Sonya off at the airport. Her time on the books was running low, but she would sacrifice for Sonya. She dialed her work number.

"Good Samaritan, this is Nancy speaking, may I help you?"

"Hey Nancy, its Trudy. Who is working the floor tonight?"

"Keisha," Nancy replied flatly. "Make sure you're here on time because she is on a prowl. And between me and you, she asked me what time you came in yesterday so just watch her."

Trudy held the phone to her ear, shaking her head in disbelief. "That bitch! She needs to go get some dick or something and stop worrying about my ass," Trudy said angrily.

Trudy thanked Nancy for the heads-up. She was disappointed that she wouldn't be able to bring Sonya to the airport.

"I'm sorry, but I can't take you. That bitch Keisha is working the floor tonight and she has it out for me. I can't afford to lose a job if I decide to punch her in the fucking face," Trudy said, still heated about Keisha asking around about her.

"Don't worry about it. If I have to catch a cab, I'll just catch a cab. I don't want you to jeopardize your job for my bullshit," Sonya said.

Trudy started to pick up her son's toys off the living room floor. "You got to call out, quit, do something. You know how our floor falls apart when somebody calls out at the last minute. Michelle told me Gloria called out last week on a Friday. Two or three patients didn't have their dressings changed the entire shift." Trudy worried about her responsibilities of the evening if no one replaced Sonya for tonight.

Sonya looked out the window again. His car was still out there. She sat back down, called the hospital, called out, and decided once she touched down in Dallas, she would provide an emergency reasoning for her abrupt resignation.

Trudy left for work at two thirty to avoid being late. Sonya called a cab and waited patiently. When it arrived, a familiar voice startled her. When she turned around, Prime approached her holding a duffle bag.

"What are you doin' around these parts?" Prime asked with a hint of trouble in his voice.

She rarely saw Prime without Aaron. She hoped that he didn't see her this morning and call Aaron to let him know that she was in his line of sight. If he knew where she was, he'd scoop her up or drag her.

"Oh, hi Prime."

Prime looked confused, not comprehending the situation because of the travel gear Sonya had on her person.

"I thought I saw that chick bounce a little while ago." He looked curiously at the bags in Sonya's hand.

Prime looked at her hard and knew something was up, not to mention the mouse underneath her eye, but didn't want to mention anything that would embarrass her. Despite his suspicions, he couldn't help but to be drawn by her. He felt a lot of empathy for her, especially since the murders the other night. He hoped that Sonya wouldn't be the next victim. Aaron was more than capable of murdering her if it came down to it.

"Tell that cabbie to go. I'll give you a ride to where ever you need to be," Prime said, not passing up any opportunity to be alone with her. He had a feeling she was bailing on Aaron.

She looked at the cab driver and then looked at Prime, unsure of his invitation. She had to be at the airport at four.

"Prime, I am going to the airport. I'm not going home. If you don't want to take me there, I am taking this cab."

"Hey lady, you're not the only one that needs a ride. Are you coming or not?" the cabbie asked angrily.

"Who the fuck you think you talking to?" Prime asked hotly.

"Fuck youuu!" the cab driver blurted as he pulled off, not realizing the back door was still opened because of Sonya's indecisiveness. Prime didn't respond to the cab driver's vulgarity. He had more important life altering matters to worry about. Through his dark thoughts, though, he shed light on one of them; he was not the triggerman. The thought of going to jail for Aaron and Flex was out of the question. If it came down to it, he would snitch instead of living in prison for the rest of his life.

Fuck Aaron, he thought as he took the suitcase and duffle bag out of Sonya's hand. He walked to his car, popped the trunk, and put her bags in it, along with his duffle bag, and closed it. He went into his car and unlocked the door from the driver's side. She slowly got into the car. Once she settled in, he pulled off. Unbeknownst to the both of them, Aaron's cokehead lawyer, Patrick, moved his BMW slowly in the parking lot, hoping to catch Prime at his client's apartment for some coke. Aaron wasn't picking up the phone and Prime was Patrick's secondary connect. He blew his horn to get Prime's attention, but he was oblivious. If they would've left about five seconds sooner, Patrick would've never seen Sonya get into the car.

Prime drove his unregistered Buick carefully on I-10W. He resembled a man torn apart. The bags under his eyes indicated sleepless nights. His clothes looked unkempt. His gray sweatshirt was dingy and he had the same jeans that he had on since the night of the murders. Sonya didn't pay him any mind so there was no way she was going to make the connection. His fingernails were caked with dirt. He secretly sniffed his sweatshirt and caught a whiff of funk. He turned off the A/C in the car and rolled down his window. He held the steering wheel between his legs and took off the sweatshirt, revealing a black T-shirt with a Marijuana plant on it. Even though he slept in it, it didn't smell half as bad as the sweatshirt. Sonya didn't smell any funk. She just wondered why he would have on a sweatshirt in eighty degree weather. He allowed his troubles and dark thoughts stand in the way of his hygiene.

"Where you going anyway?"

Sonya didn't want to tell him where she was going. He was affiliated with Aaron. In addition, the two men grew up with one another. It was definitely nice to get a ride, but she didn't trust him until she finally noticed his disheveled appearance. Prime's guilt was revealing. He looked as if he was involved with the murder the other night. If anyone was hiding something, it was definitely him, she thought as she began to gradually put her guard down.

"Texas. I'm going home."

Prime smiled and nodded his head. "I know. You said you wasn't coming back. Shit, I bet you Texas is better than this South Central shit. I'll do anything to get out of this bitch."

Sonya glanced at Prime and decided to probe.

"What happened the other night?"

He didn't change the expression on his face. He kept his eyes on the road and to the oncoming traffic coming off the ramps. He took a short breath and closed his mouth. He looked at her and returned his eyes on the road. The look he gave her was enough to answer the question.

"But why?"

He held one hand on the wheel and wiped the right corner of his brow; he felt overwhelmed.

"You better off getting out of here, believe me," he said as he got off exit 3B.

"You didn't answer my question Prime. What happened and why did y'all do it," she pressed.

"You better off not knowing Sonya."

"Did Aaron kill anybody, that's all I'm asking?" Sonya asked with desperation in her voice.

"You can't answer questions that you don't know the answers to. Just make sure you don't come back."

She decided to leave it alone; his silence about it was a

guilt indicator.

Prime and Sonya pulled into the LAX. When he parked the car, he expected a kiss. He didn't want to pass up on his opportunity. When she returned his leer, she took out the money she was going to give to the cab driver, but he respectfully declined. He decided against forcing a kiss on her. He felt relieved that he didn't have to endure any embarrassment by being rejected. She gave him a hug and thanked him gracefully. Prime had a cold feeling that he would never see her again. He felt that he saved her life.

As he pulled away, he looked at her in his rearview mirror. *"She could've at least gave me her number,"* he thought as he lit the piece of blunt that he started to smoke before he saw her. He knew Aaron was going to be on a mission to find her; she'll be thousands of miles away.

9-Waterbury

The knocking stole Claude's sleep. He took his time getting off the couch. The longer he took, the louder the knocking. He looked at the clock; hours passed since his sister took Destiny. He had no idea who was pounding on the door until he looked through the peephole. Claude smiled radiantly. When he opened it, Rocks and Tommy stood on the porch. Rocks held a bag of fresh gear and had a blunt burning between his fingers.

"What the fuck is up my nigga?" Rocks asked good-naturedly. The men embraced Claude tightly. It was the first time they've seen him in fifteen years. Rocks did three and a half years for his role in Claude's shooting, but never came across him in the system.

"What's good?" Claude asked excitedly, noticing the blunt burning between his fingers. Rocks passed it to Tommy and beckoned him to put it out. "Bout time y'all motherfuckers came through."

"We would've came earlier, but we wanted you to chill solo for a minute," Rocks said. He handed Claude a bag of fresh gear and sneakers.

"Yeah, we wanted you to settle an' shit. Just coming from New York with that fresh leak," Tommy said casually. Thomas "Tommy" Jacobs was an intelligent, witty, and quiet individual. He was dark-skinned with average height and build. He had dark brown beady eyes and his eyebrows seemed invisible. His hair was cut into a bald Caesar. He wore a black Affliction Motor Spirit v-neck t-shirt, baggy blue jeans, and a pair of all-white old school Reeboks. He hid his positive qualities with his thuggish demeanor. He was brought up in the catholic school system, but went to public school entering high school because his mother couldn't afford the tuition. That was when his morale, ambition, and potential went out the window. It wasn't the public school system that ruined his ambition and potential; it was the influence of his peers in public school that included Claude and Rocks. They introduced Tommy to a lucrative underworld of drugs, money, sex, and power. He had been locked up at least five or six times since Claude's incarceration.

Jerome "Rocks" Watts was a tall caramel complexion man with thick corn rows. He wore a LeBron James home jersey on top of a crispy white t-shirt with a pair of baggy gray Sean John jeans. He had soft, boyish features with a light goatee. He had the wicked smile of a villain. His eyes were soft and easy, but he was dangerous and calculating. He was cautious and cagey. He kept guns on him at all times. He was clever on the streets and highly battle tested. Four generations of his paternal side of the family had been incarcerated. Many people familiar with him would say that he was either going to get killed or he was going to end up with a murder on his hands.

Claude was happy that they kept their illegal business to themselves because it had been a long time since he had been home and didn't need any extra shit. He thought about the conversation he had with Domino and the reputation that Rocks had gained. Since he didn't want to spoil the occasion, he figured it would be best to ask him later.

"So besides all that shit, y'all good?"

"Always C. Just trying to eat just like everybody else, nah mean? But me and Tommy working extra hard. You how how do fam; niggas that work hard come home to shit dream that American dream only to wake up hearing an alarm clock, but me and Tommy making it a motherfucking American reality."

Claude chuckled. "Jail is the American reality, but I ain't trying to preach to y'all niggas. Eat how you can and how you want, but I'm getting a job. Hopefully, I'll be waking up to an alarm clock. Call me lame if you want to, but that fifteen-year bid ain't cool. I ain't going back."

"We ain't trying to go back either, but fuck it, the risk is worth it. Who knows? We could probably pull off a caper that could lead us to retiring from this shit," Rocks said nonchalantly.

A cloud of dread and uncertainty started to plaque Claude's mind. Rocks and Tommy were two of his closet comrade, but they were on the path to destruction while he was on the path to redemption.

"Y'all got any legal method of making money?"

"Robbin' OT niggas wit' black masks and black gloves, especially around election time. Drug dealers tend to hoard pounds of drugs during that politic stretch," Tommy said offhandedly while he looked at the African sculptures and paintings in the living room.

Claude didn't want to get too philosophical with his friends about their attributes because he was on the same criminal grind, but he wanted to put that lifestyle behind him and give the legal life a shot. His friends were well aware of the consequences and knew every rule to the street game. They were cautious and picked their drug dealing vics carefully.

"Y'all hot?" Claude asked.

"Yup," Rocks said.

Claude gave Rocks a flat stare.

"Just fucking with you C. You know damn well I don't do that high school shit. Besides, we ain't trying to go back either."

"What y'all getting into?" Claude asked, changing the tone of the conversation.

"Fuck you mean what *y'all* getting into? You mean what *we* getting into? You about to put this shit on so we could get the fuck up outta here. Since yo' convict ass can't smoke, we 'bout' to get you twisted off of some of that brown water," Rocks said.

"Some is right. I haven't fucked around with that shit in ten years. A few shots would be straight, but let me wash my ass before I do anything."

...

Claude's thoughts drifted away from his friends as Rocks made a right from East Farms to Walnut Street. The blunt circulated in the truck while he sat soberly. He placed his shirt over his mouth and nose so he wouldn't catch a contact. He heard stories about non-weed smokers having dirty urines because they were around people that smoked; he also heard it was a myth. He didn't want to take any chances.

"Zane comin' home in a few months," Rocks said.

"I heard. I didn't get the full version of the story. What happened?" Claude asked.

"Fucking wit' that bitch Mindy. Zane had her whole head fucked up. Saw Zane up in Hartford with some bi-racial chick. She didn't know Mindy was on her like that. As soon as she left

Hartford and came back here, she got pulled over and bagged. She tossed out the two bundles of dope that was on her, but didn't know about the three Mindy stashed in the back right hand corner of the trunk of the car. That fucking crab ass bitch called the cops and told them Zane had drugs in her car and gave them the license plate number," Tommy said.

Rocks and Tommy updated Claude about their inner and outer circle; family, associates in the underworld, associates and family in jail, ghetto secrets, and society. He thought it was a good time to talk to Rocks about his encounter with Domino since they were talking about the streets.

"What's good with you and Domino? He was talking kind of reckless about you up the way."

Rocks's facial tone didn't change. He accepted the blunt from Tommy and pulled on it.

"So y'all bumped heads?" Rocks asked.

"He coming at me like I'm still fresh in the game; he was talking that association shit. If I wasn't going home anytime, I would have broke his eye socket."

"Believe me C, it ain't nothing. You know the deal with that snitchin' ass Link, but Domino just mad cause he need Link to make money. Link getting money right now, but not like me and Domino hate me because of that shit. He mad 'cause he can't create his own way in life, his fucking old ass. He'll always be just a worker. You ain't the only dude he vented to. I got my eye on his ass though."

"Domino is hating on you to a point where his bitch ass could have you killed," Claude said gravely.

"Already thought about it," Rocks replied truthfully. "Domino is straight pussy and you know that, which gives me more of a reason to watch him, but fuck him, we 'bout to get yo' ass twisted!"

. . .

Rocks whispered something in the oversized, bald headed, burly Puerto Rican's ear regarding Claude's identification before discreetly placing an undisclosed amount of money in the bouncer's hand. The only ID Claude had on his person was his jail ID. Although Claude was a licensed driver, he lost his driver's license a few days before he shot Twalique. That piece of plastic was long gone. After Rocks and Tommy walked in the club, Claude was at their rear getting ready to enjoy the night's festivities.

The latest music roared out the speakers. Claude had seen many men in big numbers within the last fifteen years, but tonight was different. He wasn't in jail anymore; instead, he was at one of the livest clubs in Waterbury looking at a diverse crowd. He looked near the entrance and saw more people filling in. Rocks pointed at the two gaps at the bar so they walked in that direction. When they settled at the bar, Claude continued to eye hustle. He saw scantily dressed women fanning themselves after twenty minutes on the dance floor. He saw a few conservatively dressed females lending him an eye. He'd been out of the loop with women so long that he felt as though he would need to relearn his game. Years of using his imagination while he jerked his dick in prison were nothing compared to a real woman's flesh.

The bartender placed drinks in eager hands while the trio waited. Claude scanned the club as if he was a foreigner. The unimpressed, thugged out cats posted on the wall looked at Claude, but resumed their attention in another direction when they saw Rocks and Tommy. They were considered hood celebrities and were respected. Those that were knee deep in the streets knew Rocks and Tommy on a personal or professional level. The younger generations of the lawless were too young to remember Claude during his youthful heyday. Many of Waterbury's grittiest dudes; drug dealers, kidnappers, extortionists, and murderers confronted him with love and respect.

The trio had three quarters of the club surrounding them shooting the shit, talking game, downplaying jail politics, building positive connections, and spitting war stories. Everyone was fascinated by Claude's size. He was always known for being slim and slender and his jail built frame shocked everyone. He received prolonged hugs from dressed up petite and curvy women. The sight of all the women made his dick swell.

Later on that night, when the music, drinks, women, and the

laughter reached its climax, Claude staggered out of the bathroom with a drunken swagger. His desire to become a highly productive, law-abiding citizen was concealed with intoxication and lust. He had not been twisted like that since he drunk the jailhouse liquor in the fourth year of his bid. Reggae thundered out of the club's sound system along with the uproar of the raucus crowd. He looked around the club and it seemed that it had spun. The strobe lights made him extra dizzy, but he was well enough to maintain his gait. He was headed back to the bar when he thought he heard a feminine voice call his name. It was so loud in the club that he overrode it and carried on his travel.

He heard his name again with more clarity. He looked in the direction the voice came from and saw a tall, slender yellow skinned woman. She had piercing hazel eyes and had heart shaped lips. She wore her hair in flat twists and knots. She wore light blue skinny jeans, a white tank top that exposed the swell of her breasts, cleavage, and a casual unbuttoned short sleeve shirt that covered the tank top. She returned Claude's gaze with a wide smile revealing evenly spaced teeth. He looked at her with a half-smirk, hoping his intoxication wasn't distorting his line of vision. She sashayed in his direction. He remembered the heartache she provided. He remembered waiting for the prison guards to kill the lights so he could cry the pain away. He remembered the nagging black cloud of depression. He remembered the anger, bitterness, and the fuck-you letters he sent to her mother's address. Even in his drunkenness, tonight was totally different. He needed to relieve years of frustration into any woman who wanted to open their legs. Darlene Ivory was in eye range and he was sure she was a willing candidate for a good fuck whether it was tonight or in a few days. He needed a steady piece of ass until the right one came along.

She sized him up as soon as she was within arm's reach from him and almost believed that it wasn't Claude. She didn't want to believe that she was looking at the same man that used her phone on his last day in a free society. She thought of the demonic, homicidal look he gave her when she broke the news about her pregnancy. She gave him a long, firm embrace, thinking that her betrayal was long forgotten. She smelled the scent of his Driven cologne on his button-down shirt and got wet.

"How's it been?" she asked shyly, unable to conceal the lust in her body language.

"Good, good, just got out today. Chilling with Rocks and Tommy. They showin' a nigga a good time." She looked so good that he felt himself pre-ejaculating.

"It's been so long…"

"Can't hear you," he said.

"I said it's been a long time," she repeated.

The DJ announced last call for drinks. Rocks and Tommy beckoned Claude to hurry his conversation with her. Rocks knew what time it was though; he knew Claude was prowling around for some pussy and didn't want to nag him.

"Do you have a good memory?" she asked

He shifted his gaze from her face to her breasts. She knew he was eyeing her so she discreetly stuck her chest out a tad further so he could get an eye full.

"I think your memory is better than mine. Besides, I just got out today and I don't need to catch a charge for bustin' a nigga's ass," he said seriously.

She didn't hear the last part of his statement, but she figured he said he couldn't remember a number because he was drunk. He read the number to her while she placed it in her cell phone. The two shared a few more moments and spurts of flirtation before they parted ways.

Claude, Rocks, and Tommy linked up with more henchmen to have a last drink. The trio made a toast to Big Chris because they hadn't had a chance because of prison. Afterwards, they left with the rest of the club goers, conversed and flirted in the parking lot with hood rats and the educated, and left. The men talked loudly about who saw what; Darlene was the focal point.

"Darlene was looking badder than a motherfucker. It's been a while since I seen her. You made out my dude. First day of of captivity and already stumbled on some guaranteed ass, but control the emotions fam. Remember…"

"I already know," Claude interjected, replaying that dreadful day when she broke the news about her pregnancy.

Tommy snored in the backseat. He had one too many and prematurely called it the night.

Rocks turned the stereo on and more Maddsonn flooded the truck. Five minutes later, Rocks turned down the music to a whisper and pulled up alongside the curb of Sahara's residence. The men were drunk. Tommy's snoring reached its climax but the men paid him no mind. Rocks dug in his pocket and pulled out a wad of hundreds. He peeled off ten Benjamins and passed them to Claude.

"Come on Rocks, you know I can't pay this shit back," Claude said dejectedly.

"Don't want it back. Real niggas do real things. That ain't shit."

"Word."

Claude knew Rocks was being generous, but he also knew he was being subtle; he was secretly enticing him back in the game. He dropped a few hints at the bar. Claude was out of the loop for a decade, but he would never forget how to be an earner. The men made a lot of money in their youth and Rocks figured that Claude's print on the hustle would enhance his. Rocks wished him the best on his journey as a hardworking, taxpaying, and law-abiding citizen, but he wanted Claude back in the game and in full motion.

"Hit me tomorrow C if you need a ride somewhere," Rocks said as Claude stepped out of the truck.

"Good looking Rocks, but its going to be eighty degrees tomorrow and its going to feel good to walk."

"Alright. Tommy, I ain't no motherfucking chauffeur. Get in the front."

After Tommy took over the passenger seat, Rocks pulled away from the curb. Claude heard Maddsonn's vocals ascend when he drove halfway down the block. He looked at the money and shook his head, knowing the motive behind the cash, but he didn't care. Sahara could use seven hundred dollars of it.

A half-hour later, Claude lay in his bed feeling fresh from

his shower. The shower sobered him up a little. He almost cut his shower short because he thought he was in jail. He chuckled at the thought. He moved around in his regular sized bed, thanking God at the same time that he was not laying on an eroded mattress that belonged to the Department of Correction.

10-Los Angeles

"Dude, my parents have money! Cars! Insurance policies! Whatever you need man! My parents are millionaires! You have my fucking word I'll take care of you guys!" Peter Sullivan begged. He looked as if he was a regular in a smoke shop. His blue eyes were red from crying and begging for his life. Aaron and Flex knew the teen was holding out.

He was thin and had a curly blond mane. He wore skinny jeans and his mouth and nose bled from Aaron's right hand, staining his Abercrombie and Fitch t-shirt. He had an eighth of home grown bud, a plastic baggie holding four Percocet, a pack of Marlboro lights, a lighter in the form of a pistol, thirty dollars, and a small marijuana pipe. His cries and pleas fell on deaf ears as he continued to make attempts to bargain with the two henchmen. His constant begging blended in with the sounds of insects and cars traveling east and westbound on the highway. They were in a discreet, wooded area on the outskirts of Los Angeles. Flex shoved him to the ground. They wanted information, and they wanted it now. He saw the truck outside of Colin's house the night of the gruesome murders, but he was too afraid to admit it when Aaron asked him the first time. He feared the repercussions of a truthful answer. He bragged to his friends that he saw the truck. If he made it through this ordeal, he would have a story to tell. The men had a hunch he was a witness, but they wanted to be sure.

"What the fuck did you see?" Aaron asked him again in the same calm tone.

"This motherfucker ain't cooperating. You asked him twice already," Flex said, pulling out his handgun. He buried it into Peter's temple.

Peter's eyes expanded. The cold steel was something he had never experienced.

"I saw your truck," Peter confessed, feeling a muster seed of hope to live.

That was exactly what they wanted to hear.

"You see, that is all you had to say," Aaron said, patting Peter on his shoulder. "Now we could untie yo' ass so you could be on your way. The truth could take you a long way. Oh, and your boy, we going to have to take your word for it."

Peter didn't see the murderous intentions. He saw himself going home, taking a shower, and smoking some good shit to temporally relieve him of the image of the horrid experience he had.

"And if we find out you're lying, we got your ID. I'm pretty sure your rich family could pay for three funerals. One for you, your father, and your mother," Flex concluded.

"I won't tell anybody, I swear to you," Peter said with a new set of tears flowing down his cheeks.

"I know you won't," Flex said flatly. Aaron pulled out the gun. Peter raised his arms in one final attempt to plea for his life, but Aaron fired two shots into the teen with no regard. Flex fired another shot into the corpse for general purposes.

...

Fatima drove on 183 East in Dallas, Texas. She picked up Sonya from Dallas/Fort Worth airport. It was a warm, muggy night. Fatima wore tight jean shorts and a short Dallas Cowboy t-shirt that exposed her pierced belly button. She looked like a younger version of Sonya, except that she was a shade darker and a little shorter. She was slim and curvy. Her black hair was styled into a chic, short crop cut.

"Wanna call mommy?"

"Not now Fatima. I just want to lie down and think. I will speak to her some time this week, but not right now."

"So what happened?"

"We'll speak about that later on. I just want to get some sleep." Sonya's patience was wearing thin.

"I can't wait until Kim finds out you're here. She's gonna trip."

"No. I don't want everyone knowing that I am down here. Look at my eye Fatima. I don't want nobody all up in my business. I hope you didn't tell anyone I'm back. I need to be alone. Or did you?"

"No…well…my boyfriend knows, but that's it, he ain't…"

Sonya sighed loudly.

"He ain't going to say nothing Sonya. I been seeing him

for five months and he ain't even like that. He ain't even from down here."

"You don't know him from a hole in a wall and you just assumin' he ain't goin' to say nothing."

"You didn't know Aaron from a hole in the wall and you moved in with him. Now look where you are now. You haven't been in Dallas a full hour and you up here judgin' my man. You got a lot of nerve."

Sonya sat in the passenger seat dumbfounded. There was really nothing she could say. She could argue that her stay in California wasn't based on Aaron, but to start a new life for herself. She did, however, allow him to control some aspect of her life. She wanted to come home a long time ago, but he had her on lockdown. Sonya started to cry. Fatima felt awful, but she needed to hear it. She was so used to having the upper hand on her younger sister that she forgot about her own situation. They sat in silence.

"Look, I'm sorry. It's just that you're down here now and you are blocking me off. I'm just happy you're back. I missed you Sonya."

"No need to apologize. You're right. I just want to put everything behind me. I was afraid. I feared for my life. Now I have to take everything out of my name from a distance, but I don't care. I'm glad I'm home."

Sonya looked out of the window and began to take in familiar territory. *It's been a long time.*

"So, who is this knight and shining armor? Is he treating you right?" Sonya asked good-naturedly, drying her teary eyes.

"He is the bomb! He moved down here last year from Connecticut. He is so nice Sonya. He is respectful and Momma loves him. His name is Mark Evans. Being that I told you I told him, he's at the house now."

"What does he look like anyway?"

"You'll see when we get there." Fatima smiled radiantly.

They talked about old times. Fatima updated Sonya on family affairs and her love life. The only thing that disturbed Sonya about the conversation was the fact that their mother was still involved with Russell. She almost lost the house because of his compulsive gambling.

Fatima took a right onto W. Walnut Hill Lane and drove to her condominium complex. She drove up to the gate, rolled down her window, and punched in a code for entry. The gate slowly opened. She drove around the parking lot until she reached her destination. She parked next to a midnight blue Mazda. When the two woman got out of the car, Fatima shook her head slowly as she leered into the car and noticed his CDs scattered all over the seats. She hit a button on her key ring and unlocked the doors. She pulled out a few of the CDs and hid the rest of them. She closed the door and locked it with the key ring.

"Whose car is this?"

"It's Mark's car. He thinks just because the community is gated that no one can't break in his shit," Fatima said jokingly.

The peach condominium was beautiful. Many of them had balconies and garages. There was a basketball court in the complex. The place was quiet compared to Sonya's dwelling around Crenshaw. Sonya smiled knowing that she would never see that place again. The women walked upstairs around the side of the apartment until they reached a red door. Fatima unlocked and opened it. The door led to a small hallway. Sonya and Fatima took off their shoes and walked down the small foyer and heard a video game.

Exotic plants were all over Fatima's living room. Pictures of everyone in the family were on the wall. Maroon furniture rested on the spotless white wall to wall carpet. Mark sat in front of the sixty-five inch Smart TV playing NBA 2K16.

"Who's winning?" Fatima asked cheerfully while the women held onto bags.

Mark was in his own world. He didn't respond because he didn't hear the women come into the apartment.

"Mark!"

"Oh, what's good baby? Did you pick up your sister?"

"Hit pause and let me introduce you to her."

Mark stood up. He was tall and muscular. He was bald and wore mustache and goatee. His dark brown eyes looked innocent. He wore a tattoo on each arm. He was a nice looking man, which surprised Sonya because Fatima had bad taste in men.

"I'm sorry. My name is Mark and it is a pleasure to meet you," he said, extending his right hand for acquaintance.

"How are you? My name is Sonya. It is also a pleasure to meet you. I am sorry that we had to meet on these terms," Sonya said, feeling insecure about her appearance.

Mark didn't grill Sonya's eye because he already knew the situation. Nothing surprised Mark. He worked with battered women in Connecticut and felt empathy for them. He worked with the criminals who committed worse crimes. He decided to move with his family in Dallas. He only hoped that she wouldn't go back to Los Angeles because he knew many females could easily get caught up in the cycle of domestic abuse.

"Don't even sweat it. I'm just glad you're down here. Let me take your bags. I'm sorry I wasn't on the look out, but this game is addictive," Mark chuckled.

Sonya liked Mark. He wasn't a bum, and that was what Sonya hated about Aaron. If he weren't a drug dealer, he'd be a trophy boyfriend just like the other worthless individuals who can't see beyond the box. She was happy for Fatima. She found a keeper.

"I don't know about y'all, but I'm hungry," Mark said, looking for his car keys.

"You read my mind baby. McDonalds is still open," Fatima said.

"What do y'all want?"

"I want that fish filet value meal. You know I get the same thing every time we go to McDonalds," Fatima said.

"And you?"

"I want a double cheeseburger and a small fry." She pulled some singles dollar bills out of her pocket. Sonya held out the money to him, but he refused it. He found his keys and left.

"So that's Mark, your knight and shining armor?"

"That's my baby."

"He's cute. What does he do anyway?" Sonya asked, looking around the living room in awe, especially at the family pictures she hadn't seen in so long.

"He is a correctional officer. His cousin plugged him in about two months before he moved down here," Fatima said. "He is doing very well for himself, but I hate it when we have things planned out and he says yes to overtime."

"Be glad the man works Fatima."

"I know, I know, maybe I'm just selfish," Fatima said jokingly.

"I don't think you're selfish Fatima; I think you're in love."

Mark came back fifteen minutes later. He ordered everything accurately. They chilled out through the early morning hours of the day laughing, joking, and sipping on cocktails. Sonya was glad that she'd finally come home.

11-Los Angeles/Waterbury

The oscillating fan on the ceiling blew nothing but hot air on Aaron's back while he slept on the queen size bed. His body was spread out across it. He was exhausted from the events that took place within the last few days. After killing Peter, the men dug a hole, covered his body with quicklime, and covered it.

Tossing and turning vigorously, Aaron woke up abruptly from a coma-like sleep. He looked at the clock and it read 10:02am. It took him a few moments to realize that Sonya wasn't in the bed with him.

"Sonya."

"Sonya," he yelled again, adding more base to his voice.

He walked through the house and didn't see any sign of her. He marched towards the nightstand and grabbed the cordless phone. He dialed the number to her job. After five rings, a woman picked up the phone.

"Good Samaritan."

"Sonya there?" Aaron sounded rude.

"She's not on the schedule today," the woman stated politely.

"Fuck you mean she not there? She got fired or something?"

"Sir, she's not on the schedule. I can't give you any more information than what I told you," the woman said, feeling uncomfortable, making incredulous facial expressions at her co-worker.

"Bitch! Is she…"

Dial tone.

Aaron slammed the cordless phone on the base and headed towards the closet. When he slid the door open, he rummaged through all the clothes only to find his own. He backed away from the closet in shock, unable to grasp the reality that she left. Most of her wardrobe was gone. He rushed back to the nightstand and called Flex.

"Grandma, let me speak to Flex."

There was a moment of silence before her response.

"Is everything all right?"

"Yeah, I'm cool. I just need to speak to Flex."

"How's that girlfriend of yours, what is her name? Sandra, Sasha?"

"She's cool. Listen, I need to speak to Flex about a job that was offered to us. We don't have much time. Can you go and get him?" He hated lying to her, but he had to; he had to get her off the phone. He cared less about his grandfather. He wished natural causes would creep up on him. She expressed more concern and told Flex to pick up the phone.

"Alright, as long as you're ok."

"Hello?" Flex voice was raspy from sleeping.

"Granddaddy ain't there right?"

"Shit, I don't know."

"Did you see Sonya when you dropped me off last night?"

"Naw, I didn't see her, but yo..."

"I'll call you back." Aaron ended the call.

Aaron sat on the edge of the bed feeling numb. The possible repercussions of the murders started to play a role on his conscious. He jumped from the edge of the bed. He ran to the dresser, swiped everything off it, grabbed the back edge of it, and flipped it in an intense rage.

. . .

Claude penned seven applications and visited parole before running into his old friend Omar "Jupe" Moore. Jupe wasn't an ex-convict, but he had his own issues. He was a short dark skinned man with a small potbelly. His hands looked rough from years of doing landscaping, maintenance, and other odd jobs. He was employed, but he was looking for a second job to make ends meet. He found relief hanging with Claude. He wasn't in any mood to go home to a noisy apartment and be nagged by the mother of his two children.

They enjoyed a few bottles of beer at Fulton Park. They spoke of current events, politics, hood secrets, and the infamous question that caught his attention every time he filled out an application, the question of his criminal past and the consequences of lying on the application. Jupe provided Claude with some reassurance.

"You could be like six months in, working your ass off,

and they could pull you into the office and let you go because you weren't honest on the application. I've seen that shit happen too many times," Jupe said

"That's fucked up though. Don't get me wrong, I have checked "yes" on all the applications I filled out, but damn, sometimes that could be an eyesore to a lot of those managers. It's like I'm stuck between a rock and a hard place. You're damned if you do and you're damned if you don't."

Jupe felt for Claude because he didn't have a criminal record and knew that it wasn't easy finding a job. Having a criminal record didn't help matters. He looked at the frustration building up in Claude's face.

"In two years, they are banning that question. There are going to be some exceptions, which I'm not sure, but I hear that if approved, on January 1, 2017, Connecticut is supposed to make it a law to not ask that question on applications."

"Word?"

"Word. As long as the job you're trying to get isn't state or federal."

Claude felt better after hearing what Jupe had to say. He wished the law were enacted now. He wondered what the exceptions were. He didn't know that law was in development. It gave him hope.

After drinking another beer, the men left the park. Silence was born between them. Claude broke the ice.

"So, what's up with Gloria?"

"It is what it is C. The only thing that I don't regret is my kids, but as for her, that bitch could go to hell. I can't blame nobody but my damn self, fucking with that slut. Y'all niggas clowned me back in the day, but that's cool, 'cause I was the dumb one." He took a swig of the beer. "I should of let a ho be a ho. If I had that mindset, I wouldn't be out here begging these white folks for a job."

Claude sat silent for a moment, thinking about the time he told Jupe how they all ran a train on her. He had no idea how Jupe didn't make a judgment call, but love was love, he figured.

"You have to learn to live with regrets. Believe me, it could be worse. You can't be knocking yourself now for it."

"Word, I feel you, but I ain't seeing no light right now. Don't get me wrong, I love the fuck out of my kids, but that's as far as it gets."

"Do you have to be with her? I'm pretty sure your overprotective mom will take you back anytime," Claude said good-naturedly.

Jupe chuckled.

"Yeah, I guess I have that option, but it's the issue of child support. That's why I'm still with the bitch. When my brother got divorced, that shit hit him hard. He's going through it. When he showed me his check, that nigga had eighty dollars to his fucking name, knowing he got a good ass job. He can't even afford to live on his own. He's going through all this court shit now so he could live a decent life. To make matters worse, his ex-wife's boyfriend beats the shit out of her. My nephew Malik be telling him that shit, so he trying to get custody as we speak. They don't need to be around that shit C, for real. He living off of eighty fucking dollars. My mom won't even take that shit from him. He can't even see his kids when he wants. I don't want to go through that shit."

Jupe dropped his head on his chest and zoned out for a minute while Claude guzzled his beer. Claude didn't know Kevin, Jupe's brother, was going through all that turmoil. He remembered going to the wedding.

"What the fuck could you do?" Claude asked to no one in particular.

The men sat there and finished their beer. While they walked around Fulton, Jupe's cell phone rang, and of course, it was Gloria.

"What? Yeah and?"

With a blank expression on his face, Jupe hit the end button.

"That's the shit I'm talking about C. She knew I took the day off to take care of business, but now her broke ass is calling me asking to bring some groceries home!" Jupe raged.

"I don't see the harm in that, I mean, not to play both sides, but there are two children in the apartment."

"No doubt C, but I just gave her two hundred for

groceries yesterday. She is trying to spend the little that I have. I mean, the rent is paid, I gave her the two hundred yesterday, and now this shit."

Jupe drove to a convenience store on Chase Avenue, next door to Bank of America. Claude elected to stay in the car and zone out to some music. He felt a buzz and didn't want to ruin it by walking through the store. He listened to two tracks and suddenly, a white Altima pulled up. Instinctively, he looked to his right.

Darlene.

When she saw him, she smiled brightly, remembering how good he looked last night. A look of lust occupied her oval, green eyes when she stepped out of the car.

"What are you doing? Stalking me?" Claude asked jokingly.

Darlene placed her hand on her hip and smiled.

"You wish punk. What are you doing here anyway?"

"I'm here with Jupe. I'm waiting for him to come out so he could take my ass home."

"I'm just getting off of work and I don't have to pick up my son. I'm free," she said, maintaining eye contact with him.

Just when Claude was about to respond, Jupe came walking out carrying three bags of food. He knew the drill. He knew that he wouldn't have to drive Claude home as soon as he saw Darlene, which was a relief because Gloria was blowing him up on the cell phone. She repeatedly left vulgar text messages because Jupe wasn't picking up the phone.

"Yo Ju…"

"Go 'head bro. Do your thing. I got some unnecessary shit to handle. Get my number from Rocks. I'll probably stop by before I go to work."

"Hi Jupe."

Jupe put his car in reverse and backed up quickly and yelled out the window. "Oh, what's up Darlene? I'll talk to y'all later."

Jupe pulled out of the parking lot like a madman.

I hope this dude don't fuck around and do nothing stupid, Claude thought as his eyes followed the Jetta moving beyond normal speed out of the parking lot.

Claude waited for Darlene. She came out of the store in a hurry, eager to be in his presence again. They made their way to his house. He knew Sahara would leave at this time to go to work. He felt for the condoms he picked up earlier because he damn sure wasn't going to do anything without them.

12-Waterbury

Claude flipped Darlene over. She spread her own cheeks while she gyrated her plush ass. He mounted her. He wrapped his arms around her stomach and stroked. His speed increased. Loud animal noises escaped her mouth as she begged him not to stop.

As Claude fucked her from behind, he grabbed one of her breasts. He removed his hand from it and grabbed the back of her neck because he knew she liked that kinky shit. *Claude, I'm pregnant. I'm sorry, it just happened.* Those dreadful words replayed in his head, but his dick was solid as a rock. He intended to hurt her by pulling on her hair, but she loved every minute of it.

Twenty-five minutes later, she was riding him. She rode his dick in perfect rhythm. He was in a zone. He wanted to be creative. He used his strength, scooped her in the air, and long stroked her. Darlene came instantly; her fluids dripped all over his dick. Claude wanted to come, but he wanted it to be special. As he neared his climax, he pulled Darlene off of him, got on his knees, took off the condom, and grabbed the back of her head. Darlene's mouth was wide opened, anticipating years of desire shoot right out of his penis. Before she entertained another thought, she had a mouthful of cum, swallowing every drop of it.

They had three sessions of sex and they were both worn out. Darlene felt no regret about going behind Lloyd's back. After she served Claude the news of her pregnancy in the second year of his bid, she felt depressed. She loved Claude and never stopped loving him. She was pregnant by Lloyd, but she never learned to love him the way he loved her. Throughout the years, Lloyd treated her like royalty, going above and beyond for her and little Lloyd, but Darlene barely met the bare minimum on her side of the relationship. She cared for him as a person, but she didn't love him.

"Claude, did you hate me after I told you I was pregnant?" She rubbed his chest while she had her leg wrapped around his.

"Yeah." He spent years behind bars; he owned only his word. He wasn't going to front for no one.

"Did you ever take my youth into consideration? If I was in your shoes, would you have waited for me?"

"Yeah, I did, a few years later, but since you put it out there, no, I wouldn't have waited for you. I wasn't seasoned like that to take that kind of news."

"If that's the case, would you ever consider starting over with me?"

Claude felt uncomfortable, but appreciated.

"Where is all this coming from?"

"It's coming from my heart. I didn't run into you at the club by coincidence."

Claude twisted his face.

"I ran into Boone and he told me Rocks and Tommy was taking you out," she confessed. "And to be even more honest, I knew you'd be getting out around this time. The internet is something else, isn't it?"

"Damn, I guess it is, but check it Dar..."

"You've been on my mind for years Claude," she interjected, cutting him off so she could get her point across. "I don't mean to be pouring it on you like this, but I just thought you would want to know that. I've never stepped out of my relationship with Lloyd until today. I don't want you to stress anything right now. I'm just putting it out there. I never stopped loving you."

Her breasts were so firm that they stood at attention while she was on her back. Her hazel eyes were enticing and her posture was provocative, but Claude knew he had to work on himself first before he stepped into anything. Besides, trust went a long way, and he had none for her. If she was willing to step outside their arrangement or marriage for a long term commitment with someone fresh out of prison, she could do the same thing to him.

"You know Darlene, all for nothing, as much as I hate to admit it, you told me yourself that Lloyd is an accountant and he provides well. I can't fuck wit' that. Honestly, I ain't got shit. This is my second day out. I live with my sister. I don't own a thing but my word. I got to relearn how to stand on my own two feet. You better off reconsidering your offer."

"I don't want to." She started to suck his nipples softly while she began to gently tug on his growing penis. Once it became erect, she expertly tongued her way down from his nipples to his crotch. She held his dick and looked at him seductively before making his shaft disappear into the warmth of her mouth. She deep throated him before climbing on top of him. Claude gazed at one of the few packs of condoms he bought from the gas station, and as if on cue, she started to ease herself on him, making his dick feel the warmth of her walls.

"We...got...to get...the condoms." His desire to use one withered as she met his every stroke. He pumped her from the bottom like he was trying to make a point. When she climbed off him, he dove for the condoms, but she held him with her legs and guided his penis inside of her. She clawed his back and drew blood as she reached her climax. She thrusted her ass into his penis, wanting to feel all of Claude's fluids run deep inside her. Claude exploded in her, filling her womb with his cream. He collapsed on top of her.

They talked about the old times and Darlene's status. She said she was on the pill and had no intentions of entrapping him. She said she was clean. No matter how much she tried to convince him that he had nothing to worry about, he still kicked himself in the head for thinking with the little one. Even though he didn't possess any feelings for her like she did with him, her pussy was good. He wanted to keep her around until he found what he was looking for in a woman.

They had another protected round of sex. They fucked until they fell asleep in each other's arms. Claude brimmed with pride. He hadn't had any pussy in over fifteen years and he was fucking like Ron Jeremy. He woke up periodically throughout the evening. Darlene's cell phone vibrated nonstop. He retrieved her cell phone stealthily. She had twenty-five missed calls. Twenty of those calls came from Lloyd. He gently removed her hold from his chest to use the bathroom.

On his way back from the bathroom, Claude looked at the clock on the microwave. It read 8:00pm. Sahara wasn't due home until midnight. He had to make sure Darlene was out before ten because Sahara didn't like Darlene. The last thing Claude needed to hear was Sahara's mouth about Darlene being in her house. When Sahara heard the news about Darlene's pregnancy, she empathized with Claude because he was already in a fucked up situation. She never liked or trusted Darlene. When Claude told Sahara what she did, it didn't surprise her. He didn't want to hear any commotion on his second day out. He just knew he had to get Darlene out of there before his sister came home.

13-Los Angeles

The smoke coming from two *Purple Haze* blunts spread across the living room like a cloud in the sky. Two blunts circulated through a triad of people. Prime, Maria, and Linda sat on the dirty orange sofa covered with plastic zoned out, each consumed in their own amoral thoughts. Linda, a short, pudgy female with more hips than tits, was craving for the white powder. She was dark-skinned with a small case of acne of the left side of her face. The other side had blemishes. Her hair was short and coarse and she normally wore weaves, but since her new friend named Addiction came along, her appearance was the least of her worries. Prime's high was interrupted because Linda kept hounding him to call Aaron for the coke. Prime didn't want any reason to call Aaron because he was still ducking him. The thought of the murders haunted him. He never killed anyone, but he was there when it happened; he was just as guilty.

He hadn't slept. He lost the small sample of pleasure in life he once had, not that he was living comfortable or enjoying life itself, but he had a little hope of progressing. He was in the dark. The only way he would see light was if he snitched. He eliminated that idea because he would just enter another world of hell. He could get killed or be labeled a snitch for the rest of his life. He was lost in a maze of shit. He came up with one solution. He was going to bounce. He thought about Sonya all day and couldn't blame her for getting away. It enhanced his motive for leaving. He decided that it would be best for him to ditch town. It was the best and only option.

Prime passed the blunt to Linda. She took several pulls, stopped, and took two more pulls before she passed it to Maria, a tall, thick, lazy-eyed light skinned woman in her early thirties.

"Can you make that call again baby? We been here for almost an hour and I don't know how much I could tolerate this weed," Linda said sluggishly.

Maria had an annoyed look on her face.

"His connect ain't the only nigga in town that's holding. The nigga ain't pickin' up so stop sweatin' it. Always on that fiend shit."

Linda looked at Maria and snapped her teeth, but knew from experience not to take it beyond that. Maria could be violent, especially when there were onlookers. Linda felt embarrassed. Prime sat in the same position. He didn't seem to be paying attention.   Although she picked up on Prime's odd vibe earlier, she was thankful he was still in it.

Maria got up off the sofa and asked where the bathroom was. She had to ask Prime twice before she got a response. Prime told her the bathroom was in the hallway, the second door on the left. Linda waited until she heard the bathroom door close before making the same request.

"Prime, can you at least call one more time? If he don't pick up, I won't bother you no more."

Prime looked at her coldly. He wondered why he fucked with her. He was on the verge of cursing her out before his cell phone vibrated on the coffee table. Linda attempted to see who was on the caller ID, but he shoved her hand out of the way before she had a chance to touch it. The caller ID read, "Flex." He hoped it Aaron wasn't with him.

"Yeah."

"Where the fuck you been hidin' nigga? I know you ain't runnin' your mouth," Flex said thickly.

Prime got up and walked into the kitchen.

"What the fuck you getting all hostile for? I was out with my moms yesterday. I don't even know why I'm explaining."

"Actin' all suspect an' shit," Flex reciprocated flatly.

Prime dropped it. He didn't know if Aaron was around. He just wanted to get Linda off his ass.

"I've been calling 'cause I got these bitches over here," Prime said, having no regard to Linda staring in his face. "Linda wants her usual. You could come through and swing that by?"

"What the fuck is you whispering for? Who is the other bitch?" Flex asked, his hostile mood changing to lust.

"Maria."

"That lazy-eyed bitch? Nah, I'll pass. How long they going be there for?"

"As soon as you bring that."

Silence.

"Have you seen Sonya?"

Prime felt a bowel movement coming along, but he knew they didn't know anything. He played it cool; it wasn't like he was going to stick around anyway. He was going to leave Los Angeles as soon as possible.

"No, I didn't see her. Why? What's up?"

"She left this nigga, that's what's up. All this work and dough we got, and this nigga is stressed over a bitch. He ain't picking up his phone. Enough talking. I'll be there in fifteen, and Prime, remember, you on notice so don't fuck around and get hurt," Flex concluded gravely and hung up.

Prime went back into the living room feeling the heat from the threat. He was determined to get the fuck out of dodge. Maria and Linda sat quietly. Prime noticed the desperation in Linda's eyes. He shook his head in disgust, knowing that she was waiting on the word so he let it out.

"Don't ask no questions. It's coming."

Prime reached into the bag and rolled two more blunts of haze. He wanted to kill time before Flex made his arrival.

. . .

Homicide Detective Jack Taft sat at his desk stuffing his face with donuts and coffee, looking over the digital pictures of the murder victims, which were taken at the house on Monteith Drive. Pictures of the bodies of Colin, D-Bone, Earl, and B-Bum were spread across his desk. The pictures of the bodies were taken before they removed them from the crime scene. Detective Taft knew that the men were killed execution style because they were lined up against the wall. All of them were shot in the head. Detective Taft, sixty, had one year left on the force. He was tall, bald, and pudgy. He was a defensive lineman in high school and college and was known throughout the fuzz for his brute strength. He had a thick salt and peppered walrus mustache and dark blue eyes. He was brash, but everyone in the department respected him. The plaques over his desk spoke volumes. He solved hundreds of cases, but the pictures of the victims contained a question mark because there were no witnesses, prints, or anything concrete that could point a finger at a suspect(s). The only thing the assailants left at the scene of the crime was a few shell casings, but they didn't have any fingerprints. He took a break from looking at the morbid flicks and focused his attention on his own family. He cringed at the thought of anyone harming his wife and two daughters. He had spent many countless nights working on cases, making sure his family received the best in life. He was thankful he didn't fall into the bracket of a divorcee detective.

Detective Samuel Rinaldi walked in on his partner eyeing the picture on his desk. A man in his late thirties who was promoted to homicide detective a year ago, he walked with a strong silence. He had dirty blond hair and had a chiseled face. He was a former marine and had a genuine obsession for following the rules. He was a firm and square detective who went by the book. Many of the veteran homicide detectives disliked Rinaldi because he was only a police officer for three years and was appointed homicide detective. It took many of them in the homicide department eight to fifteen years. Unlike Detective Taft, he struggled to maintain his marriage. He sought the pleasure of going to work to leave his unstable home life. Everyone was also aware that his wife was having multiple affairs. He was considered a prick by many, especially the two DEA agents he snitched on for taking money during a drug bust. He was, however, a U.S. soldier from the Nemesis troop, 3rd Squadron, 2nd Stryker Cavalry regiment. His childhood friend was coincidently in the same regiment, but was killed after the stryker vehicle he was riding in was hit by an improvised explosive devise. Those that were close to him, which were very few, state that the incident in Iraq traumatized him and he was walking around with untreated PTSD.

Rinaldi saw the pictures of the murder victims on Taft's desk and knew he was just as baffled as his partner. He stood there holding some files. Taft was so consumed by the case that he didn't hear Detective Rinaldi come into the office.

"Is this case kicking your ass or what?" Rinaldi asked nonchalantly while he looked through the files he brought into the office.

Detective Taft put the picture of his family back in its

place, looked at his protégé and spoke.

"Kicking my ass huh? It should be kicking your ass too. If we don't crack this case open before the captain starts feeling heat from the commissioner, our asses will be in the can. You said you wanted a case that will help your career; this case could easily end our careers, especially yours. We don't have a lead to lean on. The only fucking thing we could assume is that the murders were drug related. Colin Jones was an up and coming player in the drug trade and he wasn't killed for nothing. Earl Moore and Byron Jenkins had extensive criminal records. That Dennis Howard kid was up and coming, but didn't have a criminal record and had an education. Either somebody wanted them dead or somebody wanted to take over their reign, simple as that."

"Well, brace yourself. When it rains, it pours. Remember that Peter Sullivan kid that we interviewed that day?" Rinaldi asked.

"Yeah, the only eyewitness we have, why?"

"His mother just called and said he's been gone since yesterday early afternoon. I know it's a myth about waiting twenty-four hours to declare someone missing, but she said it wasn't like him to disappear for an entire day. She didn't even know the person he was with the night of the murders, so she had no information on him. But the woman was pretty hysterical."

Taft sighed. "That kid is probably as dead as a fucking tree right now. A witness is a guaranteed ride to prison."

"Just hold your horses. Let's not jump to conclusions. The kid probably went partying and got cocked and realized that he wasn't in the right state of mind to come home. That is the least of our worries now," Detective Rinaldi said, minimizing the situation.

Detective Taft looked at his partner long and hard and shook his head like he was out of his fucking skull. Throughout his years of being a detective, twenty at that, he knew from prior experience that the kid was dead. There was no doubt about it. If the assailants could leave no concrete evidence behind, they damn sure wouldn't leave an eyewitness alive.

Rinaldi only had a year of being a detective and lacked the extra nuts and bolts to declare such a thing, so Detective Taft ignored his ignorance. Rinaldi was assigned to be Taft's partner by design so he could learn to use his sixth sense, but so far, Detective Rinaldi at times seemed clueless.

"I know we're dealing with some heavy shit here, but use your head. Whoever committed those murders knew what the hell they were doing. There were no signs of forced entry or anything. We combed the area all night and we still couldn't come up with a single goddamn fingerprint. The shell casings weren't any help because they were dipped in solvents. There were no drugs in the house, if there were any in the first place. The kid said the individuals in the truck made eye contact with him. What makes you think that those fucks didn't think about that? They knew they were seen and they did something about it. They kidnapped him and killed them. Put yourself in a killer's shoes. What would you have done if you knew you could get away with a murder and realized that someone could place you at the scene of a crime? Admit it Rinaldi, whoever did it is pretty elusive."

Rinaldi was dumbfounded, but understood his partner. He only hoped for the best, but that didn't get far in the homicide division. Experience allowed one to have a sixth sense, to have that first instinct. A good detective never ignored or disregarded their first instinct, so he knew he was not capable of making an argument.

"I understand your point, believe me. If that kid is dead somewhere, it's a classic case of being at the wrong place at the wrong time," Detective Rinaldi stated, putting the files on his desk.

"That's an understatement, but you're right. How old was that Peter kid anyway?"

"Sixteen. That kid should've been in the house."

"Maybe it's a good thing Peter's mother didn't know about that other kid. I will ride over there after work and tell her if he calls or shows up, tell him not to come around anymore, or at least until we get to the bottom of things. We'll just have her give him our number in case he knows something. If that kid shows up looking for Peter, hell, who knows, those guys could be camped out somewhere on that street, willing to do what they have to do. I just hope the kid doesn't live on the next street over. We may have to get an unmarked cruiser and park and make that part of our routine just in case we see something out of the ordinary," Detective Taft said.

"It would be bizarre if Peter's friend was the key to this entire case," Rinaldi hypothesized.

"It seems a little far-fetched, but we can't rule out anything at this time. Either someone is hiding something or nobody knows a goddamn thing. Colin Jones's girlfriend found the bodies and there is a question mark over her head. She's fucked up over this shit, but we can't even rule her out as a possible suspect. Dennis Howard's sister only identified someone who was with Howard the night of the murders, but it's not enough information to build from. There are a lot of light skinned, droopy fucks in Los Angeles. I even tried to get information from Byron Jenkins's family, but no one knows anything. I'm even wondering if his family even gives a shit. Earl Moore isn't even from California. His family requested his body to be shipped to New York. They knew he was involved in some shady shit, but they don't have a clue. If we don't do anything to get a lead on this case, we're fucked."

14-Dallas

It had been a week since Sonya landed in Dallas. There was still a slight blemish under her eye, but the swelling was gone. She was riding in the back seat of Mark's car with Fatima riding shotgun. Mark was en route to their mother's house. He really didn't want to go because he was in no mood to be caught in a web of drama. He looked in the rearview mirror and noticed the grim expression on Sonya's face. He loved Fatima, but he wanted no part of the family drama. He had his own drama and didn't want to drown off of anyone's misery.

As he made his way on South 35E, he wondered if his cousin in Connecticut came out of the slammer. He called a few times two weeks ago. He made a mental note to call him to see if he made it home as soon as the opportunity presented itself.

Mark made a right onto Greenville Avenue and made a left hand turn onto Marquita Avenue, drove straight, and went past three houses. The house was the fifth one on the right. He pulled in the driveway behind a light-green Dodge Intrepid. The house was small compared to the rest of the houses on the street. The house was flat with a lawn that had seen better days. A quarter acre of soil had patches of grass from a lack of lawn care. A few slides of the blue siding hung from the house, but it was decent.

Sonya had a sullen look on her. She didn't want to be there because of Russell. For years, Julia had a habit of putting him before her own children. It caused years of turmoil. Sonya would only visit her family on holidays and split a day later. Although she loved her mother, she wasn't in any hurry to bury the hatchet in the past as long as Russell was around.

They stepped out of the car. Fatima walked around it and took Mark's hand as they made their way to the door. Sonya stood behind them. She saw Fatima release Mark's grip from his hand and knocked.

A few moments had passed but there was no answer.

Mark heard ruffling noises in the kitchen. Despite Julia's car being in plain view, he hoped no one was home.

Damn, he thought. He heard footsteps approaching the

door from inside the house.

An older version of Sonya moved the small curtain away from the glass with her eyes deadlocked on Sonya. Her mother's eyes widened, displaying the shock she felt seeing her first born. She opened the door and rushed past Mark and Fatima and embraced Sonya. Sonya had the same grim expression on her face and patted her mother's back with one hand while her other hand was drooped to her own side.

"My baby is home!" Julia started crying. It didn't matter how Sonya felt towards her at that time. Her mother was just glad to see her. The short visits and the lack of phone calls weighed on Julia's conscious. She spoke to Sonya a few months ago, but the conversation was brief. Julia's embarrassment and shame had prohibited her from calling her daughter consistently. Julia finally released her grip and stepped back. She was so overwhelmed with joy that she didn't notice the blemish under Sonya's eye.

"You look good girl! Why are we standing outside? Come in y'all."

Sonya appeared emotionless as she followed Fatima and Mark into the house. Fatima couldn't blame her. She hoped they could be civilized.

Julia led them into the living room. Sonya noticed that nothing had changed since she visited on Christmas of last year. The portrait of a Caucasian Jesus Christ rested in the same spot. The walls were eggshell white. A large portrait of Julia, Sonya, and Fatima hugged the wall between other relative's framed photos. The portrait was taken when Sonya and Fatima were teenagers, a few years after their father was murdered and a year before Julia met Russell.

"So Fatima, when were you going to tell me that Sonya was back in town? There you go hidin' things from your mother."

"Please Momma, don't start. Sonya had a long week and she just wanted to rest, that's all. It ain't nothin' to look into, trust me."

Julia glanced at Sonya and noticed the blemish under her eye.

"Girl, what happened to yo' eye? I know you aint…"

"It's no different then what that nigga always did to you," Sonya said defensively.

"I haven't heard your voice in two months and you gon' talk to me like that? I am still your mother and I will not tolerate that kind of talk in my house," Julia said calmly.

Sonya rolled her eyes and kept quiet.

Mark sat on the small brown sofa opposite of Sonya and Fatima playing on his Galaxy. He felt the tension before the comment, but now the tension escalated. He felt that it was only going to get worse the longer they stayed. He wasn't in any mood to be a peacemaker.

"Boy, you gon' sit there and play with that phone or are you gonna be anti-social to your future in-law?" Julia asked jovially.

Mark couldn't help to crack a smile as he was caught off guard, but he liked the in-law part of Julia's question.

"Oh, I'm sorry. I didn't mean to…"

"I'm just playing. How come you ain't workin' today? I hope you got sense enough to save yo' time-off. You keep burnin' yo' time and you ain't gon' have no choice but to go to work, even when you sick."

"Momma, stop hounding him like that. Today is his day off and he's using it to spend time with us. Dang. Always tellin' folks they own business."

Julia ignored Fatima. "How long you in town for Sonya?"

"For good Momma," Sonya said flatly.

"You mean you ain't going back to Los Angeles?"

"That's what I said."

"I got an extra room that Russell keeps all his shit at. I'll have him…"

"No thank you momma. I'm fine."

"Excuse me, you must have a job or something 'cause Fatima ain't going let you stay with her without a job you know."

"Momma, Stop it! We're not over here to argue with you so…"

"Julia! Where the fuck is my motherfucking shoes at woman? You clean this goddamn house five times a day and I can't find shit!" Russell roared from down the hall in his deep, gruff voice, unaware that she had company.

Russell was home. Sonya had an evil look on her face when she heard his voice. Sonya caught Mark's eye and beckoned him that she was ready to go. Mark couldn't read lips but knew what she requested. She was in no mood to hear any of Russell's bullshit. Sonya gave her mother a look of dissatisfaction.

Just when Julia was about to answer his ignorant ass, Russell beat her to the punch.

"And who the fuck are you on the phone with anyway goddammit? It better not be no long-distance call, I tell you that much!"

"Momma, I am so sick and tired of him talkin' to you like you're a piece of trash," Fatima said loudly, not caring if Russell heard her.

"Fatima, please," Julia said in defeat, her happy demeanor deteriorating, feeling Sonya's eyes all over her.

"Last week, you was giving me a *I had enough* speech and now he is telling you how to run your household," Fatima blasted.

Heavy footsteps were heard coming down the hall. As soon as Russell reached the doorway of the living room, he opened his mouth to say something but bit his tongue. He was unprepared for her arrival. He caught Sonya's evil glare and decided to mellow out.

It was Mark's second time seeing the chubby, tall, dark-complexioned man. His beard was heavy and his head was shaved bald. His teeth were disfigured. Julia was a beautiful woman in her mid fifties, but Mark never understood what she saw in him.

"Hey, hey, what it is Sonya, uh, long-time no see, you want something to eat?" Russell asked, not knowing what else to say, feeling stupid.

"No," Sonya said curtly.

"Ah, yeah, I got to find these shoes for my job interview. I was worried that you was tying up the phone," Russell lied smoothly. Russell hadn't worked since Sonya and Fatima were teenagers. Mark was an outsider looking in to the family and he knew Russell was full of shit.

"Yeah, this trucking company got some spots open. You looking for a job brotha?"

"Nah, I'm straight, but thanks for asking," Mark responded politely. He played the neutral role.

"What, you got a job or something?" Russell pressed.

Just when Mark opened his mouth to answer, Fatima stepped in.

"Yeah, he has a real job. He doesn't need the imaginary job that you're making up," Fatima said coldly.

Mark dropped his head in his hands, not wanting to be the focal point of any argument. Even though he wasn't at fault, he still felt uncomfortable being the man in the middle of a family dispute. He attempted to get up, but Fatima sat Mark down with her eyes. It was ninety seven degrees outside and Mark would gladly sit in the car and let them slug it out.

Russell pulled out a Winston, put it in his mouth, and lit the cigarette, having no idea what to say. All eyes were on him. If he could fly away or drop dead, he would.

"Why you got to be so goddamn cold? I'm the nigga that raised you and you talking to me like one of them motherfuckers out on the street."

"Let me get something straight. You ain't nobody's daddy up in this bitch, so I suggest you take yo' black ass back where you came from!" Fatima said belligerently, waving her hands and snaking her neck.

"Julia, you better tell your daughter about runnin' her goddamn mouth in my house, 'cause she could get the fuck out!"

Julia shook her head like she had enough. "Stop it! Just stop it! Both of y'all need…"

"What you need to do Momma is stop defending this sorry ass nigga! He ain't shit and he never going be shit! Talking bout he got a job interview. That dumb ass nigga got an appointment with the loan shark. Look how he talks to you!"

Mark was stunned, his head going right and left, listening to everyone's side of the story. He looked at Russell and knew that he couldn't spit a single word over Fatima's fast talking ass.

"I ain't going to sit here and listen to this shit!" Russell yelled as he made an attempt to walk away. He was unable to speak his mind.

"While you're at it, try getting a job so you could pay momma's phone bill since you like to complain so much about tying up lines. This ain't your house, you got no say, job, life, and etc. My daddy, a real man, paid for this house with cash, so fuck you and your *my house* bullshit. He left it to momma!"

Julia attempted again to deescalate the situation, but her attempts fell on deaf ears. Fatima drilled him for the next five minutes while Mark adjusted himself to all the yelling and watched.

"Momma, you lost valuable time with Sonya behind him. You might lose some with me if you keep this piece of shit around. It's either us or his peasant ass," Fatima said, giving her mother a brutal ultimatum.

"No, she lost time fuckin' with that nigga out there in California," Russell said, managing to squeeze in a little venom.

Sonya lost her cool. She grabbed the picture of her and Fatima off the coffee table and threw it at Russell. The edge of the picture frame nearly caught him in his eye. As soon as the picture landed on the floor, the glass protecting the twenty-year old picture shattered into pieces. Sonya leaped forward with a flurry of punches while Russell put up his arms in defense. Mark jumped between them and grabbed Sonya by her waist with the intentions of removing her from the area while Sonya kept kicking and swinging. He managed to take her outside to the car. While outside, Mark held on to her until she stopped her aggressive movement.

"Sonya, calm down! We don't need any trouble from the cops," Mark stated desperately while he scanned the area. There were onlookers looking at the house.

"Ok Mark, I'm fine! Mark, let me go, I' m fine!"

"I ain't going to let you go until you calm down, for real. Believe me, we would all go to jail today. I ain't fuckin' with these Dallas cops!" Mark said while releasing his grip.

Sonya got into the backseat and broke down. Meanwhile, Fatima was heard from the outside yelling. The arguing started to become an attraction. Mark was about to go inside the house to grab Fatima until he saw her storm out the door. She got in the car. Mark backed out of the driveway and drove off.

Julia rested on her knees, holding the shattered picture crying, knowing that she was the real cause for putting Russell before her own children. Russell sat on the couch watching her. He felt nothing but embarrassment and shame. Julia wept some more as she realized that Russell would have to go.

15-Waterbury

Claude rested on his bed during the downpour. He looked for jobs all morning. He had been out of prison for a week and had not received one phone call from an employer. Rocks became persistent on enticing Claude back into the game, telling him that the nine to five shit was for the birds and with the money they could make, it wouldn't even be a struggleHe knew that the only thing Rocks was doing was giving him a recipe for disaster.

His room was quiet. He could hear Sahara scolding Destiny about jumping on the furniture, which brought a little life inside his room. The smile on his face faded as he thought about his job hunt and the struggle that came with it. He had been to several locations looking for jobs, but had no leads.

Claude reached inside the junk drawer and pulled out all the completion certificates he accumulated over the years in prison and thumbed through them. He pulled out his GED diploma and realized that the GED alone was not going to earn him a spot in the corporate world. As he thumbed through more completion certificates, the telephone rang.

"Claude, pick up the phone!" Sahara yelled from the living room.

He hoped it was an employer.

"Hello?"

"You better pick up the phone to talk to me. How you holding up?" Delores stated and continued. "I knew you were home because the letters that I wrote you came back. Oh, TeeTee was running her mouth up here about your homecoming but I didn't believe that gossiping bitch until she showed me the letter one of her people's from Waterbury wrote her…"

How did she know I was home! Damn how shit gets around. That bitch is a lifer!

"…she said she knew you was home because I guess you, Rocks, and Tommy saw Darlene and some other peoples that was around y'all that night."

"Ma…how did she…"

94

"Be careful. You seemed so focused when you wrote me the last letter. Don't get caught up with Darlene. I ain't judging her, but I always had a bad feeling about her. That shit I heard she pulled on you at the jail confirmed it, even though y'all was young, but still, once a sack chaser, always a sack chaser. You strap up with her and I ain't even playing."

"I ain't takin' her seriously, if that's what you're trying to insinuate. It was just a one night thing, that's all," he said defensively, feeling ashamed that his mother knew the deal and not to mention that he hit it raw.

"Claude, I know y'all men. Especially being locked up so long. You take heed 'cause I know you got more sense then that. Pussy comes with consequences. I ain't got much time on this phone but how is the job hunt going?"

"Still hunting," Claude answered unenthusiastically.

"Keep trying. Nobody said it was going to be easy," she said, already knowing what he was going through. "I gotta go Claude. I love you and tell Sahara I love her and for her to give my grandchild a kiss…"

The line went silent until it reached a dial tone.

Claude placed the cordless phone back on the base. He plopped down back on his bed and realized that the purpose of his mother's call was to greet and warn him. She couldn't say everything over the phone, for she might be on phone review. Everything vital for Claude to know would be included in a letter. Darlene was the main focus of that collect call. Throughout her incarceration, she had learned how to summarize her information in a small amount of time. Collect calls didn't last long.

Claude watched TV until he nodded off. Sahara woke him up by calling his name from the living room.

"Claude, pick up the phone!"

"Hello," Claude said groggily.

"What's good my nigga?"

"Who's this?"

"Who the fuck you want it to be?"

Claude looked at the caller ID and saw a 214 area code. Out of state.

"Come on man, for real, who is this?"

"It's your mans and 'em."

"Alright nigga! Enough of these fucking games. Either you tell me who the fuck it is or…"

"Or what nigga!? What the fuck you going do you eight hundred push-up a day doing motherfucker."

Claude's smile broadened.

"Mark!"

"Its about time!"

"What it do cuzzo?" Claude was excited.

"I told Sahara not to tell you it was me cause' I wanted to fuck with you."

"I was passed the fuck out. This rain got me feeling lazy as hell. I was looking for some jobs this morning and brought my ass in the house when I saw that bolt of lightening flash across the sky. How's that Dallas life treating you?"

"I will never come back to Connecticut again. I will visit, but it's so much shit down here to do. I was up in Waterbury six months ago to handle some shit and I became excited."

"Excited? You just said you ain't coming back. How could you be excited looking at Waterbury?"

"Excited because I knew I was going back the next day. That place has not changed a bit. It ain't nothin' worse than the same nigga with the same fucked up ass attitude."

"I hear you. I been out for a week and the only things that changed is some of the buildings. Other than that, niggas is doing the same shit that I did before I got locked up and the shit is depressing."

"So C, how you doing dawg?" Mark asked seriously, changing the mood of the conversation.

"I'm doing. I don't know man. I been on the hunt for the last week and I didn't get a call yet. Temp services never even called me back. I ain't placing no blame on nobody, but damn, once you get that label as a felon, you might as well consider yourself blackballed."

"I feel you, but yo, how long do you got that parole shit over your head?"

"Another year and I'm done with that invisible bar shit."

"You need to try to bring your ass down this way. Your record is everywhere you go, but you could find a gig a lot easier down this way than the 'bury.' Loads of jobs down here. A determined parolee could make a decent living. Dudes be comin' home off of major bids doing it bro."

"That definitely sound like an option. New beginnings an' shit."

"Yeah man. It's like another world down here. Too bad you on parole. You could've came down here to at least get a taste. Like I said, there ain't no way in hell I'm coming back up there to live. It ain't shit up there."

"So how's the females down there?"

"You have no idea. You would lose your fucking head cousin. There ain't nothing but video broads down here!"

"You dipping or somebody got you in the house on weekends?"

"We been together for a year and some change."

"Alright, alright, she a keeper?"

"No doubt about it. She got the three C's."

"The three C's?"

"Career, car, and crib."

Claude heard women arguing in the background.

"It seems like your girl cussin' somebody the fuck out."

"Hold on C." They were loud because the bedroom door was shut and Claude was able to hear it.

He slid open the patio door that led to the balcony and closed it once he stepped out.

"I didn't want them to hear me, but check it, my girl and her sister had a war over at their mother's house today. That's why they in the room arguing an' shit," Mark said while he looked through the glass to see if they stepped out of the room.

"She got a sister? Hook me up," Claude joked.

"I could put in a few lines, if you want me to, but you may be on your own. She got some shit going on."

"I feel you. I'll let that one pass. I'm pretty sure she don't want no jobless nigga anyway."

"You need some dough?"

"I'm straight for the moment, but good lookin' though. I

97

appreciate it."

"No doubt but check it, I got to get up off this phone before my girl start asking a thousand questions. If you need anything, I mean anything, do not hesitate to call your 'cuz.' I'm here for you."

"No doubt cuz. I'll definitely keep that in mind. All y'all have a joyful evening," Claude concluded.

"You do the same...one."

"One."

As soon as Claude hung up, he smiled at the thought of Mark being in Texas. He knew Mark had potential as youths growing up in Waterbury. Mark was the only relative that took his word seriously.

He plopped back down on his bed with a new vision. He didn't want to use the lack of opportunity in Waterbury as an excuse, but he envisioned a better opportunity in Texas. A new beginning was definitely the first step on achieving the American Dream. He also wandered idly on what Mark's girlfriends' sister looked like. The conversation inspired him.

16-Waterbury

Darlene looked around for her bra. Claude stared at her body and couldn't help but to be amazed. At twenty six, she had the body of a supermodel. Despite the conversation he had with his mother, he knew he couldn't just kick Darlene to the curb. She was the only one he was sexing. He'd rather have an ace in the hole before deciding to kick her to the curb because of some hearsay shit. He had too many lonely nights jerking his dick to be ridding himself of pussy. He didn't want Darlene as a wife, but he appreciated her pussy, and that was as far it would go.

She wished she could stay a little longer, but she had to go to work. She arrived an hour after Sahara left the house. Darlene stood up after she put on her jeans while her breasts were still exposed. He had secretly hid her bra under his pillow. She looked at him in the mirror and caught his smirk and knew he had it stashed. She turned around and walked towards him. With her jeans on and her thong on display, she crawled on the bed and licked his leg until her tongue reached his scrotum. She held it in her mouth while she stroked his penis, and a moment later, she expertly placed his manhood in her mouth. Claude's eyes turned to whites from the pleasure. She sucked his shaft and deep throated him. Her nipples and wide, dark areolas turned him on. When their eyes locked, she saw the lust in them as they both moaned. She was too deep in her head game to stop so she kept going. She gyrated the small space between his legs as she continued to bob her head on his jewel. While in motion, he looked at her slow head movement and the passion in her eyes when she looked up at him seductively. Without warning, Claude exploded in her mouth, releasing every drop of cum into her pretty mouth. Darlene got up, grabbed her pocket book, and went to the bathroom.

The day was still fairly young and he had the itch to enjoy the rest of the day outdoors, and possibly hit the club with Rocks and Tommy tonight. It had been a long week of filling out job applications and being told the same bullshit so he figured it was only fair that he enjoyed that luxury. He reached for the cordless and dialed Rocks's number.

"Yo," Rocks answered sluggishly.

"Come get me," Claude said flatly.

17-Los Angeles

Ali Ward and Wade Smith made their way through the small, dark, and crowded bar. People of all races blocked the henchmen's path as they inched their way through the crowd using elbows and small shoves. The atmosphere was tranquil and peaceful until the men walked in. The men were not physically gifted with bulging muscles or massive bulk, but their guns could take down men of all shapes and sizes. Their body language spelled a bloody incident waiting to happen.

Strategically placed mirrors decorated the walls of *The Room* for a full visual of many couples who took their bedroom duties to an open scene. The city's top DJ spun hip-hop and r&b records wildly for the diversified crowd. Everyone seemed to be in tune with the Rihanna song *Work* except for the two cronies. Ali was a short and wiry brown skinned man who was grimy, heartless, vindictive, and impulsive. His hair was either in cornrows or tied into a ponytail. He wore a pair of baggy jean shorts, a James Harden Houston Rocket jersey, and a pair of black Air Force Ones. He had a horseshoe mustache that was connected to his three-inch long goatee held together by an elastic band. Only twenty-six, he wasn't going to be anything more then a career criminal. His mother died giving birth to him so he was raised by his maternal grandmother, who also housed a few of his cousins, but she couldn't keep up with none of them. He spent the majority of his early adolescence in behavioral group homes and the late part of his adolescence in juvenile prison. Two days after celebrating his eighteenth birthday, he was arrested for an assault, sent to county jail, sentenced a few months later to four years, and got shipped to California State Prison. He had been out of prison for four years, the longest stretch he stayed in society since his early childhood, but he was a court case waiting to happen. He contributed a few bodies to the unsolved murder files in the Los Angeles Police Department.

Wade, also twenty-six, was the lesser of two evils. He was a dark skinned, medium sized man with a baby face. His hair was like a dark sea of waves. He was dressed in black jeans, a pair of all white uptowns, and a short-sleeve Rocawear buttoned down shirt. He lived for the moment. He had no ambition but to live to see the next day. His attribute in society used to be car jacking, but he did three and a half years because of it. The two felonies over his head would not stop him from killing someone if it was necessary. Ali and Wade knew each other since they were teenagers placed in juvenile detention. They were officially crime partners who had a high disregard for life.

Wade asked the attractive bartender to send over two shots of Hennessy. He retrieved the shots from her and gave one to Ali.

"Its some bitches in here tonight!" Ali said excitedly.

"Yeah, but all of them is hugged up wit' niggas. We probably the only two motherfuckers in here that came without nothing to poke on."

"That's they fucking problem for bringing sand to the beach. I wasn't trying to bring my girl. I'll approach any hoe in this bitch. I don't give a fuck if they brought niggas with em' or not," Ali stated loudly.

"I'm with that. But the way I'm feelin' now, I could damn near rape a fuckin' bitch and make her nigga watch! That's the shit I'm on right now." Wade rubbed his hands together deceptively wearing a grin on his face.

The men laughed. Two songs later, Ali went to the bar and ordered two more shots. He noticed an oriental man trying to get the bartender's attention, but Ali cut him a cold look. The man fronted like somebody was calling him in the crowd and kept his attention there. The bartender took Ali's order and came back with the drinks. Just when he turned around to give Wade his drink, a young white man bumped into Ali's left arm, causing him to spill his drink on his James Harden jersey.

"What the fuck…"

"Dude, I'm so sorry man! Here, let me buy you another drink. Fuck man! I'm so fuckin' clumsy! What are you drinking?"

"Yo, you got this drink all over my shit! Damn…"

"Order him another Hennessy," Wade interrupted, knowing his friend too well.

Under any normal circumstance, Wade would have co-signed, but he didn't feel like getting kicked out of another club. The young man wasn't a threat and it was crowded as hell. The bartender rushed another shot of Hennessy. She recognized the situation and knew the man that spilled the Hennessy. Ali accepted the drink and didn't say a word. The man quickly hurried away, fearing that if he stood there another moment, something would've happened.

"Damn, let's get some hoes tonight. That motherfucker didn't do it on purpose and he bought you another drink."

Ali grabbed some napkins off the bar and followed his man's advice. He admitted internally that he did overreact. Wade understood that Ali had been going through some shit though. The amount of rage he carried with him could cause him to hurt someone. A day after his cousin's death, Ali shot and killed a base head for a twenty-dollar debt. He justified it by saying it was the principle. He punched another fiend and broke his jaw because he was a dollar short to buy crack. Ali was violent, but his cousin's death added more wood into the fire. They remained quiet for a moment before they recognized a woman approaching them.

"What y'all fools doing on this side of town?"

"Damn Raven! Lookin' good as usual," Wade stated with a hint of seduction.

Raven was a petite, red bone woman with salient hazel eyes. Her skin was smooth. She had gone to school for cosmetology with her sole focus on hairstyling, but had to drop out to attend to her ailing grandmother. Her hair was tied into one long braid that rested over her shoulder. She wore tight jeans and a halter top that displayed the swell of her breasts. Wade almost lost his head staring at them. She noticed him staring, but it was nothing new for her. She was used to getting attention. She was a deity in the human form. She wasn't there to gain any male attention, although prior to her brother's death, she secretly yearned for it. She was there to relieve some stress. Ever since D-Bone's murder, she had flashbacks of the last person she saw her brother with the last night she seen him alive. She often wondered if the droopy dude had anything to do with it.

Despite her breathtaking looks and sex appeal, her and her brother transported tons of cocaine and heroin within and across state lines for Colin and broke bread. They hid their leisure activities with their jobs, even though Raven's job wasn't official, but official enough to make ends meet on her half of the expenses. She had a fake cosmetology license for hairdressing so she could conduct her hairdressing business at her condominium, a condo that she bought and shared with her brother. However, things took a dramatic turn. D-Bone and Colin's death placed a heavy toll on their pockets, especially Ali, and knew she couldn't keep up with the mortgage on her swank condominium with her fake hairdressing business, although she had decent clientele. With her brother and Colin gone, the connect they had got locked up and won't be out anytime soon. She was looking for another come-up and a solid and consistent connect.

Ali smiled slightly, realizing that they both had something in common. Wade didn't pick up on it. He eventually did and toned his flirtatious ways down a notch. Ali looked into Raven's hazel eyes and knew she was only there to get her mind off of things. Ali was there to do the same.

"So how you doing?" Ali asked with sincerity.

"I'm doing," Raven responded with a loud sigh.

Wade left Ali and Raven so he could order another round of shots.

"Too bad I can't say the same thing for momma. Her supervisor told her to take as much time off as possible to grieve, but she won't do it. She says she needs to stay busy."

Ali listened. He thought about his cousin Colin and felt empathy and rage. He wanted to kill anyone who was responsible for the senseless killings. He didn't give a fuck about Earl and B-Bum, but had respect for D-Bone. He had absolutely no clue on who was responsible.

"Did you hear anything?"

"Huh?"

Ali came in closer to ear shot range so Raven could hear him.

"Did you hear anything?" Ali yelled in her ear, trying to yell over the roaring techno music.

"I didn't. These two detectives came by a day before the funeral trying to put something together, but I don't know anything. I told them what I told you the day after they were murdered. I saw him with this droopy, light skinned ugly dude, but that's all I know."

"If I find them motherfuckers, them two detectives don't got to do a goddamn thing." Ali accepted the drink from Wade. Raven did the same. As soon as someone moved away from the table, they sat down. Ali made a toast.

"To Colin and D-Bone. Rest in peace homies," Ali said while he kept his glass high.

"Toast," Wade and Raven said in unison before downing their drinks.

Raven broke the ice during the brief silence.

"A day after my brother and your cousin were killed, some white boy that lives on the same street was all of a sudden missing. Ain't that some shit?"

"It is. Maybe that's the reason why they are so persistent on solving the case. They don't give a fuck about niggas gettin' murdered in a house. They care about that white boy's disappearance. If that white boy would've never came up missing, them pigs would've threw that shit in the inactive files and stuck the murders on dead niggas," Ali stated.

"I know. But check it, if they didn't find that white boy by now, that motherfucker is dead," Wade interjected.

Ali no longer felt the thirst that overcame him when he and Wade made their intimidating entrance in the club. The mystery suspects that killed his cousin occupied his mind. Raven's mind pondered the same shit, but she didn't feel any rage. She just reminisced about D-Bone and how she used to watch him when their mother had to put in overtime at the job she still worked. Instead of grieving and venting in silence, Wade got off his seat and made his way through the crowd to mingle.

. . .

Aaron scanned the bar for Sonya. The effects from the liquor started to settle, making his mind a hazy mess. Instead of escaping the real world, he invited himself into a world of misery and depression. There was no doubt that he was wearing a mask to cover his front. He thought about Sonya so deeply that he blocked off the techno music. The only light that shed on Aaron's thoughts was the kilos; however, he knew that they would have to move with caution in the process or else word could hit the street that some up and coming cats pushing dope got picked off. Aaron had been watching the news vigorously since the murders; very little had been said about it. When he watched the news yesterday, the reporter stated that there were still no suspects, but Peter Sullivan's disappearance was emphasized. Anyone who dealt with Colin knew that he held weight where he shitted. Some street level soldiers who Colin supplied had plans of robbing him but were heated because they were picked off before they had a chance to snatch Colin's wealth. If Aaron and his crew busted in the scene, suspicions would be born. His empire in the making would have to grow slow to dispel suspicions.

While Aaron's crew shot the shit, he was absorbed into a world of loneliness. He continued his unrealistic search of her discreetly while Marco gave everyone a visual of a broad he fucked the day before. He had a hunch she was in Dallas, but he still had hopes of her being local.

The DJ switched the music from techno to smooth, baby making music, which snapped Aaron out of his black cloud. The petite white bartender took over for the male one as she moved with the swiftness of a school trained bartender. Flex aggressively flagged her to serve them. She gave him a signal that she'd be over in a minute. After the bartender finished serving some customers, she scurried over to serve Flex.

"Could I get a bottle of Moet?" Flex asked loudly into the bartender's ear.

"We don't serve drinks by the bottle."

"What?"

"We don't serve drinks by the bottle," she repeated loudly.

"This ain't the hood motherfucker," Marco said good-naturedly.

"Damn, y'all fucking people act like y'all don't want no money," Flex snarled, ignoring Marco's comment.

"Well, I'm sorry, I don't make the rules," she said nervously.

Marco eyed the waitress seductively. He noticed the uneasiness in her demeanor so he decided to ease the tension. He beckoned the bartender to come closer so he could say something in her ear.

"I know you don't make the rules. My man here drunk as hell so don't mind him. Just start a tab. Feel free to join us. I would love to be in the company of a beautiful soul like yourself. And if you don't mind, I would love to have your autograph with your number underneath it," Marco said smoothly while the bartender smiled bashfully.

Marco Valentine was a pretty boy with perfectly boxed teeth. His eyebrows were plucked into a perfect shape, looking like two McDonalds French fries. His mane was dark and sleek. His sidesburns looked like two knives pointing at his chin. He normally hides his hair underneath fit-it baseball caps. At thirty, he had a medium build. Marco was a replica of a movie star, but he was a killer. He had a body in Puerto Rico and one in Florida. The murders were all unsolved. Even though his transgressions were ghoulish, he was resourceful, well connected, and loyal. He wore a St. Louis Cardinal hat and was dressed in blue jeans, a long white tee shirt, and a pair of crispy red, suede, old school Pumas.

Flex watched the encounter between Marco and the bartender with hate. The bartender was a petite blond with blue eyes. She looked like one of the Olsen twins. Flex wasn't a bad looking man, but it would be a cold day in hell before he'd pull something like that. Flex never cared for Marco and wouldn't mind putting a bullet in his skull if he ever crossed him, even though they talked like they knew each other for years.

As soon as the bartender placed their shot glasses in front of them, everyone grabbed their shots and held them high. The bartender placed an inked napkin on the bar away from the fellas and looked at Marco. He understood the cue and decided to wait to retrieve it. Flex felt a sting of jealousy.

"Salute motherfuckers," Aaron said.

"Salute," they said in unison.

The men guzzled their shots. Flex looked at the napkin and wondered what was on it, but his thoughts were led astray after Marco asked a question.

"When are we going to make these moves man?"

"When its time to make them," Aaron responded.

Flex had a look of disbelief on his face. Marco didn't have to break a sweat to get the cash and the kilos, yet he was asking about power moves.

"I don't think you'll even be a suspect," Flex said sarcastically.

Aaron cut Flex a cold stare, but knew Flex was right, but he didn't have Marco's resources. Besides, if it weren't for Marco, Aaron would've fallen into the trap the inmates made for him when he was locked up. Some people he crossed were plotting to kill him, but Marco intervened just in time by tussling with Aaron's adversaries at his side, receiving the sharp end of a shank in the process. Aaron felt forever indebted to him.

"Yeah, I know I won't, but Prime ain't no different than me. He didn't even know the drill. And what are you bitching for anyway Flex? I know I wasn't there, but I ain't asking for no handouts either, so stop fucking with me," Marco said while he quickly sized Flex for any possible confrontation.

"Nigga, I know you ain't...," Flex started, but was interrupted.

"Yo, both y'all chill the fuck out, end of fucking discussion," Aaron said sternly.

Flex and Marco engaged in a stare down. If it weren't for the loud environment, everyone at the bar would have heard what the argument was about. People tended to their own business and laughed and joked while the two men were being hostile.

"Flex, whether you like it or not, Marco is down with us. Marco came through for your fat ass numerous times, so stop that shit!" Aaron snarled.

They disengaged their stare down but still kept the tension. They diverted their attention to the occupants in the club. Aaron declared it a dead issue.

"I don't know about y'all motherfuckers, but I'm about to find me a bitch," Aaron said as he disappeared into the crowd.

Flex left the bar without saying a word. Marco dissolved his anger towards Flex when he saw the cute bartender. Marco made his way over and left her a generous tip, as well as a promise to call her later on that night.

Flex spotted a short, pudgy light-skinned female dancing by herself. He didn't regard her at first, but her eye gazing was consistent. As he began to look at her with total lust, she began to dance in front of him from a distance. Reggae thundered out the speakers. Flex was so drunk, weeded, and coked up that he kept looking around him to see if she was trying to get someone else's attention. The more Flex grilled her, the more he knew that she was beckoning him. He reluctantly walked in her direction in a drunken swagger while she continued to dance. As soon as he approached her, she spun around and stuck her ass in his crotch, moving it in a smooth, sexy rhythm. His penis grew instantly while she continued to move her ass in a rhythmical motion. The DJ played a slow-paced reggae tune as Flex found himself pre-ejaculating. He grabbed her thick thighs and followed her rhythm with his crotch. She touched the floor with both of her hands while she circled her ass in a rhythm that Flex was too drunk to handle. She slowly got off of her hands and turned to face him. She ran both of her hands on his chest. She spiraled her body to his waistline and spiraled herself up slowly. As soon as the song was over, the DJ switched the reggae to house music, breaking the moment. Flex liked what he saw because she was his type. He knew he was in for some ass tonight.

"What's your name?"

She looked at him and started smiling.

"What is yours?" she reciprocated, making herself a mystery.

"You can call me anything you want baby," Flex said, avoiding giving this strange woman his government name.

She moved the front of her weave from over her left eye.

"Can you buy me a drink? If you do, you can call me any name you want."

Flex had something against women asking for drinks instead of being offered one, but the head on his penis replaced the thinking for the head on his shoulders. He didn't plan on marrying the bitch, so why not supply the fuel that would strengthen her sexual appetite? Before Flex could ponder another thought, she took him by the hand and led him to the bar.

Aaron bumped his way through the crowd to get a closer look at the chick that caught his interest. He noticed her walking behind two men going towards the entrance. He sighed in disbelief because he never bothered to look at the two men who were standing at least arm's length away from her. He was more than confident that she was at the club alone. As he watched her leave through the main entrance with her company, Sonya popped in his mind. He missed her.

. . .

Prime was packing his shit hurriedly. The weight of the murders was too much to bear. After Flex brought the goods for Linda the other night, he put himself back in his box and vowed to never see his henchmen of a team again.

A few minutes after his mother left for work, he wrote a letter explaining vaguely about his sudden departure and gave her stern instructions in which she would comply. He was so paranoid that he didn't leave a number. He ensured her that he'd keep in contact with her. He knew that his mother would be a wreck, but he had to do what he had to do.

As he put the remaining unfolded clothes into his oversized duffel bag, he thought about Linda. He didn't feel like he owed her an explanation, but he felt some type of obligation to let her know he was leaving town. He quickly disregarded the idea. He figured that she'd leak some information about him leaving town for a snort. As he shuffled through his thoughts, he went into his safe and pulled out the money he stashed from hustling. Although eight grand wasn't the type of money one could use to stay out of town for good, he knew he was going to flip it wherever he decided to lay his hat. He grabbed the stash and put it in another duffel bag.

Ten minutes later, he was standing at the door with a freshly rolled blunt in his hand, along with his traveling bags. He rode another thought while he stood at the door and was wondering if he was doing the right thing by leaving town. He answered his own question when he walked out of the door.

18-Dallas

A strong marijuana scent drifted under Sonya's nostrils. When she opened her eyes, she saw Mark sitting on a chair he got from the kitchen playing *NBA 2k16* online while he had a blunt dangling from his mouth. He didn't know Sonya was awake. He cursed quietly as the other team picked off one of his passes.

"You are going to have high blood pressure playing that game," Sonya joked. "That weed you're smoking isn't going to help either."

"Why don't you take a few pulls?"

"I think I'll pass, but thank you," Sonya said while she still pondered the idea of taking a few hits.

"I got some applications and some job postings for you on the kitchen table that I got from my job."

Damn, this boy is always high but he's on point and resourceful.

"Thank you so much Mark for remembering. I really appreciate it."

"Don't even mention it. Fill out that application quick. The closing date is a week from now. If you get hired, you'll start within a month. If the myth is true about second hand weed smoke, you will have more than enough time to clean up before the piss test."

Sonya continued to look at the burning blunt between Mark's fingers. *I might as well enjoy it while its here.* She hadn't smoked in four years. She figured that a few hits wouldn't do any harm..

"On second thought, I'll have a few drags."

Mark paused the game and passed the blunt to her. Sonya pulled on it gently, coughing in between totes. She passed the blunt back to him as if she were afraid of it. Mark refused it for the time being.

"Man, you better stop frontin' and smoke that shit," Mark said good-naturedly.

Sonya took two more pulls before passing it back to him. She coughed uncontrollably and moved smoke away from her face.

Sonya was high. They shared a lot of information about one another. She told him how a married man approached her earlier in the parking lot and how embarrassed he felt when she made reference to his family. Of course, Mark knew the dude and thought the shit was funny. She was happy that Mark was a part of the family. She felt a good level of comfort being around him. She told him about the high and low points of her relationship with Aaron and the steady abuse he inflicted on her.

"You want to know why I'm really here?"

"Why is that?" Mark asked.

"Because I was tired of getting hit and verbally abused, not to mention that he raped me. And he..."

"And?"

"And I think he killed somebody."

He got up and walked to the refrigerator and pulled out two Heinekens. He came back into the living room and passed one to her.

"Fatima know?" Mark lit up a Black and Mild cigar.

"No, not yet. Mark please don't tell her. Fatima runs her mouth to something wicked."

"You don't need to remind me. I hope you didn't tell anybody else about it. You're telling me that you think he killed somebody. How do you know for sure?"

Sonya told him everything that led to her theory. She told him the last time she saw Aaron, Flex, and Prime together, and the last time she saw D-Bone. She even went into detail about the look Prime had in his eyes when she asked him about it.

"The reason why that dude looked at you when you asked him was because he felt like you didn't need to know."

"Why wouldn't you think that he didn't want me to know?"

"Because you can't answer the questions that you don't know the answers to. That look he gave you was all you needed."

Mark gave Sonya a moment for his words to sink in.

"Is there anything in your name?"

"Yeah, the truck, but it's paid for."

"You should be straight then. If he was smart, he would have made the truck disappear."

"Yeah, he did."

"It is definitely a good thing that dude didn't tell you. If you're ever questioned, if the shit hits the fan, you don't know anything, and you're honestly telling the truth. You're only telling me that you think he killed somebody. As for right now, assume he didn't do it, but don't ever answer any questions for what you think, not even for what you know."

Sonya stared into open space as she replayed Mark's advice. She began to enjoy her high because she felt as if she got some heat off her chest. Mark was right; she didn't know for sure about Aaron's involvement in the murders. Why should she stress something that had nothing to do with her? She began to feel a little relieved. She figured that if she never opened up to Mark, she would have indirectly involved herself in a murder case that she never witnessed.

"That dude Prime you mentioned? He gave you a ride to the airport because he knew that nigga was going to kill you one of these days, but on the other hand, he put his life in danger behind this ordeal. If your ex ever finds out, he might end up killing him, that's if he is sweating you like that."

The last thing she needed on her conscious was Prime being killed because of her. *Damn, I should have just taken the cab.*

"No one saw us."

"Maybe not, but there is always a possibility."

When Mark was ready to add more emphasis to his point, Fatima walked in the door, coming in from work. She walked to where he sat and gave him a kiss. She looked at Sonya laughed.

"Girl, I know you ain't up in here getting high."

"Sonya a grown ass woman. She don't need yo' punk ass makin' comments," Mark joked.

Fatima playfully dismissed Mark. She continued to look at Sonya with a grin on her face. Even though she didn't know Sonya's complete story, she knew that she wasn't herself and something traumatic must have happened. As much as Fatima wanted to know what really went down, she knew her sister didn't trust her with information.

Mark rolled another blunt, collected his weed works, stepped out onto the balcony, and reminisced. He looked around and felt comfort in his current environment. The majority of his family lived in the star state. The more he thought about his current environment, the more he thought of his birthplace, Waterbury, Connecticut, the city of hills. The more he thought of it, the more he began to think of Claude and his whereabouts in the small city. He visualized his cousin standing on the corner of East Farm and North Main talking to the goons standing in front of the bodega. He pictured him robbing someone, taking their shit, and pistol whipping the vic for GP.

Claude and Mark were on Orange St when a short, petite Puerto Rican woman in her early to mid twenties approached them. She wanted to know where she could cop an eight ball. Claude told her that he knew where to get it, but she had to follow them.

"I'm saying though. We got to go up Long Hill to get that shit and I ain't trying to walk around hot," Claude told her.

Mark began to think that they were going to get their dicks sucked. She didn't look bad. Mark's manhood began to swell as he pictured his dick deep down in her throat.

Claude, Mark, and the woman walked all the way up Long Hill Road. They walked through a store's parking lot and took a short cut through a patch of woods. They walked up Traverse Street.

"Are you sure your friend has the coke. We've been walking for twenty minutes and my legs are starting to bother me," the woman whined.

Claude turned around and had a scowl on his face.

"What the fuck did I tell you? I told you my man got the shit. You're only with us because I don't feel like walking down that hill, so shut the fuck up until we get there!"

Mark thought that Claude's attitude was going to leave them with "blue balls." He wanted to get his dick sucked. If it wasn't dark, Mark would have gestured Claude to relax. To Mark's surprise, she bit her lip and didn't say anything. She'd been through hell tonight trying to cop. She was shoved out of a slow moving vehicle just before she spotted the strangers. They walked up Hope Street, cut on to Warner, and went to the park as if going in the direction of Berkeley Heights. When they entered, the woman began to panic discreetly. She had fallen into another trap and there was no telling what the two teenagers were up to. She found out when Claude punched her viciously in the face.

The impact of the punch made her drop to the ground hard. He removed a .22 from his jacket pocket and poked her temple with the barrel of the gun. Her nose bled profusely.

"Please don't kill me!" she said fearfully.

"Shut up bitch. You say another word and I'll put a hole in your fucking head," Claude said with calm aggression.

Mark was shocked. His mouth was wide open while he watched Claude forcefully yank the pocketbook off her person. He found lipstick, a Newport box holding two squares, loose change, and a few condoms. He knew she had to have some trap money stuck somewhere on her body. His look was grim and grave when he pointed the gun at her vagina. She knew what he was thinking. She dug deep into her bra and pulled out her earnings for the night. She handed him the money. She voluntarily took off her clothes in the middle of a dark park because she wanted to prove to them she had no more money. She attempted to give up her body to avoid being murdered. She didn't care if the men raped her; she just wanted to see another day. When Claude took everything she had, he jetted back through the entrance. Mark was close behind him, running like the police was on the verge of catching him. They ran behind Malik and Kevin's house. They had their backs to the house trying to catch their breath. Mark was no thug, but he grew up with many of them, especially his cousin Claude.

"What the fuck was that all about?!"

Claude didn't answer him. He didn't care too much about what Mark had to say. He just cared about the hundred dollars he found stashed in her bra.

"What the fuck you do that for?" Mark asked again.

"Chill. We got a hundred from her. I'm giving you fifty. It's done."

Mark thought about jail. He thought about his dreams and ambitions. He saw them go down the drain the minute Claude pulled out the gun. Mark was scared to death. He wanted to get home before the woman started to sing to a neighbor who more than likely heard the commotion.

"Fiends get robbed on the regular. No one gives a fuck about a fiend. I robbed a lot of these motherfuckers and didn't get caught yet! I ain't going to jail nigga, you could forget about that shit. And if I ain't going to jail, you ain't going."

116

Claude read Mark's face and knew he was scared. He knew that Mark didn't do that kind of shit, so he understood where he was coming from, even though his moral principles didn't apply to anyone else. He gave Mark his share of the money and pocketed his.

"That should take your thoughts off that bitch back there. I gotta bounce. Me and Rocks got some shit to handle. Take the money."

Mark felt like a force was controlling him. He felt like he was in a dream. He told himself that this couldn't be happening. Claude was about to take off before he decided that Mark should bounce first.

"Yo, just bounce. You live right down the street. I'll wait here another two minutes and then I'll bounce. If five-O is out, it would be better if we were by ourselves. Try not to be seen. Stay in the dark."

"Alright yo, I'm out. Call me when you get to Rock's crib." Mark was sweaty and fearful. He was unable to stop himself from shaking.

Mark left Claude behind the house and darted though the dark. He ran down the street and made a right on Traverse. He cut through Mr. Jones's yard and landed in his own backyard. He frantically searched his pockets for his keys, only to realize that he left them inside his house. He looked in the garage to see if his mother was home. Her car wasn't there. He rang the doorbell aggressively. His sister was home. She was asleep, but she was inside. As he waited impatiently for his sister to come to the door, he heard a car drive slowly up the street. He peeked around the house and saw a police cruiser ride up Traverse. Mark began to panic as he rang the doorbell once again. He pressed the doorbell so hard that it broke inwardly. He pounded on the door. When there was no answer, he lifted his fist to pound on the door again, but stopped it as he noticed his sister dragging her ass to the door. When she opened it, Mark rushed by her and fled to his room, not noticing the anger on his sister's face for waking her up.

. . .

"Mark, are you going to sit outside and chill with that blunt, or are we going to smoke it?" Fatima yelled from in the kitchen, snapping Mark out of his thoughts.

"I'm coming," Mark said flatly before drying the blunt off with the lighter. He rose from his chair and went back inside the condo.

19-Los Angeles

Detective Taft looked into the eyes of Mrs. Sullivan and saw pain. The dark circles around her eyes signified a lack of sleep. Peter's parents hadn't slept since he was discovered missing. The pain they felt was unbearable. Mr. Sullivan's blue eyes were red from crying and sleepless nights. Peter Sullivan Sr., a frail, graying man in his mid-fifties, was a man apart. He had four days of growth on his face. Clair Sullivan, a petite, brunette woman around the same age as her husband, looked as if she never stopped crying. They sat in front of Detective Taft's desk holding hands remaining hopeful, waiting for Detective Taft to finish his report about their son. He had the same information he had a week ago, which was nothing. Detective Taft had learned through experience to soothe the nerves of worrisome parents without leaking unnecessary information. If he knew a loved one was dead, his opinions about the case remained neutral. He had a silent hunch Peter was dead. He told Detective Rinaldi he was willing to put his pension on it.

"Mr. and Mrs. Sullivan, I ensure you that we are doing the best we can to find your son. Our men are working around the clock expeditiously to make sure he returns home safely. I understand that this is a difficult time for the two of you and your family and friends, but I want you two to put your trust in our men," Detective Taft said smoothly.

Mr. Sullivan squeezed his wife's hand as he took a deep breath and absorbed the information. The Sullivan's yearned for good news, but it was the same news from last week. The kidnapping had made headlines. The Sullivan's were hearing nothing but the same results. They figured the two detectives could issue some news that would point the Sullivan's towards a better day. They wanted the detectives to add a little more emphasis to their string of hope.

"Thank you so much for talking with us and being honest. We know you two are busy, but thank you for going above and beyond your duties. We know our son is out there and every effort is being made to find him, but thank you once again for

118

your time," Mr. Sullivan said as he gently took his wife's hand and led her to her feet.

"Thank you detective," Mrs. Sullivan muttered as Mr. Sullivan escorted her out the door.

Detective Rinaldi bumped into the Sullivans as they made their exit out of the station. Detective Rinaldi spoke to the them briefly before he joined his partner in the office.

"You changed your theory about Peter's death," Detective Rinaldi said as he handed Taft his Duckin Donuts coffee.

"And what theory is that?"

"That we'll find him."

Detective Taft took a sip of his coffee before he responded.

"Why would you ask that?" Detective Taft asked bluntly.

"I just ran into the Sullivans and they told me that you..."

"Hold it right there," Detective Taft interrupted, holding his hand up. "I never gave them the impression that we have high hopes of finding their son. I told them that our men our doing the best they can on their efforts to find him. What the hell do you want me to say Rinaldi? That yeah, your son is dead, but we're doing the best we can to find him?"

Detective Rinaldi caught on. He knew he angered his partner. He felt stupid because he should have known what his partner's intentions were. He didn't want the Sullivans to feel any worse than they already did. Detective Rinaldi looked around sheepishly before he decided to break the silence.

"Hey, I didn't mean to offend ya. I was just..."

"Don't worry about it. I overreacted, that's all," Detective Taft said apologetically.

Detective Taft placed his head on his desk and ran both of his hands over his it. Rinaldi knew that the meeting between Taft and the Sullivans was unexpected. He recounted the many times in the last four or five days that Taft stated that he believed Peter was dead. The Sullivans were under the impression that Peter was still alive. The situation was too linked. A key witness gave a description of the truck and two days later he mysteriously disappeared? Rinaldi started to see Taft's point because it wouldn't make sense if Peter was alive.

Detective Rinaldi was about to say something until Taft maneuvered himself in a position to speak.

"I gave the same information to the Sullivans that I provided them with last week, but I didn't want to tell them what they didn't want to hear. I've been doing this for years and it's finally started to take its toll on my conscious. I try to look at this job from a business standpoint, but it's hard not to take it personal when there are devoted parents or friends counting on us for the safety of their loved ones. People always say that the hardest part of our job is looking at bodies. I think that's a crock of shit. I think the most difficult part about this job is lying to someone's parents while you look them directly into their eyes. That is something I never got used to in all the years I've been doing this shit. I wish we were never assigned to this fucking case because we don't have a clue to the quadruple murder and Peter Sullivan's disappearance and it's been almost two weeks."

Detective Taft reached in his desk and fished for a cigarette but came up with an empty pack. He crumpled it and threw it in the garbage can.

"We are going to need help with this case. Do you have any sources?" Detective Taft asked.

"The informant that I have is no where to be found. When I do find him, I'll make sure he'll get that second strike like I promised him. I don't give a shit how much of a necessity he is to his family. Detective Meaks from the narcotics division has a few informants getting information whenever he feels that there isn't enough, but being that this case was headlined nationwide, a person with loose lips might think twice before letting the cat out of the bag. Peter Sullivan's disappearance poses as a deterrent. We're in a situation where we may have to rely on an informant to keep his ear to the street that is outside of our jurisdiction. Believe me, someone who is not involved, or maybe involved indirectly knows something. Even a ten thousand dollar reward, if there was one for this case, is a turn off for someone who enjoys being alive."

"I'll get Jacobs on the phone. Call Mancini and Meaks. In the meantime, we need to get to work," Detective Taft said while he looked through some more files on his desk.

...

Linda had hit rock bottom. After numerous attempts on contacting Prime, she gave up. Aaron's abrupt appearance came in the form of a blessing. Aaron thought Prime was hiding out with her. When he realized Prime wasn't there and that interrogation was useless, he made her an offer that was difficult for her to refuse. She couldn't afford to live in her apartment. She lost her job at footlocker to addiction. Her co-workers put her onto the drug, but Linda had an addicting personality; she was turned out in no time.

Scoot, Jimmy, and Snake were cutting up drugs on the same table her son ate and did his homework on. Scoot was a short and fat brown skin man that recently completed a thirteen-year stretch for robbery. Jimmy was Aaron's right hand man that stuttered. He wore shades and sat stone face at the table doing his part. Linda felt she made a deal with the devil as she watched the men naked. The only one that shot her naked body a glance was Snake, a rail thin dark skinned nineteen year old that had a high disregard for life. Linda being naked was part of the deal. Aaron and the rest of the crew didn't trust her. If she had no pockets, there would be no theft.

...

Hours after leaving Linda's apartment, Jimmy rode around with Aaron contemplating moves. Jimmy may have a speech impediment, but he was street saavy, dangerous, and not afraid to die. He was a thick muscular man that lived for the streets and nothing but the streets. He couldn't wait to get a piece of the pie. He even offered Aaron Prime's life on sight if he was susceptible to snitch.

"Jim, we got to make this shit stretch like a motherfucker. We could rub shoulders with the big spenders if we do it quietly and accurately.

Jim spat out the window.

"We...we...need...t...t...t...to find another spot...f...f... f...for us to break this sh...sh...sh...shit up. The b...b...b... bitch is a true fiend."

Aaron kept his eyes on the road and made a left hand turn

on to Adams Boulevard. Homicide Detectives Taft and Rinaldi pulled up next to the black Maxima at a red light. The detectives were just following the flow of traffic. Unconsciously, Detective Taft leered in the passenger window of the Maxima and caught a glimpse of the men. He maintained brief eye contact with Aaron until he cut his eyes back onto the road ahead of him. Aaron knew the men weren't ordinary civilians so he played it cool because there were rocked up kilos in the car. Jimmy peeped the suits as well and gave them no eye contact. When the light turned green, Detective Taft pulled away and signaled into another lane. Aaron and Jimmy blew a sigh of relief.

"I'm already on that, and on another note, call Flex. Time is money."

. . .

Flex woke up with a pounding headache. He looked at the time on the digital cable box converter on top of the entertainment center and it read 2:00pm. He cursed himself for sleeping that late. He was supposed to meet up with Aaron, Scoot, Jimmy, and Snake to set up shop five hours ago. He scooped his jeans off the floor. He went through one pocket and then the other and retrieved his cell phone. He turned it on and set it down on the junk drawer. His cell phone vibrated on the dresser from all the unheard messages. He debated whether or not to check his voicemail because he knew most of the messages were from Aaron. He decided against it and placed his cell phone on the carpeted floor. He turned over in the bed to find Trudy staring at him.

"Good afternoon, sleepyhead," Trudy said in a quiet, tantalizing voice.

"What's up?" He tasted the overnight debris build-up in his mouth.

"You hungry?" she asked flirtatiously, lying with her legs mounted together in a spoon position. The see-through lingerie she wore revealed her dark, thick nipples and wide areolas. Her breasts protruded through the gown as if they were on the verge of popping out. The pounding headache did not stop Flex's manhood from rising. He grabbed his dick   and lusted at the sight of her thick body. He played with her nipples until they hardened.

"Yeah I'm hungry…for this thick ass body of yours." He pulled the strap down her arm. When her breasts were out, he pulled one in his mouth and sucked it softly. Trudy breathed heavily, enjoying his soft strokes with his tongue. Flex sucked on her tits until she beckoned him to chill. The more he tried to break through her resistance, the more adamant she became at stopping his advances.

"Bill stop…stop…stop…wait a minute Bill."

Flex slowly retreated to the other side of the bed, feeling a little awkward behind the rejection.

"I'm sorry. I think we are moving a little too fast, don't you think? I just want to know who I am dealing with, that's all." She pushed her breasts inside her gown.

Flex was drunk last night, but he wasn't that twisted to not remember what happened during their encounter. He remembered everything that stood out, especially the fact that he didn't have any condoms. She told him she was on birth control. That was all he wanted to hear. They had sex all night and well into the early morning hours. *It's a little too late for that shit*, Flex thought as he began to remember the many times he came inside her.

"What do you want to know?" He lit up a cigarette, inhaled, and exhaled.

"Anything that you are willing to tell me," she said, unconsciously rubbing his forearm.

Flex inhaled and exhaled the smoke as he pondered the idea of telling her his real name, but he didn't want to throw caution to the wind.

"My name is William Morrison. I work construction for my grandfather. Been doin' the shit for years," Flex lied.

"So how come you don't have a girlfriend?"

"The same reason why you don't have a boyfriend."

"I'm pretty sure we have different reasons for not having significant others. And I don't even think I ever told you," she said playfully.

Flex managed to flash a smile. There was something about

Trudy's personality that made her extra attractive despite her mediocrity.

"Well tell me."

"Tell you what?" Trudy asked stupidly.

"Why are you single?" He grabbed the bait.

"Because all y'all men are dogs."

This bitch going to tell me men are dogs but I've been fucking her raw since I got here last night. Bullshittin' ass bitch, he thought coldly, looking at her with a blank expression.

"All men are dogs. All females are dogs. That's just an excuse to cover up the real reason why you're single." He died the cigarette out into the ashtray.

"So what's the real reason why you're single?" she pressed.

"I had to get focused. It was my choice to be single. Can't get shit done wit' the wrong bitch, I mean the wrong woman who nags at a nigga over little shit. As soon as she becomes a headache, I bounce."

Trudy smiled. She had a decent impression about Flex, even though she regretted being irresponsible for not using protection last night. He seemed to be a straight-up person. She was definitely interested in his company. She dated many men that said the same shit, but there was something about him that she seemed to enjoy. After all, she had no commitment to anyone. She did, however, have a few dudes, including her child's father, that came by the apartment every now and then for relief, but she could modify the situation if the man was serious about a relationship.

"I'm single because my child's father and I didn't work out. We weren't on the same level and we both realized it. We are still friends to this day. We both attend outings together for the sake of our son. He is very involved in our son's life," Trudy stated, hiding the fact that she still had feelings for him.

Flex reached for his pack of Newport and lit another cigarette. He has had enough experience to tell whether or not a female was still fucking her baby's father. His first instinct told him she was. But there was still something about her personality that he liked.

"That's cool. It ain't nothin' wrong with a father taking

care of his. I wish I knew who my pops was. I don't even got a picture of him."

"I'm glad you understand," she said as she crawled towards Flex and gave him a kiss on the cheek. She picked up his arm and wrapped it around her neck. His dick was getting hard again. Despite her saying that slowing down shit, she stroked it and felt his pre-ejaculation. He had to piss, but he didn't want to break the mood. She released herself from the position she held when she was in front of Flex and positioned her face near his stomach. She slowly licked around his navel area and worked her way towards his inner thigh. Flex looked at his dick and saw dry cum on it. While Trudy had Flex's dick in her hand, Trudy looked at it with slanted, seductive eyes. She stuck the tip of her tongue out of her mouth and circled his shaft. He let out soft moans. She opened her mouth wide. She deep throated his dick using no teeth. Flex grabbed her head with both hands and humped her mouth. After five minutes of oral, he ejaculated in her mouth.

Flex was in the bathroom pissing. Trudy turned on the television in the bedroom. He smiled as he thought of that bullshit Trudy was kicking about getting to know one another. *Yeah right,* he thought as he heard her television volume ascending. He couldn't make out what was being said, but he could tell that she was watching the news. He knew he couldn't lay up with her all day, but he'd come back over when everything was settled. Business had to be taken care conducted. He realized that he'd already wasted enough time. Flex looked in the mirror one last time before stepping out of the bathroom.

Trudy was setting the ironing board in place, preparing to iron her uniform when Flex walked into the bedroom. He looked at the void expression on her face and wondered what the hell happened since he'd been in the bathroom. Whatever it was, it changed her mood.

"What's wrong with you?" Flex asked, not knowing how to approach her.

She looked at him with an unreadable expression.

"Just more bad news, that's all. Well, it ain't really bad, but it could be good news if they find those bastards that killed my friend."

"I don't know what you're talking about." He was growing suspicious of her behavior.

"I'm sorry. I should've explained that to you more clearly. The police are still looking for the victim's murderers. I just wasn't prepared to see that on the news," Trudy said, secretly seeking sympathy.

"Why, who got murdered?" Flex asked, having a feeling that she was going to say what he thought she was going to say.

"Did you hear what happened out there on Monteith Drive a few weeks ago?" She turned her uniform over on the ironing board.

"I don't know. People get killed everyday. I may have heard about it along with a few others."

"I only knew one person out of the group," she said.

"Which one did you know?" he asked, sparking another cigarette to ease the nervousness he'd built since Trudy brought up the murders. He knew the murders were out there in the open, but the mere thought of her knowing one of the victims caught him off guard.

"Did you know someone named Dennis Howard?"

"Nope."

"He went by D-Bone," Trudy added, hoping Flex knew who he was.

"Doesn't ring a bell," Flex said, thinking of a wrench to use to change the subject.

"Oh. It just makes me mad Bill. These niggas out there in the street is just some jealous ass niggas, that's all. Why can't everybody just make money and leave the next man alone, you know what I'm saying?" she said, talking like she was down. She didn't even know D-Bone like that. He only acknowledged her when she went out of her way to acknowledge him.

"I feel you. That's why I'm trying to get outta L.A. It ain't nothin' for me out here," Flex said, easing off the subject of the murders.

"Why, where are you trying to go?"

"Probably Atlanta. Me and my granddaddy had to do some work down there and I was thinking about buying some property."

"You going take me with you?" she asked flirtatiously.

"We'll see, you never know. Your baby father might come through and sweep you off your feet," he said sarcastically.

"Yeah right! That would never happen. But anyway, I do know one thing about you."

"And what's that?"

"You have goals. I don't know too many brothas out there that's trying to invest in some property. Maybe you could show me a thing or two."

Flex nodded his head as he noticed his phone vibrating on the carpet. Flex looked at his phone. It was Aaron. He answered the call. Trudy grabbed her bathroom basket and went into the bathroom to shower, giving Flex the opportunity to talk in private.

20-Los Angeles

Ali drove carelessly through downtown L.A. while Wade was trying to break up weed on a CD cover. They were on their way to the east side to re-up. They had been trying to get in touch with their new connect for the last two days, but his phone kept going to voicemail. The men got suspicious and decided to make an unannounced appearance. As always, the men had weaponry in the car. Wade gave Ali looks of irritability and anger, but that didn't stop him from driving like he didn't have a care in the world.

"Why don't you slow the fuck down! All these fuckin' guns in the car and you want to act like a damn fool!" Wade snarled.

"Nigga relax. It ain't even no cops out here. Stop bein' a bitch."

Ali bounced ferociously, toying with the hydraulics every time he hit a straight-away. Wade looked at Ali coldly because they were riding dirty.

"Nigga, what the fuck? What the fuck is wrong with you? And you almost made me spill this shit."

"I didn't know you had on a pad. Must be that time of the month. You been cryin' like a bitch all day," Ali said flatly, leaving the hydraulics alone and bringing the blue 1967 Chevelle hard-top to a normal level.

"Whatever." Wade poured the weed into the cigar wrap. He continued before Ali cut him off.

"I ain't going back to jail. If I go back, its gonna be for something big, not no dumb, careless shit."

Silence invaded them for a moment until Ali destroyed it.

"Ain't no sense on worrying about some shit that's out of our hands."

"That's our only source of income right now and I don't feel like being a stick up kid. What the fuck is you so cool about this shit for anyway? Simone been hounding the fuck out of you about money and you ain't worried?"

"Trying to think positive. We ain't going to know shit until we get there. I'll worry about whatever I need to worry about later," Ali said.

"Alright man, whatever, but we should still form a plan C 'cause plan A is gone, and something is suspect about plan B. We need this money and I mean fast," Wade stated with emphasis.

Ali nodded and knew his partner was right. Ali was getting harassed at home about unpaid bills. He thought about Colin being in his grave not even for two hours and Simone started talking that money shit. He thought about Colin all day and how they were thick as thieves that grew up in the same household, along with Colin's older incarcerated brother.

"Remember what Colin told us a day before he got popped? We got to look at the big picture. We can't just look at whatever is in front of us and settle for this shit."

Ali remained quiet, but heard Wade's words. As he drove through Westwood, he passed Wade the burning blunt while he took heed to caution. They knew they weren't in the core of the hood. They were in a city where one would have to pay twenty-two hundred a month for a single unit inside a condominium building. Ali looked at the odometer and slowly pumped the break. When he stopped at a red light, his phone vibrated on the dashboard. He sighed when he recognized the phone number. It was his cousin Rayshaun calling him for his incarcerated cousin, Colin's older brother. He called Rayshaun so Rayshaun could connect to Ali. Ali wasn't in any mood to talk with him because he was going to ask him the same question.

"What?" Ali answered rudely.

"What the fuck you mean what? Rayshaun, stop listening and get the fuck off the phone."

Rayshaun snapped his teeth and put the phone down.

"Did y'all fools find them dogs that bit my other half?"

"Naw, but we'll find em' before they eventually hit the dog pound," Ali said flatly.

"Alright, alright. But try your best. Those dogs need to be put to sleep before they bite some more, especially the wrong niggas," he stated and continued." If you hear anything about them pit bulls, call Rayshaun. I'm out," he finalized before hanging up.

"Your cuzzo?" Wade asked.

"Yeah."

Minutes later, Ali parked two doors down from their destination. Before they stepped out of the car, Scott, a short fifteen-year-old brown skin boy wearing a Los Angeles Dodger fit-it, baggy jeans, and an oversized black t-shirt bopped mildly to the driver's side of the vehicle. It wasn't a cool bop; it was a bop to mask the .44 he clutched in case the men decided to act stupid.

"Y'all didn't hear?"

"Hear what?" Wade asked, fearing the worst.

"Locked up. They got him a day before yesterday and from the looks of it, he ain't never going to see daylight," Scott said dejectedly.

"Fuck!" Ali banged the steering wheel.

"So what the fuck are you still doing here?" Wade asked, knowing that Scott didn't live there and that his presence didn't fit the environment he stood in. The area was swank and Scott fit the profile of a hand to hand drug dealer in a destitute neighborhood.

"To collect from y'all niggas. Y'all got that?"

Ali and Wade looked at the young man like they wanted to kill him. As pressed as they were for money, Ali wanted to peel off, but disregarded the idea because they noticed the four goons coming out of the residence. As 'bout it' as Ali and Wade were, a shoot-out in broad daylight for a couple of grand wasn't worth it. Wade reached in his pocket and threw the elastic wrapped money at him. Scott looked at his people to ensure that if the men sitting in the car got out of hand, the car's interior would be soaked in blood.

"What's up with that? I'm just letting y'all know that the shop is closed. We don't have any work so what the fuck?"

"Y'all motherfuckers could've called us and save us some gas money. Goddamn!" Ali growled.

"What the fuck do you want me to do? We hurtin' just like y'all. And besides, I don't remember any number exchanges. I was just told to collect the money niggas owe him. If y'all want to still fuck with us, cool. If not, be out. We up in here busting our ass trying to find this dude's stash so we could give it to the nigga Leech fuck with so we could work. You think we want to be in this hot ass neighborhood waiting for cash?"

The men saw the kid's point, but they didn't have time to wait. They needed work now. Ali started his engine.

"Take down this number," Ali said.

...

Ali and Wade walked into Ali's apartment that had seen better days. The paint from the walls was coated with years of cigarette and weed smoke, CDs were scattered around the nineteen inch television, and there were clothes all over the living room. The apartment was a big disaster. Simone Tucker was tending to their crying infant son Khalif. Simone was a honey colored, nice looking woman who gained a little weight from having their son, but she was still curvy and sexy. She wore long extensions and her eyes were oval shaped. She wore a long t-shirt and black spandex pants. She was stern and never held her tongue.

She looked at Ali with scorn and continued to rock the baby to sleep. She stood up with the baby and went to the next room as if the men's presence irked her, but her attitude was directed at Ali. He gave Wade a puzzled look and brushed it off. Ali told Wade to have a seat while he walked over laundry, infant toys, and other miscellaneous shit. He opened the bedroom door and closed it. Wade knew it was going to be a verbal warfare.

"You asking me what the fuck my problem is? You know what my problem is Ali. All that nickel and diming bullshit you be doing ain't putting food on the table. The rent is way past due and I had to get diapers from Nica. It's embarrassing that you can't even take care of your family."

"I just gave you a fucking hundred dollars!"

"Nigga, a hundred dollars ain't shit! A hundred dollars ain't going to prevent us from getting kicked out into the street. I don't see your ass all day and you come back with a hundred fucking dollars. You need to be a man and get a job! I'm sick of this broke shit. I..."

"I ain't seeing you out there getting a fucking job, you

always…"

"I'm taking care of our son all day while you out making a hundred damn dollars! I could sit in this raggedy ass apartment all day and make more than you. You could've made some big money wit' your cousin Colin. He even knew you thought small and that you and that nigga out there were too trigger happy to hold on to big money. That's why he kept y'all at a distance!"

A light went off in Ali's head. Although what Simone said was true, he wasn't trying to hear that shit. Colin always thought Ali and Wade were too reckless minded to handle big responsibilities. That explained the tension Ali and Wade had with Earl and B-Bum. Ali kept quiet, but he wasn't sure how much of her insults he could take. Colin loved Ali like family should love family, which was why he didn't play Ali too close when it came down to high stake business. He paid Ali just enough for him to provide for his family and have a little extra on the side. The same thing went for Wade. He bit his lip; he damn near drew blood biting his bottom one to try to keep his composure.

Simone went into the dresser and pulled out three hundred dollars to prove her point.

"Where did you get that?" Ali asked suspiciously.

"Does it matter? You didn't give it to me and it still ain't enough," she said, stuffing the money into her bra.

"I ain't going to ask you again. Where the fuck did you get that!?" Ali was a notch under his boiling point.

"It doesn't matter where I got it from. It's more money than you got to bring home." She was provoking him.

Ali breathed hard, using his hand to rub his face because he assumed who gave her the green.

"Tony gave you that shit?"

"Maybe," she said nonchalantly with her back turned. She had just situated the baby. She, at that point, broke the switch. Ali grabbed the back of her neck and tossed her on the bed. She bounced off quickly and made a feeble attempt to retaliate. She was smacked open handed and landed back on the bed. He went for her neck and got a firm hold of it. She tried to squirm to break his hold, but her strength didn't match his. He was squeezing the life out of her. Ali had the look of a madman. His lips were pursed tightly, droplets of mucus coming from his nose. Wade burst through the door. He pried Ali off of her. In the midst of it all, Ali called her all kinds of bitches.

"You ain't a man," she managed to say as she struggled to regain her wind as she held her neck. "I'm gonna get my cousin Tracy to shoot your ass!"

The threat only increased Ali's adrenaline. Before Ali got a chance to get at her again, Wade picked up Ali and led him out of the bedroom to prevent further damage. Wade knew what kind of state of mind his friend was in. He knew Simone was provocative. Wade knew that Ali, including himself, were hungry and thirsty for more money, but he understood Simone's beef. They had a child to feed, no excuses. Simone didn't bother to open the door when Ali was dragged out of the apartment. She wrapped her arms around her legs and cried, thankful that the commotion didn't wake the baby. Although her ex-boyfriend Tony was a made man, he wouldn't have given Simone a dime. She got the three hundred dollars from her mother. She'd been with Ali for years and knew how to push his buttons. She felt bad because she knew that he was still grieving Colin and that he was trying. It was a fucked up time for him, she figured, but they still needed a home to live in and a baby to feed. She hated the way they were living, but she loved him.

. . .

"Bitch talking 'bout she got that money from that nigga Tone. The nerve of that fucking bitch!"

Ali was driving out of anger while Wade licked the blunt in place.

"Ali, she didn't get that money from Tone," Wade said nonchalantly while he licked the blunt in place.

"How the fuck would you know?"

"Because he locked up."

"Locked up?"

"Simone said that to get under your skin, and that's what women do. Get under niggas skin. I don't agree on how you choked her, but I understand. But listen, the more you put you're hands on a female, the closer you going to get to killing her. She's mad Ali. Everything she said was out of anger."

Ali parked in front of Wade's crib. They were finished with the blunt they burned down. Ali regretted what he did to Simone.

"Wade, I'll just check you tomorrow. I got to straighten up some things at home."

"Alright, check you tomorrow," Wade said, giving Ali dap.

When Wade stepped out of the vehicle, he closed Ali's passenger door. Ali peeled off as usual. Wade watched him drive around the corner and knew he regretted choking the mother of his child. He was going home to amend.

21-Los Angeles/Waterbury

Raven's apartment was stylish and swank. The Colonial Revival living room had an antique Persian rug with modern icons on it, pine chests, wicker chairs, a steel, glass table, and an earth toned Ethan Allen paramount sectional. The earth-toned walls were decorated with two large Picasso abstract paintings. Long exotic plants hung from hooks screwed into the ceiling and a 60 inch 4K was mounted on the wall.

All the luxury in the apartment couldn't take away the pain she had regarding her brother's sudden demise. Raven and D-Bone bought the apartment a month before his murder. Her only source of revenue was gone. She tried to visualize the ugly bastard that was with her brother the night of the murder. She only remembered that his skin sagged, but she'd damn sure would recognize him if she saw him.

She thought of the two detectives that probed her with questions. It seemed as if they were trying to paint a picture off a vague description of the mystery man that was with her brother the night he was killed. They were just doing their jobs and all, but damn, what else could she tell them? The mystery man's appearance was lost and there was little she could do for the desperate detectives.

Although the apartment situated in Westwood was lavish, Raven couldn't see herself being there for long. In time, she'd be moving in with her mother in New York. The apartment will remain vacant until she could find a buyer. She knew that she had to move on with her life because sitting around the apartment feeling miserable wasn't going to help. She thought about Ali and Wade and their encounter that night at the club. The bulk of the conversation focused on their dead relatives and the question on who murdered them, but they never once spoke about money. If she had a clear mind that night, she would had ask Ali and Wade if they had a connect. They did, but unknowingly to her, their connect got caught with kilos and guns. Ali and Wade were fucked up. Raven had two grand to her name, way more than what Ali and Wade had combined. She knew she had to come out of her black cloud.

....

Claude spent the afternoon penning applications. He made a detour to the block because he knew Rocks and Tommy would be there. Ty and Tank, two young and up and coming thugs, flanked the street veterans. The youths gravitated to every word that came out of Rocks's mouth. Claude played the background; he noted Rocks's powerful influence.

"C, that's why I fuck with these niggas. They don't measure; these motherfuckers just come through on demand. They task, they don't ask."

Alphonso "Tank" Williamson was a stocky, reserved goon who wanted a slice of the crack game to pay for his mother's AIDS medication. His crime partner Ty was the opposite. He wanted the shine and notoriety of a street legend. He looked like a tall, oversized kid. Claude kept his eye on him. He looked familiar. He didn't see him in prison. He placed his face on someone from his past.

"You Wiley's brother?"

The mention of his Ty's older deceased brother caught his attention.

"Yeah."

Ty looked at Claude but couldn't place him.

"Do I know you?"

Claude nodded.

"It's been a long time my boy. You looking at one of the baddest motherfuckers in the city," Rocks interjected.

Ty was so full of himself that he looked down on Claude until Rocks mentioned Twalique. The mention of Twalique's name secretly gave him the creeps. Past or not, Twalique resembled a man without a soul. Many feared him. Dust and cocaine enhanced his violent personality, but Claude put a bullet in him. Twalique didn't die, but the pronounced wound he currently had on his chest was an indication that Claude was aiming for murder. Ty respected that. Any association with his brother was automatically game in his book. Claude was a street legend and Ty yearned for that status despite lacking the heart to achieve it. Ty dapped, embraced, and kissed his ass. Claude didn't want the attention. He was focused on the two police cruisers coming down the street. Without looking obvious, the men parted ways.

....

Claude felt a stream of relief the second he stepped out of Rocks's truck. As usual, Rocks's rode dirty and Claude wanted no association. It didn't stop him from accepting another grand from him. He knew Rocks's motive, but Sahara needed the money and he had zero job prospects.

He thought about Tank and Ty. He liked and respected Tank, but his gut feeling told him not to trust Ty. He never trusted his brother Wiley when he walked the planet. Wiley wanted the glory and fame of a street soldier but he received a bullet for his dreams. The apple didn't fall far from the tree.

Claude fished for his keys until the front door opened. Claude etched his face into a scowl as Sapp, Destiny's father, made his way out the door. Darnell "Sapp" Worthy wore a du-rag to cover his spinning waves. He was a brown skin, slender man. The stylish Oakley shades he wore added more style to his cocky demeanor. Although he was short and had a wiry built, he held his own. He normally carried a gun to avoid getting dirty, but he cursed himself inwardly for not having one now on his person. The chrome four-pound he had in his car glistened, but it didn't do him any good because the gun was in the car. He didn't know what to expect from Claude.

"What's goin' on C?" Sapp asked weakly. He felt intimidated because of Claude's size.

Claude half nodded.

"Just chilling man, you know? Out here getting this money an' shit. So what's good baby?"

Sapp wished those words didn't come out of his mouth.

"Ain't nothin' good in the crib nigga. My sister screaming that broke shit. Don't even have enough dough for Destiny's school clothes and you telling me you out here getting money? Get the fuck out my face with that bullshit before something happen," Claude said calmly.

Sapp was shook. He just wanted to leave Waterbury as peacefully as possible. He figured that he see Destiny, give her a few outfits, and make up another excuse to keep more money in his pocket, although he gave Sahara a hundred dollars in which she threw back in his face. He knew the wolves were out for him and that he took a big risk seeing his   daughter, but that was a chance he was willing to take. Now, Claude stood in front of him with a solid, threatening position. He wished he kept the rod on his hip. Sapp's life was miserable and his days were gloomy. He would have no problem murdering his daughter's uncle if he had to. He told himself repeatedly that he shouldn't have to bring a gun to see his daughter, but he'd think twice the next time around.

"Oh word C, it's like that?"

"It ain't no other way," Claude said. When Sahara opened the door holding Destiny, Sapp felt relieved because he knew she wouldn't let Claude go beyond his threat.

"Destiny wanted to say good-bye to you," Sahara said with attitude. She came out there with Destiny because she heard Claude's voice. When she looked out the window and saw Sapp's car parked across the street, she knew something was wrong.

Claude walked in the house and didn't look back. Sahara cut her eyes to Sapp.

"Bye Daddy," Destiny said as she walked towards him with opened arms. He picked her up and spun her around playfully. Sahara looked at Sapp with disgust. The one hundred fifty dollar Jordan's he wore gave Sahara the impression that Sapp wasn't living that bad, despite being a fugitive of the streets. The brand new Audi A4 he drove didn't help matters.

Sapp put Destiny down and looked at Sahara. Sahara caught his glare and dismissed it. She turned around and led Destiny inside the house. Sapp saw the door slam behind Sahara. He shook his head coolly and let out a chuckle. *I should've walked over here with some funky ass clothes on. When I handle my come up, they straight. Sahara ain't broke like she claiming and I bought Destiny some clothes,"* Sapp pondered while he thought about the two outfits he bought her while he reached for a cigarette.

His mood changed when he thought about the encounter he had with Claude. *I don't give a fuck it that's my daughter's uncle. He*

138

ain't getting in my way. Fuck around and shoot him.

The swagger in Sapp's walk was a bit harsh to be walking to the car, but he rocked it anyway. *Something going to have to give with that nigga. Him, Rocks, and Tommy. Fuck around and kill all three of them,* Sapp thought sinisterly as he lit a Newport and pulled off.

. . . .

"I don't want to hear no "don't start no shit speeches Sahara" 'cause nobody ain't starting shit. But when this nigga starts hollering how he getting that money, it made me feel uncomfortable 'cause you up in here struggling and I'm still looking for a job. Man, I'll smack the shit out that motherfucker, for real, telling me that shit!"

"That's Destiny's father and you're going to respect him to that degree. And keep your voice down before you wake up Destiny," Sahara spat heatedly.

Claude sat up in his bed as the words Sahara shot at him sunk in.

"I know you know that nigga stunting his ass off..."

"I'm not going to argue with you C. As long as my point got across to you. That's Destiny's father and you're going to respect that."

Sahara knew that Claude didn't care for Sapp and knew that he wasn't telling a lie. She just wanted them to be civil towards one another for Destiny's sake. When Destiny appeared at the doorway of Claude's room, their voices faded. Without saying another word, Sahara left Claude's bedroom.

Claude started to call Rocks, but he decided against it to dispel any trouble that may come from a single phone call. He looked at the clock and it read 5:03pm. It was still early. He picked his book bag up off the floor and placed it on his bed. He began to thumb through it, looking for a folder holding applications. His mind began to drift on Rocks and Bronson. Claude thought about his surroundings; he felt a steady flow of helplessness. He pulled the grand from his pocket and placed the money next to an application. *I'll probably be making this three hundred dollar shit in a two-week period fucking with these dead end jobs. American dream my ass.*

He put all the applications into one pile and placed them on top of the junk drawer. Sprawled out across the bed, Claude's mood was so dark that it turned to fear. A familiar feeling overcame him. He wanted money and he wanted it now. As all the feelings of succeeding legally and going back to more familiar, comfortable routines began to collide in his thought process, he dozed off.

Claude would fight many battles in his mind and produce more questions about his own placement in society. He would wonder if he would join the dogs and get fleas or rise above the common mentality of his peers that consisted of acceptance of an inferior role in society.

22-Los Angeles

The Jordan Down apartment, normally infested with fiends, tricks, dealers, and hustlers, was abnormally quiet. Twenty- four year old Ruth Banks kicked the last straggler out to spend Christmas Eve with her six year old son. She managed to clean the dilapidated apartment, scrubbing and cleaning all kinds of shit. The apartment hadn't been cleaned in weeks. It produced a funky odor caused by an accumulation of dirty addicts, sex, a clogged toilet, and filthy clothes. She felt a hint of relief as she looked around and thought she was looking at a brand new apartment. The mopped kitchen floor produced a Pine-Sol aroma, eliminating the foul stench. Luther Vandross song "Forever, For Always, For Love" played smoothly from the small radio in the living room. The Christmas lights blinked on the Christmas tree that stood tall in the corner.

She placed an ashtray on the coffee table and lit a Virginia Slim with two John F. Kennedy matches. She reflected on her own life. When she was fifteen, she blossomed into an hourglass figure. Her body was perfect. Her skin looked as if it was untouched. Being a privileged child that obtained her needs and wants from her parents, she ran into a smooth talking, violent hoodlum on her way home from Catholic school. Aaron was three years her senior. She loved his smooth, dark chocolate skin. His built, solid frame was supported by a perfect set of teeth. Fascinated with his charm, wisdom, and swagger, she fell in love with him. Aaron expressed himself kindly to her, but she was completely ignorant of his other side. He was a young murderer and was wanted dead on the streets. Over a brief period of time, Aaron gradually led her into the underground world of Los Angeles. She did anything for him; she allowed him use of her bedroom as a safe haven for his money, guns, and drugs. Her life took a wide turn when she found out she was three months pregnant. Her parents were outraged and embarrassed, particularly her father. No longer able to bear with her father's harsh treatment, she moved in with Aaron and his boy Leon, his crime partner. Two days before she gave birth to their son, Aaron and Leon were machined gunned down coming out of someone's house. Seven years later, her presence, mentally and physically, had withered. She had a large abscess on her neck that leaked pus. Her hair thinned on one side. She smiled radiantly, displaying rotting and missing teeth. Her smile faded when she thought about when and where she'd get her next fix. She scratched at her shoulder. Aaron moved stealthily towards the Christmas tree, trying to get his mother's attention.

"Boy, if you don't get from around that tree, you ain't opening shit tomorrow," Ruth warned motherly, happy that she was able to provide a decent Christmas for him this year.

"Mommy, can I ask you a question?" Aaron climbed on the sofa next to his mother.

"What is it baby?" She died the cigarette out in the astray.

"How did daddy die?

Ruth sat back in her seat calmly and sighed. It was the third time in a week that he'd asked that question. Each time he asked, she would beat around the bush. Growing tired of dodging his question, she decided to be straightforward with him. It bothered her to think that Aaron was exactly like him. The knife incident at the school convinced her that her son inherited most of his father's genetics. She knew that Aaron was a troubled child, but she didn't think he was capable of stabbing anyone.

She looked at her son tiredly and beckoned him to join her on the couch. He snuggled up under her arm and stretched his arm over his mother's frail stomach, feeling the love he seldom received. Ruth loved her only son, but her addiction prohibited her from displaying the love a child was supposed to get. Aaron had many lonely nights while she worked the streets. She looked at her son and felt shame. She would honestly admit that she favored dope over her son. The demon had her and she knew it.

"How did daddy die mommy?"

"He was killed." She pointed her head opposite of him while she coughed.

"How was he killed?" His curiosity was brewing.

"He was shot...several times."

"Where?"

"When you get..."

"Where mommy?"

Ruth sighed.

"He was shot twice in the chest and once in the head," she said impatiently. "You are too young to be hearing about this shit, you hear? Now I want you to stop asking me all these goddamn questions and bring your ass to bed!"

"Was daddy bad mommy?" He disregarded his mother's impatience.

Ruth took a deep breath and exhaled. Silence flooded the apartment. Throughout her experience living in the underworld, she knew Aaron understood the deadly game he played and knew that all the people he crossed would catch up to him. The same applied to her. She knew the dirt she did for months, especially in the last week or so could mean death, but she didn't want her son having another lame Christmas. On numerous occasions the week prior, she ripped off enough money from her pimp Muddy to buy Aaron's bike and other toys and clothes. She figured she could come up with a few excuses on why she didn't have her quota. She didn't think nothing of it until now because it wasn't the first time she's done it. Her son's curiosity gave her a reality check, but she quickly disregarded it because if Muddy felt a hole in his pocket, he would have created a nasty scene already.

"No, your father wasn't a bad person; he just did bad things," she answered slowly, still thinking about her own deviance. "He's in a better place."

"I heard grandpa tell grandma that my daddy's burning in hell."

Anger overwhelmed Ruth. She knew that her father held a grudge against her son's father, despite the fact that he'd been dead for seven years. He held a grudge on Aaron Sr. because he was to blame for Ruth's downfall. He held high expectations for both of his daughters. Little Aaron's birth was considered a curse, according to his standards, but he adored his other grandson, four-year-old Walter. He nicknamed him "Flex" because he always tried to form biceps out of his fat arms. Aaron felt the stepchild treatment and he hated his grandfather for it. Every fucked up remark he said around Aaron Jr., Aaron Jr. would report it back to Ruth. Growing tired of her son's complaints about her father, as of two weeks ago, she stopped Aaron from going to his grandparent's house. Despite his hatred towards his grandfather, he loved his grandmother unconditionally. She was the warmest and most kindhearted person in his orbit. Aaron's comment about his father irked her, but her agitation wasn't directed at Aaron; it was directed at her father.

"Your father is not burning in hell. Your granddaddy don't mean nothin' by it. He's just an angry man. When you get older, you're going to understand why he is the way he is, but I ain't even going to start explaining now because you the only little boy in the world that's up late night on Christmas Eve asking questions an' shit," Ruth said.

"Is Santa going to bring me a bike this year or is he going to forget like he did last year," he asked disappointedly, changing the subject.

Ruth looked at him motherly.

"Now why do you think you deserve a bike? You cut that poor child and you think you deserve a bike? And not to mention that woman bringing you back here at like eleven thirty at night, sneaking out, embarrassing me like that. Do you still think you deserve a bike?"

She looked at him with a grim face. Aaron could do nothing but look back into his mother's eyes.

"Now bring your little ass to bed before Santa miss your ass again," she demanded seriously.

"Ok, ok…good night mommy," he said, his demeanor turned colorful at the mention of Santa Clause.

"Good night baby," she said, planting a kiss on his forehead.

With that being said, Aaron ran to his room and shut the door behind him. As soon as Aaron's door closed, she sunk into the couch, absorbing all of Luther Vandross lyrics, and went to sleep.

…

Three hours later, Ruth was snoring over Sade's "Smooth Operator." An hour after Aaron went to sleep, she unlocked a closet and pulled out all of Aaron's gifts. A brand new BMX rested on the side of the tree near the window, along with an assortment of toys ranging from action figures to toy machine guns. If Ruth was a light sleeper, she would have heard Muddy and Slim kick the door open.

Muddy, a caramel colored thin man with a thick mustache, long goatee, and long processed hair that stuck out of his cowboy hat, and Slim, a heavy set, six foot five dark-skinned, clean shaven, bald man scanned the room until their eyes rested on Ruth's sleeping body.

"Slim, wake bitch up," Muddy demanded calmly as he removed his cigarette from his mouth and discarded it on the floor.

Slim hovered over the smaller figure and began to tug at her arm.

"Ruth, wake up."

She didn't bulge.

"Wake up."

She opened her eyes and turned over, facing the cushion side of the sofa.

"Wake up bitch," Slim snarled, smacking her sternly with the back of his hand.

"Wha…what? Damn, what did you do that for?" she asked, thinking as if she was in a dream while she looked at Muddy's thin figure leaning on the wall.*

144

"Slim and I was just in the neighborhood and just wanted to wish you and that little nigga a Merry Christmas," Muddy said smoothly, stroking his long goatee. "I see you doing quite well for yourself. Motherfucking gifts under the tree. I don't remember paying you all this goddamn money."

The worried look on Ruth's face betrayed her, but Muddy decided to play it off. He knew he had her, but he wanted to engage in a little foreplay before he put Slim to work.

"You know what I was thinkink on the way over here? Correct me if I'm wrong Slim. It's kind of like de je vu. Six or seven years ago, your boyfriend and that fool Leon thought they was the shit, thought they were high on life until Slim and I found out them niggas set my workers up and killed my brother in the process," Muddy said coldly, not taking his eyes off of Ruth.

Ruth didn't know whether she was dreaming or if it was real life. She didn't know who killed Aaron and his partner up until now. She was too afraid to be angry over Aaron's murder.

"Muddy, what are you talking about? I never stole anything from you. If that bitch Precious told you, she's a goddamn lie, and you know that!"

"Bitch, how the fuck you know Precious told me? I'm tired of talking. Slim, off this bitch."

Ruth was terrified. She looked at Slim and then Muddy as if he had a chance to save her, but Muddy's mind was already made up. He could tolerate a lot of shit, but he couldn't tolerate anyone stealing from him. She didn't think it was possible for Muddy to find out that she'd been stealing from him. Muddy knew from the beginning when she first dipped into his pockets, but he allowed it to accumulate so he could have a better reason to kill her.

"Please Slim, I have a son to raise. Please don't kill me! You don't have to do this! Please!"

"You shouldn't of done it Ruth, you shouldn't of done it," Slim said as he removed one of the couch's cushions and placed the barrel of his .38 caliber pistol on it. He stared into her frightened eyes and placed the cushion on her face as she attempted to squirm, but it was too late. He pulled the trigger, forming a gaping hole in her forehead.

"Kill that little nigga too. It's fucked up, but he got a set of eyes," Muddy ordered, wiping down everything he touched. He even picked up the *cigarette butt he discarded on the floor.*

Almost robotically, Slim headed straight to Aaron's bedroom. When he opened the door, Aaron was sleeping peacefully.

"Boss, he didn't see shit. That nigga is knocked the fuck out," Slim said, almost relieved that Aaron didn't witness anything that transpired in that living room. He was mainly relieved that he didn't have to kill someone so young, but he would have done it to save his own ass.

"You sure? I don't remember seeing his door ajar when I walked in," Muddy said sharply as he made his way to Aaron's bedroom. When he opened the door, he walked over to Aaron's figure, looked at him, and didn't find it necessary to kill him.

The men did another wipe down and casually walked out of the apartment.

As soon as the door closed, Aaron opened his eyes and ran to the living room. He witnessed the tragedy. He heard the door get kicked in. As soon as Slim killed her, Aaron tiptoed back to his bed. He held his breathe as Muddy stood over him, his heart beating rapidly with his eyes shut.

He walked to his mother's opened eye corpse, which he discovered when he removed the couch cushion, and screamed at the top of his lungs. Blood from her headshot leaked all over the couch, including Aaron's pajamas. He held his mother tightly on his person until Ms. Sealy, the only one that heard Aaron scream, pried him off of the corpse.

...

Aaron sat up in bed abruptly. Beads of perspiration dripped off of his muscular body. He scanned the room thoroughly, making sure that he was no longer in the apartment that he last seen his mother alive. An afternoon nap turned into two hours of heavy sleep. All the money him and his crew accumulated in the last two months couldn't erase his horrid past.

When he got up from his bed, he walked to the dresser and took out a Newport. He lit the square and inhaled deep, still thinking about Sonya's whereabouts. His new success in the drug game couldn't stop him from missing her. After his cigarette shrunk to the size of a butt, he pulled out his latest trends and prepared for another wild, exotic evening consisting of money, drugs, fast whips, and women.

23-Waterbury

It had been two months since Claude started working as a Porter at Waterbury Hospital. Claude was high on life and beamed with confidence everyday that he worked. His interaction with Rocks and Tommy was limited because he spends the second half of the day working. Whenever he caught rare, quiet moments to hang out, Rocks and Tommy clown him for being a Porter because they would say that it was just a fancy name for a janitor. It was all out of love though. Rocks and Tommy were proud that Claude was gradually turning his life around. Rocks still hounded him about returning to the streets, but it fell on deaf ears. Sahara was proud. Claude made more than enough to split everything down the middle with her; moreover, he bought a 2003 Mazda 626 crasher to get him around. Since he worked second shift, he waited with Destiny at the bus stop every morning to make sure she gets on the bus safely. He sends his mother money so she could have commissary. His mother spends her days in Niantic bragging about her son's accomplishments.

Darlene was still trying to persuade Claude into a relationship, even though she lived with her son and her son's father. He still fucks her at least two to three times a week, but he was tired of that kind of arrangement. He wanted something more, but he didn't want it with Darlene. He viewed her as a quick and easy fuck. He vowed that he wouldn't make the same mistake twice.

He was twenty-five minutes into his break watching Sports center in the staff lounge on the fifth floor when Lester Howell, an older, dark-skinned man in his late fifties with a heavy salt and peppered beard walked into the lounge. He was exhausted for contributing his share of the work on the other side of the building.

"Les, I don't know why you think that the Cavs got a shot at the against the Warriors."

"Look it here young blood. All of a sudden you a Warrior fan. I haven't heard of a Warrior fan," Lester said comically.

"I've been a Warrior fan since Tim Hardaway and Chris

Mullin. Its my team's time to shine right now."

They enjoyed a laugh. Lester had been a porter for over twenty years. He took a liking to Claude because his own son was incarcerated. They had many things in common, especially Lester being a heavy player in the game back in the day. Unknowingly to Claude, Lester had a body in the eighties. He was the only one that knew Claude did some time. Most importantly, he knew Claude's mother. He ran with Claude's father before Claude was born. He knew Sahara, but hadn't seen her since she was a child.

As the men gathered their cleaning supplies to finish out the rest of their shift, Steve Jacobson, a heavy set white man in his mid-fifties with thick bifocals, their supervisor, met Claude at the door. He gave Lester a nod as Lester proceeded down the hallway.

"Hey uh Claude? Can you meet me in the office in about ten minutes," Steve asked timidly.

"Alright, not a problem."

Ten minutes later, he knocked at the glass door. Steve beckoned Claude to enter. When he sat in front of the desk, Claude read the nervous look on Steve's face, but couldn't put a finger on any reason besides the overtime on why he would want to see him.

"Mr. Porter, I have watched you perform your custodial duties and I wish I had an entire crew with your work ethic. Unfortunately, it is with great sadness to inform you that we're going to have to let you go," Steve said apologetically.

Claude was stunned. He rubbed his temples and was at a loss of words. He looked at Steve incredulously.

"Why?"

"To be frank with you Porter, you weren't truthful on your application. Under any normal circumstance, we would've caught it before you were hired, but this kind of thing happens all the time where a background check wasn't fully investigated prior to hiring. This was not an isolated incident. We have to pre-screen all of our applicants. Don't get me wrong, we have felons working here, but your case was a double-edged sword. One, you lied on your application. Two, you were charged with attempted murder. Even if you were truthful about what you did, we still wouldn't have hired you if the background check were processed correctly because of the graphic nature of your crime. A few drug charges here and there wouldn't kill anyone, but your case was different. And on top of that, you are on parole," Steve said, telling Claude the entire scoop over the brim of his glasses.

Claude's world caved in. He knew he wasn't truthful on one application, but being that he filled out so many of them, he was sure he was truthful on the application at the hospital. He thought of all the people who were proud of him for taking the steps to change his life, especially Sahara. He thought about the struggle she had endured before he was gainfully employed. Steve pulled Claude's application out his miscellaneous pile of paperwork. When Claude reviewed it, he discovered that the proof was in the pudding.

"Porter, it is not easy for me to be the one to break this to you. According to staff, you were one of our best employees. I'm sorry, if it was up to me, I'd keep you because we all make mistakes, but it's completely out of my hands."

Claude shook his head before he spoke.

"I'm not blaming you, but I've been here for two months and I always work overtime whenever I'm asked. I worked for two weeks straight without a day off. There is no way this could be reconsidered?" Claude asked, almost pleading with him.

"I'm afraid not. I'm sorry Porter, but like I said, it is out of my hands."

Claude was quiet and his anger was brewing. He contemplated on throwing the chair he sat on, but he thought better of it.

"Alright. Thank you for giving me a shot," Claude said with a hint of anger.

Claude got up and walked out of the office without looking back. Steve opened his mouth to say something, but he knew it was worthless.

When Claude walked to the break room, Lester came in with two bottled waters in his hands.

"I figured you could use one of these."

After Claude accepted the water, he had a look of disappointment. Lester got suspicious when he saw Keith, the ex-marine second shift security guard that wore a buzz cut. He was there to ensure Claude's removal from the building.

Lester looked at the security guard and at Claude and figured out the situation.

"Its not what I think it is, is it," Lester asked carefully.

"Yup."

"Claude, what the fuck happened?"

"I got fired. They said I lied on my application." Claude flipped his book bag on his shoulder.

"So that's why Steve is here late, but I never expected that."

"I'm out." He was angry and stunned.

"Hold on C," Lester demanded. Keith sighed, but he obeyed. Claude knew Lester meant well, but he didn't feel like hearing shit. He stopped in his tracks though; he respected Lester as a person as well as his opinion.

"Don't let this bullshit here steer you down the wrong path. You may wobble but you too strong to fall. When a boxer with determination gets knocked down on his ass, he'll pick himself up from the mat, think of another way to outclass his opponent, and win the fight. You do the same C."

"But Les, you're damned if you do and your damned if you don't. These motherfuckers is going to wait until I'm halfway done with my shift to fire me? They got me working for two months. I pay rent Les and now my sister is going to be supporting her grown ass brother! This is some bullshit!"

Lester understood where he was coming from. Even though Claude was getting loud, he didn't want to interfere. When Claude ceased, Lester said that he would follow him outside. He wanted to smoke a cigarette anyway. Once they were outside, Lester pulled out his Winston and lit it.

"C, I can't sit here and tell you to calm down because the entire situation of them having you work for two months and then firing you is fucked up. You saved a lot of asses around here. When people wanted to go on vacation, you filled the vacancies. Don't let these motherfuckers see you sweat. Things happen for a reason."

"I wish I knew the reason now. Bills got to be paid Les. My sister is goin' to fucking flip because I saw her struggle when I was out scrambling to get a decent job. But Les, you got my number; I got to bounce and figure something out."

"C, listen to me. This to shall come and pass. This is not the end of the world. If this shit here ain't going to kill you, it's just gonna make you stronger," Lester said, giving Claude a firm embrace. He gave him some more words of wisdom before he put his cigarette out.

As Claude walked down the stairs to the first level of the parking lot, Lester stared at Claude's back until he left Lester's line of vision. *All that boy wanted to do was get his life straight, and this shit happens. It's just a matter of time before he hits the streets*, he thought as he went back inside to finish the rest of his shift.

When Claude walked in the house, Sahara was chasing Destiny so she could tickle her. Destiny giggled while being chased. She ran behind Claude's leg, making a feeble attempt to hide. Sahara caught up to Destiny and retrieved her daughter from her hiding spot.

"I got you," Sahara said cheerfully.

"Mommy stop," Destiny said with laughter as she was being pulled from behind Claude's leg.

Sahara looked at Claude and noticed the grim expression on his face and knew something was wrong because he was home early.

"Why are you home?" she said out of breath while she kissed Destiny on the forehead.

"I got fired," Claude said flatly.

"What for C?"

"Lied on my application."

"Claude, you've been there for two months. They are just now getting around to your background check?" she asked incredulously.

"Yup."

Sahara sighed. She told Claude about the consequences of lying on an application.

"Damn C, I told you not to…"

"I know, but I only lied on one Sahara. I filled out so many of them shits I forgot which one I lied on."

Destiny read her uncle's body language well and knew something was wrong. She thought the world of her uncle. She walked up to him with her arms stretched so he could pick her up. He picked her up and gave her a kiss on the cheek.

"Uncle C, are you ok?"

"I'm ok sweetheart; your uncle is just going through a tough time, that's all. Now you go and play."

Destiny walked to the couch with her hands behind her back. She had a sad look on her face.

"Well, just try again. Ain't no since on dwelling on it now. There are a million jobs out there," she said warmly.

Claude sat on his bed holding his achievement certifications from prison and told himself that they don't mean a damn thing. He crumpled the papers up and chucked them to the other side of the room. He felt hopeless. He felt less of a man because Sahara would have to carry the load. Steve wasn't the blame for him losing his job because he was just the messenger, but he still wanted to choke the fucking life out of him. He was too embarrassed to call Rocks or Tommy. They would drill him with the *I told you so* remarks. All of the voices of discouragement came to life inside of his mind, starting with Bronson. Bronson told him about that legit shit, as well as Rocks, Tommy, and a host of others. He knew that a step to being knee deep into the game was only a phone call away, but he didn't want to take that route. Although it was tempting, he bypassed it as taking the easy way out.

24-Beverly Hills

Aaron and his crew were enjoying the festivities at the mansion that was owned by their connect, Freddy Cai in Beverly Hills. The mansion came from the creative minds of two notable architects. It contained five spacious bedroom suites with full bathrooms, five and a half bathrooms, eleven walk-in closets, and six walkout balconies. A movie theater, office, and wine cellar/tasting room occupied a portion of the spacious residence. The grand living room had giant bay windows with a piano area that Freddy barely used. Outside of the mansion was a spacious backyard with five patio areas, sprawling lawns, a basketball court, a hot tub, and large eucalyptus trees.

The guests of the party were enjoying themselves in the early afternoon, eighty-three degree weather, which was rare in October, near the infinity pool. The DJ played a combination of light jazz and electronica to give the people an erotic feeling. There was sensuality throughout the formal affair. Women from different ethnic backgrounds walked around wearing one and two-piece bathing suits; some were topless. There were even a few females who were sharing light, passionate kisses in the swimming pool. There were two female couples who ordinarily wouldn't call themselves lesbians, at least to their standards, hugged up in the pool, but one particular couple got everyone's attention who were either in the pool or standing around it.

Aaron and Marco stood stone-faced on the side of the pool despite the erotically charged environment. Flex, Jim, Snake, and Scoot were off to the side hooting, hollering, and gawking at the topless lesbian couple making out in the swimming pool. A beautiful woman on the other side of the pool caught his attention. He placed her at the club a few months back. He wondered what her deal was.

Raven, sipping on her mixed cocktail, didn't like the lesbian scene. It wasn't that she had an issue with lesbians; she figured that they shouldn't have done it in an open area.

"Girl, you know you liked that shit; I know I did. I'm strictly dickly, but I'll fuck that Colombian bitch in a minute," Octavia stated.

Octavia was unattractive and it wasn't a surprise that someone as fine as Raven, who wore a two-piece blue bathing suit, would hang out with her. She wore a separate bathing suit that exposed her seven child bearing body. Raven tried to discourage her from wearing it, but in Octavia's mind, the separate bathing suit fit her perfectly. Every woman at the party was something to look at, but no one gave her the attention she secreted craved. She was a short, obese brown skinned woman who had raisin-sized moles all over her neck. She thought she was hot shit and looked down on everyone else as if she was superior. If she had a decent personality, she probably wouldn't be lonely, but she was a bitch.

"Then you ain't strictly dickly," Raven said nonchalantly while she took another sip of her drink.

"Girl please. I don't gets down wit' that. Me rubbing my pussy on another bitches coochie ain't gon' make me bust. I need dick," Octavia said while she held up her hand for Raven to slap it.

Raven slapped Octavia's hand and put her drink down.

"Bitch, you would fuck her if she asked you," Raven said good-naturedly.

"That bitch better have a twelve inch strap-on then," Octavia said and continued. "So Raven, when is your lame ass gonna get a man?"

"As soon as you get one."

"Yeah right. I'll get a man when a nigga proves he's worthy. My pussy is too golden for niggas to be running up in. For a nigga to fuck, eat, and suck this coochie, that nigga better have some serious cash 'cause I don't fuck niggas for free," Octavia said arrogantly.

Raven looked at Octavia flatly and knew her friend was full of shit. Octavia would fuck anything with a dick. Octavia didn't think Raven knew about her promiscuity. She had been known to give super head on both genders. She had been in a series of threesomes, not to mention that D-Bone walked in on Octavia sucking B-Bum's dick while Earl pounded it from the back. She believed the promise that D-Bone made to her about not saying anything about what he witnessed, but Raven was his sister and all the information was shared. D-Bone was dead, but she still wasn't going to tell Octavia what she knew about her.

"That's right Raven; niggas got to pay to play."

"I'm not ready for a man though. I got a heavy load of shit on my mind," Raven said.

"I hear that, but look at that fine ass nigga congregating with his boys," Octavia said while she steered at the muscular brother with lust.

"Who?"

"The one staring right at you."

Aaron was in awe as he spotted the light skinned women sitting at the table nursing her drink. He remembered her from the club a few months ago when Flex and Marco almost came to throwing blows. He made eye contact with the ugly one and didn't want her to think he was staring at her. He was with Sonya so long that he lost the vigor in his game, but that wasn't going to stop him from advancing.

As Aaron made his way to the plantation grown teak leisure table stationed on the other side of the pool, he began to get nervous. There were four exotic women sitting at the table. He didn't want to get rejected in front of the beautiful onlookers. She was engaged in a conversation with an unattractive woman. When she stopped talking to take a sip of her drink, Raven looked at Aaron while he approached. She took her eyes off of him and continued talking to her friend.

"You seem like your enjoying the festivities. Mind if I flag that butler down and get you a drink," Aaron asked civilly. "I hope I wasn't interrupting. Seem like y'all was talkin' somethin' deep."

"We were, but now that you're here, we gotta find somethin' else to talk about bein' that we don't know you like that. But we could use another round if you don't mind. By the time you come back with the drinks, we'll be open for discussion," Octavia interrupted.

"I came over to talk to your friend. I said I'll flag the butler down to get her a drink, not you," Aaron said curtly.

Raven thought about saying something in her friend's defense, but didn't feel the need. Octavia had that coming. The man came over respectfully and didn't need to hear that bullshit. The man was defending himself. He represented himself like a man. It was one of the qualities that she desired.

Octavia wore a stupid look on her face. She underestimated him. She rolled her eyes and redirected her attention.

"Like I was saying; do you care for a dri…"

"I'll be back Raven. I'll get my own drink," Octavia interrupted with scorn. She was under the impression that the man was staring at her. She was jealous and upset because Raven didn't defend her.

"What's up with your homey?"

"Why, are you interested?"

"No, but she running her mouth like she the shit. And with all due respect, you might want to watch her. The more attention you get, the more she'll hate you."

He wasn't the first one to give her warning about her childhood friend. As she pondered the thought, she noticed how handsome the man was. His cornrows were done to perfection. He wore brown khaki pants, open-toe sandals, and a long black T-shirt that stuck to the overall mass of his upper body. She fixed her eyes on the tattoo he had on his forearm and figured out his government name. She shifted her attention on her unfinished drink and didn't want to send off a signal that she was interested.

"So Aaron, what brings you out on this nice day?" She kept her eyes on the people walking by.

"I don't know Raven. I was wondering the same thing about you. Your man must be worried sick about you being around all these predators," Aaron gamed. He started to get excited. Her jet black hair was on one side of her shoulder, covering her right breast. Her hazel eyes were cherries on top of the ice cream. She sat with her legs crossed looking sexy.

"I see you're a good listener," she complimented, remembering that Octavia said her name before she abruptly departed to pursue the butler for a drink. "And believe me, I don't need a man to keep me away from predators. If these men around here are predators, what does that make you?"

"Interested. And besides, I have to have a good ear. Its part of what I do," Aaron said.

"Oh yeah? What is it that you do?"

"I make sure supply and demand is met, consultant, shit like that."

"Yeah, I bet," she said sarcastically.

"Enough about me. What do you do?"

"That's for me to know and you to find out," Raven said.

"Here comes your disgruntled friend," he said flatly. *Now that is one ugly bitch.*

"I'm ready to go. These is some tight ass rich niggas around here. Can't even buy a bitch a drink," Octavia complained.

"I don't want to hold you. Number exchange?" Aaron asked, knowing he had her in the bag.

"I'll take yours," she said.

"Alright, I don't give my number if it ain't gonna be used."

"It won't be used if you don't give it to me," she replied and winked her eye.

Aaron nodded his head with a boyish smile because not going home with her number was better than her having a boyfriend. While she was saving the number in her phone, Octavia looked on with disgust. She wished she were saving someone's phone number in her cell phone.

"Hope you get home safely," Aaron said gently, lifting Raven's hand to his lips for a gentle kiss. Octavia's mood went from dark to medieval while witnessing that.

"Can we go?!" Octavia asked hotly.

"Not a problem. There is no need for us to be here anymore," Raven said nonchalantly, smiling at Aaron as they turned to walk away.

Aaron stared at Raven's back they made their way through the guests. He knew he had her. He blushed when Raven winked at him. He watched her until she left his line of vision. Marco crept up behind him and patted him on the shoulder.

"I know you just didn't pull that! I was stalking her when I was on the patio! Did you get her number?"

"What the fuck do you think? I ain't going to be devoting

all my time for one bitch if she ain't given a nigga a taste. Hell yeah I got her number," Aaron lied.

"You lucky cocksucking motherfucker," Marco said good-naturedly.

"Naw Marc, it's all about game and how I represent it. You should've been taking notes."

"I see you been reading all of mine," Marco said with a laugh before walking away.

25-Waterbury

Claude was in the kitchen preparing dinner for Destiny. Sahara was working the second shift at her job and Claude was babysitting. A week passed since he lost his job and he had been filling out job applications. Destiny watched *Frozen*. He was at his breaking point. He didn't even get a call from temp services; they were all filled to capacity. At that point, he didn't know which way was up and had given up hope at succeeding and living a better, productive life. A familiar feeling knocked on the door of his conscious. It was a feeling of defeat. No longer was he afraid of violating his parole or disappointing the people who only wished the best for him. He didn't give a fuck about proving his crew right by giving up the legit path. He wanted that quick money. It bothered him to see Sahara taking care of the rent, her daughter, and himself. His pride was taking a beating. He began to have urges to smoke weed. He wanted to put his mind in a different world; he wanted a break from the reality he lived in. His existence didn't mean shit to him. His positive, ambitious mood deteriorated. The Claude from the past was taking over the present. The only thing that shined in his life was his niece and his sister. His mother knew about his job loss and constant struggle, but she could do nothing but encourage him to not give up.

After he prepared Destiny's plate and sat her down at the kitchen table, the phone rang. It was Sahara.

"What's up?"

"It ain't nothing. Callin' to make sure everything is alright. Did mommy call?"

"She did while me and Destiny went to the store."

"Tell her as soon as she's done eating to get her butt in the tub. I should be out of here by 12:15. Anybody call you?"

"Nope. Same shit. I called all them though and they gave me the same bullshit I've been hearing all damn week; they'll keep my application on file."

"Just keep trying. You'll find something," she encouraged.

"I will."

"Call me if y'all need anything."

"Alright." Destiny realized it was her mother on the phone and wanted to talk to her.

"Destiny wants to talk to you. Hold on."

"Hi Mommy!"

"Hey baby. What are you doing?"

"Eating."

"After you eat, you better bring your butt in the tub."

"Ok, but can you bring me back a toy?"

"No. I told you this morning that I don't have any money."

"Please," Destiny begged.

"Des, what did I tell you about begging? I told you I don't have any money for no toys. Now you give your uncle back the phone and you go finish eating."

"Ok," Destiny said dejectedly.

"I love you," Sahara said.

"Love you too."

Claude read Destiny's body language and knew Destiny was upset; he laughed inwardly as his niece gave him the phone. She sat down in front of her plate of food, poked her lips out, and folded her arms.

"Yeah," Claude said.

"Did you save me…"

"I just put a plate aside for you. You straight."

"Alright. See y'all when I get home. And tell Destiny to unfold those arms and finish eating before I tear her behind up."

"Will do. See you later," Claude said.

Claude looked at Destiny and smiled while he prepared his own plate. After piling up a large portion of food on his plate, he sat himself down at the table.

"Destiny, I don't want to see no sad faces. I want you to eat."

Without saying a word, Destiny grabbed her fork and scooped up some macaroni and cheese. She was pissed, but the look Claude gave her was a message well received. Although Claude never raised his voice at her, he had Destiny in check. His strong silence when he looked at her when she was out of line was enough for her to listen.

"Des, let me ask you something."

"Yes."

"Were you starving before we went to the store?"

"Yes," she answered softly.

"Would it be right for me to buy you a toy instead of this food?"

"But we can't eat toys," Destiny said, her disappointment clearing up.

"Exactly."

"What do you mean Uncle C?"

"I mean that all of your needs are being met. I want you to understand that in life, we can't always get what we want. There are people who can't even get their needs met."

"What are needs?" Her stubbornness was falling victim to hunger.

"Food. This home. Money."

"Some people don't have food Uncle C?"

"Yes sweetheart. Some people don't have money to eat."

"How come?"

"Depends Des, but it's because people simply don't have it like that or they made bad choices in life," he said, making sure he wasn't too technical with her.

"Have you made bad choices Uncle C?"

"Yes, plenty of them."

"Why?"

"Because I was stupid."

"You're not stupid Uncle C," she said playfully.

"I know, but your uncle made stupid choices."

"Uncle C, why did you go to jail?"

"It's a long story D…"

"Tell me, please!"

"Destiny, when you get a little older, you'll understand exactly what I mean when I said I made stupid choices. I don't ever want to see you follow my footsteps. You're too young to hear what I did, and every time you ask me, I give you the same answer. Now finish up before your food gets cold."

"Ok Uncle C."

Over a span of an hour and a half, Destiny took a bath,

put on her pajamas, played, and bullshitted with Claude until she went into her room to play. When Claude noticed the silence, he went to go check on her. He found her sound asleep on the floor holding on to a Barbie doll. He picked her up and carried her to her bed. After he tucked her in, he took a moment to observe her while she slept. He secretly wished he were in her shoes because as young as she was, she didn't have a worry in the world. She didn't have to worry about jobs, money, or any other problem that can weigh on the mind. He closed his eyes and said a prayer. He prayed to God to make her aware of the dangers in the world and for her to have enough strength to fix, conquer, and solve any trial and tribulation that may come her way. After he said his prayer, he kissed her on the forehead, left the room, and closed her door gently.

Claude fell asleep on his bed and woke up three in the morning. He had difficultly sleeping lately, especially after losing his job. He'll ponder his problems until he falls asleep; he'll wake up and ride the same thought that rode him to sleep. He'll stay up all the way until it was time for him to escort Destiny to the bus stop. He finally reached his breaking point. He knew Rocks was a nocturnal human being and he was either high or getting some pussy. He spoke to Rocks at least twice within the last week or so, but he had to tell Rocks something important. His phone was on silent and he noticed he had seven missed calls, five from Darlene and two from Rocks. He called Rocks; he answered on the second ring.

"What's good my nigga C-Note? Haven't heard from your bitch ass. You alright?"

"Nah."

"Why, 'cause you lost your job?"

"How the fuck did you know I lost my job?"

"I got my ways, but fuck all that. Something got to be fucking with you for you to be calling this late. Let a nigga know the deal," Rocks pressed.

"You busy?"

"Man, I ain't ever too busy for my nigga C. I'm coming through in fifteen," Rocks said.

"Alright yo."

"Oh, and Rocks," Claude asked, hoping Rocks didn't hang up.

"Yo."

"Bring some smoke," Claude said.

"Alright. 'Enough said. One."

"One."

. . .

"Me, you, and Tommy going run this shit for real. And C, we got a knack for robbing niggas…"

"Say no more," Claude said, heavily into his euphoric state. "You know how I get down. I'm on some no mercy shit for real," he added.

"C, you been on that no mercy shit. You could have been locked down for fifty years and still be the same nigga coming out that bitch. But it's about time you're doing what you know how to do best," Rocks said.

"I didn't want to take this route though. I feel like the route chose me. So what's first?"

"Getting money. Ain't shit changed but the weather. We going to the city tomorrow for a little rip and run, feel me?"

"What time you picking me up?"

"Now that's the Claude I know. The crazy shit is that I was waiting for this day to come. You was on that nine to five shit and you play the game better than all of us. But yeah, we pulling out around eleven tonight."

"Alright, but you know I'm fifteen years removed from this shit. The game changed," Claude said.

"But your criminal grind is the same. Look in the glove compartment."

As soon as Claude opened it, a .38 sat on top of the paperwork for Rock's truck, along with the zip lock bag sour diesel. Claude looked at Rocks for his approval. Rocks gave him the go ahead to pull the gun out.

"Take that. That's all you. It's clean."

"Alright, alright," Claude said off handedly.

"So what's good with this mission we 'bout to embark on?" Claude asked curiously as he examined the gun closely.

"Nothing out of your comfort zone," Rocks said.

26-Los Angeles

Two weeks after Aaron and Raven met, they were seated at the Traxx restaurant in downtown L.A. Previously, Aaron lost hope that Raven would call him and fell into another deep depression because he needed Raven, or any woman that was deemed replaceable, to take his mind off of Sonya. When Raven finally called him, the number came up unavailable. Under any normal circumstance, he wouldn't have picked up a blocked call, but he and took the phone call anyway. During their conversation, they agreed to meet at the Traxx.

Life had been great for him because his cash flow got large. The money did, however, slow down his yearning for Sonya, but money wasn't a replacement for someone he loved so deeply, despite his violent behavior towards her. His crew was set; they brought bundles of money in everyday. Freddy got the whitest shit imported from Mexico. Aaron bought a car, clothes, and a townhouse beachfront in Long Beach as a compliment of his criminal grind. Aaron was oblivious to Raven's game plan. She knew Aaron was fucked up on her when they first met at the party. She didn't, however, hear about Aaron through the pipeline, but she knew nothing about him was legit.

The table they sat at had a white tablecloth over it with two wine glasses to add some elegancy to fine dining. The people around them who were dining were upscale; the place was too high class for Aaron's taste, but that was where Raven wanted to meet. He would have preferred a thick cheeseburger with some seasoned French fries.

"Have you ever been here before?" Raven asked.

"Nope, but depending how the food tastes, I may credit you for putting me on."

"I guess I don't have to worry about that. The food here is delicious," Raven said.

Aaron looked at Raven while she read the menu. She looked better than she did when they first met. Her long hair was tied into a bun. Her attire was simple, yet sexy. She wore Apple Bottom jeans and a Henley Tunic shirt that was buttoned down, displaying the swell in her breasts. She felt Aaron's eyes and looked up briefly and noticed him staring. She smiled and directed her attention back in the menu. She saw him when he stepped out of his brand new 2015 Acura TSX. His thug appeal made her wet because his jeans were baggy and he wore an oversized white t- shirt. Even though a fat man could have worn the size of his shirt, she was able to make out his true definition through the shirt. His cornrows were done to perfection. She loved his hair and couldn't wait to run her hands through it.

"Why are you staring at me? You could be staring inside of your menu so you can decide what you want to eat," she said playfully.

"I can't stare at you? Besides, I already know what I want. I made sure that I should make a quick selection so I could take the time to admire your beauty."

"Please. It's not like I'm dressed up or anything," she said, blushing behind the compliment.

"You don't have to be. What you got is natural. You could probably wear anything and shine," he flirted.

"Ok Mr. Perfect, since you know what you're ordering, then what is it then?"

"You'll have to find out when the waitress comes and take our order," he teased.

"Whatever," she joked back.

When Aaron opened his mouth to say something, the young, brunette waitress came to the table and introduced herself.

"Would you like any appetizers? Something to drink?"

"No, no appetizers for me," Aaron said.

"No, no thank you," Raven said.

"What can I get you to drink?" the waitress asked.

"Sprite."

"Lemonade," Raven requested.

"Where ready to order now," Raven said, looking at Aaron slyly.

The waitress looked in Aaron's direction.

"I will have the Wild Virginia Stripped Bass and whatever this beautiful woman in front of me desires." Aaron winked at her.

Raven smiled. She was letting her guard down. She was impressed. She knew that she was in no shape to start or maintain a relationship, but Aaron was making it complicated. His charm was extraordinary.

"Yes, I will have the Louisiana Jumbo Lump Crab Cake."

The waitress finished writing their orders in her small notepad and removed the menus from their table. Aaron continued to look into Raven's beautiful, hazel eyes until she looked away, unwilling to show him her interest.

"What took you so long to call me? I told you that you should've given me your number."

"Where's the fun in that?"

"It wasn't fun waiting for you to call."

"Poor baby. You'll get it later on," she said playfully. "Can I ask you something?"

"You can ask me anything you want."

"What kind of leisure activities do you do?"

"I'm a drug dealer."

"Why didn't you say that at the party?"

"Where's the fun in that?"

"Alright smart ass," she replied joyfully. That was what she wanted to hear.

"How long have you been in the game?"

"Years."

"Have you ever been to jail?"

"Yeah, quite a few times."

"What was your longest bid?"

"Five years. I got locked up when I was twenty and got out when I was twenty-five. I went back five years later for a nine month stretch. I ain't going back though."

"Are you any good in the game?" she asked.

"I'm great. The only time I got locked up for drugs was when I was with my homie. Fucking Jim ran a red light...we get pulled over and them pigs searched the car and us. I wore a jacket that I haven't worn in months and I didn't know I had crack in my inside pocket. Got hit with possession."

"So why were you getting locked up before? And that five year bid?"

"Assaults…gun possession."

"Assaults? Damn, I would hate to piss you off," she said.

"Just street related shit. Never a woman," he lied.

"I see you are very open. I like that."

"I just like to lay everything on the table so they'll be no questions asked later. I'm a drug dealer with a fucked up past."

"How come you don't have a girlfriend?"

"She left me for another nigga that was making money when I was locked up. She moved to Texas with him."

"You?

"He left me for his baby mother," she replied truthfully.

"Sorry to hear that."

"No need to be sorry. I feel even more sorry for you though. She left you when you were down and out. That's pretty fucked up if you ask me."

"Yeah, it is, but that's how the game go. Enough about me; what's your story?"

Before Raven got a chance to answer, the waitress placed their drinks on the table. She waited a moment until the waitress left.

"Nothing intense. I do what you do, but been out of the loop for a minute to focus on some personal things, but other than that, I own a beauty salon, but its in my apartment. Don't have a license and never been to school; I just know how to do hair."

"I guess I'll start coming to you," he said, winking his eye.

"You better. But as far as the hair business, it's slow. I got clientele, but half of them ain't shit. When you're generous once, people expect that generosity shit all the time. When you can't do a handout, they go elsewhere."

"So the money is slow, huh?" he asked, sipping his soda.

"Yeah."

"Do you have a problem with my profession?" he asked curiously.

"No, not at all. In fact, I need to ask you something," she said, putting all her cards on the table.

"What's that?"

"Can I get down?"

"I knew you was gonna ask that." Aaron knew she was game the minute he sat down with her. She literally threw herself out there by saying she doesn't do much, meaning she was dealing with a lot of free time. He liked her style and character and found her attractive, but there was something strangely familiar about her. He couldn't put a finger on it.

"How did you know I was going to ask?"

"I'm a good listener."

"Was I that obvious?"

"Not really. I have a good sixth sense, that's all. I hope you're not a…"

"Please. I ain't no fucking police…FBI…DEA… nothing…I do hair."

"How do I know that?" he asked seriously.

"You should. You're the one with the sixth sense."

They both laughed.

"Alright Raven, I will see what I could do. If I put you on, loyalty is a must. This game is dirty…"

"Been in the game before. I've been in hiatus. My brother was heavy."

"Was?"

"He was killed, but I don't want to talk about that. No offense."

"None taken. Me and my people need some muscle. I don't got time to put niggas in they place and handle business at the same time. I rather pay somebody to do that kind of shit."

"That's not a problem. I know just the right duo," she said.

"They trustworthy?"

"As loyal as a dog to his owner as long as their getting paid. They're hungry. They ain't the biggest brothas in the world, but their trigger finger makes up for their size."

"Alright, alright, got to meet 'em though. I made a lot of enemies so I got to make sure we never bumped heads."

Their conversation was cut short by the waitress's arrival. She sat their food on the table and told them to enjoy their meal. They had no shame eating in front of one another. They were so hungry that few words were exchanged. Their focus was the food on their plates.

...

Aaron and Raven were at Aaron's beachfront condo sitting on his leather sectional sofa, smoking weed and listening to an R & B mix. The blunt was smoked down to a roach. They were quiet; they talked themselves to silence. Raven adjusted herself on the seat and made a comfort spot on Aaron's chest. He wrapped his arm around her iron board stomach, getting comfortable himself. He took Raven's level of comfort as a cue to make his move. He rubbed her stomach softly. When she didn't resist, he kissed her softly on the back of her neck. She tilted her head to the side to give him more exposure. He planted little kisses until he reached the point of using his tongue. She moaned softly when he worked his way up to her earlobe. She felt Aaron's warm mouth breathing passion into her ear. She turned around slowly and tilted her head back, making her neck accessible. After sucking on it for a few minutes, she got up slowly and sat on Aaron's lap facing him. They shared light, sweet passionate kisses until the lust took over. They kissed aggressively while Aaron fondled her breasts. She pulled Aaron's shirt off while they kissed. He stood her up and slowly unbuttoned her shirt. He undid her bra strap. Her pink silver dollar sized nipples complimented her skin tone. He took one of her erect nipples and sucked it. He unbuttoned her pants, pulled down the zipper, and pulled her pants down to her ankles. She wore a black thong. He laid her down, still hungrily sucking her breasts. She wrapped her arms around his muscular body, pressing him to suck more. His tongued traveled from her breasts to her navel. She adjusted herself so she could help him take off her thong. Once it was off, he nibbled and sucked on her clit, tasting all of her sweet juices. She moaned while she grind her pussy against his mouth, adding more emphasis to her pleasure. After a few minutes of eating her out, he stood up. She was on her knees. She unbuttoned his pants, pulling them off along with his boxers. He stepped out of them and brushed them to the side. His dick was rock solid. She stroked it smoothly. She licked the shaft of his penis until it disappeared into her mouth. She licked and sucked his manhood for a few minutes until she could no longer stand the foreplay. She lay back down on the couch. She took Aaron's dick and massaged her clit with it.

"I have to go get a condom."

"Hurry up. I am so horny."

Aaron rushed to the bedroom, looked in the drawer he normally kept them in, and didn't find any. He suddenly remembered that he gave Marco the last one the other day. *Fuck!* He moved hastily back to the living room where he found Raven playing with herself, softly stroking her hairless vagina. Aaron didn't have a condom in hand. They didn't want to jeopardize the fire they started. She stood up in front of him slowly and pushed him down onto the sofa. She climbed on top of him, kissing him while she stroked his dick. She held it in place, inserting the shaft, teasing him. She did it a few more times before she guided his penis in. After starting out with a slow pace, she pumped harder on his dick. Aaron held her by her waistline while she rode the hell out of him.

"Oh my God! Fuck me Aaron! I need this dick! Fuck me harder! This is your pussy now! Fuck me harder you motherfucker," she said passionately, receiving Aaron's powerful thrusts.

After fifteen minutes, Aaron flipped her over. He spread her ass cheeks while entering her and deep stroked. He slid his thumb in her anus.

"Oh, that's what I'm talking about! Fuck me! Fuck me! Keep your thumb there. Fuck me Aaron! Oh my God you motherfucker! Fuck this pussy hard! Fuck me! Fuck me harder! Oh yeah, right there...yeah, right....I'm cumming...I'm cumming...oh my God!"

When Aaron noticed her body jerking, he felt the urge to cum. Four hard thrusts later, he exploded right into her womb. She used her womb muscles to tighten the grip on his dick, trying to squeeze every drop of cum out of him. They fucked all throughout the night into the early morning hours before falling asleep.

Raven was comfortable underneath Aaron's arm, her arm wrapped around his chest, toying with his nipples. Although it was nine o'clock in the morning and the sun shined outside, his curtains prohibited the sun from entering his bedroom. Aaron had a long day ahead of him and he wanted to stretch the time further so he could enjoy Raven's warm body. They just finished another session of unprotected wild sex and the two were exhausted. Aaron was a temporary relief to all her problems. She wanted to spend as much time with him as possible. She dreaded the emptiness of her own home so she tried to stretch time as well.

"What do you have planned today?"

"The usual. I got to meet up with Freddy and re-up. Since you want to be down, you got any clientele?"

"Yeah. People still inquire. Especially these upscale folks that dabble."

"Upscale huh?" Aaron smelled money. "You could make something happen today?"

"Yeah, and I'll ensure you that it will be gone by the time the sun sets."

"What about your homies? You sure I could trust them cats?"

"What did I tell you the first time?"

"Just asking, but you know I'm puttin' them to the test today."

"How are you going to do that?"

"You'll see."

"Ok...why are you doing it?"

"Because an ungrateful motherfucker double dipping our shit, that's why," he said calmly.

"How do you know that?"

"The coke is always lovely, but Marco handles the fiends out of the street. Marco called this morning while you were sleep and told me the streets is bashing our product, forcing them zombies to get the shit from the competition. The shit has been going on for a month. We just wanted to see how far he'll go with it. It turns out that the motherfucker been adding shit to our product making it stretch longer than his dick. We don't got time for snakes."

"So it's official," she asked. She knew exactly what Ali and Wade would have to do to enter the roundtable. She didn't feel good about it, but it shouldn't matter if she felt good about it or not; she needed the cash. She allowed the thought of money ward off any guilt because she knew that someone was going to die.

"Hell yeah, 'cause if he could get away with some shit like that, then another motherfucker is gonna take the honors. That ain't happening."

"Wow," Raven said.

"Tell me about it."

"Not trying to move off the topic, but can I ask you another question?"

"Shoot," Aaron said, lighting a Newport.

"How does your mother feel about your lifestyle?"

Aaron looked at the ceiling and blew smoke at it. He set the cigarette in the ashtray.

"I wish she was around to feel something, but she's dead. Been gone since I was seven."

Raven felt like she broke a switch. She was comfortable with him. She didn't want to spoil the mood.

"I'm so sorry. I didn't know…"

"Don't even stress it."

"If you don't mind me asking, how did she pass?"

"She got killed by these two dudes that she stole money from."

"Did you know for sure that she was stealing money, I mean, you were young."

"Yeah, because it happened right in front of me."

"Oh my goodness! You've been living with that for over thirty-one years? Were you forced to watch? You know what, I am so sorry. Here am I telling people I'm not willing to talk about my past, and look at me? I am diggin' in yours."

"Naw, no worries. I wasn't forced to watch. They didn't even know I was watching. When I eavesdropped by the door, I heard them say something about I must be payin' you all this fuckin' money or some shit like that 'cause they saw the bike my moms bought."

"A bike?"

"It just wasn't the bike; I missed out on every Christmas

up until that point..."

"It happened on Christmas?"

"Yes. My mom had to steal money from this nigga to give me the Christmas I never had."

"Damn, what kind of bus..."

"She was a fiend Raven and she sold her ass to keep food in my mouth. One of them niggas was her pimp, but he had his bodyguard kill her. He put a cushion over her face and squeezed the trigger. I knew if I would have kept my eyes glued to my moms any longer, they would've killed me to. I tip-toed to my bed and acted like I was sleep. When they walked in my room to off me, I held my breath. I thought for sure they was gonna kill me, but they didn't. My moms dead on that couch. I could never get that shit out of my head," Aaron said, his demeanor quiet, calm, and sad.

"Oh my God. Where was your father?"

"He was killed by those same two niggas before I was taken out of the womb."

"How...?"

"Because I overhead them."

Raven held Aaron tight and empathized with him. A lone tear fell from her eye. She knew what he meant when he said he was a drug dealer with a fucked up past. Now that he told her about his past, she figured that he didn't have to, but he did. She knew that she wanted to be more than just Aaron's employee. She wanted to learn to give him the kind of love he never received. She thought it was only fair to tell him about her brother. After a few more moments of silence, she broke it.

"Remember I didn't want to get into my brother's details about his murder?"

"Yeah."

"He was killed two months ago along with some others. Did you know someone by the name of Dennis Howard...D-Bone for short?"

If it wasn't dark in the room, the facial expression Aaron created on his face would have given him away. Shit formed in his stomach and he wanted it to come out. He could not believe what he was hearing. His mind drifted back to the night he and

Flex killed him, Colin, Earl, and B-Bum. He saw the resemblance between D-Bone and Raven because they both have the same color eyes and the same complexion. The cigarette he was smoking almost dropped from his fingers. His body felt numb. He knew that he had to contain himself. His head spun. He glared at the ceiling and kept his mouth closed. *Of all the females at that goddamn party, why the fuck did I have to meet her? Fuck!*

"I didn't hear about it. Man, there is so many murders out here, I lost track a long time ago. Sorry to hear that."

"No need for apologies, but thank you. Anyway," she said, thankful for her own openness. "What time are you going to start handling your business? I'm not ready to let you go yet," she said playfully, removing herself from the small past she shared.

"I need to rest. You wore my ass out!" The fact that Raven revealed her brother's identity wore him out.

As soon as Raven left, he ran to the bathroom, took a big shit, and called Flex.

"Yeah homie, I need to talk to you face to face," Aaron said.

"On my way," Flex said.

27-Dallas

Sonya, Fatima, and their mother, Julia, stopped at Whataburger after walking and shopping for three hours at the Royal Shopping Mall. The ladies were exhausted and hungry. Sonya and Julia rekindled their relationship a month ago when Julia called Fatima crying about Russell's sudden disappearance. Even though it was a norm for Russell to leave for long periods of time, a month had passed and Julia had a feeling that something was wrong. Sonya was still bitter about the verbal warfare that transpired at Julia's house, but Julia was still her mother and she loved her. Sonya and Fatima drove to their mother's house to console her after her call. Ever since then, the two had been talking.

Sonya ordered a garden salad with cheddar cheese while Julia and Fatima ordered the grilled chicken salad. They all ordered small vanilla milkshakes to go along with their meals.

"Since when did you start to eat so light? I thought you were fittin' to get a cheeseburger and some fries," Julia said to Sonya.

"I'm just trying to maintain my hour glass figure. You and Fatima ain't too far behind me eating those grilled chicken salads. Besides, these milkshakes is high on calories so none of us ain't that far behind a burger," Sonya said jokingly.

"Times have changed, boy I'll tell ya. I remember when I use to buy five or six pounds of hamburger meat and you used to waste it by making them big ass hamburgers," Julia said with a laugh. "Now you sittin' up here eating salads."

"Those burgers used to be good momma, and you know it. They were all big and all. Russell used to come home saying Sonya wastin' all this meat on them motherfuckin' burgers," Fatima said in a deep voice, mocking Russell. The ladies laughed.

"I had to beg y'all to eat salad, especially when I used to grill them steaks when we used to cook out in the back. I took pride when I prepared salad and y'all used to let it go to waste, but I'm sitting here watching y'all eat it at this fast food spot. I tell y'all one thing though; I'm doing some ribs, corn on the cob, baked potatoes, and salad. You two better eat the salad this time."

"Don't worry about that momma. I can't get enough of it now. I try to get Mark to eat it, but he don't be having it," Fatima said.

"Speaking of my baby, that's him calling right now." Fatima got up from her half finished meal and stepped outside.

"That boy must be prince charming or something. My baby is sprung."

"Yes she is. He is so nice momma. I told Fatima not to mess that up. Believe me, the way I am now, I don't even care about looks, although it helps, but a nice man that makes a decent living would do me just right," Sonya said.

"So whatever happened to that boy out in L.A.? When you first met him, you was just as sprung as she is now," Julia said nonchalantly.

Sonya didn't want to get into it, but as she looked into her mother's eyes, she saw the warmth in them, something she hadn't seen in years. Sonya and her mother weren't on the best of terms in recent years, but her mother has never lost the power of her eyes. Julia looked at her with concern. Sonya grew weak looking at them. She knew her mother knew something was wrong in her relationship with Aaron, but Julia wasn't known to press.

"I think he killed somebody momma. If not one, maybe more," Sonya said gravely.

"What?! Do you know this for sure?"

"No."

"But how do you…"

"The pieces fit in the puzzle. The only piece that's missing is whether or not he did it."

"That black eye I saw you with. I knew that nigga did it and was up to no good."

Tears formed in her eyes. "He even raped me momma." The tears rolled freely, but she kept her composure for the sake of the onlookers.

"Fatima know?"

"No, but Mark does."

"Sonya, Fatima is blood. I'm blood. Why does only Mark know?"

"You know how Fatima is momma. That girl can't hold water."

Regret overcame Julia because she somehow felt responsible. As she looked at her eldest daughter, visualizations of Sonya and Fatima as little girls growing up showered her mind. She'd do anything to bring those times back. She questioned her own task of being a parent because Sonya told someone she barely knew and it bothered her, but she knew jealousy would not heal her daughter's past. She looked at Sonya through watery eyes, not able to conceal the pain behind them.

"Do you think Mark told somebody? After all, you barely know him."

"No," she said calmly.

"What did he say when you told him?"

"He told me to keep my mouth shut."

Just when Julia was about to dig for more detail about Sonya's revelation, Fatima walked in with a smile, which disappeared when she noticed her teary-eyed mother and sister. When Fatima sat down at the table, her ears were filled with horrific stories of murder, rape, and many other horrid acts of violence inflicted on Sonya. When someone sat down at the table behind them, the trio placed their finished meals on trays and departed. Fatima walked out of Whataburger like a woman that just saw a ghost. She had no idea what Sonya had went through with Aaron in Los Angeles.

. . .

Mark sat out on the deck smoking a blunt, enjoying his only day off. His entire week consisted of overtime. As his elevated mind began to drift back into time, Claude was the only one he could think of. He cracked a smile when he thought about his cousin, Rocks, Tommy, Big Chris, and their total disregard for anyone who seemed vulnerable.

. . .

"Man, I told niggas that I was going to cop a whip and we still footin' it," Claude bitched. Claude, Rocks, Tommy, Big Chris, and Mark just walked out of the mall after spending hours walking around aimlessly

with no intentions of buying. They did, however, scoop up phone numbers from the other mall rat females who had nothing else to do. All of the teens searched their pockets, looking for some money so they can all chip in for a ten dollar bag of smoke.

"But fuck a whip though. Y'all niggas got enough? I got four fifty," Claude said.

"I got two dollars nigga. How much you got Tommy, and don't be holding out on niggas either," Rocks growled.

"I told you in the mall that I only got a dollar. I ain't got a job, shit," Tommy complained.

"Neither do the rest of us motherfucker. Mark, I know you got some dough and don't front. Don't be on that "I ain't smoking shit" either 'cause I know you," Claude said.

"I got seventy five cents. Check my pockets if you think I'm bullshitting."

"I got nothing," Big Chris said.

"Fuck, so between all of us, we got eight twenty five. We'll just have to see that nigga Jack. If he won't let us fly wit' eight twenty five, I'll snuff his fucking ass," Rocks said.

"We may not even have to worry about coming up with the extra buck seventy five," Claude said quietly as he rubbed his chin.

"Why you say that?" Big Chris asked.

"Look across the street," Claude said.

While they waited for the cars to pass so they could cross Wolcott St, the teens spotted a brand new silver Ford Taurus surrounded by two male white teens and two brunette teenaged females. They were shooting the shit, drinking, and smoking cigarettes. They weren't loud and they weren't bothering anyone. When the white teens saw the raucous group of blacks approaching them, their postures stiffened, but they didn't want their female peers to recognize their fear. The blond male teen had curly hair and red pimples on one side of his face. He wore a black heavy metal t-shirt and tight Levi pants with holes in the knee areas. The red head male teen's hair was long. He looked older than his sixteen years with a heavy beard and thin mustache. He had on the same attire except his black t-shirt had the rock and roll group "Kiss" on it. His jeans were torn.

"What's up guys?" Claude asked jovially.

"Hey, how's it going?" the blond asked nervously.

"Nothin' much. We on our way up the "Hill" and we figured we stop by to check out this ride of yours," Claude said, concealing his deviant behavior. He rubbed the hood of the car in fake admiration, attempting to throw the whites off balance by displaying kindness. The whites, including the brunette female teens who sat in the back seat, had a sense that the blacks were up to no good. The red head teen scanned all of them and thought about running, but decided against it because maybe they were just admiring the car. On his second thought, he knew he may have to put up a fight if things did go wrong. The black talking was just as frail as he was, but he didn't want to take a chance because it was too many of them. Besides, he knew that he wasn't much of a fighter as well as his friend, but he would have to play the situation at hand by ear.

"Guys, it was nice talking with you, but if you guys don't mind, we have to take these girls home because they both have curfews," the red head said.

"Alright, don't let us hold you, but there is one more thing I would like to ask," Claude said.

"What is it dude?" the blond asked.

"See, my man here got a curfew too and I notice your ride don't got enough room for all of us. Was wondering if y'all could spot us a few dollars to take a cab up the way, you know what I'm saying? This nig-I mean, this dude right hear got to get the fuck home because if we don't get him home right now, he won't see another night like this until it gets cold, you feel me?" Claude referred to Big Chris.

"Dude, I'm fucking busted," the blond lied.

"So am I," the red head co-signed.

"What about these girls? I know their rich parents gave them dough to be out here with you boys," Claude said humorously.

The brunette teenaged girls in the back had a disgusted look on their face because they wrote the black teens off by being harmless. They have never been confronted by a group of blacks. They lived in the suburbs and never experienced violence. The brunettes were attractive. They had long, brown hair. The only differences between them were the color of their eyes. One of them had hazel eyes and the other one had blue. The one with the hazel eyes had an oval face; the blue eye brunette had a narrow one. If they knew what the black teenaged youth's real intentions were, they would have kept the nasty facial expressions to themselves. The girls had uppity attitudes and were mad at their male peers for being cowards. The four white youths have never encountered street thugs. They had no idea what *they were up against.*

"Listen guys," one of the brunettes said from the back seat, "we don't have any money and it's getting awfully late. You guys are holding us up. If you don't mind, I want to get home so I won't be grounded for the next month," she said with an aura of irritability.

"Ain't no reason for the fuckin' attitude bitch!" Rocks growled loudly.

"I don't have..."

"Shut up Beth!" the red head snarled.

"Yo, fuck all this shit. Tired of fucking playing with y'all. Either give us the goods or get hit off with the bad," Tommy said sharply.

"Dude, we don't want any trouble. Whatever Beth said is on her. She's just worried that her parents are going to ground her," the blond said desperately.

"That sounds like a personal problem to me," Claude said eerily, his joyful demeanor turning horrid.

"Give us the dough motherfuckers," Mark stated harshly.

"Dude, we don't..."

Without any more hesitation, Claude punched the blond on the side of his jaw, making him fall hard to the ground. He stomped on the blond ferociously while he made a feeble attempt to use his hands and arms as shields. While the blond was being stomped, the red head was being smothered by kicks with different shoe brands. Mark took off his belt and whipped the red head while the others stomped him. The girls in the back screamed at the top of their lungs.

"Shut the fuck up before we fuck y'all up to!" Claude yelled thickly. The girls ceased the screaming and replaced them with crying and whimpering. One of the brunettes looked out the window and saw that the blond was a bloody mess. While the teens slipped into an unconscious state, the group of young black males beat, threatened, and looted their pockets. The women gave up their money willingly. Satisfied, the young black males fled into the darkness of the night.

...

Sonya and Fatima walked in, snapping Mark out of one of his usual daydreams about the past. When he came in from the front deck, Sonya walked by him. Fatima gave him an odd look and walked into the kitchen, throwing Mark's food on the table like she had an attitude.

"What's your problem?" Mark asked, discarding the blunt

roach he had in his hand.

"You Mark. Come here," she said.

Mark wondered why she was uptight. He couldn't think of one valid reason why.

"Why didn't you tell me about Sonya's ex? Don't lie to me Mark because I know she told you," Fatima said curtly.

"It wasn't my place. I just didn't want to get involved. Damn, you mad over that shit?"

"Sort of Mark. What the hell? I tell you everything."

"Understand the position I was in Fatima. If I would have told you and if she would've found out, it would have been hectic in here. I figured you were going to find out anyway. I just let sleeping dogs lie baby, you know what I mean?"

"I wouldn't have told her if you didn't want me to. I just hate when you keep things from me."

"I promised her I wouldn't say anything and I didn't. If I promise you something, I always come through for you, right?"

"Yes Mark," she said, letting her anger slip away because she knew Sonya always kept things from her. "And I appreciate it. Me and momma feel like shit 'cause you knew and the both of us are just finding out."

"How would that sound if I just leaked that to you? How would that make me look?"

"I hear you, but damn, it kind of sucks that Sonya told water over blood, but I guess she had her reasons for not telling us. And you're right; I guess that this proves your trustworthiness. If my own sister could trust you, than I could trust you." Fatima planted a kiss on Mark's cheek.

Fatima opened the refrigerator and pulled out a Dutch Master. Sonya came out of her room as if she sensed that Fatima was about to roll a blunt. She looked at Mark with apologetic eyes because she knew Fatima was going to confront him. When Fatima finished rolling the blunt, they sat on the couch. Mark popped in a movie. They let the smoke settle into their lungs and enjoyed a nice high.

28-Los Angeles

Detectives Taft and Rinaldi were leaving the two-month-old crime scene trying to decipher the little evidence they had. They were baffled and frustrated because they didn't have a suspect or a clue on who committed the murders out on Monteith Drive. Detective Taft kicked himself in the head, wishing he had retired last year. They have been taking a lot of heat from the administrators because of the unsolved homicides. The detectives, however, received light when a drifter came across a skull on the outskirts of L.A., but that could be anyone besides Peter Sullivan. The detectives remained hopeful because the skull had strains of blond hair sticking out of the cranium.

"We can't feel this stressed because there is a shit load of crime scene investigators back there that are just as baffled as we are," Rinaldi said, sipping his coffee.

"Yeah, I know, but it's fucked up that there are only five number tags for evidence that's worthless. What the fuck is four spent shells and goddamn blood on the wall? Its not that the blood belongs to the pricks that did this shit or like there are fingerprints on the shells. If that was the case, we'll be further than we are right now. Those fucks either knew how to cover this shit up or they had no idea that they were getting away with a perfect murder," Taft complained.

"Tell me about it. But even if that skull belongs to the kid, it would only add closure to the disappearance, not on who's responsible. We combed through that entire area on where the skull was found and we didn't find any other body parts. Either some animals moved them or those sick fucks scattered them. I don't know, but I feel as though where chasing ghosts; it's a shot in the dark," Rinaldi said.

"We exhausted everything we can do at this point. I feel like entrapping some worthless fucks that are going to kill anyway and call it a case. If your theory proves correct about the cadaver being gutted and scattered, we're dealing with killers so violent that not even Hollywood itself could dream them up. I've always said in my career that I am a dogged detective that wouldn't give up, but I'm biting my words as we speak," Taft said. "Not to change the subject, but have you ever got a hold of that informant?"

Rinaldi said," Yeah, while we were back there looking for a needle in a haystack, I called him because he owes me big time. I could've had him pulled from the block he was selling on since he was released, and I made that known to him when I called, you know, about me seeing him. Also, I threw the strike in his face because he was in denial about selling drugs, or shall I say, his diminishing product. When I brought that shit up, I had his full, undivided attention. The kid is young, probably not even twenty and he has a strike already. He will be pushing for two if he doesn't cooperate. We'll be meeting him later on. I didn't get into any details about what I need him for, because if I did, he'll probably be too chicken shit to sing, but I can't really blame him. I know somebody else knows about those murders and the streets are certainly not talking."

"What about Dennis Howard's sister. Did you even touch base with her?"

"Yeah, I called twice and got no answer. I even stopped by there, but I don't think the broad knows anything to tell you the truth."

"We can't even rule her out as a suspect, even though it may seem unlikely, but I seen too much in this career to ignore the unexpected. We'll bother her one more time. If she doesn't cooperate, will leave her alone for a while until we get some more tools to start building the case," Taft said, lighting up his second Marlboro in ten minutes.

"Man, that broad has a set of tits on her though."

Just when Taft was about to reply, his cell phone vibrated.

"Detective Taft speaking."

"Yeah...yeah....yeah...you gotta be shitting me! Ok... yeah...well I'll be goddamned. Does anyone else know about this? We'll be right down."

"What was that all about?" Rinaldi asked.

"That was Tony Calluzo, the deputy medical examiner. Peter's dental records are a positive match with the skull they've examined. Looks like the drifter found our missing person. He said the body was gutted so your theory about the animals proved correct. Peter Sullivan is dead," Taft said gravely.

They remained quiet to absorb the news. The detectives were trying to figure out subtle ways to let the Sullivan's know that their son was found deceased. It was one of the worst tasks of any detective, whether they were rookies or seasoned vets, to let a family know that their loved ones expired. The Sullivan's remained hopeful and maintained a level of faith, but their worlds were going to crumble once they find out that their only son was now a memory.

"After we come from the coroner's office, we'll tell the Sullivan's about the positive identification. I have been dreading this fucking day where we have to be the bearer of bad news. It's one thing to let them know that their son is dead, but it's another to tell them that we only found his skull." Taft lit another cigarette.

As they made their way to the coroner's office, they were quiet, thinking about their own offspring and wondering how they would feel if they received news like that about their children. All of Peter Sullivan's hopes and dreams went down the pipe because he was at the wrong place and the wrong time. The detectives had a chapter closed for them in the case, although it wasn't a desired result because they would rather have found Peter Sullivan alive.

. . .

Linda was sucking Snake's dick. Slurping was the only sound in the living room. They have been messing around for a month. Even though Snake was ten years her junior, Snake always had the white rock. Every time she asked for it, he knew she didn't have any money. He knew that he was in store for some good head. However, the more he fed her and any other fiend that didn't have any money, the more he fucked up his street distribution. He'll dip out of the package just to get his dick sucked and replace it with any shit that had the same color. He knew the fiends complained, but he didn't know that members of his own team were on to him.

When Linda rode by Crenshaw and spotted Snake in the mix of things, she wanted some coke, but Snake only had crack.

She never smoked rock before, but she wasn't about to give it any thought because she needed a high. One of Marco's runners normally served her the coke, but he was nowhere to be found. She tried a few other coke connects but their cell phones were either out of service or they were unable to provide her the goods. Snake saw a potential slave in Linda because he knew she wasn't getting anymore cash from Aaron because he no longer needed her apartment to cook and bag. Snake sold her a few grams of crack and knew he had her right where he wanted her.

When Snake tilted his head upwards and saw her head bobbing back and forth between his legs, he wanted to reach a climax and bust a nut inside of her mouth. He grabbed the back of her head and humped her mouth. When Linda felt Snake's legs tremble, she slowed down her speed and *deep throated* him. When he came, she swallowed. Snake maneuvered himself away from her.

"Damn, that was some good shit! Fuck!" Snake said. Linda wiped the remaining semen from around her mouth and wiped it on the couch.

Snake looked at her like she lost her mind.

"That's some nasty shit you just did," he said as Linda got up from her position and fixed up her untidy appearance. She flipped her dingy bra back over her small breasts and put back on her dirty t-shirt.

"Nigga please, it's only you and my child doesn't even live here anymore. Shit, what's more nasty, me swallowing your nut or me wiping the shit on the couch?" She searched the floor for her panties. Snake didn't fuck her, but he loved to see a woman naked while she gave him some head. He did that to the rest of the fiends he supplied. Snake twisted his face as he looked at her wild bush and wondered why she never trimmed it.

"Whatever. That alone just told me that you probably put some other nigga's nut where I'm sitting at so don't give me your shit. I bet you Prime's nut is all over this motherfucker."

"Nigga fuck you! I ain't trying to let you disrespect me Snake, for real, and take Prime's name out your mouth because he got nothin' to do with me and you."

"Me and you? Go 'head with that shit. If I wasn't supplying your funky ass, you wouldn't have given my dick a chance so don't talk that me and you shit. Ever since that faggot ass Aaron stopped using your crib to bag, you been a broke bitch. If I wasn't around to serve you, you would have somebody else's dick in your mouth."

Linda was about to respond with venom, but she thought better of it. She wanted crack. She didn't have a job and she was on a verge of getting evicted. She didn't want to burn any bridges so she swallowed her pride because she knew, at that point, that she needed him. If worse came to worse, she would move in with Maria, but that was a last resort.

"Damn Snake, you use to be so sweet to me. What happened?"

"I don't know, but I need to borrow your car. I need to handle some business," he said, disregarding her attempt to reconcile the situation.

"Ok, but can you leave me a little something before you leave…please," she begged.

"Look in the cabinet Linda."

He knew she was going to ask for some rock if he would ask for the car so he planted it there. He needed the car so he could drive down to the station to secure his job on the streets. He knew he was being watched and would do anything from catching his second strike. Linda handed him the keys and he bounced.

A few minutes after Snake left, Linda decided to wait until later to break in the new crack pipe. She sat on the couch and thought about how her life had spun out of control. At the pace she was going, she would be a trick out in the streets in no time. Her habit was known throughout the family. Her son was living with her mother. She didn't want him to grow up thinking that his grandmother was his mother. She figured the only way to avoid that was to kick the habit.

When Linda woke up o at 3am, she wondered where Snake could be with her car. She looked out of the window and saw her car parked in the same spot from which she left it. She saw him in the car. She felt as if something was wrong. She grabbed a pair of sweatpants from the dirty pile of clothes and put them on. When she opened the door, she felt uneasy at the sight of Snake from her porch. She figured that he must have gotten himself drunk and high and was too fucked up to come inside the apartment to return her keys. When she walked to the driver's window, her eyes bulged. She covered her mouth and stopped herself from screaming. The reality check she worried about was right in her face. Snake's blood covered the front seat. He sat in the driver's seat with his throat slit. The dirt he did caught up to him. To add more insult to injury, Snake found out where Aaron hid some of his stash money. He was going after those greenbacks after he dropped the dime on Aaron and his team about supplying the streets. To say he was an unappreciative dude was an understatement; he was naturally a snake and his name wasn't given to him for nothing.

Linda ran back into the house and called Maria instead of calling the police. She was so hysterical that Maria didn't know what she was talking about on the phone. When Maria confirmed that she was on her way, Linda called the police. When the police dispatcher asked the name of the victim, she couldn't honestly tell them because she didn't know Snake's government name. Detective Taft and Rinaldi would not meet him at the station; they'd see him on the coroner's table.

29-Waterbury

It was a cold Friday November night. Lloyd and Darlene's one level home was located on Cooke St. The sound of the old dishwasher was the only noise in the house besides the rerun of the Golden Girls. The house was cleaned to perfection with the exception of a few of Lloyd's scattered X-Box video games lying on the floor next to the television set. Darlene was fully dressed and ready to pick up her friend Pamela. She wore a long sleeve blue blouse buttoned down that exposed the swell of her breasts. The jeans she wore covered her boot's full length. Darlene became annoyed at her friend because Darlene wanted to hit the club while free drinks were being passed. She was also avoiding Lloyd. She wanted to see her son, but she didn't feel like being under the red light. He would have copped a cold attitude about her going to the club. Darlene was looking fly and sexy.

She sighed when Claude came to her mind. When she called him earlier, as usual, his phone went to voicemail. She knew that what she was doing behind Lloyd's back was wrong, but she couldn't help herself. After all, Claude took her virginity. Even though she got pregnant a year after his incarceration, she was never over Claude. She thought about the sad, depressed look on his face when she broke the news to him. That look on his face hunted her for years. She secretly hated Lloyd for bringing her to the prison and telling Claude face to face about her pregnancy. At that time, she thought ten years was more like a million. Now that he was no longer incarcerated, she regretted what she did, even though her son, Lloyd Jr. was a blessing. Her ten year relationship with Lloyd was deteriorating. Ever since Claude got released from prison, she couldn't stop lusting and loving him. Lloyd definitely was suspicious and he felt the distance between them. He asked if she was fucking anyone, but she denied it. She tried to act like it was an insult on her for Lloyd to ask. Lloyd wasn't stupid. When Lloyd had enough of being kept in the dark, he found himself following Darlene. When he followed her to Griggs St yesterday, he didn't know Claude lived there. As her car remained parked in front of his house, he decided that he wasn't going to wait any longer because he waited for two hours for her to come out. Growing tired of looking to see if one of the doors to the multi-family house would open, he decided to leave. This morning, when Darlene went to work, he went back to Griggs Street after he dropped Lloyd Jr. off at school. When he thought about the possibility that Darlene could have been visiting a female friend, he smiled at his paranoia and started his car, but that's when Claude and Rocks walked out of one of the front doors to the multi-family home. Her affair with Claude was confirmed. Lloyd sat in his car stunned. He knew it would be a while before he confronted her because he had to work, take Lloyd Jr. to his game, and take him over to his mother's house.

She called Pamela.

"Pam, I'll be there in fifteen minutes. You better be ready bitch," Darlene said jokingly.

"I was just about to call you. I'm ready heifer."

"Alright, see you in a few."

When Darlene got up from the couch, Lloyd walked in the door holding a sleeping Lloyd Jr. Lloyd was a tall, brown skin large sized man that sported a mini-afro. He was big and burly. At thirty two, he was well accomplished. He had a degree from Southern Connecticut State University and was an accountant in Hartford. He made good money and worked hard to take care of Darlene and their son. Darlene had a job in a non-profit group home, but she didn't make a quarter to what he made a year. They had a few problems here and there, but nothing out of the ordinary. Since Claude's release, however, Darlene was acting brand new; Lloyd had been feeling the distant vibe.

The look he wore on his face was cold and bitter. Darlene knew that she was going to be late picking up Pamela.

"Hey," Darlene said flatly.

Lloyd didn't say anything. He made his way to their son's room so he could put him to bed. Lloyd Jr. had a long day because after school, he had a basketball game. After that, Lloyd took their son to his mother's house to eat pizza. It was planned for him anyway, but since he hit the game winning shot, Lloyd and his mother called it a celebration meal. During the basketball game, Lloyd was zoned out, thinking and visualizing Claude's dick in her womb. It took him a few seconds for him to realize that his son hit the game winning shot. At his mother's house, he had to be an actor, but his mother knew something was troubling him, but she didn't press it.

As soon as Lloyd took his son's clothes off so he could sleep, he walked out of his room and closed the door gently. He knew that his son was knocked out and was too deep into his sleep to hear the drama he was about to unfold.

"Where you going and why are you home this early? You said you had to work late. I wouldn't have kept Lloyd out so late if I knew you were home," Lloyd said gloomily.

"First of all, I never said I had to work late. Secondly, I'm going out with Pam tonight. Is that alright daddy?" she replied curtly.

"Alright, alright, just thought I'd ask, you know? Considering how you're dressed, I figured you were going out on some late hot date."

"Don't start Lloyd. I just want to go out and have a good time. I don't need to hear this shit now. We've been down this road many times."

"Is that so? You are one sneaky ass bitch. I know you been fucking Claude."

"Excuse me? I know you just didn't call me a bitch Lloyd." Darlene was shocked. Her mind scrambled. She thought she had him in the dark.

"Yeah, I called you a bitch, bitch. I only call it how I see it."

"Besides your insecurities, what's the problem Lloyd?" she asked with her arms folded. She stood in front of him.

"I know you've been fucking that nigga, you slut bitch."

Darlene had enough of him calling her a bitch. His nonchalantness pushed her over the edge.

Smack!

Darlene smacked Lloyd so hard that he fell against the entertainment center. A framed photo of them shattered when it hit the floor. When she tried to charge at him, he grabbed her with one hand by the neck and twirled her on the coffee table.

The legs of the table broke. She was surprised. He never put hands on her until now. She got up slowly. She knew that she was no match for him, but the truth always hurt. Darlene, in her heated state of mind managed to crack a smile.

"You know what Lloyd?" she asked between gasps of air, "Yeah I fucked him. I fucked Claude. I've been fucking him since he got out. And you know what? He fucks me good! I cum every time, even when he cums in my mouth. When he does, I rub my own pussy. When I fuck your weak ass, I think of him! My pussy turns to sand when I fuck you!"

Lloyd was so enraged that he wanted to kill her. Instead, he absorbed the truth while his pride as a man fell to rock bottom. He pushed her violently against the wall, causing the sheet rock to cave in. When she was on the floor, he wrapped his hands around her neck. Their son came at the perfect time.

"Get off mommy! Get off mommy!"

Lloyd Jr. tagged his father's back with fists. Lloyd came back to reality and released his grip.

"Go the fuck to your room and don't come out," Lloyd said thickly. Lloyd Jr. was only nine years old and he saw the evil in his father's eyes. He had never seen his father that enraged. He ignored him stood by his mother. She made it to her feet clumsily, stumbled to her pocketbook, grabbed her keys, gave him an angry teary eyed look and stormed out the door.

Lloyd remained on the floor. He was coming to his senses. Tears fell freely down his face. He was never harsh on his son; he was never harsh to Darlene like that either. Lloyd Jr. was just protecting his mother.

He knew that Darlene was going to the club. He had a hunch that Claude was going to be there. Making a vital decision during his angry state of mind, he called his sister so she could watch Lloyd Jr. After he placed the call, he waited impatiently for her. She arrived at the house twenty minutes later. When she saw the wreck in the living room, she asked what happened. Lloyd dropped a fifty-dollar bill on the end table and left without saying a word.

30-Two hours later...

Women were dressed conservatively for the cold weather outside or scantily dressed, despite the November chill. Either way, Claude and his team were having a good time looking at the eye candy surrounding them, but Claude and Rocks discussed business.

Claude had been knee deep in the game for a month. His mind for dirty business had generated him major gross. A lot of the money accumulated came from drug money and strong arming out of town drug dealers. Business was booming and Claude's addiction to money grew. He told his sister he had a job working nights, but she knew better. She knew he had a foot in the game, but kept quiet. She didn't condone it, but she was no longer struggling with bills. Destiny even had a babysitter. Although he was more dangerous now than he was as a youth growing up, his focus was set on saving money to open his own barbershop. He figured he'd open up shop down in Texas. Waterbury was out of the question and any inner city neighborhood surrounding it because he knew during his money making campaign he would make his own share of enemies.

Claude and Rocks made sure Zane came home from York Correctional Institution in style. Despite business, Zane's release from prison was the reason for the celebration. She was locked up for eighteen months for possession and was ready to take a major plunge into the game. The club was near close time and Rocks went to go gather the herd, leaving Claude and Zane to converse.

"You all big and shit. I know its been fifteen years, but damn." She took a swig of her beer. "Them bitches I got with me is down for whatever, but I think Mercedes wants a taste of your thick ass. You and Rocks need to ditch Tommy and those other two young dudes y'all with if y'all want to tear that pussy up just as long as y'all have that powder. They coke heads."

Claude laughed and eyed Zane's friends. Diamond was a short, petite, dark skinned Puerto Rican that had styled, short hair. She wore a nose ring and had a large tattoo of a giant butterfly and heart covering the small of her back. Mercedes was a tall, thick brown skinned Trinidadian that wore a strapless one piece white dress. Claude noticed the swell of her breasts from where he stood.

Zane was a thick, caramel complexion female with long dreadlocks. She wore baggy jeans, a Sean John sweatshirt, and light grey Timberlands. Zane was a lesbian that was constantly surrounded by a barrage of model type females. She was pretty in the face, but her body was a great asset in which she concealed by wearing baggy clothes. She was like one of the dudes. She was cool, but she could be dangerous for those that oppose her. Claude and Rocks made sure Zane had a spot on their roster when she was released.

"Fifteen fucking years Zane. My physical appearance changed, but my mental is much deeper. I see the whole picture. I used to see it partially. Just want to make my cash explode and get out this shit, for real."

"I feel you. Motherfuckin' white man with his bullshit. Fuck em' though; we got to make our own way in this fucked up world, you feel me?" Zane asked, guzzling her beer.

"Best believe I do," Claude said as he clicked his beer bottle with Zane's bottle as a small toast for new, illegal beginnings.

They caught a quiet moment and analyzed the occupants in the club. Claude was feeling good. He was drunk, Zane was officially home, and he was set to get his swerve on with Mercedes. He looked near the DJ booth and spotted Rocks spitting game to Diamond. When he looked at the end of the bar, he saw Pam, a big boned dark skinned woman that was always with Darlene. When he didn't spot her, he blew a sigh of relief because she had been blowing him up all day.

"Yo nigga, what the fuck is wrong with you? I left your mom up the way today and she told me you still fucking with that bitch," Zane said.

Claude turned towards the bathroom slowly and saw Darlene walking out of it.

"Damn!" Claude grunted.

"I know she ain't coming over here. She probably don't

recognize me, or if she did, she got a lot of audacity 'cause she know I don't like her."

Claude watched Darlene through his peripheral vision walk to where they stood. He noticed her approaching them, but he paid her no attention.

"What's up Claude? Can I talk to you for a minute?" Darlene asked quietly, awaiting Claude's answer. "Oh, hi Zane, I didn't even recognize you," she lied. "How are you?"

Zane took another swig of her beer and walked away without saying a word.

"Ok, what is her problem? You fucking her C? That's why you don't return any of my calls?"

"What did you have to talk to me about Darlene?" he asked flatly.

"Why are you dodging my calls?"

"Been busy."

"Been busy, huh? Been busy fucking that dyke bitch? Been busy preparing yourself for jail C? Been busy selling drugs? What the fuck happened to you?"

Darlene was pissed. Despite getting slammed into the coffee table a few hours ago, she still made it to the club after she took a few Motrin. She wore a different change of gear. She borrowed some of Pam's younger sister's wardrobe just to see Claude at the club and give him a piece of her mind.

Claude felt the urge to bark on her for talking about his friend. They have known each other since grade school and their friendship was solid. To add more wood into the fire, she talked openly about his living. He came up with a solution.

"Bye Darlene," he said plainly and walked away.

"Don't turn your back on me! I got my ass whipped by Lloyd fucking with you," Darlene spat angrily, grabbing him by the arm.

"So what the fuck do you want from me?! Take a hint Darlene! I don't want you! You are ruining my high with all this extra shit," Claude said through clenched teeth while he forcefully pulled his arm from her grip.

"Fuck you Claude!" She spat at him, missing his face by a hair. The saliva did, however, land on his sweatshirt. If he didn't think for one second in his anger, Darlene would have been a goner. His team didn't notice the stunt Darlene pulled, but the close onlookers did, especially Pam. She followed Darlene hurriedly into the bathroom.

Claude grabbed some napkins that were given to him by the bartender. She witnessed the entire incident as well as a few others. The bartender gave him a Hennessy and Coke on the house. When he accepted the drink, someone tapped him on the shoulder. When he turned around, Lloyd stood behind him, towering over Claude's five foot eleven frame. He didn't notice the incident, but he remembered Darlene's words of betrayal. When Lloyd left his house, he called his friend Wendell who was already at the club. Wendell verified that Claude was there. Lloyd sat in the car for twenty minutes drinking E & J straight from the bottle, realizing he was putting his career as an accountant on the line. His drunkenness was overcoming his common logic and it gave him a false sense of power. When he gathered the balls to go inside, he had to wait in line until it was his turn to be frisked. He spotted Claude a few minutes after scanning the place.

"Long time no see playa. I see you doing your thing. I mean, you wasted no time breaking up my household an' shit. Stay the fuck away from my girl nigga," Lloyd spat calmly, his breath smelling like alcohol.

"You need to tell your bitch then," Claude said sarcastically.

"I think you need to watch who you calling a bitch motherfucker," Lloyd said hotly, balling his hands for battle. "That's my kid's mother!"

Claude leaned coolly on the table, not feeling threatened by the large mass of man before him. He sipped on his drink as if Lloyd wasn't there. Without looking at him, Claude adjusted his body slightly so he could respond.

"Yo, my bad, you need to tell that foul ass slut to stay off my dick," Claude said evenly.

Lloyd looked at Claude and his anger had gone to the max. Claude displayed no fear of Lloyd's presence. He was dealing with pride. Lloyd was used to intimidating people because of his size. Lloyd had always played the aggressor, despite his education. Lloyd laid down a lot of people in his college football years and drunken nights at clubs. He gained a reputation for himself. Lloyd knew Claude longer than Darlene and he was never afraid of him, despite Claude's violent reputation. Claude minimized the seriousness of the situation. That drove Lloyd over the edge.

Rocks, Tommy, and Zane stood together and noticed the brewing action. Zane just finished telling them about Darlene's presence. Seeing Lloyd where Claude stood told them everything they all needed to know. Rocks placed two of his fingers in his mouth and whistled through the roaring hip hop. Since Tank and Ty were close by, they picked up on the signal for distress and moved in Claude's direction.

"Who the fuck do you think you talking to?" Lloyd said loudly, drawing attention to himself. Wendell saw Claude's team file in, but he wasn't getting involved. He decided that it would be best to be smart because he wasn't that cool with Lloyd to side with him to battle. He acted as if he didn't see anything and walked in the opposite direction of the growing commotion.

"Talking to an oversized cocksucker," Claude said arrogantly and smoothly while he sipped his drink.

Lloyd shoved Claude harshly, causing him to lose balance and spill his drink, the second time that happened. He used the edge of the table to gain his balance. Lloyd tried to follow up with a right hand, but Claude caught his balance in a nick of time. When he dodged Lloyd's looping right hand swing, Claude countered with a short, stiff right to the side of Lloyd's face. The punch was short and sharp. His knees buckled from the impact of the punch. Lloyd was on the floor, unable to get up from his sprawled out position.

Claude was about to follow up with a kick to his face, but Rocks grabbed him just in time. Darlene and Pam burst through the shocked crowd of onlookers. She saw Claude standing over Lloyd and a rage overcame her. She tried to attack Claude, but before she got a chance, Zane, Diamond, and Mercedes jumped on Darlene like a pride of lions attacking prey. Darlene was off her feet in no time. While she was getting stomped, Darlene made a subtle, feeble attempt to fight back, but being on her back, swinging like she was on her feet made her ass whipping worse. Zane and her two friends left Darlene on the floor wounded, swelled, and bleeding. Claude regained control and jetted out of the club with his team, including Diamond and Mercedes.

When the commotion simmered down in the club, Pam helped Darlene off the floor. She looked at Pam and gave her an evil eye. While Darlene was getting jumped, Pam looked like a spectator watching the fight. Pam was too frozen with fear to help her. She walked over to her fallen common law husband, who was still on the floor holding the side of his face, and tried to help him. Pam couldn't even make up an excuse because if the shoe was on the other foot, Darlene would have helped her.

Luckily for the crew, no cops were posted outside. The cops who were present were inside the club to make sure nothing went down. The two cops were too busy shooting the shit with the attractive ladies on the dance floor. They didn't see anything but a large man sprawled out on the floor after the fact. By the time they saw the fallen man, Claude and his team were on the road with Diamond and Mercedes following behind in Diamond's car. They were on their way to pick up some powder and Zane's other lady friend. Darlene and Lloyd were embarrassed to death, but they were from the hood and knew best not to snitch. When asked by police on what happened, Lloyd said they were out of town 'cats.' When they asked Darlene, she said she didn't know and just wanted to go home. Since the cops felt like assholes for not knowing shit that happened right underneath their noses, they didn't press them. After Darlene and Lloyd refused medical attention for the umpteenth time, they left the club. Darlene had no choice but to ride with coward ass Pam because when she attempted to hop in the car with Lloyd, he locked all the doors, started the car, and drove off.

31-Manhattan/Brooklyn

Sapp walked with a cool, drunken swagger. A blunt dangled from his mouth as he walked on 23rd St and Broadway coming from the 40/40 club with a brown skinned, voluptuous woman at his side. He looked like a sitting duck for an armed robbery as the thick link on his neck glistened in the cold, brisk night. He grabbed the back of the young woman's ass as they strutted through the thickness of people to get to Sapp's Lexus. His clothes were crisp. He was wearing a New York Crew Series Premium bomber, a black and white checkered Vanguard woven shirt underneath it, Gilyard denim jeans, and a fresh pair of classic black Timberlands. Alexis, the woman he was courting, wore a jean jumper with fur neck trim and a pair of high-heeled Gucci boots. They had met an hour ago and he knew he had Alexis in the bag.

Alexis was in awe when she saw the exterior of Sapp's 2015 silver Lexus GS 300 as they approached it. Sapp saw her reaction and produced a sinister sly smile because the way she was looking, he felt as if he was the luckiest motherfucker alive. As they settled in the car and allowed the vehicle to warm up, she reached over the gear shift and slowly ran her fingers from his leg to his crotch. Sapp's manhood rose as she stroked his dick through his jeans. She leaned over and licked his neck. Sapp was too drunk to control himself. He attempted to unbutton her jacket, but she casually stopped him.

"We'll be where we need to be as soon as you leave. Hurry, because I'm so fucking horny," she said seductively as she ran her hand from his chest to his stomach before resuming her position in her seat.

Sapp couldn't take the grin off his face. For the hell of it, he grabbed her breasts before he stepped on the clutch and put the car into first gear and took off.

While Sapp slowly weaved in and out of traffic on the Manhattan Bridge, Alexis grilled the side of Sapp's face. Sapp noticed her in his peripheral vision, but maintained a grim look. He was trying his hardest not to grin, but he couldn't help himself.

"So, a fine ass nigga like yourself should be going home to his baby momma and his kids, especially at 4:30 in the morning on Thanksgiving. What's really good with you? Do I got to fight off some bitches over your blazin' ass? What's your story?"

"No ma, you don't got to lift a finger. I'm just a simple ass hustlin' nigga. I got a daughter though, but her moms be on some bullshit, talkin' that I can't see her unless I was with her, you feel me? The bitch is crazy. I'm tryin' to get custody an' shit, but I got to show the court some papers," he lied.

"Shit, you got money. That's all the paper you need."

"I wish it could be like that. She struggling like a motherfucker and my daughter is better off living with me. I mean, despite all her bullshit, I take care of em, you feel me? I bought her whip, pay most of her bills and all that shit and the bitch won't let me see my daughter. Her jail fiend ass brother benefitting from my money, that bitch ass nigga," he said with a bold face lie.

"If we get together, are you gonna hold me down? I can do for myself, but it's good when a man of your character has my back. I can't stand these triflin' ass niggas these days. With all due respect, your baby momma should appreciate a nigga like you 'cause it ain't many like you."

"We'll see ma."

In his mind, he came a long way, even though he had to step on a few toes to get where he was at. The fucked up thing was that he felt that he had to do what he had to do. In 2007, Rocks and his cousin Danny were making money. Sapp used to be Rocks and Danny's mule. He was given a few thousand dollars to make trips to go get kilos from New York. Doing a 100mph on 95 North in Stamford coming from the city would be the beginning of his downfall. Sapp was oblivious to the state trooper who was camped out in the grass waiting for someone who was in a hurry. Sapp was the only unlucky one. He cursed the people in front of him in his lane for braking on the highway. The brake lights were just an indication of everyone's awareness of the state trooper, but Sapp caught on a second too late. He almost took a shit when he saw the bright flashing lights in his rearview mirror. Since the gold, dark tinted

Nissan Altima smelled of exotic weed smoke, he knew he was a done deal. There was no way he was able to make the scent of weed go away. When the trooper walked up to his vehicle, he thought about taking off, but that was just a thought. When the trooper saw his droopy red eyes and took a whiff of the scent coming from the dark tinted Altima, the trooper had probable cause to search the car. Before he did that, he called for back-up. When two more state troopers arrived at the scene, he wished he had reacted off his first instinct and peeled off because there was no way he could of justified the four bricks of cocaine resting in the trunk. He knew he would have to bring someone powerful down. He didn't have it in him to do four bricks worth of time and he knew it. He sat in the back of the cruiser handcuffed while the suits rummaged through his car.

Some of the inmates in Whalley grew weary of Sapp's constant legal calls. Many people knew that he got bagged with four bricks. As the weeks turned into months, four mid level drug dealers got nabbed and lost their cases, resulting in ten to fifteen year sentences with the exception of Julio Santiago, who received a life sentence for being a persistent felon. When it was Sapp's day in court, he received six years. The six years he received didn't ease his satisfaction. He figured bringing down the four drug dealers should have erased the entire sentence that was given to him because they were all major suppliers.

The first week in November in the year 2007 was hectic. Election time was in full swing. Many city officials were applying pressure to law enforcement officials in Connecticut to crack down on high ranking, nondependent drug dealers. Law enforcement officials conducted citywide raids, but were unsuccessful with each one that was carried out. Sapp heard about the unsuccessful attempts, thanks to Sahara, and he knew the jakes were looking in the wrong places. He had an idea, but of course, he was going to step on more toes. Danny and Rocks were living large while he sat in Carl Robinson doing a six year bid. It infuriated him because he felt as if they owed him something. He was the one carrying the weight across state lines. He placed his life on the line everyday and Rocks and Danny never sent him commissary money, naked female photos or anything. That was the least they could have done. As he sat in his cell pissed off, he made up his mind. It was time to drop another dime.

A few months later, Rocks and Danny got too comfortable. Claude wrote Rocks repeatedly and warned him about Sapp, but Rocks didn't think Sapp had the heart to put his life on the line. Reality hit hard on a cold, January night. Danny was resting comfortably in his home with his girlfriend and their children when his crib got raided. Twenty kilos and all sorts of weaponry were found on his premises. Rocks drove around the corner when he saw the abundance of police cruisers. Rocks made a quick detour just in time. He hurried home and got rid of the two kilos he had to the weed roaches in all of his ashtrays. As expected, the police kicked down Rocks's door with the intention of catching him with his thumb up his ass, but they didn't; however, since Rocks had a warrant, he had to sit for eighteen months, but his sentence was a vacation compared to Danny's sentence. The kilos Danny got hit with were huge, but he also had warrants stemming from robbery and assault. In June of 2008, he received twenty seven years for the kilos, five years for the guns, and ten years for the second degree assault and the armed robbery. He was sentenced to forty two years. If Danny would have had a public defender, he would have received a sixty year sentence. Danny's criminal record was taken into consideration. He had been doing time in Connecticut and New York since he was thirteen. He spent his twenty sixth birthday doing the first day of his life sentence. The government imposed Rule 35 in Sapp's favor…twice. Sapp only did three years. If he would have trooped it out like a true soldier, he would have done twenty five. His betrayal ignited an everlasting beef. Sapp did three years and disappeared. He had only made cameo visits to Waterbury to see Destiny and his mother. Seeing Sapp twice a year has been a norm for Destiny, but she savored every moment spent with her father.

Sapp had his plan set. He was going to fuck Alexis, drive out to his spot in the Bronx to retrieve a grip of money, and ride up to Waterbury, CT to wither some of the storm that had been over his head for years. In prison, Sapp and Link created a bond. Link was the only stupid motherfucker that believed that Sapp was true to the game, despite the shit he heard about him. Link was released in jail in June of 2008. Sapp was released two months later. Two days after Sapp left the system, he went to Link for work. Link gave Sapp two kilos of heroin off of consignment after Sapp promised him that he would have Link's money in a week in a half. The week and a half turned into two years. When he called Link out of the blue, after two years, Link didn't even have time to issue a threat on Sapp's life because Link's fantasy of killing Sapp for the last two years died when Sapp said he wanted to meet up with him to give him fifty grand, including a little interest for his troubles.

Sapp drove on Lafayette Avenue, took a left on to Classon, and took another left onto DeKalb Ave. He rode slowly on the street until he found a parking space near St. James Place. There were many cars parked on the one-way street, but it seemed deserted. Sapp felt a little uneasy because he didn't know anyone from the area. His first instinct kicked in when he noticed Alexis looking around, which was a little strange for his gathering. She was drunk, but now she was acting nervous. She was so engulfed in her scanning that she didn't know her own hands were trembling.

"What's wrong with your hands? You know something I don't," he asked coldly without a hint of drunkenness.

"Damn daddy, why are you so paranoid? My hands were shaking ever since we left the club. It takes a while for them to warm up. I'm anemic. Let me find out you a shook one. I ain't going let nothin' happen to you baby," she said, stroking his goatee.

"Nah, nah, I ain't shook. I just don't know these niggas like that, you know what I'm saying? I'm a CT cat with CT license plates. CT and New York niggas don't get along."

"Baby, it ain't even that type of party down here," she said as she opened the mirror implanted visor, went into her Gucci bag, and pulled out her lip gloss to add some moisture to her well-defined lips.

A red light went off in Sapp's head. He couldn't put a finger on it, but he was sure something was wrong. His sixth sense kicked in. If Sapp had common sense, he would obey his sixth sense and get the fuck out of there, but his little man between his legs was doing all the thinking. He reached under his seat and pulled out a Ruger SR9 to ensure his own safety.

"Baby, like I told you, it ain't that type of party. You better put that shit away before you catch a charge," she said while she was getting out the car.

"You must be out your fucking mind if you think I'm putting away my heat," Sapp said as he stepped into the blistering cold weather.

As soon as Sapp was completely out of the car, he felt a piercing cold piece of steel on his neck. Sapp froze with fear as he stopped dead in his tracks. When he was in the car, he would have noticed a figure creeping slowly to the driver's side of his Lexus, but he was too busy talking shit. He didn't even scan the area for anything out of the ordinary. His gun was useless. He saw Alexis standing outside of the passenger door unfazed by the stick-up. She had a cold look in her eye.

"Well, well, well, if it isn't snitching ass Sapp. Long time no see cocksucker. Put the gun down nigga…slowly," the voice demanded.

When Sapp looked at Alexis, she had a smirk on her face. Sapp felt stupid that he let his guard down, but he had to weigh his options, which were little. In fact, he had none. He recognized the voice immediately. The triggerman carried a vengeance so strong that he knew that this would be his last day on Earth. He didn't think he was ever going to see Rocks again, but here he was, standing there with the tool that would end his life. Sapp looked at Alexis like he would do anything to get out of Rocks's grasp and kill her. He cursed himself for leaving his man's and them hanging. They told him repeatedly not to leave alone with her, but the little man between his legs got the best of him. He gently placed the gun on the ground.

"Yeah motherfucker, I know what you thinking. You thinking like, this bitch set my ass up. Well you know what? Hell yeah I set you up, just like you snitched on my brother Danny you coward-ass bitch," Alexis spat.

"I got fifty g's at my crib…"

"I got the Nike duffle in the whip nigga. Been there, done that," Rocks said slyly.

Sapp knew he reached the end of the road. He couldn't deny that he snitched on Rocks, Danny and many others. He accepted his fate. He was tired of running. He managed to squeeze in thoughts of Destiny. He thought about the first time he held her when she was a newborn and the last time he seen over the summer. A lone tear fell from his eye.

"Move away from the whip and get the fuck on your knees," Rocks demanded.

He did what he was told. Sapp trembled with fear, but he knew this day would come. He continued to think of his only offspring. He created, in that short period of time, visuals of Sahara and Destiny holding hands. His thoughts were quickly interrupted by the sound of Rocks's gun and the sudden pain he felt in his left thigh. Sapp grabbed it to make a feeble attempt to stop the blood from pouring profusely from it, but it was useless. Through all of that, he saw Rocks standing over him with the gun pointed to his head. Rocks pulled the trigger and Sapp's images of most of the people he came across in his lifetime, including Rocks, turned to black. Sapp was dead at thirty-five. Rocks and Jada, as known as Alexis to Sapp, pulled off in the Dodge Viper, a car borrowed from a fiend, heading towards I-287. The precinct was only down the street so they had to move fast. Sapp's open-eyed corpse rested in a pool of his own blood next to his Lexus with the driver's door wide open.

32-Waterbury/Los Angeles

Claude's bedroom was filled with drunken, holiday laughter as Claude and Rocks were playing NBA 2K16 for the Xbox One. Rocks bitched as Claude enjoyed an eight to zero run to finish off the second quarter, putting him in the lead for the first time in the game. Zane spoke on her cell phone, ignoring the vulgar, shit talking in the bedroom. Tommy was on the recliner chair knocked out. The video consoles that were live before Claude's incarceration was Playstation and Dreamcast. Throughout all the battles Claude, Rocks, and Tommy had when it came to video games, Claude always had the upper edge. It never took him long to adapt to video games, not even in adulthood on a new level of gaming.

"Fuck you mean computer assistance? Your getting your ass whipped, that's all. And this is my third time playing this shit. I'm that nigga," Claude boasted while he and Rocks let the halftime show play on the video game.

"Whatever motherfucker. That ain't you that's beating me. The computer is. And stop fronting 'cause this ain't the third time you played this game. You been playing this game just as long as I have."

"You've been playing these basketball shits since they came on the market. As for me, I get out of jail after fifteen years and continue to bust your ass. I mean, you're nice, but I'm great."

"Hit some jump shots C. All you do is dunk and hit free throws," Rocks said flatly, frustrated because of Claude's momentum.

"Yeah alright. You've been hitting threes wit' Dirk. I ain't complained once. My post game is on point. I'm untouchable."

"You ain't shit. You using fucking LeBron James. The sun is just shining on a dog's ass. You stink C," Rocks said, adjusting his hands for the second half of the game.

"You haven't beating me since…I don't even know the last time you beat me. I consistently smash your ass Rocks. Maybe you need to complete some drills before you decide to unhook your shit and bring it over here. See, this is yo' Xbox One; I'm just the only one man enough to rape you in your own game," Claude said arrogantly.

"Whatever motherfucker. Hit start."

Claude won the game by ten points. Rocks begged repeatedly for a rematch while Claude taunted him good-naturedly by flexing his biceps.

"I got winners," Tommy said, waking up from a snooze. The Thanksgiving meal provided a lasting effect on him.

"Tommy, let me just play this nigga one more time," Rocks asked desperately.

"Hell no. I ain't watchin' again. Besides, you lost. Pass the stick."

"Yeah nigga. You lost. Pass that shit. Always trying to stunt like you the shit," Zane interjected.

"Hey Zane, how about getting off the phone and tend to yo' niggas, you know what I mean? Roll a blunt, fix us some plates, do something. You been on that goddamn phone since we finished eating," Rocks said.

"Fuck you nigga. Just pass the handle to another contender. You had your chance," Zane joked.

"It don't matter who I play. It's gonna be the same result. I'm nice," Claude chimed.

Claude had Tommy up by fifteen late in the fourth quarter while Rocks and Zane rolled blunts. As soon as the game ended, Tommy put the joystick down and retreated to the comfort of the chair he napped on. Claude checked his stats on the game. Rocks and Zane applied the finishing touches to the neatly rolled blunts. Claude's phone vibrated on his junk drawer.

"Zane, see who that is that's calling me. Fucking Darlene texting that Happy Holiday shit, trying to get me to call her. If it's restricted, it's her; don't pick up."

"It's Mark. 'Sup my dude!? Long time no hear from," Zane spat excitedly into the phone.

"When is that bitch ass nigga coming up here to check niggas," Rocks asked loudly. The last time Rocks seen Mark was the day Mark left for Texas two years ago. Rocks resided in a half-way house at the time. Mark swung by to say good-bye to him. He left Rocks with two hundred dollars and a pair of

Timberlands. Tommy would have been excited to hear from Mark, but he was snoring on the chair so no one bothered to wake him.

"Mark said he should be up in a few months," Zane said before starting her conversation.

Claude told Zane to have Mark call on the house phone after their conversation. Zane spoke to Mark for five more minutes before hanging up. After a few moments, Mark called the house. Claude picked up the phone after the second ring. They exchanged happy holidays, talked about general stuff, gave the phone to Rocks, and the conversation was over. As soon as Rocks hung up with Mark, Claude's phone vibrated again.

"Hello, this is Melanie. Is Sahara home?" she asked as if something was wrong.

"No she's not, but I'll tell her you called. Is every..."

"Please tell her to call me," Melanie said before hanging up.

What the fuck was that all about?

They were putting on their jackets, anticipating on getting high in Rocks's truck. Since Zane's phone was running out of minutes, she made it a habit to use Claude's phone. When Claude closed the door behind him when they all stepped into the arctic weather, his phone vibrated in Zane's pocket. Zane answered the phone without looking at the caller ID, thinking it was one of her playmates calling back.

"Yeah, I'll accept. 'Sup Delores. Happy Holidays..."

Claude was waiting for his mother to call. Claude reached to grab the phone from Zane, but she beckoned him to hold off for a second. He noticed the look on Zane's face as Delores revealed information that Claude was eager to hear. Claude backed off because the expression on Zane's face spelled bad news.

"Alright...alright... Here go Claude. Love you too," Zane said as she handed Claude the phone.

"What's going on?" Claude asked.

"Talk to your mother Claude. She don't have that much time left on the phone."

"Ma, what happened?" Claude asked with concerned.

"Destiny's father was found shot to death in New York. Listen, I don't have time on this phone. I don't even know if Sahara knows, but tell her I'll call her tomorrow at the same time. Love ya'll." The phone went silent.

"Yo, what the fuck is really good? What the fuck just happened?" Rocks asked, hoping it wasn't what he thought it was.

"Sapp is dead. My moms said they found him this morning."

No one seemed surprised and taken by the news.

"With all due respect C, fuck that nigga. He was living on borrowed time anyway. Fuck him. Let's get high," Tommy said ignorantly.

"For real, he was destined to die young anyway. He probably snitched on some niggas in N.Y. and got caught out. Let's not let that snake ruin the evening. I'm trying to decorate my lungs with this chronic and set up some pussy for the night," Rock said comically as if he caught amnesia on what happened early that morning.

Claude said, "It's about Destiny. I don't give a fuck about the nigga, but I worry about her reaction, especially Sahara. I'm sure she'll get over it, but now she gotta think of a way to tell Destiny."

"You think Sahara know already?" Zane asked.

"Probably not, 'cause some woman named Melanie called when I was on the phone with Mark actin' kinda suspect, like something was wrong. That could have been his mom calling."

"Killed in N.Y. huh? He ran away from here, but gets killed in New York. I'm saying though; did he call the crib or come by every now and then to check on Destiny? Of all the places he could have hid, he slid to New York to get caught out," Rocks said, shaking his head.

"He was over here three months ago. I caught him coming out the front door all blinged up an' shit. Me and Sahara got into it because I told her about her homeboy and about him being here. I wasn't trying to stop him from seeing his daughter, but I didn't want that hot nigga around here 'cause he had a price on his head."

Rocks looked at Claude strangely.

"He was up here? Damn nigga, when was you going to tell me?"

"I'm telling you now, but what if I did tell you at the time?"

"Today's news would have been old news," Rocks said gravely. "Let's smoke. I ain't even trying to get into this shit. And Claude, I thought about Destiny. No offense, but Sapp better off dead anyway. It could save her a lot of embarrassment. Everybody would think your niece is a snitch, na' mean?"

No one thought deeply about Rocks's comment except Claude. He became irate at Rock's statement about Destiny until he began to read between the lines. Claude knew Rocks always wanted Sapp dead. He figured that Rocks exposed himself to a murder. After all, he hadn't seen or heard from him in the last couple of days. He decided not to press it. Anything in the dark shall come out to the light.

Forty five minutes later, they got out of the truck after smoking the two blunts. As soon as they reached the porch, Sahara pulled up to the curb. When she parked, the car was damn near in the middle of the street. The second she stepped out of the car, Claude had a feeling that she already knew Sapp was dead. Sahara seemed as if she was in a zone. Her movements were almost robotic.

"Sahara," Claude said while he and the crew walked in her direction.

When Claude stood within arm's reach of her, he noticed her make-up smeared from crying.

"He's dead C. He's dead."

Claude and Zane consoled Sahara while Rocks and Tommy stood a few feet apart from one another. Tommy was locked up when Rocks, Danny, and Sapp were on the grind so he didn't give a fuck. He just wanted to get inside the house because of the frigid weather. Rocks maintained a stone face while he and Claude's eyes locked briefly. Rocks unlocked his eyes quickly, signaling guilt, according to Claude's standards. The comment he made about Destiny only added emphasis to his suspicion. If Rocks killed Sapp, he figured, that would put him between a rock and a hard place. How could he face his sister with him knowing who killed the father of her only daughter? How could he ever roll with Rocks living under his sister's roof? He only hoped that his sixth sense was just a false alarm.

. . .

Simone rested her head on Ali's chest, listening to his heartbeat. The rhythm and blue music played quietly from the small radio rested on the nightstand next to the bed. They were resting their bodies after having intense, rough sex. They spent the holiday over Simone's mother's house, enjoying the holiday meal her mother cooked. Her mother agreed to take the baby for the night. As soon as they came back to the apartment, Ali pressed Simone against the wall and started sexing her. An hour later, they cuddled comfortably, enjoying each other's vibe. Things have been going well for them lately. The bills were paid, the rent was paid all the way up to February, and the storm that existed in their relationship had withered. Even though Ali kept Simone in the dark about where the fast money was coming from, she knew the money Ali brought in was dirty, but it placed food on the table and clothes on their son's back.

"Baby, just promise me that you be careful on whatever your doing. We need you," Simone said softly.

"Come on now, I'm Ali. Everything is cool, but I want you to stop thinking like that. When you think something is gonna happen, it probably will. Maintain good thoughts sweetheart and nothing could stop us."

"Not trying to be negative or anything, but I just don't want your luck to run out. I love you Ali and I want you to be careful on whatever you are doing."

"Listen, I can't blame you for feeling how you feeling but I got a plan. I ain't no dumb ass nigga and I know I can't do this shit for the rest of my life. The money I'm stackin' right now is for the long run."

"Yeah, whatever that is…"

"Why you wanna know so much?"

"Because I have a right to know. We have years invested

and the least you could do is let me in. If I kept you in the dark, you'll lose your head," she said truthfully.

"You can't answer the questions you don't know the answers to; just protecting you."

"Baby, protect me from what? Are you saying you can't trust me?"

"Here we go again. I thought we wasn't gonna talk about this shit," he said, his patience wearing thin.

"Let's enjoy our time together. I'm sorry baby," she said as she started to kiss his neck softly.

Ali's intent of putting Simone in her place about her intrusiveness was put to rest by the warmth of her tongue. She slowly jerked his growing dick until it reached its full length. She readjusted herself in the bed, causing her breasts to become fully exposed.

"Damn, after all these years of being together, your tits still turn me the fuck on." He grabbed one of her breasts and sucked softly on it.

"Do you still think I'm beautiful and sexy?"

Simone put on a little weight since she had her baby, but she was still voluptuous and sexy. Ali never looked at her differently. Throughout the love and the war they've been through, the love between them was never lost. He kissed her on her lips. He caressed her body gently for reassurance.

"Stop asking stupid questions. You know my thoughts about you never changed."

"They better not. From all the money you've given me within the last month, maybe I shouldn't ask you anymore stupid questions. I would be able to afford school!"

"Damn, I'm bringing home that much? I remember you use to give me a hard ass time for being broke. Now that I'm bringing home some money, you talking that school shit. What kind of bullshit they teach up in them schools that you already don't know? Fuck college. With the money we going to have by then, you could buy any motherfuckin' degree you want."

"Don't be no bad influence Ali 'cause by me going to school, its going to benefit all of us. We just got to paint a bigger picture for ourselves. We got to rid ourselves from petty attitudes like that dude you work for."

"Aaron? Why, what did he ever do to you?" He eyed her suspiciously.

"Nothing Ali, but it's something about him. He rubs me the wrong way. I have a feeling about him and it ain't good."

"Nah, he alright; he just about his business, that's all."

"It's a small world Ali. He could have been the one that killed your cousin."

Ali didn't have a response because he never thought about the possibility. People get murdered everyday in Los Angeles so it could have been anyone that killed him. He simply overrode the thought.

"Whatever is in the dark shall come out in the light. If that's the case, then he one dead ass nigga," he said seriously. "Why would you say that anyway?"

"Baby, I didn't mean to plant a seed of thought in your head, but it's good for you. I say it because I know you work for him. Where do you think he gets all the money to pay you? People who got money like that got bodies like that."

Simone's words sunk deep into Ali's head. He wasn't going to ponder her words all night, but he'd keep the thought in mind. He could've easily thought about the possibility of Aaron killing his cousin, but he never did, and neither did Wade. He just thought about the money. He decided to not share the theory with Wade. It was just a thought.

"You love me?" Ali asked, intentionally throwing her off the subject.

"Yeah I love you, but I want you to be careful," she said as she pulled herself on top of him. She kissed him softly. As her head went from his nipples all the way down to his dick, they spent the entire Thanksgiving holiday exploring each other.

33-Waterbury

"That motherfucker got to go, simple ass that. Who the fuck does he think he is? That nigga been living on edge for a long time and I think it's about time that we push him over it. Twalique, tell Domino what the fuck happened in New York," Link demanded. Link had a low-toned, raspy voice that was heard by everyone in the empty kitchen of his stash house on Bishop St. The place was vacant aside from the compartment underneath the floor that concealed a safe. The four fold up, steel chairs was the only furniture in the apartment. Link wore a bubble North Face coat with a black skully. The apartment wasn't equipped with heat so it was cold. Link was a pudgy, bald, five foot nine, dark complexioned man in his late thirties. Feared and hated by many, Link was a clever, criminal minded individual that was desperately seeking a come-up. The three days of growth on his face symbolized stress, but mostly anger. He was vexed about the fifty grand Rocks lifted from Sapp. He wouldn't have been pissed if someone else took the cash.

Domino gained his freedom yesterday. Link didn't even formally acknowledge his presence. He didn't bother to give him a pound, hug, handshake or anything. He knew Domino was coming home so it wasn't a surprise. He had something planned for later though. His hatred towards Rocks overshadowed the human side of him.

"What the fuck? Glad to see you to. That's the thanks I get for me takin' the rap for your shit? It could have been you walking through the door," Domino said calmly, stroking his long goatee.

"My bad dawg, but shit is that real right now. Glad you home, but you mind as well clock in 'cause we got some serious shit to handle," Link said, given Domino the dap and hug he deserved. Domino's demeanor changed because he understood his friend well. He looked into Link's blood shot, weed-ridden eyes and knew something was up.

"What's good? Let a nigga in," Domino said, giving Twalique dap. Twalique took a blunt out of his sunglasses kit and attempted to hand Domino one.

"Nobody ain't checkin' your piss, right," Twalique asked as he held back the blunt out of respect.

"Nah, I'm end of sentence. I don't owe them crackas shit. Bless your boy with that fine greenery kid. Niggas need to put on some heat in this bitch. It's colder than two motherfuckers in here."

"Peep it, first things first. Sapp dead," Twalique said as he lit his own blunt.

"What? Who put him to sleep, not that it's a fucking surprise an' shit, but what happened?"

"I'm 'bout to get to that. Link told me to follow him 'cause Sapp wanted a shot at redemption, na' mean? Sapp called this nigga out of the blue and told Link he got fifty grand for him if he called off the wolves. To make a long story a tad bit shorter, Sapp mentioned that he was going to the 40/40 club the night before Thanksgiving, which was Wednesday. I went down there to scope him out just to see if Sapp's proposition was righteous. I go down there early just so I could see him come in, to see if he flossing. I was looking for any sign of money. I'm in that bitch for two hours and still no sign of Sapp. Just when I was gonna call Link and tell him that Sapp was just running his mouth, this nigga came up in there decked the fuck out, but nothin' to connect him to a mill' or anything like that, but there was something substantial about his appearance, I don't know, but I had a feeling that I made a trip to N.Y. for nothin' 'cause I knew that fifty grand probably wasn't nothin' to him. Anyway, he came in the club wit' like four, five shined out niggas. For like an hour, I'm watching him. He ordered four rounds for whoever was near him of that expensive ass shit, including himself. If I would have been around him and he recognized me, he would've got suspicious and probably would have thought twice about giving Link back the money," Twalique said as he kept untwisting his corn rows.

"Not only that, but you wouldn't have left New York alive. Sapp was a snitch, but he wasn't stupid. If Sapp had it like that, those dudes around him was his muscle," Link interjected.

"Peep it though. Sapp was rollin' like he on the come-up an' shit. I don't know if he was flossin' or he was just a made nigga. I don't know, but one thing is for sure though. I wasn't the only nigga hawkin' him," Twalique said mysteriously as he paused to tote on his blunt.

"Who?" Domino asked.

"Chill, let me finish. I'm squintin' my eyes, trying to make out the side of his face. I inched through the crowd until I was at least six or seven feet from him. Fuckin' Rocks kid."

"What? You telling me Rocks killed that nigga and took fifty grand from him? How do you know for sure?"

"I know he got the money 'cause criminal minds think alike. For Sapp to be incognito that goddamn long, Rocks invested a lot of time to find out Sapp's whereabouts. He got my money. This ain't about Sapp, 'cause I wanted to kill him. This is about him stealing my money. I ain't havin' that shit. This nigga is a thorn on my side. Even if the motherfucker didn't have my money, he took the life of a nigga that had my meal ticket in his hands."

"Check it," Twalique blasted. He wanted to finish his story without being interrupted. "I backed off and dropped in a deep cut. My eyes is on his back for twenty minutes. He start talking to this bitch, nothin' sexual, but more business like, na' mean? After seeing that cocksuckin' ass nigga, I put myself out of his eye sight. After Rocks stopped talking to shorty, he bounced. I tried to go outside to see what kind of car he drove or something, but that nigga was gone. I smoked a cigarette, still scanning for him, but he was long gone by then. I go back in and walk around until I could spot Sapp. I saw the nigga alright; the same bitch Rocks was talking to was grinding Sapp on the dance floor."

"You saying that Rocks and that bitch set him up?" Domino asked.

"Yeah 'cause the pieces to the puzzle fit in place too easily. If I wasn't in the club that night, nobody would have not known shit," Twalique said, leaning on the wall with his tattooed arms crossed. His dark skin face bore no expression, but it seemed as if the snarl on his face was a permanent fixture. At six feet even, his chiseled body required years of jail time.

"What do we do?" Domino asked.

215

"The obvious," Link said casually.

"It should be no time soon though. No on sight and all that extra wild shit. Just got out yesterday and I don't want no parts of jail, true story fam."

"It goes without sayin' Domino. Keep this also in mind. Rocks ain't the only problem."

"So what are you sayin' Link? What do we..."

Twalique froze in mid-sentence, the problem that Link had in mind popping up like an answer to a pop-up quiz. When Link looked at Twalique, he didn't have to say no more.

"Claude," Twalique said flatly.

"Surprise nigga! That bullet scar on the side of your torso ain't ever goin' away," Link said, trying to get Twalique motivated.

"It's funny that you mentioned him because he slept under the bunk that I was on. He was on this gettin' out the game shit. He was frontin' like he was on this legit power move shit when I kept tellin' him that Rocks was a hot commodity that was steppin' on toes, feel me? I even told him about him settin' up Blanco, but that nigga said nothing, tryin' to run that silent game on me, but I played his game though. Now niggas is tellin' me he back on the set. But damn, I didn't know he shot you," Domino fronted as he looked at Link telling him that he knew why Twalique was in the presence of them.

Claude and Twalique never bumped heads since the incident. They never crossed paths, not even in prison. However, over the years, during Claude's incarceration, Twalique harbored ill will towards him. Claude and Twalique were bona fide natural enemies. Link knew this, which was the only reason Twalique was there in the first place. Link was a thinking man. He knew that the scar Claude left on Twalique had affected him. Link could care less about him, but Twalique was a golden pawn that he could use on the way to the come up that he desperately wanted. Link wanted to get back on top.

"Yeah dawg, them niggas got to go. I don't give a fuck who's wit' em when we decide to make it happen, even if it's that thick lesbian bitch and them young niggas. We put a couple in 'em and drop 'em and our pockets will be bulgin' yo! Room full of money, plenty for us to break bread an' dip, 'na mean? We'll just act like everything smug though,   keep 'em off balance, let 'em breathe for awhile, maybe two, three months, maybe sooner than that…whatever. We gon' run into them motherfuckers, best believe, so keep yo' chest guarded at all times. The talk about this shit here…you already know," Link said, making sure the conversation doesn't leave the room.

Link went into more details about his plan of destruction. He mentioned that he didn't want to make any sudden moves, but he still wanted Rocks dead before the spring.

Trudy cursed under her breath as she wiped down the counters to her kitchen. Many of them had weed debris on them left there by Flex, displaying no regard to her and Jason, her eight year old son. Flex was chilling hard, lying on the couch with just his boxers on. His huge gut protruded over his waistline of his underwear while he channel surfed and smoked weed. He looked like a trophy boyfriend, but Trudy couldn't bitch about the security he provided her and her son. The only satisfying part about their relationship was the money factor. Other than that, their relationship was on the rocks. Their soul connection was built on a fable.

Trudy still didn't know anything about Flex. She was still under the impression that he worked construction. She believed he had no affiliation with crime. She still didn't know that his nickname was Flex. It was his plan to keep her in total darkness. She never saw anyone who was associated with him. They have been together for three months, since the so-called one night stand. She narrowed the quality of their relationship down to zero. She was a person that had always stepped into relationships blindly, including the one with her child's father.

Flex was comfortable in his ways because she rarely spoke on her frustrations about the relationship. She dropped indirect hints with the hope of him catching on. She watched him through scornful, slit-sized eyes as the phone rang. Flex acted like he didn't hear it. Instead, he rested his big body on the couch that was too small for his big body. He had a blunt burning between his fingers, making no attempt to hide the weed. He kept to himself as if he was in the room alone, especially when Jason brought the phone to his mother.

"Its some woman named Sonya mommy. Can we go to the park today?" Jason asked.

"Maybe sweetheart…hello," Trudy said.

"Hey girl. Just callin' to see how you doing," Sonya said.

"Thank you for the birthday card, I appreciate it. Now I have your address. So when I come down there in a few months, we are going to have a blast. And by the way, Mrs.

Patterson died the other day."

"Are you serious? I just thought about her this morning. I could still remember the last conversation we had before I moved. Life is so short Trudy, I swear."

"She *just* asked about you. She wanted to know how you were holding up. At least she is not in any pain anymore." Sonya heard Trudy curse loudly. She figured she may have dropped something. "I work all day and come home to some nasty shit," Trudy said with agitation. It wasn't directed at Sonya, but at Flex. The comment got his attention.

"Damn Trudy, I thought your man was something out of a fairytale book. Are you ok?"

"No, not at all. It's just a big fucking mess..."

"Who the fuck are you on the phone with?! It better not be that bitch ass baby daddy!"

Sonya tried to make out the voice in the background. She thought that it sounded familiar, but she didn't want to ask any questions, but the man was yelling like he built Trudy and the apartment from scratch.

"Look, I got to go right now," Trudy said while Flex slowly approached her.

"Ok, but Trudy, keep in..."

Dial tone.

"I know you ain't telling your friends or your baby daddy about us 'cause I don't like that shit. Fucking bitches got nothin' better to do but to run their goddamn mouth. Anything that happens in this apartment stays in here, fuck that!"

"Please. You think 'cause you pay to live here means you own this place. I could talk to anyone I want 'cause it's my phone. Believe me, me and my son was doing fine before I met you. If you want to leave then..." She stopped talking when she looked into his dark, menacing eyes and realized that she may have started a war she didn't have the heart to finish.

"Then what Trudy? Don't hold your tongue now. Spit it out. If you want me to kick rocks, just say the word."

Trudy sighed deeply before she spoke.

"I'm saying baby. I'm not happy, but I think its something we can work out," Trudy said unenthusiastically.

"This is the fucking thanks I get for taking care of you and a little boy that's not even mine?"

"Bill, that's not the point."

"Then what is it then," Flex tested. He was surprised by her sudden abruptness. During their relationship, she was never the one to voice her desires or needs. Flex, on the other hand, was oblivious to his behavior. He figured that money was the main key point to operating an effective relationship. He saw it no other way.

"You don't respect me and my son. You leave all your paraphernalia all over the place, you don't clean after yourself, and you keep me in the dark about a lot of shit. I'm just not happy Bill. My son wants to be a construction worker just like you, but I don't want him fuckin' wit' drugs either. He don't need to be around that shit. You wanted to know the truth and now you got it," she said sternly.

Flex was so stunned that he was at a loss of words. As she continued to tell him a little more about himself, he knew she was right. As she piled more truth about his existence, she blasted him from his childish personality to his hygiene. Flex decided that he could no longer hear the truth.

"Alright, damn, what the fuck," Flex blasted. "You should have told me this shit before. A closed mouth doesn't get heard. I ain't into reading minds and shit like that."

"Well, you know now," Trudy said before heading towards the shower, leaving Flex standing alone with something to think about.

Flex unconsciously thumb through the mail while Trudy showered. He wasn't being intrusive or anything. He figured that something may have arrived for him. Just when he realized that Trudy doesn't know his government name and knows him only as Bill, he dropped the stack of mail on the table, forcing one envelope from the pile to stick out. Flex didn't wear glasses, but he squint his eyes as he read the contents of the letter. Jason was in his room playing Xbox One, keeping himself occupied. Flex picked up the small envelope and read the sender's name. A look of panic etched in his face, his paranoia coming at him at full blast when he read the name, Sonya Williams. Does she know? Once the shower stopped, he knew that he had to act fast. He found a pen to write with and a paper towel and quickly wrote Sonya's Texas address and stuffed it in his pocket.

Flex put two and two together. He'd just realized that Trudy and Sonya may have worked together in the same hospital. During their three month relationship, he never knew what hospital she worked. If he would have brought her to work on any day during their relationship, he would have made the connection a long time ago.

Trudy walked out of the bathroom with a towel around her body. She gave Flex a look that told him she didn't feel like being bothered with. She went straight to the bedroom. After Flex heard the door close, he heard her locking the door.

"Trudy, open the door," Flex said calmly.

She didn't respond. Flex was so anxious that he could have kicked the door down, but he didn't out of respect for her son.

"Open the door," Flex said, the volume on his voice increasing.

"Bill, I just want some time to relax. I need some me time. I've given you three months. Can I give myself today?"

"I just want to ask you some shit an' I'm out."

After a few moments, she unlocked the door.

"Who was you on the phone with?"

"It was my friend Sonya, why?"

"My homie Lester looking for some fresh meat. He just got out two weeks ago and I got him a job doing what I'm doing," Flex lied. He was indirectly trying to get Trudy to talk.

"Sonya is not available. She's not accepting any applications. She's healing Bill. Her boyfriend used to beat the shit out of her."

"Who she used to fuck with?"

"Don't know, don't care, but she don't need no jail fiend ass nigga all up in her life. She's been through enough."

Trudy sat at the edge of the bed putting on baby oil. He couldn't ignore her half-naked, plump body. He inched his large frame over to where she sat. She seriously didn't want to be bothered with, but that changed once he snatched the baby oil from her. He squirted some on her back.

"Bill, please stop," she said faintly.

"Why, your arms ain't long enough to do this shit by yourself," Flex said smoothly. He was rubbing the baby oil on her, rubbing her back in a circular motion, hitting the spots she always wanted him to target.

"But I'm supposed to be mad at you," she whined.

"Only dogs get mad, people get angry."

"Whatever."

He slowly lowered his head. He licked the side of her neck. She leaned away from his advances.

"Let's not go that far. You need to earn this pussy. I'm not that mad 'cause I know I've been spoiling you, but it has to stop. You just trying to walk all over shit. It stops now," she said, putting on her bathrobe.

"My needs are so simple Bill. I just want to be pampered every now and then. I know we have money, but it ain't buying us happiness. Your good to my child, but he needs a father figure, not just a man who drops cash and toys all the time. You need to take some responsibility for my child. I need you to feel that void Bill. When I dealt with his father, he just wanted to fuck and leave, but he's going to be sorry when Jason is old enough to realize who stepped up to the plate. I want that person to be you."

Flex looked at her wearily. He didn't hear a word she said. He was thankful that Trudy didn't have a clue.

"Now if you excuse me, I will like to call my friend back since I damn near hung up on her. By the way, you said you were going to watch Jason tonight. You didn't tell me about any change of plans. I signed up to do third shift."

"Don't even trip. Wasn't planning on going anywhere anyway," Flex said as he grabbed his towel to take a shower.

"Yeah, I bet, but as long as you heard what I said," she said, feeling relieved that she put Flex in his place.

I hear you talking that bullshit. "I hear you," he said. He retreated back to the sofa, wondering how Aaron would react one he received the address.

35-Waterbury

Claude applied the finishing touches on the blunt as he awaited Rocks's arrival. Three weeks had passed since Sapp's murder. It was a week before Christmas. The death itself wasn't what was bothering him. Rocks killed Sapp knowing that he was Destiny's father. That was the main thing corrupting Claude's mind. He was tired of the awkward feeling that he felt. He needed a way to destroy it. He figured that the simplest solution was to charge it to the game. Rocks did what he felt he had to do. Claude empathized with him; he put himself in Rocks's shoes. He would have done the same thing. People did not have time for snakes, especially when heavy money was involved. He also felt it was too bad Destiny was too young to understand the severity behind Sapp's ordeal. He promised himself that he would put Destiny on to what happened to her father when she was old enough to understand the game. Lastly, he had to see his sister's face knowing that he had the answer to her question that would be embedded in her mind: Who killed him?

Claude pushed all that shit in the back of his mind and focused on the task at hand. He knew that he didn't have time to reflect on the past, even as little as a minute ago. Yesterday, he received a surprise phone call from J-Rock, the thug he left in Webster. He got released a month after Claude. J-Rock told Claude that he had a gig in creation that could get him and a few members of the crew set for an early retirement from the game. He also told him that he had to be careful on his selection of his people because the job was too high risk to be fucking around with rookies. There was a big probability that death would happen if the operation goes south. Claude didn't want to consider J-Rock's proposal at first, but the thought of a big face negotiating with some heavy pushers from New York meant big money.

He was so deep into his thought that he didn't hear knocking at the door, but he heard the next set of knocking. He walked to the front door and opened it. It was Rocks. They embraced brotherly at the door before leading Rocks to the living room.

"It's charged to the game. We got some heavy shit to handle," Claude said as he took a pull of the fire he just rolled. Rocks understood what Claude meant. Claude didn't have to tell him twice of bringing it up. Although the circumstances surrounding Sapp's death was fucked up, being that Sapp was the father of Sahara's only child, Sapp's murder was bound to happen. Rocks felt awkward being in the presence of his best friend, but if it was charged to the game, it is what it was.

"I hope the heavy shit you're referring to got something to do with heavy money," Rocks said, taking the blunt from Claude.

"Best believe, but there is some shit I want to look into before we make that happen, you feel me? You remember me ever telling you about J-Rock?"

"The stick up kid from Bridgeport?"

"Yeah. That's him. He work with Jupe at a temp agency. He gave J-Rock my cell number. I spoke with him yesterday. The only thing he told me about the job was that it involves a big face, stacks of money, and that its high risk."

Rocks had a twisted look on his face.

"High risk? What the fuck? Do you know this nigga like that C? With all due respect, I did my fair share of strong armin' niggas, and still do, but I always make sure my dirt ain't high risk."

"Rocks, you study your vics all the time, but if you study the vics that he'll explain to you, your days of illegal life, as well as mine, will be out the window. Our livelihoods is high risk so what difference would it make? I realized that my past is too fucked up to work in a working class society so fuck it. I'm takin' everything. My life will be the shit when I'm done takin' money. Besides, these niggas ain't regular civilians so who gives a fuck?"

Rocks remained quiet and listened to every word Claude said. He was down for whatever, but he needed more information about the heist. If Claude had a hand in some shit, Rocks would have a hand in it as well. He couldn't wait until he was familiar about his role in the premeditated robbery. He was curious to know how thorough J-Rock was with his blueprint.

"So when do we look into this shit some more?"

"In about a half-hour," Claude answered.

. . .

Forty five minutes later, Claude and Rocks pulled up on the side of Fulton Park near the baseball field. They were looking out for an old, black Camero with tinted windows. They remained silent, watching the old, weathered leaves and sand being blown away by the cold breeze of Mother Nature. Claude looked out the window and saw adolescences playing football in the brisk December weather. He cracked a smile as he watched the teens play. It brought back vivid memories of his own youth.

"I remember when I was out here bustin' ass on the field, but if you ask me to play in this goddamn cold weather now, it ain't happening."

"I was just thinking the same thing. That's when we didn't have anything to worry about," Claude said when he noticed the black Camero in the rearview mirror of Rocks's truck.

"That's him."

J-Rock bopped slowly in the frigid wind as he made his way to the truck. Rocks saw him, but didn't recognize him. He wore some black baggy sweatpants, a skull cap, and a heavy coat. It was so windy that J-Rock had to put his hood on. Rocks unlocked the doors so J-Rock could hop in.

"What's poppin' my nigga? I'm J-Rock," he said to Rocks with his hand extended for a pound.

"Rocks," he said, returning the formal greeting.

"C, what's good? Your boy Jupe told me you stepped up your game. You the only nigga that I thought of anyway. Rocks, if you don't mind, we should move around so we can smoke and talk. My man said shit be hot over here and I'm dirty."

"Cool," Rocks said as he started his truck.

A half hour later, Rocks rode back to Fulton to drop J-Rock off to his car. Everyone agreed on the heist. Everyone was aware of the high risk, but the high reward was too tempting to let pass. The men believed they could pull off the caper, but they weren't sure if the other members of their team were ready. J-Rock went over the plan three times in the thirty minutes Rocks drove. J-Rock asked them if they had any questions or any nagging thoughts about their premeditated rip and run. Rocks wanted to know the reasoning for the target. J-Rock told them that Calvin King was a made man from Bridgeport that had him on his payroll since he was thirteen years old. For years, he did bids here and there. Most of them came as a result of handling Calvin's business. Since J-Rock's return to the streets, he had been treated like he was brand new despite all the work he had put in for Calvin over the years. Calvin had his hand in many subcategories of crime that included drugs, prostitution, bootlegging, extortion, murder for hire, but his biggest focus was drugs. When J-Rock got released from prison, he was demoted to the lower part of Calvin's command hierarchy of illegal business. Everyone J-Rock came up with had increased rank and authority over him. He wasn't having that so he decided to do what he had to do.

"I'm just thinking big, man. The nigga don't respect me and I've been grinding half my life making that nigga money an' he treat me like a number. Fuck that. I lost respect so instead of wasting my energy hating this nigga, I mind as well do something about it," J-Rock said.

They were impressed with the plan of action, especially Rocks. There was nothing about the blueprint that he would have changed. Even with this in mind, Rocks still didn't want to take what J-Rock said about the plan at face value. He trusted Claude's judgment though. When it came to the streets, according to Claude, J-Rock had a Ph. D. J-Rock was a career criminal that would never change. The men understood J-Rock's reasoning for wanting to rob his boss, but they also understood that there were two sides to every story. But either way, Calvin was going to get robbed. Claude and Rocks gave J-Rock a pound before J-Rock hopped in his own vehicle and took off.

"I hope your man's shit is official. The plan sound like its smooth sailing as shit, but goddamn man, we ain't fucking with an ordinary nigga," Rocks said with a little concern.

"Fuck it. The niggas we deal with on a reg ain't ordinary either. Fuck consequences dawg. Ain't no niggas like us. It will be just like old times," Claude said as he discarded the roach blunt out the window.

"C, we moving up in weight class wit' this shit, best believe. If the reward is comfortable, than I guess it's worth it. We are going to have to be on point. We can't sleep on this," Rocks said.

"Who you telling? I'm calling Tommy now. We all got to meet. We got some serious shit to discuss."

...

Calvin King snapped his fat fingers expertly, beckoning one of his muscle, Bam, to snap open the briefcase. Bam did as he was instructed and opened it with caution as if there was a bomb inside of it. There were greenbacks in the briefcase. Benny's face was expressionless, but he was concealing his excitement because he knew he was about to blow. It wasn't that Benny never saw money ranging over six figures. The money in the suitcase wasn't bad for a person to receive just two weeks out of prison. The heroin Benny brought exceeded Calvin's expectation; everyone was happy. Bam and Roscoe smiled with greed seeping out of their teeth. The heroin was so pure and rare that the henchmen planned a takeover. There was nothing like the dog food they had in front of them. The only thing missing was the celebration. Calvin had to kill some more time by supplying drinks to eliminate any suspicion that his high class neighbors may have.

"Yo Roscoe, grab some of that brown water so we could celebrate new beginnings," Calvin instructed smoothly while he lit up his Cuban cigar. Calvin had lots of things to celebrate. All of his illegal businesses were growing on all cylinders. There was more money to be made. In reality, money was the only thing going on for him. He was a six foot three, obese, dark-skinned man with pink lips and a nappy beard. He wasn't attractive, but his money was long and it gave him a much needed sex appeal.

"Just a few drinks; you was here for five, six minutes. Its seven thirty now. You have an hour and a half, two hour ride. It's too early to leave. Wait until eight fifteen, maybe eight twenty," Calvin said nonchalantly, sitting with his leg over his thigh, blowing smoke rings with his cigar.

"With all due respect Cal, Carter is waiting for us outside and we want to get the fuck out of here as soon as possible. Besides, the CD player in the car doesn't work and Carter probably starting to get reckless 'cause it's all quiet an' shit," Benny said politely, wanting anxiously to get out of there and head back to the Bronx. He wanted to start handling business. His partner Roland sat across from him, the end of his right fist pressed against his lips, wanting to shut Benny the fuck up for being in such a hurry. He knew Calvin didn't want to draw unwanted attention.

"I guess your business is going to have to wait," Calvin said, flicking his cigar, growing impatient with Benny.

"I'm saying though…"

"Look motherfucker, if y'all leave out of that door before eight fifteen, the deal is off and niggas won't leave this bitch alive," Calvin said gloomily, his beady black eyes piercing Benny's person.

"Alright, goddamn, what the…"

"I could use a drink, if you don't mind," Roland said quickly, interrupting his partner before he fucked around and got them both killed. Benny was smart, witty, and quick, but his temper was his biggest drawback. He was the talker because it was his greatest asset. Roland, on the other hand, was resourceful and very mindful of his surroundings. If Benny would have walked into Calvin's home alone, he would have gotten himself murdered on the strength of his mouth. Roland promised Randall, Benny's newly incarcerated brother, that he'd assist Benny on his come-up and to keep him alive.

Roscoe prepared the drinks on top of the marble topped bar that was built in the corner of the living room. He placed the drinks on the coasters that rested on a glass coffee table. Bam and Roscoe were on alert after hearing Calvin make his threat, but acted as if they were oblivious. Benny had to repress his true feelings of anger because he got put on blast in front of everyone. Benny would fight and shoot with anyone, which was the problem; he had limited self-control. That was the reason why his brother needed Roland to look after him. Benny was dangerous and needed to be supervised in his interaction with the underworld.

Benny accepted his drink. He was starting to understand Calvin's obsession with timing. The money he just received for the heroin wiped away his foolish pride. If he wanted to be on some gung-ho shit at the moment, he would have easily gotten him and his partner killed.

"My bad for attempting to make the spot hot," Benny said apologetically.

"Apology accepted. Just wanted to keep my shit safe, you know what I mean? If you leave out of here after you just got here, that makes my spot hot." While Calvin talked and lectured Benny on being safe, Roland was nodding his head, agreeing with everything Calvin said. He didn't like Calvin's threat, but he understood Calvin's position.

"I hear you, but goddamn, what the fuck did you do to get some shit like this? A nigga like me want to get up on some top of the line shit," Benny said, amazed at Calvin's long awaited, well earned come up. He looked around his surroundings and realized how much bread Calvin was sitting on. The spacious, expensively furnished living room was an example of Calvin's success. Paintings from foreign countries occupied the walls of the mini-mansion located on a cul-de-sac in Southington, Connecticut. Benny looked at the two soldiers Calvin had under his lead. George Richards, as known as "Bam," had been loyal to Calvin from the beginning. Bam was a six feet four, bald headed light skinned man that used to be called "Freckles" during his youth until he fucked up the teen that originated the nickname. From that beat down alone, he earned the nickname Bam. During his stay at a juvenile facility in New York, his mother died of cancer. When he was released, he had no where to call home. Since Calvin was in the early stages of being a severe, hardened criminal, he had enough influence to place Bam under his wing. Roscoe, on the other hand, was just someone Bam befriended on Riker's Island because of some rescue shit. Bam got into it with some Brooklyn cats over some stolen commissary. When it was time for shit to go down, Roscoe had Bam's back. That incident was the reason for the bond that he and Roscoe share in the present.

"If I tell you, I'll have to kill you," Calvin replied humorously.

"Then I don't want to know," Benny countered while he raised his arms playfully.

"Nah, but really, I worked hard for all this shit here. I had to live and learn, make sacrifices and all that shit to get where I'm at. Business and Christmas is why I'm up here," Calvin said.

"You can't hate the cold that much considerin' Christmas is a week away. Big spenders could find a comfort zone in hell," Benny said.

"As soon as Christmas is over with, I'm out. Aye Roscoe," Calvin said, changing the subject, "go get Carter from outside and have him join us for a drink. We got time to kill, right?"

He looked at Benny for any sign of resistance being that he had to threaten him about making sudden moves out the house. Benny was a quick learner; he offered none. He didn't know Calvin from a hole in a wall and didn't care to know him. Calvin was a major player that his brother dealt with; however, Randall warned Benny in that letter he wrote him about Calvin and his obsession with power. As Calvin schooled Benny and Roland about the dos and the don'ts of the game, Calvin noticed that his goon Roscoe didn't bring Carter in to join in on the drinks. When Benny was about to utter the same question Calvin had in mind, three ski masked men came in the room hastily with guns.

"Alright y'all, you know what it is; let me see them hands!" the stockier of the three demanded. "We ain't tryin' to hurt motherfuckers, but we will if we have to. Come off your shit!"

The taller gunman noticed the light skin dude make an attempt to conceal the briefcase as if it had a chance of not being seen.

"Well, well, well, look what we have here," the taller gunman approached Benny with his gun drawn. "Open that shit!

Benny took his time getting the briefcase open. The money he harbored was his foundation. He didn't feel like going back to square one. The money in the briefcase was all he had. He was now seeing his future being sucked into the barrel the gunman was holding. Getting annoyed at Benny's reluctance to open the briefcase, the tall gunman punched Benny viciously in the face with his nine millimeter.

"Open the fucking briefcase before this motherfucking gun go off in this fancy shit," the stockier gunman co-signed.

Benny popped open the briefcase.

"We hit the jackpot! We got ourselves some major players! Since these niggas is ballin' an' shit, there got to be a safe up in here. Yo, my man, watch them eyes before I put a bullet in one of them shits," the stockier one said loudly, referring to Roland. He just happened to look at the masked man at the wrong time. Roland wasn't a fool. He took his eyes off the mask man as instructed and hoped and prayed he, Benny, and Carter could make it out of the house alive.

Calvin looked at the stockier ski masked man and couldn't recognize his set of eyes. His deep, deadly voice didn't ring a bell either, but Calvin knew the men meant business. The tall masked man didn't look familiar. He tried to look for other routine mannerisms that he would be able to place with his enemies, but he was unable to do so. The assailant's movements were robust. There was no hesitation in their step. He wasn't trying to test them and call their bluff. He made a gesture to Bam to cooperate. Roscoe and Benny's other partner Carter didn't return. Although Roscoe was expendable, Calvin wanted to know what the fuck was going on. Just when he began to relax and take the heist on the chin, he heard footsteps descending down the stairs in the other room. The fourth ski masked man escorted Calvin's Asian fiancée at gunpoint. Their infant daughter was securely tucked in her arms. Calvin inwardly panicked, but didn't want to give the goons the satisfaction of witnessing him sweat. *They were already in the house*, he thought as the newest masked team member sat Jessica and the infant child on the sofa. After he got Calvin's family situated, he whispered something in the stockier man's ear. Calvin and Bam looked at one another wondering how the men knew about the home in Southington. Nobody besides his fiancée, Bam, and Roscoe knew he had a house in the high classed neighborhood. Calvin had to label everyone as a suspect, but he had a hunch that Roscoe had something to do with it.

"I will only warn you once. I don't want to hurt your family, but I will if I have to question you twice. What is the combination to the safe," the taller gunman asked sternly as he made his way to Calvin's woman. He put the gun on the side of her head. One of the masked men walked up to Bam and held the gun to his head for extra emphasis. Calvin had to display a poker face. The goods in the safe could satisfy a young thug's come up if flipped properly. The drugs and the money out in the open in the living room was the main course though. After giving the taller man the combination to the safe, he sent the newest ski masked member back upstairs.

Calvin saw the terror in Jessica's eyes. She held their sleeping infant tightly against her chest. She didn't have a shirt on underneath her robe and didn't want the men being aroused. She prayed that the men would take what they want and leave. She had never been victimized or exposed to crime. Calvin kept her in the dark about his involvement and investment in the underworld. Jessica and the baby were being taken care of. She didn't ask questions, but she would if they make it out of the heist alive.

The masked man sent upstairs to undo the safe came downstairs with one of the duffel bags Calvin brought up from Miami. The duffel bag bulged with cash and jewels. Calvin didn't like the swagger in the goon's step as he placed the bag along with the rest of the shit they planned to take out of there.

"Alright man, what the fuck? You niggas got what the fuck you want and then some. Why don't y'all cocksuckers take a hike," Calvin said evenly. His pride had him in a choke hold. He had never once been robbed until now. In one quick motion, the stockier gunman pistol whipped Bam, knocking him out. Calvin cringed as he witnessed the impact of the blow. Calvin anticipated a sharp pistol whipped blow as well. He prepared mentally for it. When the stockier of the henchmen signaled the others to leave, Calvin sighed, thankful that the men didn't cause any major damage. The thugs grabbed all the goods and proceeded to leave, but the tall one stopped in his tracks. He walked back to Jessica and stared at her. Jessica looked into the man's eyes and froze with fear. He gently pulled the baby away and placed the baby on the two-piece sectional. Acting on animal instinct, Calvin sprung from his position on the floor and lunged at the gunman. The gunman hurriedly positioned his hand on his .22 and fired a shot. It struck Calvin above the knee cap. He collapsed to the floor, screamed, and clutched tightly to the wound.

"You stupid motherfucker! All I wanted was the ring! I ain't tryin' to rape your bitch!" the taller one said. The stockier gunman stomped his foot and beckoned them out of the house.

While Calvin lay in Jessica's arms, suffering and grimacing, his eyes followed the backs of the gunmen, vowing to kill them all if he ever got wind of their identities. He now declared the men living on borrowed time. It would be a while before Bam and Benny recuperate and find Roscoe and Carter tied up in the small shed in the backyard. Carter was barely conscious. Jessica, the baby, Roland, and Roscoe were the only ones who didn't have a scratch.

Four hours later, Calvin's on-call, personal doctor had finished dislodging the bullet from the entry wound. Roscoe and Carter had to be touched up also because they got the shit stomped out of them. Both of Carter's eyes were closed, but Roscoe only had a few scrapes and bruises. He got his fair share of blows, but a lot of them were to the body. His body ached, but a plan was a plan. Calvin and Bam acted as if they didn't notice, but they did on first sight. Roland had definitely noticed and wanted some answers to everything that went down, but he knew everyone was just as stunned over the shit as he was. He thought Calvin set it up, but after seeing the stress, anger, and pain in his face, he knew it wasn't a set up, at least on Calvin's part. Calvin promised Benny and Roland he would give them the money that was stolen from them in a few days. He said that they could stick around until the money arrived. Benny and Roland agreed to stick around for Carter's sake. Besides his eyes being wide shut, he had three broken ribs and a broken jaw. For now, Calvin had some researching and investigating to do, starting with Roscoe.

36-Waterbury

The hole in the wall joint known as Pacos was a major attraction for the inner city working class, thugs, fiends, pimps, hustlers, and high rollers. The music was at a decent level. The other major players and goons conversed loudly, shooting the shit to kill some time before they pull off their next caper. The other heads in the club were either playing pool or darts, and gambling hard earned money. Link and Domino stood side by side, conversing secretly away from everyone else.

"Since these niggas got my money and fucking up my pockets, they don't have any reason to hang down here," Link said to Domino in a tone that only Domino could hear. The men were down there to see if Claude and Rocks were easy access. Unfortunately, this was their fourth time down there in a week. It wasn't that they were hiding; Link and Domino would miss them by a hair. Timing was the reasoning for Link and Domino's inclusive results.

"I tried to tell you that shit from the get. These niggas is living large. They hiding the money by not showing it...at least Claude ain't. My cousin Solomon told me he saw him yesterday pushing that beat up Mazda. Best believe, them niggas is sitting on some cash," Domino said, lighting up a Newport.

"Tell me something I don't know. Those motherfuckers getting my money out there, not to mention the fifty thousand dollar bonus that Rocks stole. It's eating me alive to even think about Rocks stealing my money and that nigga Claude having a hand in it," Link said coolly, rubbing his beard.

"You keep saying Claude had something to do with this shit, but I don't think that's the case," Domino said.

"Why do you say that?"

"Because I think Sapp got a baby by his sister, 'na mean? Rocks was probably on his own with that one."

"I don't give a fuck. Association breeds similarity. If he wit' him when its time for shit to pop off, he gon' get it too. He probably drove the get away car back to CT. Twalique may have witnessed the connection, but he probably missed all the extra shit that mattered. He gon' slide to," Link said without blinking an eye. The bitterness he had towards Rocks transferred onto Claude. It had been a month since the key to Link's fifty thousand dollars had to meet his maker. Sapp's death came at a surprise to no one, but his death was the hottest topic on the streets.

"I could bet you everything in my safe that Claude didn't give a fuck about Sapp. His sister is just someone Sapp fucked along the way and just happened to impregnate the bitch, at least that's how Sapp put it."

Domino had a confused look on his face by Link's comment. Link nodded his head to the entrance of the club. It was time for them to go.

"So you knew that Sapp got a baby by Claude's sister?" Link didn't say anything until they were outside.

"Yeah. That's why I think Claude was involved," he said to Domino as they crossed a live East Farm street to get to the car.

Link and Domino watched the nocturnal thugs through their weed ridden, red eyes through tinted windows. The ones lingering around the entrance in the club were trying to figure out who owned the dark blue Lexus GS. The men were among the most notoriously elite, ruthless motherfuckers in Waterbury, but no one noticed their brief appearance in the club. Link was pleased that he recognized only a few of the old heads who knew best to only acknowledge them with a nod.

"It's a good thing we was just there five minutes. I didn't feel like putting no one in their place for coming out their face reckless wit' that hood celebrity shit," Domino said, borrowing some light from Link's shine. Domino actually liked the attention; Link knew it.

"What's up with their muscle?" Link asked as he lit one of the rolled up blunts in the ashtray.

"You know, fucking Tommy, those two young niggas, that sexy dyke bitch. We could run right through em. I'll call Wise and Spunk…"

"You talking stupid Domino. We can't have thirty niggas involved in this shit. It's out of me, you, and Twalique. Either way, it's time for them niggas to feel the flames, find a way to squeeze our way through that muscle and just make it happen, you heard?"

"I hear you, but I don't think manuvering around the muscle is a problem. Them niggas is young and inexperienced. We could tie them niggas up when we ready to slay them clown ass niggas," Domino said, choking on the blunt while he laughed.

"Don't sleep. Claude and Rocks know this game just like I do. They keep them cats around for a reason. You know better than that nigga," Link said.

"Yeah, it make sense considering that they may have their hands in more shit. They saw you as a target, takin' your workers and that money Sapp had for you. Them motherfuckers got a lot of nerve and a lot of money," Domino said, indirectly striking back at Link for treating him like a protégé, knowing that they came into the game at the same time. Link picked it up quick, but didn't take the bait.

"That's why something is going to get done, 'na mean? But fuck all that, who's that walking out of the Lux?

She looked familiar, Link thought. He'd definitely seen her around. He couldn't put a name to her face. Aside from the familiarity, she was a dime. Her short hair was styled with gold highlights. She wore some simple blue jeans and a small, brick red colored bubble goose down jacket. Link wanted to be incognito, but he couldn't resist. He gave himself a self-prep.

"That's Claude's ex Darlene! Yeah, talk to that bitch. She probably know where that nigga rest at, 'na mean?"

"Word? Are you fucking serious?" Link couldn't believe their luck.

"Yeah. I heard he was crying over that bitch up the way!"

"Here she come," Link said abruptly, interrupting Domino's gossiping trip. Darlene's arrival and presence couldn't have come at a better time.

"Was sup shorty? Could I assist you with something? An excursion? Little vacation? Whatever you want. What's good ma?" Link asked as she looked at him like he had two heads.

"Do I know you?" Darlene asked.

Link stuck out his iced up wrist to beckon her to come closer. Darlene didn't feel like being bothered because she had her own issues. She was now living with her mother. Lloyd kicked her out of the house. He also had custody of their son. Those were her primary issues. Her secondary issue was her insane attraction to a man that viewed her as a slut. Her third issue was that she didn't know which way was up. She was still hanging out with Pam even though she fell back when she got jumped last month. The problems in her life were overwhelming, but like many other people in similar situations, her problems were self-inflicted. She had no one to point the finger to but herself.

"Could I help you?" she asked, standing a few feet away from the car. Link and Domino marveled at her, capturing her well-defined body in a single eye shot.

"Yeah, you could start off with your name," Link said with a smile that revealed evenly spaced teeth. He had a small gap between the two front ones.

"Stop frontin' Negro. Domino knows who I am so stop actin' like you don't know."

Her demeanor caught Link by surprise. He liked every second of it.

"Alright, alright, no need for the formalities then. I'm Link. You already know Domino. What's good?"

"Do one of y'all have any smoke?" she asked, getting to the point. Link smiled and beckoned her to the backseat of the car.

"Come on, it's fucking brick out here. I want to roll up this window. We ain't gonna kidnap you. Just blaze with your new friend," Link said smoothly, waving the blunt under his nose.

Darlene eyed Link suspiciously, but she was cold. She smelled the exotic blunts in the whip. She yearned for weed all day to temporarily cloud her existing problems. Her connect was out of town. She called Pam to see who had it, but she didn't know. The men in front of her looked too high and humble to set off some rape shit. Besides, the chunks of diamonds on his wrist spoke for itself. Darlene figured that he probably fucked a bitch or two, so why not? Darlene got into the car.

"I'm going to be honest wit' you shorty. This shit we

smoking is laced wit' cane. You still want to smoke?" Domino asked, looking at her in the rearview mirror of the car.

"Sure, why not?"

"Just being honest ma, that's all," Link said slyly.

"I appreciate it, pass me the blunt," she demanded.

Once Darlene finished toting, she pulled on it again, but moderately. Darlene smoked weed, but she never smoked anything laced. She never smoked with Link and Domino.

Darlene was feeling the effects of the laced blunt. She couldn't stay still, talked uncontrollably, and her mouth was dry. Link didn't mind hearing her ramble, but when she started talking about Claude, she had his undivided attention. She spoke about Claude for about an hour. The fact that Darlene stepped out of her boundary to fuck with someone from the past fresh from prison was beyond him. Link liked her though. He wanted to fuck her badly, but he decided to be a gentleman and pass.

As Darlene lay snuggled underneath Link's right arm sound asleep, a sinister smile flashed across his face. Her loose lips were Link's utensils to get at Claude and Rocks. During a course of an hour since he and Darlene arrived at his mother's three bedroom house out in Bunker Hill, Darlene told Link just about all of Claude and Rocks general whereabouts without Link's implication. Darlene smoked herself clueless. When she woke up from her power nap, she had no idea that she gave Link a recipe for war. She just aided and abetted a blue print to death.

37-Los Angeles

The women in the kitchen were loud while they played spades. Raven, Octavia, Simone, and Noemi spoke dirty about Natalie, the Mexican woman that came to the New Year's gathering with Marco. He had the petite young woman pressed against the wall, sucking on her neck as if there were something sweet on it. Raven laughed at Marco and his guest, but didn't throw any hate at them. After all, she coordinated the party at her place so everyone could unwind after a tough year. It had been a horrific year for her. Four months had passed since her brother's death. Raven had taken her trial and tribulation on the chin in full stride. She had no choice to be strong because her mother was the weak link to holding her own on coping with the loss of a loved one.

Raven's life had changed gradually. When she met Aaron two months after her brother's murder, he had minimized the pain she suffered as she dealt with the mental anguish of accepting her brother's death. He was the sunshine in her life, if not more; however, Raven had a feeling that the honeymoon was over. She understood that she may be on the verge of driving Aaron away with her emotional outbursts, but the party she threw, in her mind, signified a new beginning.

Octavia, Simone, and Noemi shot daggers at Natalie. Simone and Noemi said she had no respect for herself. Octavia, on the other hand, talked shit about Marco and Natalie's sensual exchange, but she wished that she was the recipient of Marco or Natalie's smooth touch and kisses. Her hating ass would do anything to take attention off herself and place it on someone else for pleasure because she was the black sheep of the party. Since Octavia was Raven's friend, Simone and Noemi looked at one another discreetly and thought the bitch had a lot of nerve trying to spit knowledge on morals knowing that she was the biggest Jezebel in the room. Other than that, the women were enjoying themselves as they prepared to bring in the New Year.

As Octavia rambled on with her bullshit, the women maintained their blank facial expression. No one wanted to encourage her by laughing at her jokes. Octavia was overdosing on her rhetoric, but she was oblivious to the woman's silent pleas for her to shut up.

"I can't stand people who have no respect for themselves. They should both just get a room," Octavia said angrily, putting the lid on the coffin of the subject.

"So Raven, how are things going with your new boyfriend? I recognize your glow," Noemi said cheerfully.

"Please, my bitch is sprung," Octavia rudely interjected. "Ever since he gave her the dick, this heifer act like she don't know nobody. I told her that his dick must be good."

"Things couldn't be better Noemi. Thank you for asking. What's up with you and Wade? I heard you and him are expecting," Raven said, growing impatient with her childhood friend's constant talking.

"Yeah, I am. I'm three months but it doesn't feel like it," Noemi said.

"Girl, be careful what you ask for. My son is eleven and my coochie still hurt from having his bad ass," Octavia blasted.

All the women remained silent until Simone broke it.

"I don't know Oct, maybe you need to get your shit checked," Simone said and laughed. The women laughed.

"I don't think that shit was funny," Octavia said with conviction.

"Oh please," Raven said. "You've been rankin' on that chick Marco got up in here and you get mad when someone jokes with you?"

"So you takin' her side Raven? I see how it is. Our whole lives you always acted funny around people. I see some things never change." Octavia was playing the victim.

"Yeah, some things never change. You need to grow out of that sensitivity shit. Can't even chill and trip out for the New Year 'cause yo' ass want to shed tears over a joke. Go ahead wit' that," Raven said coldly. Octavia was a scary looking woman, but she would never cross the line with Raven, at least not to her face.

"Whatever," Octavia said, feeling everyone's eyes on her.

"Is Wade excited?" Raven asked Noemi, shifting the subject.

"Yeah, I guess, but I think he would be even more excited

when the baby arrives."

"Girl, you askin' all these questions about our relationships. What's up with yours? Ever since you met that fly ass dark nigga, you fell off the edge of the Earth. Either you sprung or he got that ass on lock," Noemi said jokingly.

Raven smiled radiantly, knowing that Noemi hit it on the button. As of right now, besides her mother, Aaron was the only thing going on for her. Simone listened to Raven and still believed that something was up with Aaron. She didn't trust him. There was something about him that she couldn't put her finger on, but the only person she expressed those feelings to was Ali. She kept those feelings to herself out of respect . If Raven wanted an opinion about Aaron from her, than that's different. She would tell Raven what she's been holding onto.

The women continued to drink and joke. Octavia seemed isolated behind Raven's cold remarks, but it was nothing new. It wasn't the first time she had to put Octavia in her place, but Octavia told herself that enough was enough. She vowed to get Raven back for putting her on blast whenever the opportunity presented itself.

While the women enjoyed the Raven-created festivities, Aaron and Flex stood on one side of Raven's highly decorated living room. The new oil stained painting of D-Bone bothered Aaron, but who was he to tell her to take it down? He did, however, refuse to carry the burden of being responsible for D-Bone's murder. *I killed the motherfucker. So what? Like I knew that was Raven's brother.* He would tell himself that repeatedly, but it never stopped him for feeling like shit whenever Raven vented about her brother's murder.

Aside from dealing with Raven, everything was on and popping in his crew. They were still stuck in a cash explosion. Every member of the crew had been living a fruitful life. It would be an understatement if one were to say that Aaron's crew was doing big things. They all have cash, cribs, bitches, and drugs. They were living a street player's dream. Aaron made sure he invested in his crew because his revenue had been growing since he formed his alliance.

While Ali, Wade, Scoot, Jimmy, and Marco did their thing,

Aaron and Flex was having a discreet conversation off to the side about some shit that had nothing to do with anyone else in the room.

"Are you fucking sure nigga?"

"Hell yeah. I didn't know my bitch and Sonya worked in the same hospital. I been with this chick for how long and I couldn't honestly tell you where she worked. I just know that she's a nurse," Flex said.

"Damn, I wished I knew where the hell she was. My guess would be somewhere in Texas, but she left without a fucking trace...'

"What?"

"I hope she didn't leave because of them bitch niggas we killed," Aaron said eerily.

"Only one way to find out," Flex said as he pulled out a piece of a paper that had writing on it.

"What the fuck is that?"

"Sonya's address."

"What?"

"Yeah, you heard me. Sonya's address nigga."

Aaron gazed at it as if it was a long lost artifact. The answer to the question he'd been asking since Sonya left was now in his face. He also knew the piece of paper was official because Sonya's roots were in Texas.

"You did good cuz, you did good. I just hope we don't have to dig this deep."

"I don't want it to come to that shit, but we ain't trying to go to jail either. Besides, I tried to play it like I wanted to hook her up with someone, but Trudy said Sonya ain't ready for no relationship because her man used to beat the shit out of her."

Aaron absorbed every word that came out of his Flex's mouth. He felt regret and opened his feelings up for Sonya. He remembered the day of the killings. He remembered the look Sonya had on her face when he beat and raped her. The good time he was having had come to a stand still because of his thoughts of a woman who left his life. Although he was an Atheist, he prayed to God that he wouldn't have to kill her.

"So she didn't say nothin' about them killings?"

"If that was the case, my bitch would have been dead. When I eavesdropped, it was just a casual conversation. We still have to worry about Prime's coward ass. Let's not focus just on Sonya. Also, those two niggas is suspect. I hope they got no affiliation with your girl's brother. But…"

Flex's statement was interrupted by the crew's arrival.

"These motherfuckers actin' all anti-social an' shit! It's eleven fifty eight, two minutes away from the new year and these niggas talking business. We could talk about that shit on the second," Scoot said a little louder than he had to. He had on a two piece black and white strip suit with a black brim Panama hat. He had his goatee tied up with an elastic band. Scoot was looking sharp, but to some, he was a sitting duck for jokes. He was the only one dressed for a funeral. Everyone else wore the crisp, urban wear.

"Business always before all this shit," Aaron said dryly, irritated of the men's sudden approach.

With one minute remaining, the ladies joined in with the men. Raven walked up to Aaron and hugged him. Aaron hugged her in return, but his heart wasn't with her; it was with Sonya. Aaron liked and cared for Raven, but he didn't love her. During the months of their courtship, Raven continued to grieve her fallen brother. Aaron was tired of acting. He was tired of providing her with fake empathy and sympathy. It would have been different if he wasn't her brother's murderer, but he was. He would have kicked her to the curb a long time ago, but he felt that he had to watch her close. She was one of his biggest assets in his come up, not to mention her old clientele who bought big. If he decided to split, in his assessment, she would probably be on some vindictive shit. He didn't need that in his life right now.

Once the New Year was official, Simone embraced Ali because they both were thankful that they had enough strength to fight off all the shortcomings that they been through as a couple. Aaron, on the other hand, felt numb as he felt the embrace of his woman. He lacked excitement in his face. Flex provided him with good news of Sonya whereabouts, but on the strength of him knowing where she resided, he was feeling

243

the same emotions the day she left him for good. Wade and Noemi shared a moment. Marco and the woman he was sexing were engaged in sloppy wet kisses. Scoot and Jimmy didn't come to the party with pretty things on their arms, but they got a kick out of the party just like everyone else. Everyone was having a blast.

As the early morning hours of the first day of the new year dwindled, the crew partied themselves into a coma-like state. The only sober person in the condo was Noemi because of her pregnancy. Octavia sat at the kitchen table with her arms folded, unsatisfied with the night's festivities. She was seething with hate primarily because of loneliness and Raven's outburst towards her. Unbeknownst to her, Jimmy told Marco he had thoughts of having her suck his dick, but Marco came to the rescue on that one. Natalie, the woman Marco had with him, could have come out of a Maxim magazine. She was a dime. She wasn't Marco's girlfriend, but she was a good fuck, a freaky one at that. Marco gently convinced Natalie to hit Jimmy off. Ten minutes later, Jimmy had her legs resting on his shoulders, pounding her like it had to be done. Flex drooled on his shirt as his drug and alcohol intake got the best of him. Wade played around with the remote control as he channel surfed. Noemi sat beside him holding her growing stomach, falling in and out of a sleep.

"Esto esta` muy malo, Marco," Natalie blasted.

"Venir en Natalie, tu' era sensacion el," Marco said sheepishly as he allowed his head to bounce on the love seat with his eyes half shut.

"Chinga usted!" Natalie was heated because Marco slipped her an ecstasy pill and took full control of her. She acted as if she were in the room by herself as she rambled on and on in her dialect.

"Tu mama' es una gorda, fea y puta," Natalie said before storming out of Raven's living room door.

Marco heard that insult loud and clear as he got up swiftly out of his seat and stormed towards the door in an attempt to catch her. Aaron stopped Marco in his route to catch her.

"Chinga usted poonta!" Aaron didn't know what was said or what was going on, but he knew the broad was going to get hell if Marco broke away from his grip.

"No, y'all can't be settin' shit off up in here! Uh huh," Raven said loudly as she descended the stairs.

"I got this Raven," Aaron said. "Marc man, you makin' shit hot as fuck. Be cool motherfucker! Fuck that bitch," Aaron said sternly, surprised by Marco's behavior because he had never seen him like that before. Marco generally had a calm demeanor and it seemed like a dream for Marco to come out of his zone. Flex was sleeping through the entire ordeal. Ali, Wade, Scoot, Jimmy, and the women remained in their positions as the drama unfolded. Jimmy didn't understand Spanish, but he knew he was the core of the problem and thought the shit was funny. Ali and Wade were brought up with commotion. They weren't moved by it.

"On that note, I'm gone. Got shit to handle in the morning. You people enjoy your night," Scoot said cordially before heading out the door. He had enough shit going on in his life. He didn't want to stick around.

"I'm sorry Raven. I didn't mean to disrespect your house like that. I normally don't let anybody talk shit about my dead mom. I don't give a fuck who it is. Motherfuckers won't be gettin' away wit' that shit," Marco concluded. Aaron didn't know Marco's mother was dead, as well as the others, but Raven still had to nip shit in the bud.

"I hear you Marco, but we workin' wit' too much to let emotions get in the way. As many bitches as you fucked? Come on Marco, the bitch ain't worth it if she's that easy to fuck?"

"With all due respect, that's not the point. The point is she disrespected my mother. I'm sorry that I dishonored your home though," Marco said in his Spanish accent. His phone vibrated on his hip. He took the phone call outside. Marco's mood went from jeers to cheers as he heard the voice on the other line. Raven closed the door behind Marco to give him his privacy.

A few minutes after Marco started his phone call, Octavia walked out the door without saying shit, but no one paid her any mind. She could have left a long time ago and her absence would have been unnoticed. Raven snuggled next to Aaron on the couch while Ali, Wade, Simone, and Noemi were on their way out. Ali and Wade's high subsided and they were ready to hit the sack.

"Y'all look like y'all could sleep a full day," Raven said, noticing the silence from her guests.

"Hell yeah. Tired as a motherfucker. We got a long day ahead of us. We mind as well get out rest now 'cause I ain't sleepin' later. We don't get paid when we sleep," Ali said, completely unenthused.

"Man, with your work ethic, you're gonna end up gettin' paid when you're past the fuck out. This world will soon be yours; yours to Wade if y'all niggas is on the same grind," Aaron said as he yawned, exhausted from the party, drugs, and alcohol.

"Yeah, I got the grind in my heart. I have no choice," Wade said, nodding to Noemi's pregnant belly. She was waiting patiently at the door, along with Simone, who looked as if she'd sleep like a rock the second her eyes close.

"We still makin' that Sacramento run?" Ali asked.

"Yeah, but I got somethin' for y'all niggas. Makin' sure y'all niggas is takin' care of. I'm too tired to even move, but Raven don't mind you goin' up in her room as long as you get what you came for and be out," Aaron said, making it known that Ali's time upstairs would be tracked.

"What is it?" Wade asked curiously.

"If Ali get the steppin' upstairs, the sooner you will find out what it is," Raven added, adjusting herself in her comfort zone on Aaron's chest.

Without saying anymore, Ali walked upstairs.

Raven's bedroom looked like a safe haven for a queen as Ali scoped out her king sized bed. Her wall to wall carpet in the massive bedroom was spacious. Cosmetics from all sorts were on top of her dresser. Her walk-in closet was huge. She had two wardrobes worth of clothes in it. A sixty-five inch television was mounted on the wall. She even had a full bathroom in her bedroom. She had everything before she met Aaron, but since their acquaintance, the money she was making was adding emphasis to her glamorous lifestyle.

Ali looked in the area that Aaron and Raven told him to look. There was a long dresser on the far side of the bedroom.

It had six drawers in it. The middle drawer on the right side of the dresser was where Ali and Wade's surprise rested. When he opened the drawer, there were two stacks of hundred dollar bills, each stack containing three grand. There was a note attached to one of the stashes that stated the money was a New Years bonus. Ali smiled wildly, thanking Raven silently for putting him and Wade on to some serious cold cash. Ali and Wade have never seen that kind of money. They were making so much cash that Ali and Simone were thinking of buying a house. Simone handled the financial side of the household. She knew Ali wasn't doing anything legit to earn his grip so she formulated a financial plan for him to get out of whatever game he was playing. Wade and Noemi, on the other hand, suffered from instant gratification. Wade actually saw himself working for Aaron for the rest of his life; moreover, Noemi co-signed his intentions. They both lived for the moment. Ali noticed Wade's heavy dive into the corporate world, but kept his opinion to himself because Wade was a grown man and his opinion would not have mattered anyway.

After Ali counted all of the money, he placed the stacks inside of his jacket. As soon as he started to leave the bedroom, he noticed a shine from Aaron's Nike duffel bag. Human nature prompted him to look inside the bag. When he did, he damn near choked on his own air. He couldn't believe what he saw. He didn't want to believe that it may be Colin's chain that was inside of Aaron's duffel bag. He knew someone else may have the same taste as Colin, but he didn't think it was possible because Colin normally customized his jewelry. For verification, he turned the star shaped medallion around. When he looked in the back of the medallion, Colin's initials were engraved in the back. His eyes watered with fiery. Tons of emotions took over his person as he instantly took out his burner. He bit his lip so hard that they bled. He held his .38 special with a firm and powerful grip. His eyes bulged as he inhaled and exhaled wildly. His teeth remained clinched as thoughts of making an ugly scene danced around in his head. He could go downstairs and pop off anyone who could have been responsible for his cousin's murder, but in a matter of seconds, he regained his composure and thought with logic.

He understood Aaron's comment about getting what he needed to get and split so he decided to play Aaron's game for now. He didn't want to flat out assume that Aaron or the rest of his people were the killers. He could have bought the chain from someone. Either way, he vowed to find out. If Aaron was smart enough to read his body language, it would be genocide in Raven's apartment. He knew he had to play it cool. He had to play it by ear. When he walked downstairs back to the action, he was back to normal.

"Appreciate that shit Aaron. Don't even know what to say. Once again, you gave niggas your full blessing," Ali said sincerely, putting an iron hand in a velvet glove.

"No need. Y'all niggas have earned your keep fuckin' wit' us. Y'all motherfuckers do the dirty shit so y'all get the bonuses. We all on the same page wit' it," Aaron said, on the verge of passing out.

"Seriously. I got a baby on the way and all that shit. We tryin' to do it big in the household. We need this…"

"For real," Ali cut in, interrupting Wade. "We need to do a little somethin' for you. You gave us nothin' but surprises since we jumped in y'all set. You could lift up your feet and then some. But Raven, like always, thank you for the hospitality. We appreciate it," Ali said civilly, hugging Raven, kissing her on the cheek.

Ali and Wade gave everyone a pound before they made their departure. Simone and Noemi said their good-byes to Raven and Aaron, and then to a passing Jimmy, who held up a peace sign and jetted out the door. Aaron and Raven felt that there wasn't a need to wake up Flex because he wouldn't move if one tried to wake him. Aaron and the rest of the crew, excluding Raven, would flip out if they found out how much they resembled sitting ducks.

Ali pulled the Impala in front of Noemi and Wade's spot. Simone and Noemi made plans on cooking later that day. The men exchanged a few words throughout the ride to Wade and Noemi's crib.

"Baby, I want to go home," Simone whined as Ali got out

of the car.

"It'll just take a minute. Can I get that?" Ali asked sarcastically, showing visible signs of a mood change.

"Don't talk to me like that Ali," Simone said, folding her arms. Ali kissed her on the cheek and onto her lips. She gently bit his lip and said hurry up.

Ali got out of the car. Wade met Ali in the back of it and walked forward. Ali handed Wade over his share of the money Aaron gave them. Noemi kept Simone company in the warm Impala while the men talked.

"Damn, you that fucked up? That nigga is throwing cash on us like we strippers an' shit. What the fuck is up with that long face man? We should be calling that motherfucker Jesus Christ 'cause he saved us," Wade said as he thumbed through his stash.

"No, he might of sent our people to Jesus," Ali said flatly.

"Fuck you mean Ali?"

"Exactly how it sounds."

"What?" Wade had a puzzled look on his face.

They locked eyes signifying that Ali didn't have to say no more.

"How you figure?"

"When I went upstairs to get the cash, I noticed some ice in his bag. Shit was brighter than a motherfucker. I wasn't goin' to take it or no shit like that. I took that shit out of the bag and realized that the link that had that star-shaped medallion was Colin's shit. I was ready to come downstairs and shoot niggas."

"Man, Colin ain't the only one with a link that got a star shaped medallion attached to it. You might be blowin' it out of proportion."

"I ain't blowin' shit out of proportion. It's Colin's chain 'cause he had his initials engraved in the back."

"Maybe he bought it from somebody," Wade proposed. He hoped his meal ticket wasn't responsible for the murders.

"I know all that shit, which is why we goin' to dig a little deeper."

"How we going to do that?"

"How else motherfucker?" Ali asked sarcastically. "We pay

more attention, that's all. I know you enjoying the grind, and so am I, but if we end up finding out them niggas did it, we gon' do them like they did Colin and them other niggas. After we get rid of 'em, we take over shit," Ali said with a cold confidence.

"We have to let Raven in."

"No we don't. She's too close. She'll fuck around and blow this shit. We want to avenge nigga, but we trying to reap the rewards from this shit. You see all that money he throwing at us? The nigga may not be that large, but he large enough to give us three thousand apiece off of general principle. I nickled and dimed my whole life. I don't see that kind of money. That motherfucker is running shit right though. I will give the nigga some credit, but that shit belongs to us if he killed my cousin and 'em. We'll let her know when the time is right. Right now, the time ain't right."

"So talk to me cuz," Wade said.

"We just break them down. The key to this shit here is to not look for shit. If he did it, the truth would leak out on its own; just give it time. But we could attack this shit from all kinds of angles, startin' wit' those safe houses."

38-Waterbury

"These niggas is out like it's the first day of summer, and they stylin' too," Pam said, scheming on a lame to pay her way through the night.

"They damn sure is. Girl, I am about to have me some Darlene time. Me and Lloyd are officially done. My only concern is my son. If a nigga want to open his wallet up for a bitch, then that's different 'cause a bitch is definitely broke," Darlene said. She called herself establishing a new wave of self-esteem, pretending all the bullshit she started was behind her, but in reality, she would forever feel like shit for ruining her own family.

"I know that's right. These sorry ass, broke ass niggas ain't shit anyway. If they ain't good for money, they better be swingin' that dick right," Pam chimed. "Speaking of niggas, you never told me who you got the weed from that night; you said the weed was laced."

"Link. He is already promising' me the world. His ass got Junior one of those X-Boxes, the outfit that I'm wearing, and a lot of other shit," Darlene bragged.

Pam raised an eyebrow at the mention of the name Link.

"Girl, you better be careful fucking around with that nigga. Heard he got bodies."

"Please, that nigga never killed anybody. I didn't meet him fresh off the prison bus you know. All these murders in Waterbury all got solved."

"Darlene, what makes you think he didn't get national or international with it? Don't be naïve; the streets don't talk for nothing."

"I will keep that in mind," Darlene said, hoping what her friend said was just a rumor. Darlene never really had a full ear on the street and she didn't know any better, but Pam's brothers grew up with Link and they provided her with enough Link stories to last a lifetime. She was familiar with Link's potential to make shit ugly.

"I guess you're over Claude," Pam said as Darlene pulled up and parked her car across the street from Pacos.

"I was never under because it was just a fuck."

Pam discreetly twisted her lips. She knew Darlene was full of shit, but if she would have told her that, Darlene would have countered with her coward act the night she got jumped and how she watched without making an attempt to help. She decided to stay mute on that topic and start another one.

"Well, don't give that nigga too much pussy. He just might give you the world like he promised."

"It's funny because I never gave him any."

"Are you serious? He is buying shit for you and Junior and you didn't have to spread your legs once?" Pam was jealous. Pam sucked dick and was a known slut. The only thing she ever got in return was another failed love connection and an anchor to once again sink her lonely heart. Many men and women contributed to the anchor. She loved Darlene like a sister, but she sometimes hated her for being beautiful. She hated herself for being a size eighteen.

"It must be nice to be as slim as you and you could get any man you want."

"Girl you know you need to stop," Darlene said as she shrugged off her friend's comment.

"You will never believe who I'm looking at right now," Pam said, staring out the window, waiting for Darlene so they could go inside the club.

"Who are you looking at?" Darlene asked, fixing the make-up on her face.

"Claude and the rest of the goons."

Darlene damn near smeared her make-up as she risked breaking her neck to get a look at the man she was fucked up over.

"Oh, no big deal. I got someone that could take his mind off those sluts that's draping over him. Two could play that game," Darlene said as she started to thumb through contacts on her cell phone.

"Who are you calling?" Pam asked flatly.

"A friend."

. . .

The cold, gusty wind blew around a few beer and soda

cans at four in the morning. The remaining few stragglers were leaving the after hour joint. The team went there after leaving Pacos, which was two hours ago. Claude, Rocks, and Zane hopped in Rocks's truck and Tank and Tyrell hopped in with Tommy. They've all been smoking and drinking since it was daylight so there wasn't too much conversation going on. As soon as Zane touched the interior of the backseat, she passed out.

"On some real shit C, what happened to you? I remember you was walking in the hood wit' a briefcase and now you got a . 38 tucked in your waist," Rocks said in good nature.

"So do I, but fuck it. You can't say that I didn't try," Claude answered back sluggishly, on the verge of falling asleep.

"I think sometimes what it would have been like to be a square ass nigga, feel me? What if I did good in school instead of digging into this game early? Do you think about shit like that C?" Rocks started the truck.

"Everyday day. I always imagine what it would be like if I never went to jail, but went to college instead. I would have been head strong in the business game. Now I got to be a crooked nigga and snatch the fucking American dream myself, you know what I mean?"

"That's society for you."

"No Rocks, we make our own decisions. We can't be always blaming society for us being criminals."

"I halfway feel you C, but we came from some fucked up stock that lacked the tools to progress in life." He thumbed through the case, trying to figure out what song from the CD could enhance his high.

"That could either make or break you. You could use the fucked up hand you were dealt with and turn it into a royal flush or you could leave it the way it is. Those fucking immigrants come over here not knowing a goddamn lick of English, but a lot of them motherfuckers go on to be entrepreneurs sometime down the line. You just got to fix the hand you were dealt with; do whatever it takes," Claude said.

They conversed some more while Zane was knocked out

in the backseat. Rocks pulled off slowly, careful not to attract any unwanted attention from the police because they patrol the area throughout the night.

"Ride me up Tank's crib before you take me home. He just texted me and said Tommy just dropped him off. I forgot to collect that dough from him," Claude said. Rocks nodded and continued his way up East Farm Street.

"Let's drop her drunk ass off first," Rocks said. The men chuckled because a dump truck would not have disturbed Zane out of her sleep.

. . .

"Let this car go by," Twalique instructed as Domino expertly maneuvered the BMW up North Walnut Street.

"I got this, but check it, it can't go down in no residential area. We gon' let em' drop the bitch off and take it from there. No leg shots nigga," Domino said sternly to validate his seriousness. "Aim for murder."

"You already know," Twalique said gravely.

. . .

Rocks took a right and entered the second parking lot of Berkeley Heights, the set of units facing Long Hill Road and parked. Rocks turned down the music to a whisper.

"C, true story, I'm thinking about changing my ways."

"Handle that then. I'm trying myself man, but right now it ain't the time for me, but you, you got to do what's right for you. If you feel like you have to make modifications to your life, do what you got to do. You watched Malcolm X," Claude said jokingly. They shared a laugh.

"Just been on some power move shit lately. I got money nigga. Its time to get that legal hustle shit on, you feel me?"

"No doubt. There is life beyond the streets," Claude said, giving Rocks dap in the process before getting out of the truck.

As Claude stepped into the early morning, his keys fell out of his pocket. When he bent down to grab them, Rocks slumped over the driver's side door and slid to the ground. Claude was so high that it took him a second longer to process what was going on. His instinct snapped into place. His high vanished. He pulled his gun from his waist and ducked. The second he ducked for cover, a bullet with Claude's name on it entered the driver's side back seat window and exited the passenger's side back seat window. Claude didn't panic. He was in a crouch position with his back against the Navigator and crept to the rear of it. In one quick motion, with both hands on his gun, he quickly turned to the direction the bullets came from and fired off two shots. By the time the bullets landed into the woods across the street, he prepared to fire off another shot, but decided against it as he saw the gunman retreat into the safety of the white Beamer. He closed the door and the driver peeled off, leaving screech marks on the road. Claude cautiously rose from his crouch position and got a good look at the fleeing car.

He turned his attention to Rocks's lifeless body. Rock's mouth was ajar and his eyes were opened. His head was tilted to the right with a gaping hole on the side of it, leaking blood and brain matter. Knowing that he didn't have much time, he took Rocks's gun, drugs, money, and his cell phone off of the corpse to minimize any suspicion of Rocks being involved in foul play. When Claude called Tank, he was standing from a small distance. Tank wondered whether or not his high took him to a disturbed, foreign land. Claude didn't want him to think the obvious.

"Don't think like that. Them cats bounced after I popped off," Claude said in a low voice.

"I saw you bust at 'em," Tank said while he looked at Rocks's body in shock.

They heard sirens, but if they stood there any longer, they would be included in an investigation. Without saying a word, they gave each other a pound and a brotherly hug. Tank dipped through the small yard, went up a long set of stairs, and went into his apartment and used it as a place of refuge because the cops would be at the scene any moment. Claude took one more look at his best friend's corpse and took off running into the massive darkness of the early morning.

39-Dallas

Sonya didn't know if she was dreaming of hearing the phone rang as it did continuously. She turned over on the sofa as if it would make the sound go away, but the phone kept ringing. When it rang again, she rose and looked at the cable box converter; it read 3:16am. She looked and fumbled for the cordless with no success until it rang for what seemed like the twentieth time. The cordless phone was on the charger, right where it was supposed to be. She allowed the phone to ring one more time before she answered it.

"Hello," Sonya answered as she yawned.

"Is Mark there?" Claude asked rudely, sounding as if he ran up a few flights of stairs.

"Excuse me?" Sonya asked irately.

"Is Mark there?" he asked in the same tone.

Sonya couldn't believe someone would have the audacity to wake everyone up in the house and have the nerve to be as rude as he was. Sonya's patience grew so thin that she didn't pick up on the desperation in the man's voice.

"I don't know who you are, but you need to have some manners when you call somebody's home this damn late at night," Sonya said, her voice becoming crystal clear.

"Look bitch, I don't got no fucking time to play games with you! Put my cousin on the goddamn phone!"

Sonya attempted to bark back at the man that just called her a bitch, but the mention of "my cousin" made her think otherwise. Something had to be up; moreover, it wasn't like Sonya's name was on the lease for her to talk shit to people calling Fatima and Mark's condo. She humbled herself and made moves to their room with the cordless phone in hand. She wondered why they didn't pick up the phone, but she remembered that they turned the ringers off in their bedroom at night. She knocked on the door, calling Mark's name.

"Mark, telephone!"

She heard Mark getting out of the bed and heard his movement as he approached the door. Sonya came to the conclusion that it may be an emergency phone call, but she still fumed about being called a bitch. Mark opened the door with his bathrobe on. The tired look on his face revealed agitation because he just came off a sixteen hour day at his job and he had to be up in three hours to do another shift.

"Who is it?" Mark asked, holding his hand out for the cordless.

"I don't know, but I think he's your cousin. Oh, and Mark," Sonya said, putting the phone on mute, making sure that the caller didn't hear her, "You need to tell your cousin that he don't know me to be calling me a bitch."

Mark gave Sonya a puzzled look as he took the phone from her.

"Hello," Mark voiced into the phone.

"Yo, Rocks dead man!" Claude voiced into the phone.

"What?"

"Niggas cut him down…with fucking silencers! I was with him, but fuck all that! You need to come up here today!"

Mark wasn't sure if he was dreaming. He sat with his mouth wide open, overwhelmed by the sudden news of Rocks's death. Sonya saw his face and replaced her anger with concern. Fatima appeared from out of the darkness of the bedroom wondering who Mark was talking to.

"You hear me Mark?! If possible, try to catch the next flight."

"Yeah, I heard you C. You know who did it?" Mark asked, a fresh set of tears rolling down his face. The women looked at him with grave concern, especially Fatima because she had never seen Mark shed a tear. Mark's display of his emotional side was brand new to her.

"Don't know, but you need to get the fuck up here. Rocks dead yo," Claude said as he broke down. Mark could hear him sobbing uncontrollably.

"Yo, I'll be on the next flight. Hold ya head C, I'm coming," Mark said as he wiped the tears from his eyes.

"Call me when you find out the time the plane lands in Bradley. I gotta go Mark, but make sure you get up here," Claude repeated with despair.

"Alright C, I'm on it. Let me get packed. I'll call you in an hour," Mark said.

"Alright yo, see you later on. Love you man."

"Love you to dawg. Hold your head high," Mark encouraged as his own weeping increased.

"One."

"One," Mark reciprocated.

"Baby, what happened?" Fatima asked softly while Sonya looked on in suspense.

"My homeboy Rocks got killed a little while ago. Claude was with him," Mark answered before he sat on the edge of his bed. He rested his head on his folded arms and continued to cry.

"Oh my God! Baby I'm so sorry," Fatima said genuinely as Mark's weeping became contagious to everyone in the room. Fatima stroked Mark's back softly as he rested his head on her shoulder. Mark told so many stories about his crew that the women felt as if they knew them. The women consoled Mark until he was strong enough to proceed with his trip to his hometown in Connecticut.

. . .

Sonya and Fatima and a few of Sonya's co-workers were out dining and drinking at The Old Monk on Henderson Ave to unwind after a long day at work. The place was swamped and had almost reached its capacity of consumers. When Patricia Willis, one of Sonya's co-workers, approached her about joining her and Amy for an informal night out, she was apprehensive at first because her days normally consisted of working and going home. When she thought about her sister, she figured that her and her co-workers gathering would be a perfect opportunity for the both of them to chill and relax. Fatima agreed to take Sonya up on the offer of joining them because she didn't feel like being alone. She was used to Mark being there. She wanted to be with him. She wanted to be his support system. She didn't want him to get stuck in his hometown because of chaos. She wanted Mark to herself, but knew she was being selfish. She missed him.

Sonya wore her hair down with the highlighted tips touching the swell of her breasts. She wore a short-sleeved black cashmere hoodie, dark blue jeans, and low-cut brown leather boots. Fatima wore tight fitting black jeans with a dark grey cable-knit sweater. Even though the sisters didn't wear anything too revealing, many heads had turned throughout the course of the night in their direction, admiring the women's natural beauty.

"Thank you for inviting us, believe me, we both needed to get out for the night," Sonya said.

"Girl, don't even mention it. We've been coming to this spot since it opened. I'm just glad y'all enjoyin' yourselves," Patricia said, pushing her long dreadlocks to the side. Patricia was a short, thick light-skinned woman. She wore a full jean skirt and a honey palm color wool turtle neck sweater. Patricia welcomed Sonya with opened arms when she started working at the hospital. Sonya and Patricia had something horrific in common; they have been in abusive relationships. They shared their stories one night about their past history. It opened up a genuine friendship. Amy Farnham, Sonya's other co-worker, was a white girl from Alabama that went to the University of Texas, but decided to reside in the star state when she graduated. She didn't have a story, but Amy was cool. She was a tall, petite woman with a southern drawl and worked the same shift as Sonya and Patricia. She wore regular blue jeans and a light blue t-shirt.

"It's about time you brought your ass out. Patricia and I thought you were a hermit who just happens to work," Amy said jokingly. The women laughed.

"That will change soon. I'm just trying to recover, but I think I'm quite there, ready to move on," Sonya said, taking a sip of her Tequila Sunrise.

"Ready to move on, huh? You ready to move on to the open arms of a man? You go girl," Amy said jovially.

"I been tryin' to get her to come out with me and Mark, but I know my sister; she has to come around on her own."

"That is the way it is. A person will know whether or not they are ready," Patricia co-signed.

"Speaking of men, I heard you had a keeper Fatima. Tell us about your king," Amy said.

"I do have a keeper, but my baby is in Connecticut for the

moment," Fatima said as she started to get comfortable around Sonya's friends.

"Why is he in Connecticut? And you didn't go? I would jump at the opportunity to get up out of here for a few days. When did he leave anyway? If you don't mind me asking." Amy sipped on her drink.

"His friend was murdered early this morning so he caught an early flight. He should be back sometime next week."

"I'm so sorry Fatima. I am so embarrassed, I didn't know," Amy said, holding her face with her mouth opened.

"Nothing to be sorry about," Fatima said, sipping on her drink.

"Please send him my condolences," Amy said genuinely.

"His cousin called and broke the news to him. He was rude as hell when he called, even called me a bitch, and I was heated, but when I gave Mark the phone and he cried, I knew something was wrong."

"I have never seen Mark so sad before," Fatima said. "We didn't hear the phone because we normally leave the ringer off, but for his cousin to call so late, something had to be wrong. Mark normally shut off his cell phone when he is tired so I know his cousin tried the cell phone first."

"Is it bad in Connecticut?" Patricia asked.

"According to Mark, it is in some areas, especially Hartford and Bridgeport, but my baby is from Waterbury and even that ain't much of a safe haven. I'm just glad he is out of there and down here with me."

"So what's up with Mark's cousin? Is he cute? Is he single?" Patricia asked, thinking of her own void in her life.

"Mark has some young pictures of him and his friends. His cousin's name is Claude, "C" for short. He just got out of jail like last summer after doing like ten years or so, but I think he plays the streets close. Don't think he's a keeper, but he is cute. Mark hasn't seen him face to face in years. The pictures of him were taken over fifteen years ago when he was with Rocks, the one that was murdered, and please don't ask me that boy's real name 'cause I don't know, and some of his other friends," Fatima said and continued. "Mark has heard that Claude is as solid as a rock," she added.

"Um, um, um, just the way I like 'em. Nice and juicy! Let me stop!" Patricia said as she giggled.

"You know good and well you're not playing Pat!" Amy said.

Everyone laughed in unison. Fatima's cell phone ranged. She excused herself so she could talk in private.

"What's good baby girl? I miss you," Mark said smoothly.

"I miss you too sweetheart. When are you coming home?"

"Next Friday or a little before."

"How is he?"

"Can't get into it right now. But check it, I'm goin' to have to call you in a little while. Me, Tommy, and Zane 'bout to step out and get something to eat. Just called to see how you're holding up."

"Mark, you be careful."

"No doubt."

"Where is Claude?" She was trying to prolong the conversation.

"In the bed high ass hell. This dude got like four or five ounces of smoke laying around with more of the shit coming, but I got to run. Love you."

"I love you too."

Fatima rejoined the group. Everyone enjoyed themselves as they exchanged stories and gossip. It was a good night for Sonya and Fatima. They both needed to fall back, chill, and vibe with good people.

40-Santa Monica

Aaron and Marco sat in the gathering room of Patrick Watson's four bedroom, four bathroom mini-mansion. The exterior design of the house was extraordinary because the ocean front house overlooked massive stone arches. There was a patio on each floor of the mansion. The mansion itself was multi-shaped and came from the gifted mind of Patrick's brother, an expert in exterior and interior design. The mini-mansion consisted of a tennis court, a large hot tub shaped like a triangle, and a basketball court. Patrick also had a fifteen foot aquarium embedded in the wall of the hallway that led to the living room on the other side of the residence. The aquarium housed small sharks, eels, and a variety of exotic fish from the Caribbean.

The gathering room where the men were seated had no sign of entertainment. The room consisted of a black leather corner sofa where Aaron, Marco, and Patrick were seated, a white wall to wall earth toned Cabana rug that ran him a few grand, a walnut writing table with an abstract painting on the wall over it, a black stain oak veneer desk that was infested with paperwork of his clients, a laptop, and a small mirror that had cocaine debris on it. The only thing that stood out in the room was its floor to ceiling windows that faced the Pacific Ocean.

"It's a hell of a shock to see you guys here. I thought those small ones were making the delivery. Those guys give me the fucking creeps. Those fuck bags don't even talk for Christ's sake," Patrick said, referring to Ali and Wade.

"They ain't supposed to. Those motherfuckers come up here for two purposes; to drop off and pick up, nothin' more, nothin' less, and speaking of that, show me the money," Aaron said, cutting through the small talk.

While Aaron and Patrick swapped product for greenbacks, Marco was admiring his surroundings, mesmerized by the scenery his eyes took in.

"You must've put away some unlucky big face motherfucker 'cause you came off on this pad. You could see the ocean an' shit," Marco said as he marveled at the scenery.

"All work and no play makes Pat a dull boy. It's not just me though. I have a wife and two kids. My wife is a scientist so I had no problem collaborating with her to get this house. But yeah, the bad weather sucks now with all the gray skies. Looks even better in the summer, especially when there are hot chicks jet skiing."

Marco said, "I could only imagine."

"Why imagine? All you have to do is come up here in the summer. You could basically extend your arm out the window and snatch yourself a babe."

"Look at you. You talking about chicks, babes, bitches, whatever, but this fine woman in this photo got your whole shit in shackles," Aaron joked.

The men laughed in unison.

"Yeah, I guess your right, but speaking of spouses, are you still with that super hot chick? What's her name again? Sandra? Sonya! Yeah, that's her name. I remember when you were two months in and she paid me off with the brick of smack you left in her apartment. She felt fucking terrible for doing that, but she was mad at you for putting her freedom on the line. I said to myself how lucky that son of a bitch was for having someone like that," Patrick said, engulfed in his own recollection.

"Good things come to an end," Aaron said flatly, knowing she still held a small piece of his heart.

"Sorry about the split A. I'm pretty sure she has a beautiful replacement. I hope she didn't leave you for that ugly bastard I seen her with last summer," Patrick said off handedly while he inspected the bricks.

Aaron and Marco looked at each other discreetly.

"What ugly bastard are you referring to?" Marco asked cautiously, careful not to make Patrick hip to his small interrogation. Aaron was about to ask about the dude he seen her with abruptly. Marco had no emotional attachments to Sonya, but Aaron did.

"I'm just fucking kidding. You know Prime is an ugly bastard. I use to tease him, but I did see her with him. That was right after I got an ounce from him."

An alarm went off in his head. He realized he just told the

men some shit they weren't supposed to know.

"She had bags. I believe he was taking her to either a bus or train station; the LAX perhaps. Maybe that's when you two broke up, but fuck it, when the season changes, you could practically fuck a celebrity," Patrick said, making a bold attempt to dispel any suspicion.

"Once again Pat, you talking that fuck a babe shit but your ass is trapped up in this bitch," Aaron joked. He concealed his anger so Patrick wouldn't think he said anything wrong. After all, Patrick was still connected to the law so Aaron fed him with a long spoon.

"If you see the first sign of a jump-off, call me, probably throw in a little extra for your hospitality," Marco said as he rose out of his seat as he noticed Aaron nodding his head towards the door.

Patrick took them on another tour of the mansion before he walked the men to the car.

"Come more often instead of sending them two goddamn robots."

"That's what they get paid for. Trust me, those motherfuckers don't like making this trip being that they are riding dirty, but they do it because they love the dough. We out," Aaron said before peeling off down Patrick's driveway, leaving tire tracks on the asphalt. Patrick grinned and shook his head before returning to his palace.

. . .

Raven relaxed quietly in her black teddy as she read a hair magazine. She didn't have on any panties or thongs so Aaron wouldn't have to pull anything off when he returned. Her pubic hair was shaped in a single strip because she knew Aaron gets off when her pubic hair was well groomed. Today, she managed to make her calls, conduct business, do drop offs, and collect money in a four hour span. She finished removing the paint from her toe nails so she could be prepared to have her them done. She stopped reading when she mistaken Aaron's entry for a neighbor's entry next door. She placed her magazine on Aaron's nightstand. When she was satisfied with a comfort spot on the bed, she clapped her hands loudly, making the lights go off. She was too tired to wait for Aaron to come home.

She heard Aaron walk in the door. Her fatigue turned into an adrenaline rush for excitement. She wanted to give him the news so badly about her pregnancy. When she had the symptoms, she knew right away that her birth shot was over its limit. She took a home test yesterday, but she confirmed it with the doctor earlier in the day. She wanted it to be a boy so she could name him after her brother.

Since she met Aaron, her life went from despair to an unlimited amount of hope because Aaron was the main jewel in her life. Although she accepted the reality of her brother's death, she still exhibited sullen moods when he sits in her idle mind. Her mother moved to New York to start a new life. She could have gone with her, but her love for Aaron was too deep.

"Hey baby!" Raven said excitedly.

"What's up Raven?" He was completely unenthused.

Her excitement level dropped.

"I miss you, but you don't seem that excited to see me. What is with your tone? Did I do anything wrong?"

Aaron had his mouth closed tightly, trying not to bark at her. In his sociopath mind, he recognized that she had done nothing to him. He just wasn't in a good mood. The mere thought of Prime aiding his ex-queen out of the state was driving him insane. Aaron would have blown Prime's top off if he would had ran into him on the way home. His feelings for Sonya resurfaced and it drove him crazy. In addition, he had to deal with Raven on a personal and business level. He knew he had to restore the balance.

"Miss you too Rave, but I just want to go to sleep and regain my energy. We got a lot of money to make and it ain't going to get got feeling all fuzzy an' shit," Aaron said as he kissed her on the cheek, failing to recognize the sexy lingerie she bought for him to see. He pulled the carpet from her excitement and she blew a deep sigh. Raven was an extremely beautiful woman and wasn't used to being ignored. Any man would kill to have her in their arms. Since she had been with Aaron, she had been very happy and uplifting, but lately, she knew that their honeymoon period was going down hill. She was embarking on his dark side. She never knew that when Aaron's mind was idle, Sonya occupied it until his mind was active. Aaron had been starting to get over her, but the news today triggered old feelings that were too hard to ignore. Whenever she playfully crept from behind and grabbed him by his waist, he would be stern with her, but when he noticed her first reaction when he was being abrupt with her, he would flip his seriousness and make it seem like a joke. She knew all too well, but she was too much in love with him to entertain any negative thoughts about him. She was not only in love, but she was getting paid big. She hoped that their way of life and prosperous living can last, but she knew she was working a high-risk profession and that the tables could turn.

"But why do you seem so irritable? It hurts me that you can't come and talk to me. I know my brother's death took a huge toll on me, but I'm coming around now. Can you not act brand new with me since I stopped bombarding you with all my misery?"

"I hear you Rave, but I think you are reading it too deep. I'm just tired. Just because I don't say anything doesn't mean that I'm actin' funny."

"I will take that as an answer. Good night Aaron," she said before turning the lights off.

Aaron was fifteen minutes deep into his sleep while Raven had her back turned, wide awake thinking of the mystery man lying next to her. She wasn't ready to tell him about her pregnancy because it wasn't the right time. At that moment, however, a little light cut through her blindness. She was unsure about him.

41-Waterbury

It was twenty five degrees and freezing rain as Claude, Mark, Tommy, and Zane were surrounded by Rocks's immediate family and friends outside the Baptist church on Pearl Street. A hearse and five limousines were parked in front of the church for transport to New Pine Grove cemetery where the rest of the soldiers rested eternally. There were two lines for two-person at a time viewing. The funeral was packed with family, friends, former ex-runners, girlfriends, jump-offs, corn balls, young thugs, ex-cons, drug dealers, babies, and many other people. They were all gathered to say good-bye to Rocks at his home going. The freezing rain was so cold that it hurt just to stand out there. The line was slow-going while people wept before seeing Rocks's body. The frantically brisk weather seemed as if it didn't bother Claude because the hurt and pain that he'd experienced kept his body warm.

Claude and his people had on baggy jeans, North Face bubble coats, and some Timberlands, reeking of sour diesel and chocolate, per Rock's request. Vanessa, Rocks's older sister, told Claude the specifics about the conversation she had with her brother a few years ago. He told her that if he were to die or get killed, he wanted his closest people to stand out like sore thumbs. The purpose was not in any way to disrespect the Lord and the church. The purpose was to let everyone know who his truest people were outside of his blood family. Rocks's mother didn't like the request, but she knew she had to honor it. Rocks wanted his closest people to be his pall bearers.

The church organs, people weeping, babies crying, relatives and friends crying hysterically were the only sounds in the church. Claude and Zane were in front of Mark and Tommy. As they all got closer to the opened casket, Zane broke down and rested her head on Claude's shoulder and cried loudly. Claude had to keep her from sliding to the floor. Claude was sobbing as well, but he had to be strong for Zane because she was so emotionally stricken that she could hardly stand. When they approached Rocks's casket, Claude lost his grip and was too weak to support Zane when they saw Rocks's corpse resting with similar attire to what he requested to his sister for Claude and them to wear at his funeral, disregarding the North Face bubble coat. He wore a black and gray sweater and baggy jeans. His cornrows were done to perfection. His lips were stretched across his face in a permanent frown. Pictures of him, Claude, Tommy, Mark, Zane, Danny, and some other people that were always in the presence of his inner circle were situated on the lid to his casket. A collage with him, relatives, and friends stood erect next to the casket. On top of the collage spelled out Jerome in gold glitter. Rocks's niece took the honors of putting his name on top of it. Included were baby pictures of Rocks. There were even pictures of Claude, Tommy, and Mark during the heydays of their youth. The gold link he wore shone mercifully. Claude and Zane leaked tears all over Rocks's clothes as they had to be escorted away from the body. Rocks's mother looked on with emotion as she recalled the days when they were little boys wrestling in the backyard. She remembered telling Claude and Jerome that somebody was going to get hurt one day. She remembered the sleepovers, trouble, mayhem, the bids, and everything else when the two came up.

"Yea, though I walk through the valley of the shadow of death, I will fear no evil; for you with me; your rod and your staff, they comfort me…"

After hearing the reverend recite from Psalms 23, he preached about the present state of mind compared to the ones who lived when Jesus Christ walked the Earth. He preached about the violence within the communities and expressed a loud disdain of the current chaotic situation of murdered young black men.

"These young black men and women are being exploited in music and television through sex, drugs, and murder which is destroying the minds of our youth. To all the young men and women in here, this is NOT television, this is FOR REAL!" the reverend screamed into the microphone, pointing at Rocks's body. He knew Jerome since he was a child. It bothered him to see someone so young being a victim of his own environment, especially individuals he knew since they were children.

As Claude listened to the reverend's sermon, vivid visuals

of Rocks being cut down ran rampant in his mind as he looked at Rocks's lifeless body in the casket. He was in so much pain that he didn't have any room for anger...yet. Mark sat next to Zane. The rest of the crew listened on with tears in their eyes, wishing that Rocks were still alive.

As the services proceeded further, Mark stood up and took his spot over the podium and shared a memory of his friend. He drew heavy laughter from the crowd as he spoke of it so vividly. When he was at the end, Mark joked his way into crying. He excused himself and went back to his seat.

As Rock's funeral services came to a conclusion, the pallbearers had to come forward. Claude, Tommy, Mark, and Jupe were among the six pallbearers. When Claude and the rest of the pallbearers wheeled his casket down the aisle and loaded it into the hearse, he noticed a familiar figure in his peripheral vision; it was Darlene holding an umbrella.

"C, I'm so sorry," she said as a stream of tears flowed freely down her face. "I am here if you need me."

She hugged Claude, but he hugged her back half-heartedly. He released his hand from her back and kept it moving while Darlene stood speechless. She was oblivious to the role she played in Rocks's death, but whatever was in the dark shall come out to the light.

. . .

"I swear, when I saw Darlene outside after the funeral, I wanted to smack the shit out that bitch. At the time, I was in no mood to look at people I can't fuckin' stand. I had to pray to God to forgive me for even entertaining those thoughts," Zane said.

"Yeah, knowing that bitch, she probably came to the funeral because she knew C was there. What a no-class bitch she is," Tommy said. Ever since Rocks got killed a week ago, Tommy's entire attitude changed for the worst. He was not taking Rocks's death well, neither were the rest, but Claude knew it would be a long time for them all to recover. Tommy had been staying with Claude since Mark arrived in Waterbury. Tommy lived with his elderly mother, but he wanted to be around his friends during the turbulent times. He was afraid to be alone because he didn't want to cope with Rocks's death by himself, and Claude knew it.

They were on their third blunt. They were flat and unenthusiastic as each one of them devoted their high thinking of their fallen comrade. Claude came into the bedroom with a half gallon of Hennessy and blue, plastic cups to add more emphasis to the celebration of Rocks's home going. He wanted to prepare them for the bomb he was going to drop on them.

"Yo, what I'm about to say stay right here in this room."

"Come on C, you already know. That's without saying," Tommy said.

"For real. What's good?" Zane asked.

Mark wasn't surprised that Claude was holding back information. He knew that there was more to what Claude told him about Rocks's murder. He figured that Rocks had a trail of enemies and it could have been anyone that put him to sleep, but Claude was on the frontline when Rocks got murdered and had to know more than what he provided.

"I can't tell you who killed Rocks, but I think I know why he was killed," Claude said.

"What's up?" Tommy asked eagerly.

"Because he killed Sapp."

Everyone held their mouths wide open, sucking in the news that Claude dropped on them. Tommy attempted to calculate every move he made with Rocks around the time of his death but couldn't come up with a solution.

"He told you?" Tommy asked.

"Nope."

Mark looked surprised. He stared long and hard at Claude as if he was trying to figure him out.

"It goes without saying Tommy. He didn't have to say shit. I know he did it. I knew he did it when my moms told me."

"How?" Zane asked.

"Thanksgiving day. That's when my moms called and told us they found Sapp's body in Brooklyn. When we walked Sahara into the house, I looked straight at Rocks when he passed me to get back into the house. He didn't even look me in the eye. That sealed the deal right there."

"So that's why Rocks said you was acting funny," Tommy said, his recollection coming to life.

"Not surprised. He played a role with you," Claude said. "He figured you would tell me so I would be under the impression that he was clueless why I'm acting like that. I knew that dude too well. But listen, two, three weeks later, J-Rock came at me with the job offer. I couldn't hold that against Rocks because for one, I needed him, and two, I could understand why he did it. I'm not feeling what he did considering that was Destiny's father he killed, but I could understand. Rocks told me in the past that he wanted to kill Sapp, and he did."

"C, you still ain't really telling us nothin' concrete," Mark added.

"Let me get there. When I called him and told him I had to talk to him face to face, he was here in ten minutes. Normally, that nigga would have showed up an hour later, but he knew what the deal was. When I let him in, the first thing I told him that it was charged to the game. He nodded his head and that's the last time we spoke of it."

"Come to think of it, a day before Thanksgiving, I hit him up in the morning. He told me he had to make moves and I didn't hear from him until the next day," Tommy said, putting what Claude told him in perspective.

"What about Sahara and Destiny C? Are you going to tell them?" Zane asked with concern.

"No."

"Why?" Zane was annoyed by Claude's direct answer.

"What do you mean why Zane? Destiny is only six and she is already aware of death itself. I had to stay home the other day because she thought I was going to die once I leave. Me and Sahara can't reach her right now. I'm not going to say anything until I feel its right for Sahara to know. Destiny ain't gonna know that shit until she's old enough to understand."

"C, I'm not going to say nothin' to Sahara. I didn't see it that way," Zane said truthfully. Zane had a soft spot for kids and didn't think Rocks was right for killing Sapp knowing that was Destiny's father. She did, however, know about the turmoil that existed between Rocks and Sapp for Danny's lifelong incarceration, but it didn't mean that Rocks had to kill him. Sapp was going to get his with or without Rocks's murderous input.

After more grim conversation, the four reverted right back to the weed and alcohol so they could rid themselves temporarily of the reality that surrounded them.

42-Los Angeles

Trudy was enjoying a rare, quiet moment while doing laundry. It had been quiet in her apartment since yesterday afternoon. Her son was with his father. He may be with him until her eye healed because Flex popped the shit out of her when she confessed that she was still fucking her child's father. Flex knew this when he first started fucking with her, but he allowed his emotions to mutate like a virus. He fell in love with her. He even went as far as paying all of her bills. She had him fucked up. Her son's father couldn't live up to any responsibilities that a father was supposed to have, but Flex filled that void in Jason's life. She needed "Bill" because he took care of all her financial wants and obligations. He would give her money whenever she asked for it.

She was dependent on "Bill" and he knew it. He used it to his advantage and tried to make her believe that he owned her. All the power and money that "Bill" had over her had never stopped her from giving up the pussy he thought he owned. "Bill" kept asking her if she was still fucking with him to a point where he sounded like a scratched CD. Fed up with his constant nagging and interrogating, she confessed that she still fucked Jason's father from time to time and that she would always love him because he blessed her with her only son. She told half the truth though. If she would have told him that there was a time he fucked her an hour after she fucked her child's father, and didn't shower, he would have killed her. Even though she was folding clothes with a black, puffy eye, she felt it was worth it to get his fat ass out of her life.

She came across his jeans and sighed. She didn't want him to have any reason to come back to the apartment. She knew it would be a struggle without him, but she felt his departure was a blessing. When she moved his jeans to the side, she figured she could find some money in his pockets. As she fingered her way into them, she found three crisp hundred dollar bills. She contemplated on whether or not to keep it. She decided to give him a few days to retrieve his money and pants. If he didn't come, fuck him, she figured because three hundred dollars should be for her troubles. She didn't want to go to work with a black eye. She ran through her personal, vacation, and only had two more days of sick time. Today was her first of the two. That three hundred would help her small paycheck next Friday. She searched the other pockets to see if there was more money to claim, but there was none. She only found his driver's license. She examined it closely, telling herself that Bill is short for William, not Walter. Secondly, she was under the impression that Jenkins was his last name. The driver's license read "Walter Banks." She held it in her hand in shock. She wasn't hurt, but she felt stupid for being with him five months not knowing his real name. Her mouth was opened and in the shape of a smile while she shook her head in disbelief. She realized she placed herself and her son in clear and present danger.

An hour after she found out her ex-man's real identity, she drew out a blueprint for her own stupidity, starting with the night they met when she fucked him with no condom and ending with her eye black and puffy. She remembered how her friend Sonya had a black eye, but managed to come to work the next day. She felt the need to talk to someone about her discovery and misery and decided to call her.

"Hey! Haven't spoken to you in a minute. How are things with you?"

"Things could be a whole lot better, believe me when I tell you," Trudy said, not really in the mood for any kind of talk outside of her own fucked up situation.

"What's wrong Trudy?"

"I would be lying if I told you otherwise. Remember I told you I was seeing someone?"

"Yeah, a few times. Can't say I don't know anything about him other than him being a contractor or something like that...I think his name is Bob?"

"No, Bill."

"Oh, but what's wrong?"

"Me and Bill got into it yesterday and I kicked his fat ass out for giving me a black eye. Didn't want to call the cops on him. I just wanted him to leave..."

"Wait a minute," Sonya interrupted. "He hit you? It hasn't

been a year and he is hitting you?" She felt empathy for Trudy because of her abusive relationship with Aaron. "What was his reasoning?"

"I wasn't feeling him like that. I was feeling his money. The overtime went dry, I have no vacation or sick time, and I only have a thousand dollars left in my savings compared to the six thousand I use to have. Anyway, the nigga breaks bread with his granddaddy. He was paying my rent and car note. He bought my son an X-Box, all kinds of shit, but I just wasn't feeling him like that."

"What was it about him that you didn't like? You made it seem like you were walking on clouds girl."

"He is just filthy. He could take three showers a day and still carry a funky odor. He smelled like an attic. It was a whole bunch of shit about him that would make a bitch's pussy dry. He has a decent face, but I'm not attracted to him."

"Trudy, I could understand that, but what would make him hit you?"

"He asked me if I was still fucking Jason's father for the hundredth time and you know the answer to that."

"Money ain't everything and can't keep people happy the way they want it," Sonya said, playing a neutral role. She couldn't blame Trudy for wanting to be happy.

"I applaud you for being honest, but, with all due respect, what did you expect? Did you expect him to be a man and take it on the chin? He probably loves you."

"I know he does. That is why I didn't call the cops."

"Is he in stalk mode?"

"Girl please. He's been calling me nonstop since he gave me a black eye. I can't send his calls to voicemail because my son is with his father. Both of my numbers will be changed tomorrow, including the locks on the doors. Oh, and by the way, I was with his ass for five months and I just found out his real name today. Ain't that some shit?"

"I see," Sonya responded. "What's his real name?"

"Fuckin' Walter Banks."

"What!?"

"What Sonya?! You know him?! Talk to me!"

"Listen Trudy, I will tell you this just once. Do not cut me off and listen. Walter is my ex-boyfriend's cousin. He goes by Flex. I never really told you the real reason why I moved back home. I believe my ex-boyfriend Aaron and Walter killed Dennis and the rest of them."

"How do you know for sure?" Trudy felt the need to take a shit.

"I can't get into all that over the phone, but trust me and realize I would never steer you wrong," Sonya said eerily.

"Why would they do it?"

"You said he was taking care of y'all, right?"

That was all Trudy needed to hear. She knew something major had to happen for her to run home to Dallas. Sonya feared for her life. Trudy feared for her life in the present. She wished Sonya would have kept that shit to herself, but it just gave her more of a reason to further distance herself from "Bill."

"Girl, get off the phone and protect yourself! Keep your mouth shut because it has nothin' to do with you."

"You don't need to tell me twice. I will call you later," Trudy said before hanging up. If she wasn't so consumed in the phone call, she would have heard someone opening the back door when she started her conversation with Sonya.

Flex overheard the conversation. His anger was beyond the hot zone, especially after overhearing that he was being used. He was hurt and he couldn't deny it because he thought what they had was real. He wasn't spending his time, energy, and money on her because he was a sucker. He felt that was the least he could do since his entire persona was a fake. He made moves for her because he loved her. On top of all that, Sonya blew their cover about the murders. He loved Trudy, but she had to go.

Trudy had her back turned, facing the window, somewhat in a daze about the news Sonya dropped. Flex was standing in the doorway of the bedroom. Trudy was oblivious to his presence.

"Do you smell me you foul chicken head bitch? I provided you with everything you need and you still fuck wit' yo' bum ass baby daddy? And yeah, my name is Walter. My peoples call me Flex. And you know what? It felt good murdering them bitch ass marks 'cause I'm livin' good right now. We killed the white boy because he saw us. How 'bout that?" Flex said all this with a cool, collect, and sinister tone that scared Trudy.

"Wh...wh...how...why are you telling me this?" she asked fearfully. She was beating herself up because her first instinct told her to change the locks as soon as she kicked him out.

"Because you and Sonya just won a few first class tickets to Jesus Christ," he said before rushing her.

He rushed her so quickly that she didn't have time to react. She put up a fight as she kicked wildly and clawed his face until she drew blood. When she screamed, it was cut short because he had his big, ape-like hands securely wrapped around her neck, squeezing it. Her nails dug deeper and deeper into his skin, but the pressure of her nails diminished. She was losing oxygen. The blood vessels in her eyes bulged from the pressure. She turned blue. Her wild kicking and clawing stopped, but he kept choking her until her body went limp. He let her go. The look on her face spelled fear. She looked as if something on the ceiling frightened her. He sat on the floor with the body to catch his breath. He looked at the corpse, breathing heavily, wondering what he was going to do with it. As soon as he caught his breath, he called Aaron. The phone seemed to ring forever before he picked it up.

"What's up fat boy?" Aaron said comically.

"I need your help cuz; I had to do it. The bitch knew too much."

"What the fuck are you talking about?"

"Can't get into that cuz. Come help a nigga. I'm up this bitch's crib. Hurry up. A nigga is going crazy right now. Had to do it cuz," Flex said frantically.

"Wipe down everything you touched. Coming right now. The spot Prime's mom used to live right?"

"Yeah."

"Hang up!"

Flex ended the call, got off the floor, and started to wipe

down everything he touched. He stopped in his tracks, looked at the body, took the comforter off the bed, and covered it so his eyes wouldn't receive an eyesore.

43-Los Angeles

"I don't know man. Just think we need to dig a little deeper into this shit. It's been like a month since you saw that chain and we still ain't find a motherfucking thing. We just need to make that money," Wade said. He and Ali sat in Wade's parked car out on Crenshaw.

Ali had his eyes on the passersby with a hostile look on his face. He understood what his friend was saying, but the chain he found, in his mind, was all he needed to see.

"What are the chances of that nigga buying that chain from somebody else? In my opinion, I think he's getting rich off my cousin's product. I also think he used my cousin an' them as ingredients to his come-up," he said before continuing. "Think about it Wade. How many niggas you know that got money buy fucking used chains that was customized for someone else?"

"You don't think Raven don't talk about D-Bone? Memories, pictures, resemblance, her crying, all that shit? That nigga can't be crazy enough to keep around the sister of a nigga he killed. Come on Ali, think about it."

"Yeah, I thought about it, but the reason for him keeping her around is a lot bigger than you think. He needs us Wade. We made his ass crazy money. If I was in his spot, I'll keep her close too. If she becomes hip to him, he could dead her on the spot. I rather kill her on the spot than from a distance."

He dropped a jewel on Wade because his silence indicated it. Wade was recanting his theory because Ali was right. He couldn't see himself making the money he was making now working for someone other than Aaron. He didn't want to fuck around and blow his grip over an accusation. He was down for the cause, but the uncertainty of not having a fat meal ticket scared the shit out of him.

"Who was that fool we knifed?" Ali asked, focusing on the cracked out fiend across the street.

"Snake."

"Didn't we leave him in the front seat of her whip?"

"Yeah, that's her," Wade said. "I ran into that chick wit'

the scar on her face. What's her name?"

"I think Maria."

"That's her name. She told me that bitch right there is strung out and how she remembered when she didn't even smoke weed. She said she used to fuck with Prime and he got her strung out," Wade said.

"You don't see a connection? That's Linda. Scoot told me they used to break product at her crib until they ran out of use for her ass. They kicked her to the curb," Ali said.

"Your point?

"We a step ahead in the game. It's obvious Aaron doesn't know we suspicious, but I'm sure he plays along when Raven talks about her brother. She told me the only dude she seen her brother wit' that night was some ugly light skin motherfucker with droopy skin, and I think that ugly motherfucker is Prime. What makes you think Raven didn't tell Aaron about him? If he ever gets even the smallest fucking hint that Prime is around and no longer MIA, he's going to kill him before Raven even see the motherfucker. Out of sight, out of mind. If it turns out that Prime ain't missing, than I'm wrong, and I'll give you a g," Ali said convincingly.

"I want my money," Wade said good-naturedly, hoping that his friend was wrong.

With that said, Wade started the car and headed in Linda's direction. As soon as the men pulled up, she made her way down to the Chevy as expected.

"Y'all holding or what?" Linda asked, her appearance disheveled. Her hair was unkempt and out of place and she had on dirty green sweatpants. She wore an extra large Mickey Mouse shirt that lost its elastic. She leaned into the car more than she had to so the men could get a sneak peak of her B sized tits because she didn't have a bra on.

"Hell yeah we holding sweetheart," Ali said smoothly, talking through the passenger side door.

Throwing caution into the wind, she jumped into the car and never gave it a second thought.

. . .

Prime had a new number every other day because he

didn't want anyone tracking him, not even his mother for her own sake. His pre-paid phone ran out of minutes during the conversation he had with Linda regarding his mother's declining health and that he needed to come back to Los Angeles. Because of Linda, he knew Aaron and the rest were doing well for themselves and that they all had money. He wanted no parts of it because he didn't want to be a target of a retaliatory hit or a murder investigation. She knew his mother's new address because she was walking down the street one day after servicing a trick and spotted her moving into the low rise flat. Prime called her two days after she saw Prime's mother and gave him her address. That was a month and a half ago.

After nearly six hours of driving from Oakland, worried to death about his mother, Prime was a block away from her domain. He wanted badly to know what was wrong with her.

He drove down a few flat level houses until he spotted his mother's Jeep Wrangler and parked behind it. He saw the lights on in the house. A moment later, he saw her through the window walking through the living room. She had on her work uniform. Something wasn't right. Linda had panic in her voice when he spoke to her. She made it seem that Prime's mother was on her last leg.

What the fuck, he said to himself as a lone figure approached him from his blind side.

"Yo' mama is ok motherfucker," the man stated as he buried the barrel of the gun in the back of Prime's head.

"Put them goddamn hands where I could see 'em," the man demanded.

"What the fuck is going on man?! This shit supposed to be a joke?"

"I ask the questions nigga."

The man pistol whipped Prime, knocking him unconscious.

...

"Prime, wake up, wake up nigga," Wade instructed before smacking the daylight out of him.

It took Prime a few moments to get adjusted to the light. His head was in pain as he tried to get adjusted to the light.

When he did, he realized he had another problem. He was tied down to a chair with his hands tied behind it. His legs were tied and his mouth was gagged with duct tape. He turned his head and saw Linda tied and gagged up in the same position he was in. The horrid look she had in her eyes told Prime that she didn't mean to set him up. Ali had placed a P89 against her temple when she called Prime and told him the bogus story about his mother being sick. However, Prime was so shook that his fear wouldn't allow him to decipher the motive. He took a good look at the two men before him and couldn't place their faces anywhere. As he began to regain a hold on his thoughts, he knew what the shit was all about. He wondered if his people were alive. While Prime gathered more thoughts, Ali took his cell phone out of his pocket. He pointed it towards Prime and snapped a picture. He walked slowly and quietly around Prime snapping shots from all angles. Prime couldn't think of any reason why the man would take flicks of him because he knew they weren't cops. When Ali was satisfied with the pictures he snapped, he put his phone back into his pocket. He pulled the duct tape off of Prime's mouth abruptly. Some of Prime's facial hair was stuck on the tape.

"You probably wonderin' why you and this bitch is tied and gagged up. I'll be wonderin' the same shit if I were you. If you know something, then speak up," Wade said flatly.

Prime sat like a rock. He didn't want to say anything to admit guilt nor did he want to stay quiet like a mute. He was in a catch-22. If he confessed to the murders, the men would kill him, but if he remained quiet, the result would be the same. He figured that the men would drag the truth out of him anyway.

The room was quiet while they were waiting for Prime's answer. Ali was about to set something off, but his phone made a text messaging chime. Ali checked it; his face became grim because of what he read on the screen.

"You know the reason why you sittin' in that chair. Come clean nigga and we'll let you live," Ali said convincingly.

Raven texted Ali back and confirmed that Prime was the one she saw with her brother. Prime's sagging skin was a dead giveaway. Ali put his phone on silent because he knew Raven was going to blow him up on his phone. Prime started to cry. He had no way of getting out of his hostage situation. He was sweating from fear. Linda was a mess. She was trying to say something with a strip of duct tape over her mouth. Wade accommodated her.

"Whatever him and them niggas did I had nothin' to do with it," Linda said while she cried and fought to catch her breath. "Please let me go! I did what y'all asked me to, I won't tell anybody!"

"Yeah, I know," Wade said before squeezing off two shots in her chest. The first bullet went straight through her heart, followed by the second one.

After Wade shot and killed Linda, Ali pointed his gun at Prime.

"Alright, alright, I will tell y'all what you need to know, but please, I wasn't the one who pulled the trigger! Come on man, I'm my mom's only child! I did not play no part in the murders! Let me live, please," Prime spat cowardly.

"Talk motherfucker," Wade said brashly. Deep down within his heart, he hoped that Ali's plan of a takeover was legit because he knew that his real meal ticket was about to become a corpse.

"Our connect Ziggy was on his way to do a bid. He plugged me to D-Bone, met up wit' him a week after Ziggy got locked up. He told me he fuck with a nigga with the potential to be top dog status. I told my people about the shit. My niggas was on something different, talking 'bout robbing niggas. I was down, but I didn't think anyone was going to get murdered." Prime felt like a rat for selling out his people, but he had a gun pointed at him. He began to reason that if Aaron or Flex was in his shoes, they'll do the same thing.

"Everything happened so fast. Once we had all the goods, these niggas started squeezing off shots. Aaron and Flex shot 'em all in the head while they were tied up."

"Oh, like this," Ali said before shooting Prime in the head at close range.

The men stared at the bodies with no remorse. They knew it would be plenty more to come.

When Ali checked his cell phone, there were eleven missed calls, all from Raven.

"I guess I could use that grand that I was supposed to get from you if them niggas weren't the killers. It's going towards the empire that we going to build. The city is ours," Ali said coldly.

"Yeah, your right. I could feel Colin and D-Bone's presence as we speak," Wade said.

"You could say that again. Let's get the fuck out of here before the pigs get here," Ali said. The men wiped down everything they touched and got out of the abandoned house.

44-Waterbury

The snow fell from the sky in abundance as the traffic on I-84 West came to a standstill. People honked horns and bitched out the window as if a single person could control the traffic. At the rate of speed Claude was driving, it would be another forty five minutes before he got home. The slippery terrain was too much for people to play around with speed. There were already three accidents on the stretch; one of those wrecks resulted in a fatality.

Destiny was having a difficult time coping with her father's death. She seemed stupefied and had been having difficulty focusing in school; moreover, she had been acting out in school and at home. In addition, Rocks's death had also taken a toll on her because she feared for Claude's life. Claude couldn't tell if she was sleep by the silence in the backseat because her days have been quiet since the tragedies.

Claude sat at the wheel in silence, engaging in an internal war within himself. It had been a month since he helped bury his number one sidekick. Rocks's death had put a toll on his conscious. Since the bullets struck Rocks, Claude's attitude hadn't been the same. He had a rough time dealing with his friend's death. He felt like he could have stopped that from happening because he could have gotten the money from Tank a day after. The pain Claude felt was unbearable. Throughout the month, his hurt and pain turned into anger. It was a familiar and heavy anger that he had no control over. All his thoughts of retaliation turned into premeditation. He felt as though he had nothing to live for. Indirectly, society had given him a license to be a fuck up. He gracefully accepted the license to kill the motherfuckers who had a hand in Rocks's death. In just a matter of time, something would have to give.

When Claude got off of exit 25 to Scott Road, his cell phone rang. He glanced at the name and number on the screen. It was so slippery that he wasn't too crazy about answering, but he did.

"What's good?"

"Fuckin' Tommy got locked up last night," Zane said.

"What happened?"

"He got pulled over at the bottom of Lakewood Road by turning right on red when he wasn't supposed to. A cop saw it and pulled him over. The cop ran his plates and took his information. That's when they told him he had two warrants."

"Damn! The car is in his name?"

"I don't even know, but he's in New Haven. When he calls you, he would tell it better than me," Zane said.

"It's always something. Do you know what the warrants were for?"

"No clue, but you know his name is probably in affidavits an' shit, but yo, not meaning to drop the subject, but we may have to place a few niggas on the suspect list. I'll rather talk to you face to face though. Can you come get me?"

"Yeah. Give me like twenty five minutes. It's slippery like a motherfucker out here. And Zane, do I know these niggas?"

"Yeah, you know them very well."

"Word? Alright, I see you in a few."

After getting Destiny settled, he eagerly went into the living room where Zane was operating the remote control to the television.

"What two niggas you talking about?"

"I don't want you to take what I'm about to say and run with it. It just dawned on me," she said.

"What dawned on you Zane?"

"I saw Domino and Twalique last night."

Claude had a serious look on his face as he pondered the information Zane gave him. It wouldn't surprise him if they were the ones responsible, but he was thinking that it could have been payback for the heist in Southington. He could have shared the same death date as Rocks. The assailants could have been gunning for two instead of one. They may have only completed half their mission.

He saw Domino's motive for killing Rocks because of what Domino told him in jail. And if Domino was involved, Link was behind it all. The only way he could fit Twalique in the puzzle was if Claude was the intended target.

"Domino and Twalique, huh? Didn't know the niggas was

out."

"After he came at you sideways about Rocks, did y'all talk after that?"

"Not at all. We never had any conflict, but everyone knew there was an unspoken tension between us."

"Damn, and he slept on the top bunk," Zane said.

"That shit didn't bother me. I was leaving anyway. You know how many cellies I had that I didn't like? You know the deal. But I'm still trying to figure out where Twalique fit in. If Rocks didn't get killed over Sapp, then them niggas could be strong candidates for suspects, including that punk motherfucker Link, 'cause if Domino is connected, than Link its behind it. I still can't get over you mentioning Twalique though."

"Jupe still fuck with Gloria?" Zane asked.

"As far as I know, but how is that relevant?"

"Because she was hugged up wit' Twalique when I saw him with Domino."

"That's not surprising."

"Does Sapp and Link know each other?"

" Link wanted to kill Sapp just as bad as Rocks so there can't be a connection there. Where'd you see them anyway?"

"At Pacos. Like I said, it is just a thought. I remember you telling me that shit with Domino when you was locked up and you already know what you did to Twalique. Coincidence?"

"For their sake, they better hope it is."

"What about Southington? I'm still paranoid about that shit Claude."

"You should, and we going to stay paranoid because we can't rule nothin' out. For all we know, he could have gotten killed over some shit that happened years ago, but I doubt it. We stole damn near a million in cash and over a half mill' in heroin. That's a lot of work in the street. Niggas like that fat motherfucker got eyes back there. We can't figure out who's who. And fucking Tommy. We can't protect him if he's in jail. That fucking flossing shit fucked him up Zane, and y'all think that I was barking on motherfuckers for nothing. Tommy blew his own spot."

"I know. Everybody turn right on red at that light. So what are we going to do?"

"This town ain't but so big. The police been on it, but we could easily find out who killed him from keeping an eye and an ear on the streets. I want to find out who the fuck did it before po-po find out. Them motherfuckers damn near killed my ass. Right now, stay real low until we find something concrete. For now though, I am going to pay my homeboy a little visit," Claude said before walking to the kitchen.

Delores Porter was lying on her back on the bottom bunk with her hands tucked behind her head, thinking about her son running the streets. She was familiar with the rules of the game and how things could unfold and get ugly. Rocks's death, in her eyes, was a tragedy, but wasn't surprised by it because she had known Rocks's his entire life. She knew how deep he was into the streets. When Sahara told her Claude got shot at, she literally lost her mind because she knew that could have been him sprawled out, bleeding on the asphalt.

Delores had beaten up a young, boisterous woman from Waterbury for gossiping about her son. The woman told another inmate that she wouldn't be surprised if Claude killed Rocks. The piece of information traveled back to her quickly. Delores had beaten the woman into unconsciousness for throwing dirt on her son's name. That was three and a half weeks ago. Now that she was in segregation, she had no choice but to dwell on her current situation and new problems from the outside that extended beyond her control.

Delores's light skin looked as youthful as it did when she arrived in York Correctional facility in 1994 after her manslaughter conviction. She became a tad stockier over the years, but she was still attractive at forty eight. Her cornrows were long enough to touch the middle of her back. Claude was a spitting image of her. Anyone would recognize their resemblance.

She felt like an asshole for catching a Class A ticket, but she refused to allow anyone to throw salt on her son; however, that was the least of her worries. Her family was her biggest concern, especially Claude. She felt it in her bones that her son was angry. She had a difficult time raising him and was smart enough to know that he was even more difficult as an adult. Claude and Rocks were like Tango and Cash. One of Delores's best friends was murdered two years after Sahara was born and she could honestly empathize with Claude. However, she hadn't seen him face to face since 1998, two years before Claude's incarceration, but she knew him better than most. She knew what he was capable of when he was crossed. That was what scared her the most.

It had been twenty-one years since she seen the horrid look Mookie, her boyfriend at the time, had on his face when he ran into a drawn kitchen knife that she intended to scare him off with. When they exchanged verbal onslaughts, Mookie had enough and told her how he'd squeeze the life out of her. Since she stood near the kitchen sink, she had easy access to sharps. She saw the biggest one and grabbed it. When he charged her, Delores's reflexes overpowered her fear. The knife went right through his heart. The look Mookie had on his face woke her up daily. She honestly didn't mean to kill him, but her public defender had too many other clients to defend to be focused solely on her case.

Lastly, when Sahara visited her a day before Rocks's funeral, she told Delores that Destiny wasn't over her father's death. Rocks's death a few months afterwards didn't help. Delores prays to God everyday for Destiny to not end up like her and Claude.

She sat up and sat at the edge of the bunk. She needed to get to her family. Class A tickets would only hold her back. Tears rolled down her cheeks because her family needed to be protected. She got off the bunk, kneeled humbly, and prayed. She prayed for her family's protection. She knew that whatever life-altering ordeal that Claude was involved with could have an adverse reaction on Sahara and Destiny. She had a feeling that something was going to go down. She was scared to death. She prayed for him to be man enough to protect himself and his family. After she got off her knees, she balled herself up on the bunk and wept because of uncertainty.

....

The traffic on I-95 North slowed down to a crawl. The heavy, freezing rain made it difficult for anyone blessed with perfect vision to see out of their windshields. Rain, sleet, hail, or perhaps any biblical disaster wasn't going to stop Domino and Twalique from conducting business as usual. The men were hungry and would do anything to put a stop to Link's steadily increasing decline from the top. They were so thirsty for cheddar that the men would gladly die with cash balled up in their hands. They would stop at nothing, even if they had to kill Claude next. Since the talk of Rocks's unsolved murder has quieted down, the men relaxed instead of visualizing the police kicking down their door. The men were almost convinced that they have gotten away with murder. Whenever Twalique gets paranoid about getting caught and charged with murder, Domino would reassure him that the police didn't give a fuck about a drug dealer. Naturally, Domino felt somewhat at ease that he wasn't the trigger man because if they get caught, he'd rather go down as an accessory than a murderer.

"Ain't this a motherfucker? It took us at least an hour and a half to get to the city. Now we tryin' to come home. Been in this fuckin' car for six goddamn hours! What the fuck?" Domino was pissed.

"And not to mention that we ridin' dirty. Of all the days to come down here, we had to come down today," Twalique added.

"Look on the bright side though; we 'bout to do it. Once we get this shit back to Waterbury, we could start choppin' the shit down. We gon' try to flip this bitch two, three times before we come back to NY, 'na mean? We gon' keep this shit movin' so our cash could explode," Domino said.

Twalique was actually going to go solo, but he didn't know Queens like Domino. That wasn't the only reason why Domino tagged along though. Domino and Twalique were constantly doing missions and clubbing together because he was watching him. Link wanted to make sure Twalique wouldn't crack. He had to make sure he wasn't stupid enough to share details about the murder or crack and turn himself in. That would be Link and Domino's recipe for disaster if Twalique decided to talk. Domino had, however, gained a liking for him, but business was business. If Twalique thought for one second to turn himself in, he would kill him before he entertained that thought. Link wanted Twalique to be kept close.

Since Domino was driving, Twalique unconsciously went into his pocket and pulled out a half ounce of some diesel, along with a Dutch.

"Yo, you could smoke that shit your damn self. I ain't gon' lie, I'm kinda shook daddy drivin' this bitch."

"The traffic ain't even movin' Dom! You want me to drive?" Twalique asked comically.

"Naw, naw, I'm just sayin' that a nigga need to focus, that's all. Why don't you spark it when we get to route 8?"

" Route 8 is a long way from here. Fuckin' wit' this traffic, we'll probably be there in three hours. I need to smoke bro, at least four or five pulls."

The men remained quiet while Twalique took his long, hard totes. As their silence grew thicker, the men thought the same thing. The foul shit they pulled last month was an unspoken event. Although Link and Domino were glad that Rocks was a memory, Twalique hid his regret in a cloud of smoke. He killed Rocks for five grand, but he already spent two grand on some bullshit. He could see that money disappearing if it only took him a few weeks to spend half of it. Most importantly, he Domino's scheme of developing a friendship with him to keep him close. Twalique was simply playing along with it. If Link was the only one putting money in his pockets, there was no way he was going to bite the hand that fed him. He was swamped in regret about the murder, but the past was the past. He would kill again if presented another opportunity, even if Claude was next on the list.

"You think Claude going to be a problem?" Twalique asked in his euphoric state.

"He may not live long enough for him to be one."

"So you sayin' he is going to be a problem?"

"Just like I said, he will if we let him."

Twalique developed a new wave of worry and stress because he was a living example of how Claude reacted when he was crossed. When Twalique, Scott, Drillz, and a long host of others stomped the dual out, Twalique had no idea that Claude would come back with full force and shoot him on the side of his torso. After all, it took Claude and his people months to retaliate. He had a feeling that Claude may be the same vindictive person he was fifteen years ago. Either way, he refused to allow Claude to catch him slipping.

"I can't believe those cocksuckin' ass niggas tried to flip 'cause we had our tools on us. What the fuck do they expect man?" Domino asked to no one in particular.

"They doin' what they suppose to be doing. Them niggas don't know us like that. If the shoe was on the other foot, our shit would be tighter. Come on Domino, you know that. Don't take it personal."

"That motherfucker damn near grabbed my dick in that pat down. Just sayin' though; I didn't like that shit."

The traffic started to let up. When Domino drove a normal flow in the middle lane, his cell phone vibrated loudly in the cup holder.

"Yo," Domino uttered. "What up?"

"Yeah, yeah…get the fuck outta here! You serious?!"

The expression on Domino's face worried Twalique. He listened in on the conversation. He couldn't read him. He just hoped that the cops didn't have any leads to Rocks's murder. He had been paranoid to the maximum lately.

"So that's why niggas hadn't seen him. Them niggas is hidin' dawg! Alright, alright, we'll touch ground when we get to town. "

Domino nodded on the phone a few more times, listening to more of Link's instruction.

"Alright yo, see you when I see you. Word."

Domino ended the conversation. Twalique was curious on what Domino learned on the phone. He knew Domino just heard some ground breaking news based on the smirk he had on his face.

"Yo, what happened?"

"Remember Wiley?"

"Yeah."

"His little brother Ty was a little stewed because he was left out of the loop when Claude and them other niggas robbed a capo."

"A Capo? What capo you talkin' about?"

"Calvin King."

"Calvin King? Get the fuck outta here! They robbed that nigga?! Those motherfuckers got a lot of balls fuckin' wit' that dude," Twalique said while he choked on the blunt he was smoking. "Trust me, that nigga is rich. He killed a lot of folks in the process of him solidifying his reign and he more than likely collected even more bodies to stay on top. I didn't think he was in Connecticut."

"Word?"

"Word. They probably think Calvin sent the boys to do Rocks, but what's wit' that Ty nigga? They left him out of the heist so he runnin' his mouth now?"

"Accordin' to Link, Ty didn't know Chester was his nephew," Domino said.

"So he just vented to the wrong nigga then."

"It appears that way, but I never told you the amount of cheddar them niggas got Calvin for."

Twalique damn near lost his escalating high as he anticipated a high number.

"How much?"

Domino smirked.

"Almost a mill' in cash and work."

"Goddamn! No wonder Ty is pissed the fuck off! I don't blame the motherfucker, but fuck all that though! When do we get a piece of that?"

"That's exactly what I'm thinking now, but pass that greenery kid 'cause this calls for a celebration," Domino said loudly.

"So what do we do now?" Twalique asked.

"We ain't doing shit tonight, but tomorrow, we going to pay Ty a visit."

"You know where he be at?"

Domino looked at Twalique with a sinister grin and moved over to the next lane.

"Not at all, but Chester, yeah, he know," Domino said, nodding his head slowly like he was on to something.

. . .

The dirty slush and the plowed piled up clumps of snow made it difficult for anyone with elite driving skills to parallel park properly on Rose Street. That didn't stop Claude from stunting like he was going to run Jupe over while he checked the amount of oil he had in his old Jetta. Jupe flinched, causing him to bump his head on the inside of the hood of his car. He parked two cars down from where Jupe stood.

"How old are you?" Jupe asked Claude sarcastically while he rubbed the top of his head.

"Yo, my bad man. You alright?"

"Yeah, I'm good, but damn nigga, it's slippery than a motherfucker out here. You should have hit me. I could sue for some of that stash I know yo' ass is building," Jupe said good-naturedly.

"So I see you checked your mother's closet," Claude said nonchalantly.

"I did. And on the dresser, I found the letters that your mother wrote me from Niantic reliving our conjugal visits."

They laughed whole heartedly and dapped. While growing up, Claude's clique engaged in the mother jokes. Their humor was crude, but the mother jokes were said out of love, never out of character.

"What's good my dude?"

"You."

"Naw, not me, you that nigga, but on some real shit, how you feeling C?"

"I'm doing alright, you know what I mean? Trying to maintain, feel me? Trying to see life at another angle," Claude said. "So what's good with you playboy? Is life treating you better today than yesterday?" Claude changed his tone quickly to avoid a Rocks conversation.

"On the real, I can't even complain. I'm doing good!"

"Whoa there partner! You're a little excited there. Run it to a motherfucker. What's new?"

"Got a new job. Been there for a few weeks. Got the gig through this chick I'm fucking with."

"New job, new woman, sky is the limit for you." Claude smiled broadly and patted Jupe on the shoulder.

"What up wit' your girl though? You got shorty on the side or you on the wifing tip?"

"It's definitely some potential. We riding' slow, taking it one day at a time."

"Wow, you on it like that? Gloria know?"

"I don't give a fuck one way or the other."

"You think she hitting the sheets wit' another nigga?"

"Yup. And you would never believe who."

"Is it somebody we know?"

"Yeah, especially you."

"Me? Who she fuck with?" Claude wanted Jupe to cut the shit and get to the chase.

"Twalique."

"Wow," Claude said flatly.

"Speakin' of the devil, here comes that bitch now."

Claude looked at the car carefully.

"Ever since her mom bought her that whip, I never see her, but that's fine with me."

"And you still livin' here?"

"Not for long. The kids been more on the move to my mom's house. They have been there the last couple days. This stupid bitch don't know that they ain't coming back."

"Word?"

"Word. It gets worst. Why did my daughter tell me she saw mommy and another man in our bed with no clothes on? And Tony told me he saw Twalique pushing her shit. When I needed the fucking car, the bitch instead gave me a ride."

Gloria made her way to the men. Claude wondered if she heard Jupe talking shit about her. The look she had on her face confirmed it.

"Who are you calling a bitch Jupe?"

"Who the fuck did you hear us talk about?"

"You know what? I don't give a shit what you said. You ain't nothin' but a bum ass nigga anyway. Can't pay or come up with half of nothing, sorry ass Negro," Gloria said coldly.

"Hi Claude," she said with attitude as if it hurt her to acknowledge him. Claude nodded as she made her way by him. Claude thought that Gloria didn't look bad. She was dark-skinned, short, thick in the right places, and had extensions in her hair. Claude was too preoccupied from the sight of the car to pay her anymore attention than she deserved. Her attitude towards life itself made her a disgusting person.

"Sorry you had to hear that shit. She'll be cussin' herself out when she realizes she can't afford to live here by herself."

"Out of curiosity, is she going to be cool with you taking the kids?"

"Yeah 'cause it'll be a relief to her C, man, you don't understand how evil that bitch really is. Whenever I ain't here, shit be poppin' off in the household like there ain't no tomorrow, for real."

"I hear you, but I got to cut out and finish my errands before it get dark. Got a tail light missing and don't want any contact with police. I'm glad some light is shining on your ass. Does your new shorty know about Gloria?"

"She knows everything. I'm just tryin' to end this chapter and start a new one."

"That's what's up. What you getting into later?" Claude asked.

"Probably rearranging some shit at my mom's crib. Why, you want to burn something down later?"

"You already know. I got this fire I want you to try, but good seeing you though. Give me a call later and we'll take it from there."

"Alright C, one love fam."

"One," Claude said.

Jupe took off down the street. When his car was out of distance, he turned his attention to the white beamer and saw the bullet entry.

Let me find out, Claude uttered before getting into his car.

46-Waterbury

Claude looked a lot different then he did when he first came home from prison. He kept his bulk, but other than that, he sported a mini-afro and a full beard. The days seemed void and silent to him; in fact, they were so quiet, Claude would swear to everything he loved that he could hear Rocks in the next room shooting the shit. He'd wake up abruptly in the middle of the night after reliving that dreadful night in his sleep. The sight of Rocks's corpse was like a picture stamped on the wall of his brain.

As he stroked his beard, a middle aged black man blew his horn recklessly because Claude was so out of it that he didn't know the light turned green. He went through the light as the man tailgated him through it. He looked in the mirror and saw the man screaming obscenities. He started to give the guy the middle finger, but decided against it as he realized the man sparking the verbal onslaught looked familiar. As they moved further down East Main Street, Claude moved into the right lane as the man pulled up in the middle lane. When the man pulled up to the driver's side, Claude saw the man he used to work with holding his middle finger with a smile on his face.

The men pulled over at the gas station. They got out of the car and embraced brotherly.

"What it is man!? Thought I was gonna have to fuck you up back there, holding up all the goddamn traffic an' shit. I'm like, what the fuck? Then I realized it was yo' silly ass holding shit up," Lester said humorously.

"Man, yo' old ass wasn't gonna do shit but ply y'self off your own windshield! What's the deal Les?"

"Ain't nothin' but the same shit. I'm 'a stop at the package store and get ready for these games tonight. What you getting into young blood? You alright?"

"Yeah, just taking it day by day, you know what I mean?"

"I hear you. Well shit, if you ain't doing nothing, why don't you come through tonight and keep an old man company? I got hurt at the job and I got nothing but time and just about enough money to get fucked up tonight. You game?"

"Yeah, I could come through. It's not like I got a job," Claude said, chuckling at his own joke.

"You know where I live?"

"You said you live on Hawkins Street, right?"

"Yeah, same spot for the last eleven years. By the way, you wouldn't happen to have any reefer, do you?"

Claude looked at Lester like he should know he always kept the good shit. Lester smiled when Claude's facial expression confirmed it.

"I'll be there right before the game starts."

"Alright, that's what it is then. See you a little before eight."

"Yeah, I'll bring that shit that'll make your head spin. Don't die on me old man."

"C, you don't die on me. This body been through it all."

They exchanged brotherly hugs and went their separate ways.

. . .

Claude was over Lester's house kicking it, watching the Suns play the Nuggets, conversing over a bottle of Hennessy and an ounce of weed. Claude enjoyed Lester and vice versa. They laughed and joked. They were sharing war and prison stories. The conversation was so deep that Claude opened up about Rocks's death and the attempt on his life. Lester already knew the situation, but it was a lot different when one heard a story from the horse's mouth. During all the laughing and joking, he had a feeling that Claude was up to something. He could almost put a finger on it. Lester has been around enough criminals and madman to tell if something was brewing.

"I could see right through you," Lester said, interrupting their rare, quiet moment.

"Alright you old motherfucker, tell me what you can see," Claude joked as he took a swig of the bottle of Hennessy they shared.

"You really want to know?" Lester was looking for a green light.

"Hell yeah," Claude responded.

Lester took a swig of the brown water and took a tote from

the blunt.

"You want to get the niggas that murdered your buddy, huh?"

When Lester asked him, Claude took another swig and looked at the old head. He was shocked that Lester could pick up the premeditation that existed in his head. His plans for the ones responsible should be for his thoughts only, and Lester knew this, but it was something about the older G that spelled trust.

"Even if I want to get the cocksuckers, setting the blueprint on how to get these niggas and getting away with it is hard."

"Look it here. Anybody could get touched. I don't give a fuck who it is. If them niggas could clap John F. Kennedy riding in a top down motorcade or poke Julius Caesar, than whoever you're looking for could get touched, just like the rest of the motherfuckers that got touched," Lester said convincingly and continued. "And as far as getting away with it, that's the hard part unless your overall thinking is advanced."

Claude looked at his older friend and smiled sinisterly.

"You sound like you're speaking from experience Les. Let a nigga in," Claude said, turning the volume down on the older model television.

"Use safe, valuable resources that don't know your name," Lester said eerily. "And burn your bridges."

Lester dropped a jewel on Claude, leaving him at a lost of words because he was thoroughly convinced that Lester had a body or more somewhere. Maybe he killed in the heyday of his youth. Claude, at that point, realized that Lester was nothing more than an original gangster with a past. A square could not provide the war stories and situations like Lester. He told each and every story with detailed description without being self-incriminating.

The men got situated in their silence, watching the game until Claude opened his mouth.

"How much money you talking for them resources Les?"

"I hear you talking the talk, but I don't think your pockets is fat enough."

"You sure about that?"

300

Lester looked at Claude, unsure on how to read the man who was thirty years his junior.

"Not really, but thirty grand is a lot of money, especially when another party is involved."

"Its not when your life depends on it," Claude said, patting Lester on the shoulder.

Lester didn't know how to take Claude's response, but he was willing to hold his hand out on whatever money Claude decided to spend. He knew he was taking a huge risk of dealing with someone he known for only two months, but it was a risk he was willing to take. Money was what he needed because his worker's compensation wasn't doing shit for him. His paper can't stack right being on worker's compensation.

"It may be a hefty fee to be a middle man."

"I ain't worried about it," Claude said convincingly.

"Then it's a done deal."

"I don't have to tell you the obvious," Claude said blankly.

"Damn sure don't. I ain't brand new to this kind of shit. There were others in the spot you're in, including myself. Anyway, call this number. Ask for Elijah. It's not his name but he goes by it. Don't tell him you're name because he doesn't care to know."

"Even better. Do I have to make a trip?"

"New Haven. Don't bring nobody down there with you. If you do, he won't fuck with you."

"Not a problem."

The gentlemen dropped the subject and continued to drink and drug well into the next game.

. . .

Claude cursed Mother Nature when he parked the car on Howard Avenue in New Haven. The wind was so heavy that he thought he needed a wheel alignment. To make matters worse, he had a hangover from last night from getting drunk and high with Lester. He wanted to make his move as quickly as possible. He knew he had to stick around to make his arrival look like a visit, but he wanted to be out of there before the storm touched ground. He put his North Face bubble coat on while still in the car. When he walked out of the car and into the wintry weather, he cursed again. The snowflakes were falling gently and fast from the sky. They were going to fall for the rest of the day. He had to come today because "Elijah" was going out of town for a few weeks. He couldn't deal with any local gun runners. This was his only time to catch him. He either had to ride down there or guard his and his crew's life while the ones that murdered Rocks still lingered around; in addition, Claude and his crew had cold cash, earned by strong arming a millionaire. If word ever got out about that heist they pulled, it would be price tags on Claude and his crew, including Sahara and Destiny or anyone who was unfortunate to be standing next to him.

He knocked twice and waited a few seconds before knocking again. It was the code knock Lester told him to use when he arrived at the gun runner's apartment. He heard some shuffling noises behind the closed door. A minute and a half after he knocked the third time, a tall, dreaded, thin man with a five o'clock shadow on his face opened the door.

"You know who sent me," Claude said.

The dude nodded, hearing what he needed to hear.

"Names aren't important. You never seen this spot and you never seen me. We straight on that?" Elijah asked.

"That goes without saying," Claude responded.

"What the fuck!" Claude uttered as Elijah pointed a small pistol a little above his kidney.

"Don't take this shit personal," Elijah said as he frisked Claude while he kept the barrel of the gun on Claude. "Don't got enough trust for motherfuckers to be hirin' security. The less eyes on my shit, the better. You ain't never been here."

"What is this?" Elijah asked as he withdrew the pistol from his waistline.

"I'm holdin' on to this shit until you leave."

"Keep the motherfucker. Hopefully I'll be walkin' out of here with somethin' better."

Elijah checked the safety on Claude's gun and stashed it in his pocket. He could understand Claude having the gun, but he didn't want to take any chances with anyone outside of his circle.

Elijah walked Claude down a short hallway that reeked of

ganja until they reached a door at the end of the hallway. When they entered through the doorway, the men walked through a desolate room separated by a colorful bead divider. When Elijah held the beads for Claude to enter, he was amazed at all the weaponry scattered all throughout the room. He understood why the man was paranoid. Elijah had everything from small .22 handguns to grenades. He had an array of assault rifles, shotguns, .38 revolvers, etc. He thought about his own presence in the house. If Elijah's pad got raided, he would be included in the Elijah package going up north.

"Silencers."

Elijah smirked because he charged big for that kind of shit. He walked to the other side of the room, opened one of the cabinets underneath the kitchen sink, and pulled out an AWC backdraft .22LR.

"The suppressor can be removed quick, returning this to its original appearance. The sound reduction performance for this steel is nothing short of excellent," Elijah stated as if he invented the gun.

"I need three of 'em."

"Goddamn man, what kind of court you holding out there in those streets?" Elijah asked, growing suspicious of his unknown consumer. He only dealt with clientele and had an idea who the vics were, but he didn't know who the young man was after.

"Crimes and names ain't important," Claude said, dropping three grand on the table.

Elijah didn't utter another word.

"All my tools are clean," Elijah reassured.

"That's what I like to hear."

Claude followed Elijah to the other side of the room to retrieve the rest of the burners. Claude reached inside his pockets and pulled out a pair of black gloves to avoid leaving fingerprints

"Brand new right?"

"I never sell used shit," Elijah said.

"Gimme two rounds of ammo and load them up for me," Claude demanded, dropping another stack of hundreds on the table.

Elijah didn't say a word. He put his own gloves on and did what he was told to do. After he finished, he taught Claude how to remove the suppressor. After showing Claude the basic usage of the silencer, he carefully tucked each gun into the thickness of his North face bubble coat.

"I'm sure my man up the 'bury told you about burning bridges. You got the number. If and when you cross that bridge, I could let him know that you will be in touch."

Claude nodded, gave Elijah some dap, and found his way out.

47-Waterbury

Ty was trying to sneak out of the house to avoid his mother's constant nagging of him being out all hours of the night, even though he was twenty years old. His older brother had been dead quite some time; therefore, his mother didn't want her second born son to suffer the same fate like Wiley, her first born. She would do anything to keep him in her presence, but the older Ty got, the more her tactics of keeping him around backfired. He was too knee deep in the streets to even consider his mother's deepest concern about him being murdered in a gutter somewhere, just like Wiley.

Ty was vexed and held a serious grudge against his people for being left out of the robbery, even though Claude, Rocks, Tommy, Tank, and Zane skimmed money off their share since they voted him off the heist. Zane was reluctant to give him anything. She figured Ty would still act funny in the long run because they stole so much money and product. Claude knew Zane was right; in fact, it gave Claude more of a reason to keep a set of eyes on him.

Ty was unsatisfied with the trust fund that his people gave him. He didn't feel obligated to be loyal to anyone. That heist could have made a dramatic difference in his life; however, the scraps his crew gave him were more short term. He understood Tank's struggle to keep his mom alive, but Ty figured Tank could have given him more money than what he gave him. Tank's mother has full blown AIDS. Selfishly, Ty figured the only thing Tank should be paying for was funeral expenses because Ty seriously thought she was going to die last week when she was rushed to the hospital.

Claude was another one on his shit list. He respected Claude, but he hated him after the heist. He figured that Rocks gave Claude too much power. He felt the hatred brewing inside him, but he didn't have the heart to express it.

Ty threw on a navy blue hoodie to finalize his thuggish appearance. His huge frame added some appeal to his thuggish style, but his bald face and head made him look like an oversized young boy.

Ty looked out his bedroom window and saw Chester parked in front of Walsh school, exactly where he told him he'd be five minutes earlier. He put on his skull cap and North face coat. When he walked into the living room, his mother was asleep on the couch while the television was on. He walked quietly out the front door.

. . .

Sahara held the ten thousand dollars in cash while her mouth was wide open in shock. She figured it was Claude's doing, but she wondered why he would place it deep in Destiny's drawer. She looked at the note that read, "One day you will understand." The note had Sahara baffled because it wasn't Claude's handwriting. She didn't understand why would anyone leave a child ten thousand dollars, but she knew Claude could come up with a better solution.

Sahara had been stressed out within the last few months. It all started with Sapp's death and Destiny's adverse response to it. Secondly, Rocks's death only created a negative emphasis to Destiny's ordeal of dealing with death. She had problems in school. Sahara had to go to a meeting the other day that consisted of herself, the principle, and a child psychologist. Sahara didn't like the recommendation of her staying back with the possibility of attending special education classes, but if her behavior didn't improve, as well as her performance, it could be an option. The last few months have been hell for her, but the money she held in her hand erased a lot of her inner turmoil.

She was oblivious to Claude's entry into the house and his approach towards the entrance to Destiny's bedroom door. She stared long and hard at the money. Claude stared at her back wondering what the hell occupied her. He figured she heard him come in.

"What's good Sahara?"

Sahara didn't bulge. She was still staring at the money like she never seen or felt a stack of cash before. She turned around slowly.

"This is good Claude," she said, holding the cash. "What is this all about?"

Claude looked at the money incredulously. His guess was

as good as hers, but when he saw the note, he knew it was Rocks's handwriting.

"Well? Are you just going to stand there, or are you going to tell me where this money came from?"

He knew the day will come; in addition, it was all in the act of good timing. He just received a letter from their mother. He figured that now will be a good time to start spilling beans.

"Rocks left Destiny that money," he said nonchalantly while he tried to quickly prepare himself for Sahara's first reaction after hearing his explanation.

"Why would Rocks leave my daughter ten thousand dollars Claude? Does it have anything to do with Sapp? Did y'all kill him C?" she said as she was on a verge of breaking down.

Claude continued to look deep into her eyes, trying to figure out a way to deal with his sister.

"Answer me dammit! What the fuck is going on?! What did y'all do to him?" she said as the tears spilled down her cheek. Unexpectedly, she took a swing at Claude, connecting to the side of his chin. She swung wildly. She hit him twice more before he grabbed her in an attempt to stop her from swinging.

"Calm the fuck down Sahara and listen! I could explain everything," Claude said loudly, using his strength to hold his sister down.

Sahara gave up her resistance and cried. She was confused about the money and had a hunch about who may have murdered Destiny's father. She knew she couldn't withstand her brother's strength so she gave him a window.

"Get off of me C," she demanded.

"Not until you calm down and listen."

"I will. Just get off of me."

He did what he was told. Sahara sat up on the edge of the bed wiping away the tears.

"I know things have been real fucked up since the deaths, and I know Destiny is even more fucked up over this shit. Since I know all this, I decided to not let you in on the truth about Sapp's murder, but first things first, I didn't kill him. In fact, I had nothing to do with it."

Claude told Sahara everything. He broke everything down

from start to finish. She knew about the grudge Rocks had with Sapp, but was surprised that the beef between them drove Rocks to murder. Claude even told her that their murders might be related. He told her that Rocks left that money as compensation for Sapp's death. It was the only logical explanation he could think of. Throughout all of his explaining, he never told her about the heist.

"Why didn't you tell me this before Claude?"

"Because it wasn't meant for you to know at the time, but that's not it. I need for you to pack you and Destiny's shit and bounce," Claude said quickly, cutting straight to the chase. He was relieved that he let the cat out of the bag without any major consequences, but there was more he didn't tell her.

"Bounce? What are you talking about C?"

"I mean what I said. Niggas is grimy Sahara. I'm telling you this right now. Shit is going to go down and I don't want you and Destiny involved."

"Involved in what C?!" Sahara was beyond hysterical. Claude took her by her hand and led her into his bedroom.

Claude went into his closet and pulled out a suitcase and two tote bags. When he opened up the luggage, exposing the contents in the bag, Sahara almost fainted as she stared in disbelief at the multi stacks of money. He told her how he knew Rocks killed Sapp, but he had to charge it to the game to obtain the money that rested in front of their eyes.

"Why did you put your own family in jeopardy Claude? Why? Is it really worth this money? Now you are telling me that me and my daughter's life is in danger,"she asked quietly.

"On the real, I did put y'all in grave danger, but I'm doin' something about it. I need for you to call your job and tell them you have to move due to an emergency with the family."

"What the fuck Claude?! Why do we…"

"Because that's the best thing to do Sahara! I'll be goddamned if I'm gonna let something happen to y'all because of my bullshit! And you know what? You are going to move tonight, and I mean tonight! Mark will pick y'all up from the airport and take y'all to Aunt Pearl's house. You could start a new life."

Sahara didn't have much to say. She had always contemplated a move somewhere down south, and it would be a good start for Destiny since she was young. There were better school systems down in Dallas. She didn't, however, want to make a move because of force, but she had to. She understood what had to be done.

"Look, don't worry about Mommy because she already know the drill. I made her a promise that I would protect y'all. Now, I need for you to pick up Destiny from the babysitter's crib and make moves."

"Do you even have tickets Claude?"

Claude reached into the tote bag and pulled out a stack.

"You could worry about that when you get to Bradley. Don't worry about this spot, your job, and your car. This is our money Sahara. You my sister and you always held me down when no one else did. It's time for you to listen to me for a change. I know what Rocks did was fucked up, and I will explain it to Destiny when she is old enough to know."

"You better C! That is my main concern. You have a lot of fixing in her life to do, just so you are aware," Sahara said before leaving Claude's room in the midst of their conversation.

Later on that evening, Claude dropped Sahara and Destiny off at Bradley. Sahara and Destiny hugged Claude long and hard. Sahara was concerned about Claude's safety, but Claude reassured her that nothing would happen to him. After dropping them off, he made a call to Mark and told him that Sahara and Destiny were on their way.

"Listen cousin, I'm going to send something huge in the mail. When you get it, follow my instructions. You one of the few niggas that I could trust so I'm not going to tell you not to cross me."

"C, what the fuck is goin' on man?! First it's Sahara and Destiny and now it's this package shit. Can you let me in?"

"You already know the deal Mark, but I'm not talking about that package until I see you in person. Should be in about a week."

"Claude, you are bugging me the fuck out?! What the hell is going on?"

"I'll see you shortly," Claude said before hanging up, leaving Mark dazed and confused as he held onto his cell phone. He knew Claude was up to something ugly.

48-Waterbury

Link, Domino, Twalique, and Ty were in Link's rented Dodge Durango at the bottom of Claude's street, waiting for him to leave it so they could boost those jewels and greenbacks from him. The Durango wasn't tinted, but it was parked on the opposite side of the street, five houses down from where Claude lived. Claude would be oblivious to the men if and when he came strolling down the street. Ty told Link that Claude and his sister have a tendency to leave the back door unlocked. He told them that one person lives above them, but she was never home; in fact, the woman won't be home for another two months. While Ty's anger grew, his desire to take some of that cold, hard cash grew as well.

Ty had some regret for siding with the enemy, but he felt he did what he had to do. He would always come up with the solution that he risked his life and freedom for those cats, and all they could give him was scraps, even though between all of them, he was given eight grand for being left out of the loop, including a kilo. Tank tried to school Ty by telling him that he could flip the kilo and the eight grand and turn his income into three digits. They gave Ty a come up and then some. It wasn't personal because Ty would have stuck out because of his height. That type of rip and run had to be drawn out accurately, and Claude and Rocks knew that. Ty wasn't trying to hear that though. He knew he was pulling a bitch move, but he wanted more of that paper.

"Yo Ty, you sure he got that cheddar up in there?" Domino asked.

"Can't say for sure, but he pays too much attention to that closet," Ty said, feeling like an undercover cop.

"That's why we in and out. Besides, he ain't the only one wit' paper, right Ty?" Link asked sinisterly, having Ty exactly where he wanted him. Link promised him the cut that Ty wanted if their mission succeeded, but he was going to replace Ty's share for his disappearance.

Ty had a pathetic look on his face. He sold his soul to the devil for cash money. He thought of all the capers he did with

311

his crime partner Tank. He thought about the good times when they parking lot pimped, the time they got stomped out at the bus stop, the time when they both jumped off the third floor when the cops raided their connect's spot while they were in it, the car thefts and joy rides, and the many other dangerous and adventurous things they did together. That went straight through his mind and out the window as he rode with the enemy.

"If Claude share ain't up there, Tank might have his stash tucked away somewhere. Tank is too smart for that kind of shit."

"And Claude ain't?" Link asked, having a feeling they were going to get a negative result from searching Claude's residence.

"Not sure. Don't really know that cat like that. As far as I'm concerned, he's just a nigga Rocks put on. They supposedly had history an' shit," Ty said.

"Deeper than what your young mind could imagine," Twalique said off-handedly, his mind going back to that night when he was shot.

"What about that bitch wit' the dreads?! We could collect from all these motherfuckers tonight!" Domino said forcefully.

Before Link could respond, Claude finally walked out his front door. Although it was dark, the porch light shone directly on him.

"There he go right there," Link said as he nodded his head in Claude's direction. Claude came out of the house to warm up his car. He left the keys in the ignition and went back inside the house. When he came back out, Twalique stared at him with disdain as he thought about the hatred that existed between them. His beady eyes followed Claude into the car. When he pulled off, Twalique eye balled Claude with a deadly fury in his eyes, thinking that he should have killed Claude instead of Rocks. Ty was damn near on the floor in the backseat when Claude rode by them. Link and Domino turned their heads coolly, despite it being night time. When the coast was clear, Ty realized that there was no turning back.

Link suggested waiting for a few minutes before breaking and entering.

"In and out y'all. If we can't find it, take some shit. We just want to make sure that if this nigga come back, he won't just think motherfuckers went for the jackpot. Don't forget the masks in case niggas is in there," Link instructed. "Ty, take us to the gold kid."

"If his sister and her seed is in there, we gon' keep 'em for ransom," Domino added. "That will eliminate all this creepin' around shit. Get it in a bundle."

When they walked across the street, Ty was at their rear with a pistol in the small of his back. He hoped and prayed Sahara and Destiny wouldn't be inside, but if they were, fuck it, he figured. He'd come too far to let a woman and a child put a wrench into his plans. By the time the men reached Claude's unlocked back door, Ty had no feelings. He was ready to get paid.

. . .

Claude drove around aimlessly until he reached Gloria's house where her white BMW shone under the street light. Ever since he picked up the silencers, he had been lurking around Gloria's house, hoping that he could catch a glimpse of Twalique because he knew Jupe didn't live there anymore.

After an hour of being posted inside his car, he made his way home. When he reached his house, he pulled up in the driveway and parked in the backyard next to Sahara's car. He grabbed his silencer, placed it in the holster, and let the Tupac song ride out since he was about to get out of the car. Claude was sitting on some life altering cheddar, but Rocks's death left a void so big in his life that his share of the cash, plus the money from the kilo of heroin he flipped a few times, couldn't bring a smile to his face.

Once the song was over, he stepped out of the car. When he reached the backdoor, he made an attempt to put the key in the doorknob, but he realized he didn't need to because the door was ajar. Claude knew the door was closed before he left the house. He acknowledged that he and his sister would sometimes leave the backdoor unlocked by accident, but the back door was never opened unless someone closed the door behind them, but didn't make sure the door was shut all the way. He looked down at his feet and looked in the direction of the side of the house and saw footprints in the snow. Instinctively, he pulled his gun from his holster and crept inside the house.

He turned on the light in the kitchen. Everything seemed normal and in place. He moved out of the kitchen slowly with the gun drawn with two hands and turned on the light in the living room. That was when it became official that someone was inside the house. All the furniture in the living room was in disarray. The flat screen was gone, as well as the stereo, and the closet in the living room had all its contents all over the floor. His heart was pounding, for he didn't know if the motherfucker was still in the house. He was so anxious that he almost took off his gloves, but he remembered that he still didn't have prints on the gun. He took a deep breath and searched the rest of the premises one room at a time. Once he searched Sahara and Destiny's room and the bathroom, he made his way to his room. His bedroom was in disarray. His closet had been picked through carefully, as if they were trying to search for something. Careful not to throw caution into the wind, he stepped out of his walk-in closet with the gun still drawn. He searched the house again until he made his way outside. He went back into the house, grabbed Sahara's extra set of keys, came back outside, and started her car so it could warm up. He took out his cell phone and called Tank.

"Yo," Tank answered as if he smoked a sack.

"Where you at?" Claude asked anxiously.

"I'm at the crib."

"Niggas broke in my crib dawg. I think niggas was looking for that cheddar," Claude theorized.

"What?! Niggas broke into the crib?"

"Yeah, but check it, I'm coming up your way as soon as this car warm up. I rather see you face to face, but it's on kid."

"No doubt. The front door is open," Tank said.

"Not a good idea Tank. If they was trying to take my paper, what makes you think they ain't coming for yours?"

"Good point fam. So niggas know we got money? How so?"

"Because somebody is talking Tank. I could only think of

one motherfucker, but I ain't going to get into that shit now. I'll be up in a bit," Claude said before hanging up.

Claude smirked and shook his head as he thought about Ty. He was the only one that knew about the heist. A wave of anger overcame him as he explored the possibility that Ty may be rolling with the motherfuckers that killed Rocks. Ten minutes later, he got into Sahara's whip and made his way to Tanks. He called Zane on the way over there and told her to get ready because something major was about to go down.

49-Los Angeles

Aaron threw a bunch of clothes out of his closet, looking for a traveling bag as he prepared for his Texas road trip. He wanted to silence Sonya as he clutched on to the paper towel with her address on it. The longer Sonya breathes, he figured, the more of a chance she had of dropping a dime. He wasn't willing to gamble on whether or not she'd keep her mouth closed so he was going through with his plan of killing her. If she told Trudy, she certainly told someone else.

His paranoia peeked when Flex called him for assistance; in addition, seeing Trudy's picture on the news a few days later only added more fuel to the fire. Although they did away with Trudy's body, her picture on the news was a tough reminder of what he and Flex did in the summer. Things were back to normal since Flex choked Trudy to death, and Aaron wanted to keep it that way. He knew the lowdown on Texas and its strict law so he knew he was taking a risk going down there. The last thing he needed was to catch a murder charge in its tough jurisdiction. He planned on executing a perfect murder, just like the dudes he and Flex shot to death last August. Taking a plane wasn't an option. A flight delay will only keep him in the star state longer than he should with Sonya's blood on his hands.

Sonya wasn't the only woman on his shit list. Lately, Raven has been very distant, which sparked his suspicions about her knowing his secret. He didn't plan on killing her, but he will keep an eye on her. Since he was responsible for her brother's death, he figured that it would be best to keep her close for an easy kill just in case she found out.

Sexing Raven was not something Aaron looked forward to these days. Fucking her dry pussy made the small amount of love he had for her decay. He didn't know that Raven was hip to what he and Flex did; moreover, he didn't know that she was once pregnant, but had an abortion after she heard word that Aaron and Flex killed her brother. After Octavia picked her up from the abortion clinic, she wondered if she jumped to conclusions without facts. When she was recuperating later on that evening, over Aaron's pad per Ali, she picked through one of his drawers and found a picture of Sonya. She recognized her immediately as she placed the woman in the photo at the hospital where her grandmother received treatment. She realized that that's Aaron's ex-girlfriend who moved to Texas. The missing woman on the news worked at the hospital as well. She could even recall a conversation they had about Sonya getting abused by her boyfriend a month before her brother was murdered. She even asked Raven if her brother was single. This led her to two questions: Why did Sonya leave? Was it because she was getting stomped out, or did she have an idea of the murders that took place? She knew now that she didn't leave him for another man.

After packing his GPS, he took one last look at Raven', wondering if it was a mistake leaving town while she rested in his bed. He brushed aside his paranoia and laughed at it. When he stepped out of the room, he called Flex with instruction on what moves that had to be made while he handled business in Texas.

When the front door closed, Raven's eyes opened. She'd been awake the entire time while Aaron packed. She was waiting for him to leave so she could check the status of the plan Ali and Wade have in motion. She jumped out of the bed wearing just her bra and panties. She was still fucking Aaron, but it was all part of the plan. Raven was so disgusted when she first received the picture text of Prime that she literally got sick to her stomach because she recognized Prime. His droopy skin was a dead giveaway and she saw that through a camera phone. The mere thought of fucking her brother's killer drove her to the brink of a break down. Although she has done her fair share of dirt, she never wished death on anyone. Her attitude has changed. She came close to killing him in his sleep. She held the .22 firm over his sleeping body, the barrel of the gun just inches away from his nose. She got her grip back on reality and returned the gun exactly where she found it.

As soon as she was finished putting on her clothes, she called Ali to find out the prognosis. The phone rang repeatedly until he finally picked it up. He spoke before Raven got a chance to put a word in.

"The plan is in full effect baby. Did he leave yet?"

"He left like ten minutes ago. I can't keep doing this Ali. Something is going to have to give," she said emotionally.

"It's going to happen sweetheart, but I'm glad you were strong enough to not blow the cover. I got these niggas here right now. If you over that cocksucker's pad, get the fuck outta there 'cause we got work to do. We gonna make sure he walk into a pile of shit by the time he get back. Pack your shit and be the fuck gone."

"Ali, before you hang up, that girl on the news…"

"Already know about it. I'll explain that shit to you later on. If your first instinct is telling you something wild is going on, than you got some good instincts," Ali said without being too direct. "And from what Flex tells us, Aaron may not be back for a hot minute. Gives us more than enough time to do what we have to do. We gonna take away his sheep and we'll save the shepherd for a nigga that got a hard on for him. And remember, don't talk. Let me get these niggas in order. I'll hit you back."

Raven held the phone for a while. She didn't know if the "eye for an eye" model would be right as she held Detective Taft's card, wondering if telling on Aaron and his henchmen would be the right thing to do.

. . .

"You and Rinaldi are not the only fuck bags with a goddamn hangnail of a case. Dobson and I just got chewed out by the chief for focusing too much on the McRobert case. Your case is fucked up, but the McRobert case could be comparable. We're being pulled off it to concentrate on two scumbags who didn't mean a damn thing to anyone on the fucking planet," Detective Jacobs bitched. His round, doughy fat face was beet red as he vented his anger about the way things were being handled in the department. He pulled Rinaldi's seat from his cubicle and pulled it up alongside Detective Taft's desk.

"I swear, Captain O' Donnell needs to be lined up and fucking shot for making all these goddamn irrational decisions. He pulled Weaver and Miller off the Dylan case and put them on a case that's bound to get cold. What a controlling bastard he is. He does all this reassigning shit because he gets a hard on from it. No wonder his wife left him."

"Exactly. Speaking of self-centered, pompous cocksuckers, where the fuck is Rinaldi," Jacobs asked sarcastically.

Detective Taft smirked, but didn't feed into it. He knew Jacobs for over twenty five years and could understand why he didn't like Rinaldi, but he'd always played a neutral role.

"By the way, I heard his wife is fucking anything that has a cock," Detective Jacobs added for the hell of it.

"Someone else may be laying pipe to his wife, but he's a hell of a detective, ain't a doubt about it."

Detective Jacobs twisted his overly thick mustache and chuckled.

"I see that case is knocking on your door to retirement made itself a home. You don't want to go out with a big bang? Or do you want to say the hell with this and put that Zodiac-type case on a dead scumbag and call it a day?"

"I didn't get my good reputation for short cutting Jacobs," Taft said.

"You can short cut the fuck outta here before this shit gives ya a heart attack," Jacobs said seriously.

"Yeah, yeah, yeah, fuck you Jacobs. I could see your fat ass hunched over a plate of pasta with your fat face in it trying to be Dick fucking Tracy, dead on the desk," Taft said comically.

"If I could fuck your wife once or twice before I depart, than fuck it. I'll die with a smile on my face and my hand on my hard cock," Jacobs said good-naturedly.

Detective Taft chuckled loudly.

"Who took your load?" Detective Taft asked, still laughing at Jacob's crude humor.

"Fucking Tyler."

"I'm not surprised. I would take that as a compliment. Tyler is an asshole and everyone knows it. What case did you and Dobson pick up?"

"Pittman and Anderson," Jacobs said, lighting a cigarette.

"Pittman and Anderson? Bodies found on Grape Street the other day?"

"Yup. I spoke with his mother. She said she hasn't seen or heard from him since the summer. Said he was pretty despondent before he vanished. She never contacted police because he left a note, but it didn't point us in any direction. And get a load of this; that Anderson girl that was found with him was the same woman who walked out to her car and found Rinaldi's informant with his throat slit."

That information made Detective Taft's day. He made a connection as quickly as he heard the word. The mass murder on Montieth Drive happened over the summer; Taft simply compared it with Pittman's disappearance. *Maybe he was running from something,* he thought as Jacobs ran down his mental list of probable leads.

"Hey, do you have the photos of the bodies lingering around?"

"I have them on me," Jacobs said, pulling the photos out of his breast pocket.

Before Taft laid eyes on the photos, Dennis Howard's sister came to mind, as well as the statement she made about seeing her brother with a light skin black man.

He rested his eyes on the flick, making possible links from the male corpse in the photo being light-skinned to the question of Pittman's disappearance. He had to be running from something, but what? Detective Taft placed the photo on the desk and looked at Anderson's corpse. He recognized her off of a first glance because she was with the informant the night he was killed. Taft was so excited about the possible lead that he almost pissed on himself.

Immediately, however, he left room for disappointment because it may be a coincidence. It was good for now.

"You look like I fed you some good shit."

"Don't get ahead of yourself asshole. These photos mean shit to me. I thought you had something for us to work off of," Taft fronted.

"I do. You owe me fucking big time," Jacobs said, walking away, knowing Taft was full of shit.

"That's if they offer any kind of merit, but yes fat ass, I owe you if this shit turns out to be a solid lead," Taft shot back

Derek Jordan

as he made preparations to contact Raven.

50-Waterbury

"This is it y'all, the moment of truth. If anyone of y'all niggas is scared, let me know 'cause we don't have any room for error. These bitch ass niggas been breathing long enough with Rocks dead," Claude said. They were in Zane's cousin's basement.

Zane stayed there with Claude for the last two days since his house got broken into. Dot wasn't home, but Claude wasn't taking any chances.

"Nobody ain't scared C, we just waiting for you. I'm saying though; we could light up that funk before we bounce?" Tank asked quietly. Although Tank was down for the cause, he was nervous. Zane was petrified, but aborting the mission never crossed her mind. Tank, on the other hand, trembled from a combination of adrenaline, anxiety, and fear. Claude noticed it.

"Ain't nothin' to be nervous about. A lot of money is being spent on putting this shit together. We straight. Get that jail shit outta your mind because it ain't on mine, but yeah, do what you do, just as long as you could handle yourself when the shit pops off."

Claude's movements were swift and steady. He carried himself like he did hundreds of killings, but he'd never killed. Tank envied him about his composure. Watching him made all the side effects to the premeditation of murder subside. Zane, however, looked like a deer zoned out to oncoming headlights.

"I hope you ain't shook. All you gotta do is drive," Claude said smoothly, pinching her cheek with a little force, which brought out some laughter from Zane. Claude looked calm, but he was just as scared as the others. His comment brought him back to when he peer pressured Big Chris into driving, the night he shot Twalique.

"Stop," Zane said, still giggling.

Attitude reflected leadership. If Tank or Zane would have noticed Claude being nervous, they would have had second thoughts about going through with the plan. He wanted to keep them calm. If his nervousness got out of control, he'd think about his money.

"Alright, so look, once we drop three, possibly four tonight, y'all could just go the fuck home because everything is going to play its way out."

"Damn C, you didn't say nothin' about no fourth," Zane said.

"You only have to drive Zane," Claude said nonchalantly. "Everything will play out, trust me."

"That means somebody else is included."

"Yeah, and that's where your money comes in."

"Say no more. If you trust the cat that's involved, then fuck it. Once we get back to Dot's spot, I'll give you that to give to him, her, or whoever the fuck they are," she said.

"Tank, is you ready?" Claude asked, pumping the young man up.

Tank smirked.

"Hell yeah I'm ready."

"Then let's get these motherfuckers!"

Everyone wore black hoodies, gloves, and ski masks. After Claude and Tank checked their guns, they followed Zane's rear up the stairs and led them out the front door.

. . .

"So tell me Ty, how does it feel to be a snake motherfucker? You sold out your people and still came up on empty with the bread," Chester said as he lit his Black and Mild. They have been going at it for the last ten minutes. They were killing time over Link's house on Deerfield Street in Bunker Hill. Twalique was playing Madden on the big screen while Link reclined in his chair with a toothpick dangling out of his mouth with his hands crossed behind his back. He was in deep thought. He watched Ty and Chester argue, but his scheming took precedence over two young dudes arguing.

Ty looked at the man who may be an inch higher than an average midget defensively and with menacing eyes. Chester was a short man, but his build was stocky and he had knockout potential.

"Yo, I don't give a fuck if you Link's nephew nigga. You'll get your shit beaten punk," Ty said sharply.

"You and what army," Chester said sarcastically.

"Link, you better tell this little nigga something because I ain't the one living off the strength from another nigga," Ty blasted.

"Well, you are, considering them niggas is sitting on jewels and cash while they got you on the block pumpin' g-packs," Chester said.

Twalique laughed hysterically. Link continued to sit in the recliner and stare into space. The argument started from a few light jokes that were exchanged back and forth light-heartedly before Chester questioned his heart, since he betrayed his people.

"What up then?! Ain't no punks over here pussy," Ty said belligerently.

They exchanged hostile faces.

"Alright, both of y'all shut the fuck up and focus on this money. Chester, go get that bag in the kitchen. Don't look in it; just bring it here," Link said, coming out of his cloud. He caught Ty's invitation for Chester for a fair one. It impressed him because he didn't think Ty had it in him. It was too bad he was going to waste him later because he didn't have any need for him anymore. He got in contact with one of Calvin King's associates, met him at an undisclosed location, and gave him a piece of paper with names on it. He liked Ty, but killing him was part of the plan.

"If you worried about me looking in the bag, then why don't you get it," Chester shot back.

Link fixed his eyes on Chester.

"Go get the fucking bag."

Chester sighed and got up. Ty grinned because Chester went out like a bitch. Earlier, Chester questioned his heart. Ty grinned because he knew Chester had a lot of nerve, but Ty didn't know about the role he would play in Link's last plan.

When Chester came back with the Jansport book bag, he was about to get comfortable, but Link put a halt to that.

"Naw, don't sit. I need you to run over Smack's crib and collect my money. I'll text you the address."

Link was an evil motherfucker to involve his only nephew with a premeditated murder, but it had to be done. Link was sure Chester wouldn't think anything of it once he decided to give him the okay to open the bag. Being that he leaked the robbery to Calvin's associate and got paid comfortably, Calvin told the associate to tell Link that there was a tag on all those involved. Link wrote down all the names and matched them with Connecticut Department of Correction photos of Claude and the rest of them, courtesy of Link's jump off, Tina, who was a correctional counselor that had access to all that shit. Calvin's associate knew it was official when he saw a photo of J-Rock. Link told him that Rocks was in the dirt so he was just one less he had to deal with. In return for the photos, he received a half of million, just what he needed to come up. Link almost had an anxiety attack. No one knew about his new fortune, except Domino, who was in the driver's seat of the car when Link and Calvin's associate met. The bag Chester took out of the house with him had ten thousand dollars in it in stacks. Chester would have no choice but to kill Ty if he planned on keeping the money.

Ten minutes after sending the text to Chester, someone rang the doorbell. Twalique paused his game, went over to the door, looked through the peephole and smiled. When he opened the door, he smirked at the woman. He reflected on his and Darlene's fuck episode the other night. He did, however, realize that if Link never turned her out, she would not had given him the time of day. Although he humped some slave pussy, Darlene was still beautiful, but her new heroin habit made her rail thin.

"What's up ma? You going to give me some more of that dope pussy tonight?" Twalique asked with a crooked smile.

"If you got the pay, then we could play," Darlene said coldly as she walked by him. Darlene had a right to be cold because she couldn't kick the monkey off of her back. The monkey was her only friend in the world. Lloyd was aware of her new drug habit. He had no problem making everyone else know, including the courts, which was why she had no visitation rights. It would be like that until she made exceptional progress in recovery. She sold her soul to Link. She lost everything, including her car, and most importantly, her dignity. Darlene fought intense battles in her life, but her addiction to heroin was the biggest of them all.

"Don't ever take your time coming here if I ask you to hurry bitch. You got that?" Link asked sternly.

The more she looked into Link's eyes, the more she wanted him to be involved in a freak accident or anything that could put her pimp, physical Satan to sleep.

"Fuck you Link! You had me waiting…"

That was as far as she got as Link got up and smacked her viciously across the face, causing her to stumble over the coffee table.

"Do you understand me?" Link asked calmly, standing over her with a grim face.

"Yes," she uttered flatly. She covered herself in case he wasn't finishing beating her.

"Now, entertain my friend right here while Twalique roll some blunts."

"Entertain him like how? He got money?" she asked, her eyes shooting daggers. She checked her face for blood, but there wasn't any as she stumbled up from the floor.

"Don't play stupid; you know the deal," Link said.

Ty and Darlene locked eyes. Link knew they had an acquaintance in common. An unspoken code of silence was made by Ty and Darlene through eye contact as she made her way to the young man. Ty quickly fumbled with his belt. He didn't get a chance to sit down as Darlene started sucking him off. She wanted to get it over with so she could have her next fix. As she slobbered on his manhood, she wondered if there was a way to get the monkey off her back. She wanted to know badly before Link became creative with her amoral sex acts.

Ty's head was leaned back in ecstasy as Darlene deep throated him. After sucking him for two minutes, Ty came in her small mouth. Darlene got up from between his legs and made her way to the bathroom where she spit Ty's semen into the toilet. Link and Ty made eye contact and smiled. Ty smiled because Link was his ticket to fast cash, cars, jewelry, and pussy. Link smiled because he had Ty exactly where he wanted him. It was time for the pawn to be sacrificed.

. . .

Tank and Zane were posted in the crasher three houses from where Link lived. It was four in the morning and they have been there since eleven. It wasn't a surprise that Ty sided with the enemies. It bothered Tank, but he charged it to the game. It took him a lifetime to realize how Ty was. Claude had some other cat that he was locked up with in the neighborhood, waiting to get at that fourth person Claude talked about, but for now, Zane and Tank kept their eyes on Link's front door.

In two days, Claude knew their movement. The hunt started when Claude, Tank and Zane were posted in front of Gloria's house. On the first day, Twalique walked out of Gloria's house at six in the morning. He went to a few stash houses, made some sells, and went back over to Gloria's house at mid-afternoon. Later on that evening, after five hours of waiting for Twalique to leave, he walked out of the house, started the car, and smoked a cigarette. While he smoked, a brown Honda Accord pulled up behind the BMW. Domino got out of the vehicle, locked it, and jumped in the passenger seat in the Beamer. Claude was in his crasher, watching their every move.

They didn't know who the guy was that had the backpack on him, but Tank had seen him around before and prepared a mental note to find out who he was. Seeing Darlene pull up and walk up the pathway to Link's door caused Zane and Tank to spill their high. They were baffled as to why she was there. She could put a wrench in their plan of destruction. Zane's blood boiled as the sight of her.

"What the fuck is this bitch doing over here?! Call C and find out what is going on. Is she the fourth person?" Zane asked irately.

"No, not at all, but I'll call him," Tank said before calling.

"Yo," Tank said once he got Claude on the phone.

"You still fuck Darlene?" Tank asked.

"No, why?"

"Because this bitch just stepped into Link's crib. Do we have to modify this plan a bit?"

"We don't have to modify shit. We'll work around it, but check it; my man got the blue whip parked up the street from y'all. He waiting for the go-ahead. Anything else out of the ordinary, just holla at me. Don't worry about Darlene. If she witnesses the wrong shit, she could easily be the fifth person; I doubt it though. The dude I got posted up there with y'all will appear like a ghost and vanish across the continent."

As Claude talked, someone driving a brown Honda Accord with tints pulled up, taking a park across the street. The car had seen better days. Zane rested her eyes on the vehicle. Tank was trying to hear Claude and focus on the figure that parked the car across the street. When the man stepped out of the vehicle wobbling, Tank froze. Claude's words fell on deaf ears.

"You hear me," Claude blasted over the phone. Disregarding Claude's tone, he made sure his gun and the silencer were still attached. His hands trembled in the leather gloves as he scanned his surroundings for any kind of activity.

"C, we see the motherfucker. Call you once we nabbed this nigga," Tank said as he ended the call.

...

Domino was so drunk that he didn't realize he had two of his tires grounded on the sidewalk as he walked out of the car staggering, having no idea on what kind of danger waiting for him across the street. His body wasn't cold because of his drunkenness, but he'll sober up once he found out what would be in store for his ass once he crossed the street.

...

Tank told Zane to stay low as he got out of the car and put an unlit cigarette in his mouth, careful not to make anything obvious. Zane had the driver's seat touching the backseat. Zane was scared shitless, but had faith that everything would run its course. She raised her head to see if whether or not things were in motion. Domino was still near his car grabbing his Dutches from his front seat. Tank walked slowly in his direction.

As Tank got closer, his trembling and fear disappeared. He was too close to his mark to lose a grip on things. He already had his gun drawn as Domino had his back turned, oblivious to the young man closing in on him. Tank crept so deep and precise that Domino didn't know he was an arm's reach away from being snatched.

"What up dawg? You got a light?" Tank asked quietly while he still held on to the gun that was in his pocket, fronting like he was looking for a light himself as the unlit Newport dangled from his mouth.

Domino screwed his face at the young man. Domino fumbled through his pockets looking for one. The young man in front of him looked familiar. By the time it hit him on who the young man was it was too late for him to think of any sudden moves.

"And while your at it, walk with me," Tank said, aiming the gun at his face.

"Wha…"

"Don't play retarded nigga. Walk."

When Domino started walking, he was wondering if tonight would be his last as all the foul shit he'd ever did started piling on him like an avalanche.

"Yo, what the fuck is really good?" Domino asked when they got to the car. His high and drunkenness was gone. He looked at Link's front door, hoping someone would come out of it and rescue him, but that wasn't happening. Seeing Zane in the front seat confirmed everything because he knew Claude was behind the set up.

Since Tank didn't answer his question, he knew a miracle within a miracle would be his only hope. Tank told Zane to pop the trunk.

Zane got out of the car and pointed the gun at Domino while Tank gagged and tied him up. Once Tank tested the strength in the restraints, he took everything off Domino's person and closed the trunk.

While Zane drove, Domino realized that the cats that kidnapped him were the same motherfuckers he slept on two months ago. Link mentioned that Claude kept those young cats around for a reason. Domino was in a world of shit.

51-Waterbury

Flip sat in the stolen car heated, thinking about a hundred ways to kill his long time adversary as he waited patiently for Claude. What cheered him up was seeing Claude's people snatch Domino. He never liked Domino from the start, ever since Claude gave him the rundown on him when they were locked up. It wasn't like he didn't have a mind of his own; he read Domino the same way Claude described him.

Out of the many men he thought of that could have cut his brother down, he never thought Aaron was responsible for Colin's murder. Since his release from prison, he vowed to kill Aaron and send him to hell for killing his brother and stealing his reign. Flip and his late brother were going to combine their masterminds and create a greater emphasis on the money that flowed in naturally. Flip taught his brother everything he knew about the game. Flip's teachings gave Colin the ability to live lavishly. Flip was unable to go to his brother's funeral, and that was something he would never forget. He hated Connecticut even more than he hated it when his foot first touched Connecticut soil.

Flip built an invisible fortress around him and grieved by himself. He didn't know his brother was murdered until a week after it happened. His mother couldn't bring herself to tell him. He found out his brother's death by Ali's letter. He had no family in Connecticut. Colin was twenty six at the time of his death. Flip hadn't seen him in ten years. When his cousin Ali wrote him and told him who had a hand in the murder, he busted through the fortress holding a can of rage. He hoped Ali did what he was supposed to do and make Aaron the last man standing.

Flip resided with a fifty-five year old overweight white woman who ran life skill groups at the half-way house he was admitted in after leaving prison. Since she was lonely and widowed, she allowed Flip easy entry into her life. Flip wasn't attracted to her, but he needed a place to stay and it would have been a process to have his parole transferred to California because of his priors. The woman provided Flip with clothes, money, food, and shelter. He moved in three weeks ago. He was bored and he sought an outlet. He wrote Claude a letter and enclosed his cell phone number. Four days later, Claude picked Flip up in Hartford, took him to lunch, and gave him a proposition. He wanted Flip to get at Link and whoever got in the way. Since Flip was in Hartford, and word on the street traveled fast, he knew Claude's road dawg was put to sleep. He knew him well enough to assume he was angry about it. Their lunch outing sealed the deal on his assumption. It would be more money towards his come-up once he arrived in Los Angeles. Flip didn't ask any questions. He didn't care either way. He just wanted to get out of Connecticut for good. Killing the dude that Claude wanted him to kill was only a tune-up before dealing with Aaron. By succeeding his mission, it gave him a valid purpose to leave Connecticut because his heart was engraved in Los Angeles. He looked at Connecticut soil like a prison without bars. He couldn't leave the state and head home to California until his parole expired in 2017. He already made his mind about staying in California once his feet touched the ground so the fuck with parole, he thought once Claude told him the amount of cash he'd receive for the murder. He told the woman he was catching the bus to see his friend that lived near the casino, but instead, he stole a crasher and met Claude in Waterbury. He had no intentions of seeing that woman again.

Flip glanced at his Armitron watch and it read 4:15am. Link was due to step outside at least an hour from now being that he had to work. Link had a bullshit job to cover up his criminal activities, which was why he rode a piece of shit car to work to eliminate suspicion, but the streets knew him well. He tapped on the steering wheel repeatedly, waiting for any sign of life to come out of the front door.

Flip knew what Aaron was capable of doing. He was one of the few people who knew Aaron caught bodies as a teenager and never been a suspect. He didn't want Ali to draw first blood with him because he knew Ali would probably meet his match. Ali was a hot head that could care less whether he lived or died, but someone like Aaron would put him in his grave quick. Aaron was too seasoned to fall victim to a cat like Ali.

Whenever Flip crossed paths with Aaron coming up in Los Angeles, he avoided him because he was afraid. He would even taunt Flip about the stabbing incident. As the years progressed, Flip's fear turned to unsettled anger. Every time he felt the scar Aaron planted on his face twenty something years ago, he visualized himself doing something ugly to him if he ever got the opportunity. Since Flip yearned to cross paths with him, he got his wish, even though his brother had to die for his wish to come true.

He would have never thought that he would kill Aaron for another reason other than the scar on his face that he's had since childhood. He even wondered if Aaron knew Colin was his brother, but it wouldn't surprise him if he didn't. As he prepared another thought, Claude banged on the window, holding a Stop and Shop bag filled with cash. Flip jumped, clutching his gun, and eased off of it at the sight of his friend.

"It's good to be on point Cali. Any action besides that shit you saw a few minutes ago?" Claude asked, settling in the car as he tossed the bag on Flip's lap. "You'll get the rest when the shit is done."

Flip nodded. "What's the official number on the drop C?"

"Maybe two, but leave the bitch out of it. My man already told me the scoop, but if you feel like you have to clip her if she makes any noise, just knock her the fuck out, but don't kill her. I ain't into that murdering women shit, despite how grimy the bitch is."

"The tall dude. The dude that violated. Put him up on the death list?"

Claude knew Tank wouldn't dead Ty, despite the foul, fucked up shit he pulled. When Tank and Zane first pulled up around Link's house, they saw Ty step into the residence. Zane called Claude and informed him about his presence. That was the reasoning of dudes breaking into his house. If Ty breathed after tonight, Claude figured, he'd be putting all their lives and freedom in jeopardy.

"Yeah, put 'im up there. I got to go Cali. It's time to get down to business. When you do that, text me the number one. I'll come and get you, but be aware we going to be driving extra funky in daylight."

"It comes with the territory C," Flip said nonchalantly, knowing exactly what Claude was talking about.

"Alright. Call you in a hot one," Claude gave Flip dap and got out of the car.

Flip redirected his focus to Link's front door, looking out for two targets instead of one. He went for his gun when he saw Link's door open. He sat back in his seat when he saw the woman. It wasn't one of the targets. He felt relief when she started the car and took off down the street. Ten minutes after Darlene jetted, Twalique walked out of Link's house. Flip looked at him and smiled before reaching for his cell phone.

"C, get ready," Flip said into the receiver before ending the call.

. . .

"How long will it be before Twalique get here?" Tank asked. It was the first question and the only words Tank uttered since he and Zane tied Domino to a steel folding chair.

"He should be here any minute, but can I..."

Domino's words were cut short by Tank's fist.

"We ask the motherfucking questions! You just sit tight and shut the fuck up."

Domino decided to do just that because it was useless to try to reason with the young male and female duo. When Tank and Zane took him out of the trunk, he was shocked when he noticed he was in the backyard of the stash house that Link put half the money he got from Calvin for the drop on Columbia Blvd. Link hadn't used the stash house since he was on top, but he was stupid to place half the money that Calvin gave him inside the unguarded house. Since no one knew about the place, other than Twalique, he knew the reason for him being bounded to a chair exceeded breaking in and entering. It was about Rocks. He knew if Claude could let off a shot when they took off, he had enough sense to store the make of the car in his memory. He knew they shouldn't have used Gloria's car. A cloud of fear developed as he looked at his silent captors. He wondered why they didn't do anything more than just snuff him. Domino knew it would be a matter of time when Claude walked through the door. He wondered if Link and Twalique were alive and if Ty set them up so they could get to him, Twalique, or Link. He disregarded the idea because he knew Ty didn't know about the stash house, but how did they know where Link lived? He always disagreed with Link, but he felt stupid for not taking his word seriously. When Domino slept and played the role as Rip Van Winkle, Claude was making moves like Napoleon.

Fifteen minutes later, Domino heard the cellar door open. He hoped that it was Twalique coming downstairs with his guns drawn. When he saw Twalique enter the doorway to the empty area of the basement, he looked at his hands and didn't see a gun in either one of them; instead, he saw Claude at his rear, wearing a crooked grin on his face and holding a gun in the back of Twalique's head.

"Finally we all meet. Too bad we had to meet in these fucked up conditions. Sit down," Claude ordered as he forcefully pushed Twalique to the floor. "Tie this nigga down."

Domino looked at Claude with dripping fear. He never thought Claude would ever have the upper hand on him, and there he was, soaked with vengeance, infested with rage over his friend's passing, holding a gun in his hand.

It took no time to tie Twalique in the chair. Claude walked around his hostages holding the gun with two hands behind his back. Twalique and Domino wished that some divine intervention would save them. Suddenly, Claude stopped dead in his tracks and shot daggers at the men.

"I got a plane to catch and no time for games. I know y'all bitch ass niggas broke into my crib. So I'm gonna ask y'all question number one, and I don't want no bullshit. If I hear some bullshit, my gun goes off. If not, then y'all niggas could walk the fuck out of here and charge it to the game. How did y'all niggas know where I live?"

"Darlene. She started fucking with Link and he got that info out of her, plain and simple, but we didn't break into your crib," Domino said.

Claude raised his gun.

"Alright, alright. Your man Ty was a little pissed off that

y'all niggas left him out of that heist y'all pulled so he sided with us. Period. That nigga was hungry so he told us where to look in your crib for the money y'all stole from Calvin. Come on C, we want the same thing you lookin' for. We didn't run our mouth like your man did. We saw it as an opportunity and we ran with it. We wanted the paper."

Claude didn't respond. The mentioning of the man's name worried him because God only knew how many other people knew about the heist. He couldn't hold that against the hostages because they were doing what the average crook did. They just fucked with the wrong one. Ty's betrayal wasn't a surprise to him so he knew Domino wasn't lying.

"Nothin' to say Twalique? You seem real quiet tied to a chair."

"What the fuck can I say C? You got us, but if you understand game, then we should call it even. After all, you shot me," Twalique said, trying his gift of gab to squeak out of his hostage situation. If he were to make it out alive, he promised himself that he would kill Claude.

"Fuck this, I ain't dying for what that nigga did."

Twalique looked at Domino in disgust. He knew Domino was pussy all along.

"What did he do?" Claude asked quickly, knowing the answer already.

"He killed Rocks! I told that nigga to keep driving when he saw y'all pull into the projects but I ain't gon' argue with a nigga with a gun," Domino said cowardly.

"Domino, you's a bitch for real! You ain't shit without Link you fucking coward ass pussy!" Twalique spat. Twalique looked like an animal held captive as he struggled and fought with the restraints.

"You killed my homeboy," Claude asked him as he approached Twalique.

"Rocks killed Sapp, but that wasn't the reason why Link had Twalique kill him. Sapp was the key to our come up. That was the money Sapp was going to give him to call off the wolves. It wasn't about Sapp. It was about that cash we was suppose to get from Sapp 'cause that was Link's money. Rocks stepped on the game plan and put niggas back to square one."

"You a pussy Domino! If I breathe tomorrow, I will kill your grandmother and daughter on site nigga."

"So my nigga got killed over fifty grand?" Claude asked gravely.

"It was the prin…"

Domino's words got stuck as Claude shot Twalique in cold blood, right in the side of his head. Blood spewed on the wall.

"Yo, the safe is upstairs in the closet of the master bedroom. The password is six, eighteen, forty two," Domino said fearfully, trying anything to see tomorrow.

"Don't let that nigga bleed out on the floor. Go get those body-sized bags from the car Zane and don't make any noise. Leave the trunk open and hurry," Claude ordered before turning his attention to Domino. A stream of piss dripped on the floor from the inside of his jeans.

Zane came back with the bags.

"Domino, I need you to delivery a message to Link," Claude said.

Domino looked relieved because it was an indication that he was going to live.

"Anything, word up, anything. What do you need me to tell him?" Domino asked desperately.

"If only he knew how much of a pussy you were when you walked and breathed the planet," Claude answered before letting his gun go off in the back of Domino's head.

. . .

Claude put Twalique's body in the trunk of his crasher while Zane and Tank placed Domino in Tank's whip. The trio had the bodies in the body bags before they leaked too much blood. Before moving the deceased, Claude went to his trunk, pulled out ammonia, laundry detergent, and a Poland Springs bottle of water. He mixed the three elements and used it as a cleanser. He scrubbed the blood stains off the dirty carpet. He didn't leave any trace of it. After closing the trunks, they went back inside and located Link's stash, finding the five hundred thousand dollars that Calvin gave Link for his services minus the ten grand Link gave his nephew. They split it three ways.

Once they were in motion, bodies in the trunk an all, Claude made a call.

"Yeah," the person answered, his voice scrappy from him being woken up out of a sleep.

"I'm ready to burn those bridges in about an hour."

The person's sleepiness subsided. He expected the call because it was about money.

"Alright, see you then," the man said before hanging up.

Claude looked at his watch. The time read 5:05am. It was time for Link and Ty to prepare for their home going.

. . .

As soon as Link went back inside while his car warmed up, Flip quietly got out of the car and left the car door ajar for easy entry once he made his escape. He discreetly made his way to Link's yard and waited at the edge of his house because it was the best vantage point available once Link seated himself in the car. Flip cursed to himself when he saw a man jogging down the street. At the same time, he heard the front door open. Ty walked down the walkway and got into the car. Link was behind him, holding a small tote bag, and had a blunt dangling from his mouth as he forgot to lock the front door. Flip turned his attention to the direction the jogger was running. He was out of sight. When he set his attention on Link, he was on his way to the car.

. . .

"Let me ask you a question. You slang for a living and make more bread than the average nigga. Why the fuck do you work? You got the kind of money where you don't have to wake up this early to make crumbs," Ty said.

"Because that's how you get the pigs off your back Ty. That's why we in this piece of shit of a bucket," Link said, tapping on his steering wheel for emphasis. "What the fuck do I look like driving around in a Mercedes with no check stubs? But yeah, fuck all that, I need you to do me a favor. I'm going to take you over to Floyd's crib so you could run him up this package," Link said, referring to the tote bag. "Hurry up back down though because I can't be late," Link lied. Chester and Floyd were waiting for Ty to step up in the house so they could assist him at gunpoint to the trunk of Chester's car. Link would be on his way to work by the time Ty made it up the stairs. He actually liked Ty, but a snake was a snake. If he could sell out his own people, he could sell out anyone else involved in his circle.

"Not a problem, but Link, you think…"

Ty's words were interrupted by someone tapping the driver's side window.

"What the fuck?" Link said off-handedly as he slipped for the first time in years by rolling the window down not knowing who it was that was knocking on it.

"Claude sent these," the man said before dumping shots into the car, hitting Link and Ty in multiple areas of their bodies. Their bodies rattled and thumped from the array of bullets. Since he didn't have enough time to search the car for jewels, he opted by taking the tote bag only that had twenty grand in it.

After Flip left the murder scene, he smiled at the gun because it didn't make any noises. He only wished he could take that shit with him to L.A., but he wanted Aaron's murder a little messier. When he started the car, he texted Claude the number one and sent it. He was ready to receive the other half of that money and travel to the other side of the country.

52-New Haven

The sky produced huge snow flakes that started to stick to the ground. Claude expertly drove the car on the unplowed, icy terrain while Flip rode shotgun, nervous because of Twalique's corpse stinking up the trunk and the road conditions. He remembered the last time he was a day away from going back to his home state; he got bagged. Getting caught with drugs was one thing, but getting knocked for a body in the trunk was another. His only objective was to hit California arrest free. He hoped Claude could make it to the destination without cops getting in the way. It could happen if Claude fucked around and got careless with his driving.

"This shit is fucked up man. It just had to start snowing out this motherfucker," Flip said nervously as the road conditions became less tolerant. They just got off of route 69 in New Haven and merged on to Whalley Avenue; that was the second part of their small turbulent road trip. Route 69 was an adventure in itself. The roads became so icy that anyone in a hurry would die on the slippery roads. There was hardly any traction on it, making the police infested route that more dangerous. The time of the day was on their side because of the work commute. That enabled them to blend in with the traffic. Whalley was congested. The traffic was bumper to bumper.

"Where does this motherfucker live?" Flip asked, trying everything in his power to mask his fear of getting caught.

"About six or seven blocks up, not far from here," Claude said, focusing hard on the road. He realized Elijah's gun spot wasn't far from where he sat in traffic. He wondered idly on how Lester's other peep was going to be like. Elijah frisked him while he held a .22 on his person. He wasn't in any mood for that kind of treatment. He wanted to get rid of the bodies and catch the next flight to Dallas.

"How do you think your peoples is holdin' up?"

"They like two cars behind us. We straight Cali. A few more lights up and we bust a right and we on the street where he lives," Claude said to shut him up. Flip had been nagging him the entire trip, but he gave Flip no argument. He understood

339

how badly he wanted to be on the next thing smoking to California.

Flip nodded and relaxed a bit.

"You scared to go back? The reason why I'm askin' is because you ain't lookin' too nervous about this shit. I ain't scared or no shit like that, but damn, you actin' like we goin' to work like the rest of these motherfuckers."

"Hold that thought," Claude said before answering his cell phone.

"Yo," Claude said.

"That shit spread like a disease. Will talk to you more about it once we touch ground," Tank said.

"The ones we got or the ones up the way?"

"Not ours," Tank said.

"Any eyes," Claude asked.

"A jogger who don't know shit."

"Talk to you in a minute," Claude said, ending the conversation.

"What's up?" Flip asked with a new stream of worry.

"Nothin' to worry about. The jakes loaded up them bodies you dropped," Claude said like it wasn't a big deal.

"Fuck!"

" What did you expect? Ain't no way two bodies ain't gonna be unnoticed with the car still running. Tank told me there was a jogger out there that got interviewed, but he couldn't identify any suspects because it was dark."

"Yeah and he jogged away from the action. He was completely out of sight when I did them niggas. It's been two hours since I clipped them. Your whole town probably heard the word. Small ass fuckin' Waterbury. It ain't nothin' like L.A. Niggas would have found that shit out like a week later out west," Flip spat.

"We ain't gonna know 'til we talk to Tank," Claude said, making a right on Ella Grasso Blvd.

Claude maneuvered the car around a Cadillac that was doubled parked in the middle of the street and prevented a head on collision with a plow truck that was coming from the opposite direction. Claude and the driver of the plow truck missed each other by a hair.

"Good drivin' C, damn, I thought that truck was gonna hit us."

"So did I. That was close," Claude said, slightly winded from his near accident. He felt his heart pound a hole through his chest.

"I would have bounced."

"You and I both, but that was fuckin' close."

After driving for another ten minutes, Claude drove the car to a crawl, looking for the address he wrote on the piece of paper he held. Tank fell back; he parked on top of the street to wait for Claude's cue to join him and Flip.

"You asked me earlier if I was scared to go back. I'm not scared of being incarcerated, but I don't ever want to be confined. If I do go back, it's going to be because of a technical violation, not the shit we just did, you feel me? I don't plan on being a criminal for the rest of my life, but for now, the risks we take is going to do nothing but reap rewards," Claude said, stopping the car. He called Tank and cued him to follow.

"We here," he told Flip.

" I guess the motherfucker smelled money from around the corner or he been stalkin' his window since I called him," Claude said, responding to his vibrating cell phone. He was just about to call the dude.

"Yo," Claude answered.

"Another car pulling up?" Red asked.

"Any second now."

"Back them cars up in the garage."

"Alright." Claude ended the call and called Tank.

"Back the car in after I back mine. Back it up right in the garage," Claude instructed as he waited for Tank. When Tank arrived, the garage doors opened.

After hearing instructions from Red Jones, the street mortician, Claude backed his car in, followed by Tank. The crooked bastard lost his license because of the stack of bodies he held at his funeral home for nonpayment from his customers. Instead of burying the deceased in plots, the fucker would come back and get the body from the cemetery hours after a funeral. He'd just store the bodies in the funeral home until payment was made.

When Lester, his friend for over thirty years, called and told him about some big money, he was all ears. Everything about Red was amoral, especially the way he used to conduct his business with his funeral parlor. Red had a medium build with a protruding gut hanging over the belt of his waistline. He was wearing a dirty baseball cap. His wild, frizzled, light brown hair stuck out of it. The heavy bags under his droopy eyes signified hardship. The scar over his throat was the price he had to pay for blatantly disrespecting the dead. A relative of the deceased he was dissecting caught up to his ass when the dude found out he was visiting an empty plot.

Red Jones was about that paper being that he had been out of business for seven years. It had been a constant struggle for him to make ends meet. He had nothing; he was in the core of rock bottom. He would climb out of it by using something that was supposed to be gone just like his license. He was going to use the retort that he and his criminal companions stole a week after the funeral home was shut down. He was going to use it to burn two bodies.

Claude and Tank backed the vehicles into the garage. Red gave everyone a suspicious glare because he didn't know who he spoke to on the phone, but he expected the talker to have some company with him. He felt strange doing business with people he had no idea existed, but those were the rules. He understood them thoroughly and hoped the youths understood them with clarity as well.

"How long is this shit gonna take? Can you do 'em both at the same time?" Claude asked, looking at the cremation chamber as he got out of the car. The others got out as well. He knew they weren't going to be able to leave anytime soon because of the weather, but he did want to see where his money was going.

"This shit here ain't designed for no two bodies at a time," Red said, twisting his thick, red mustache.

"What difference does it make? Niggas is going to burn regardless. It ain't like you gon' get a surprise inspection," Flip said sarcastically. He was itching to get out of Connecticut and return to his roots.

Claude beckoned Flip to chill. He knew Flip wanted to get the fuck out of dodge, and so did he, but Claude didn't want anything sloppy and wanted the snow to subside before they made any moves.

"How much do them motherfuckers weigh anyway?" Red asked, ignoring Flip's ignorance.

"Why don't you just see for yourself," Claude said. He told Tank to pop the trunk of his vehicle. Claude did the same.

Red helped Claude with Twalique's body. Zane caught a chill as the open eye corpse seemed to be staring at her. Tank and Flip pulled Domino's cadaver. The bodies were securely wrapped up in body bags. There were no signs of any blood spill in either trunk. Rigor mortis started to settle in the bodies because it was a bitch taking them out of the trunk. Two cardboard containers were ready for use. Claude and Red placed Twalique's body in one of them.

Red instructed Claude to help lift the corpse onto the retort. The temperature of the cremation chamber was already set at 1800 degrees. It was ready for use.

"Again, how long is this shit going to take?" Flip asked.

Red shot Flip a look of annoyance, but held his composure because he was thinking about the money. He couldn't blame the young man for being in a hurry. Red had done the shit numerous times and everyone's response was the same. Killers wanted to burn the bodies and slide out of there.

"I know y'all in a hurry, but the weather is fucked up and this is going to take a little more than a minute anyway. I will say two to three hours for each one. Y'all lucky they ain't bigger than they are. I cremated three, four hundred pound motherfuckers and those could take four, five hours. If y'all really want a clean slate, y'all got to be patient. If y'all want to leave, then leave, but if a man like me dropped off some bodies, I will stay my black ass there until the motherfuckers turn to ash. Make sure you placed your money in the right investment."

Claude released his hope of getting out of there early, but he did want to make sure that he was getting his money's worth.

Flip treated himself to a seat and decided that there was no use for him to bitch. Zane and Tank remained quiet. Tank was naturally a man who didn't say much. It was hard to read him. Zane, on the other hand, looked worried and regretful of what they did. It was a look that Claude had never seen. He walked behind her and massaged her shoulders. He wanted to reassure her that everything was going to be fine. Zane had a criminal grind, but she had never been associated with murder. Red saw Zane's face and became concerned, not for her, but concerned on whether she'd crack under pressure if the shit hit the fan. Flip didn't give a fuck if she was scared or not. Once he left for California, he was going to stay there.

"You alright Zane? Come on now, we need you to be strong. What's done is done, you feel me? You getting us a little nervous here," Claude whispered, away from the others.

"Don't worry about me, C. I'm just shocked that we're doing this. I just want to get this over with," she said quietly.

"It will, but just what the nigga said, we got to be patient. Just be cool and relax, you know what I mean?"

Red took notice of the discreet conversation and became paranoid.

"What's with all that goddamn whispering an' shit?" Red asked belligerently.

"Motherfucker, you just do what we paying you to do! You don't know our names and we don't care to know yours. Just handle the business. What we say under our breath ain't none of your concern," Claude snapped.

With that being said, Red humbled himself and continued to make final preparations before the first body entered the chamber. He wanted that money and couldn't think of another way to land that kind of paper.

"Since we gon' be here for a while, I know you don't mind if we smoke," Tank said, the first words that came out of his mouth since they backed the cars into the garage.

"Whatever could make y'all feel comfortable," Red said, trying to make his task easy. He didn't want any added tension. It was easy money and he'd be damned if he fucked it up.

After undressing the bodies, he made sure they didn't have

any extra shit on them, especially a pacemaker, which could blow up the entire machine. He rolled Twalique's grotesque corpse into the retort for it to be burned.

. . .

After Domino's body was thoroughly cremated, Red took an industrial sized push broom and used it to gather the rest of Domino's ashes. He placed the remains into a cremulator. He did the same procedure for Twalique. While all that was happening, Flip paced the floor while Tank and Zane watched him through their high, red eyes. Claude sat coolly in the corner of the garage, smoking his own blunt of purple haze. He felt excited when Red placed the ashes in large, zip lock bags. They were there for about four and a half hours. Claude was thankful that it didn't take longer than expected. Their cell phones rang nonstop about the grisly deaths of Link and Ty. Questions mounted about Domino and Twalique, but no one was pointing fingers.

Claude held Twalique's ashes in one hand and Domino's ashes in the other, having no remorse. He set the ashes to the side and told Tank to slide the tote bag containing sixty grand. When he did, Red thumbed through the money with greed on his face, thankful the ordeal was done.

"You have those with you?" Red asked.

Red was surprised that everyone still had on their gloves. Since they never touched any part of the guns, he didn't intend to touch the guns either, but he was going to collect some more money by discarding them.

Claude pulled out a wad of cash, knowing exactly where the man was going, and handed it to him. Red counted the money as if he were a bank teller at some point in his life. He counted seventeen hundred dollars.

"Everybody put your gun on the table," Claude told everyone. "So where are these shits going?"

Red may be grimy, but he understood the game well. Claude took his silence as confirmation.

As they gathered themselves to leave, Claude pointed to the back room where he wanted to have a private chat with Red.

"Good looking out even though I don't know who the

fuck you are. Just wanted to know that there has to be an understanding, you dig?"

Red knew what Claude was insinuating; in fact, he was going to drop it on Claude first. He felt relief when he realized the young man took the silent code as seriously as he took it.

"All day. I ain't no stranger to all of this shit. Live your life to the fullest. Sometimes we all got to do shit we don't want to do to get ahead. But yeah, ain't no snitches over here," Red said seriously.

Claude smiled and gave him a pound and a half-embrace. There was an unspoken recognition of realness between them.

"You want the crasher my homeboy pulled up in?"

Red looked at the exterior of the Toyota Corolla. He popped the hood and knew what needed to be done to make the car more durable than it was.

"Shit yeah I'll take it," Red said after closing the hood.

Claude and company took off, leaving Red feeling a little empty because he hadn't had company in a long time. His lonely thoughts turned to excitement when he thought about the money his unknown guest paid him. The money was his ticket out of New Haven.

All four of them packed into Sahara's Nissan Maxima, thankful that the storm subsided. Claude had to run through Waterbury to drop Zane and Tank off. Zane was headed to Virginia with the intention of settling. Tank was moving his mother and brother to South Carolina, his mother's homeland, so his mother could live out her years comfortably around family.

When Claude took a left and landed on Whalley Avenue, he called Jupe. He offered him a sweet deal.

53-Dallas

As soon as Claude got off the terminal in the Dallas/Fort Worth International airport, his eyes scanned for his cousin Mark. Although the many faces he glared at were unrecognizable, he was still paranoid about the murders; moreover, he still didn't want to sleep on Calvin. A man of his power could have eyes anywhere, even in the lone star state.

He checked his watch and it read 1:30am, but it was actually 12:30am because of the time zone difference. He walked the airport slowly, recalling all the events that happened early that morning. He didn't know how he felt about taking two lives, but he knew that he could do it again. He knew the consequences if he were to get caught, but it was a chance he was willing to take. The gloves came off when Twalique and Domino killed Rocks, so he knew he had to kill them before they get the chance to get at him. Operating on animal instinct, he felt exhausted after living a stint without a conscious. Twalique and Domino may have been fucked up individuals, but they were children of black women who had nothing to do with the beef.

He wondered if Mark had the time mixed up because he had been off the plane for fifteen minutes. He waited impatiently at the baggage claim, wondering why it was surprising for him to be late. Mark had always had a habit of not being on time.

Claude smiled when he thought about the expression on Jupe's face when he gave him Sahara's car as a token of his appreciation for taking him and Flip to the airport. He didn't ask any questions which was even better. The more he thought about Jupe, the more he thought about the people in Texas and how they may differ from the folks on the east coast. He hoped that they were good people. He planned on planting a few seeds so he could enjoy a new life in another environment. Although he was excited to be in Texas, he was exhausted. The day's events took a toll on his physical being; he needed to lie down. The icy road conditions also contributed to his sleepiness. He slept the entire flight and had to be woken up by the woman

347

sitting in the middle seat of the plane.

When he and Flip finally arrived at Bradley, they parted ways. Claude waited an hour before he boarded a one way flight to Dallas. When the plane landed, he turned on his cell phone. He had a few unread text messages and no calls. The first one was from Flip. He was now leaving Bradley airport. Claude snickered as he thought about his friend's anxiousness and hurry to get out of Connecticut. Three and a half hours after he and Claude arrived at Bradley, Flip was still in Windsor Locks, waiting impatiently as ever for the plane to depart.

After retrieving his bag from baggage claim, he decided that he'd stick around the terminal he got off at when the plane landed. Ten minutes later, Claude spotted Mark in the massive crowd looking around for someone. Claude walked in his direction instead of hollering his name. Mark saw Claude coming in his direction so he stood there until Claude approached him.

"It's about time motherfucker," Claude said humorously as he embraced his cousin.

"Check your phone asshole. It was a car accident on the highway. Traffic was moving slow as fuck. I'm here though," Mark said good-naturedly.

"You got your shit from baggage claim?" Mark asked.

"Yeah, but yo, did you get…"

Mark nodded his head before Claude finished the question Mark knew he was going to ask.

"Good. When did it come? Did it look like somebody tampered with it?"

"Not at all C. Let's get the fuck outta here," Mark said, grabbing a bag and wondering what the hell was in that big package Claude sent.

Claude and Mark walked coolly through the airport and onto the parking lot where Mark parked with luggage in hand. Mark had a feeling that Claude did something fucked up for him to be down there in Dallas. He was unusually quiet. There was something void and evil about him. Why would he jeopardize his parole to be out of state? Why did Claude send Sahara and Destiny to Texas? Mark was clueless to what was going on, but

Mark knew that Claude would never discuss anything illegal over the phone. There were many questions Mark would like to ask, but he didn't know what angle to approach him.

Once they got settled into the car, Mark opened a compartment of his car and pulled out some weed.

"Ah, I see you got some of that funk. How is the smoke down here anyway?"

"Ain't no different than what we smoke back home, but it's a lot cheaper down here," Mark said, backing the car out of the space.

"How cheap?"

"You could get a pound for 750."

"That's sweet as fuck."

"Yup."

"I would make a killing down here, but I heard it's hot as hell down here though. Fuck around and get locked up forever down this motherfucker."

"You heard right, but yeah, you could make a killing," Mark agreed.

"Claude, do me a favor and call your sister. She calls me over and over telling me she can't get a hold of you," Mark said, trying to get Claude to talk.

"You know how I do Mark. That is the reason why I dodged her calls. I can't afford to jeopardize my freedom for talking over the phone, you know what I mean?"

"Yeah, I hear you, but I think you could've told her something C. After all, she deserves some kind of an explanation on why you rearranged her life on short notice."

Claude didn't say anything; instead, he checked out Mark's CD collection, trying to figure out what CD to play until he landed on a mix tape.

"C, what's good man?" Mark finally asked.

"Twalique, Domino, Link, and Wiley's brother Ty…dead, that's whats good."

...

After hearing a detailed account of what happened from start to finish, Mark sat in stone silence. Mark pulled out a baggie that had a little weed left in it and placed it in a blunt wrap.

"So Claude, where did y'all leave the bodies?" Mark asked without hearing the rest of the story.

Claude looked Mark dead in his eyes.

"Had them cremated, end of story. No bodies, no case. It had to be done Mark. Niggas tried to kill me along with Rocks."

Claude got silent and looked out the window as they coasted down the highway. Mark knew that was a silent cue to drop it. Mark didn't want to know any further anyway, but he would take what Claude said to the grave with him and Claude knew that.

"How much of that fire you got at your crib?" Claude asked.

"I think I got enough for three blunts."

"Damn Mark, that ain't enough. Why don't you call your weed man and tell him to bring four pounds of that fire?"

Mark's eyes grew wide.

"You sure C? Four pounds?"

"Yeah, that's what I just said. If I came down here to get out of that dark life, I mind as well step into the light high."

"C, they got you on paper?"

"My urine hasn't been checked since the summer, but fuck all that legal shit. Call that country motherfucker and fill in the order. Is he even holdin' like that?"

"We will see."

"You got to work tomorrow?"

"Yeah, but when I get out, I'm calling out for the next three days to help y'all smoke up that choke."

"Speaking of y'all, I think I owe your sister and law an apology for calling her a bitch," Claude said admittedly.

"I think the circumstances were fucked up, but I think an apology would clear the air a little," Mark said as he pulled off from Lake Arlington and headed home.

"If that's the case, let's stop at a store. Watch your cuz in action."

"Alright, action speaks louder than words. If you could pull that, than I'll ease off the ass whippings that I will give you in 2K."

"No need for the charity. I heard Rocks use to give you a problem in 2K. I use to stomp Rocks," Claude said playfully.

"Different kind of style C, different styles, just like boxing," Mark said as he continued his focus on the road.

. . .

Sonya browsed the internet on her new lap top while sipping on a glass of wine. Since she was working half of shift in the morning, she didn't think sleep was a necessity for the moment. She felt relaxed. She felt high from the blunt roach she smoked. The strong wine added more zip to her buzz. She had just taken a shower and applied some "smell good" lotion to her flawless smooth caramel complexion. Her hair was pulled back into a ponytail where it extended to the small of her back. Her hair had grown a lot since she came home in the summer. Since she started working out after work at her job four months ago, there wasn't an ounce of body fat on her petite body. Sonya had numerous opportunities to date, but elected not to. She didn't want any drug dealers, pimps, or capos. She wanted a stable man that wouldn't offer her any drama. She wanted someone that could provide her with protection and security. Aaron was now a mere glimpse of her past. She rarely thought about him. She was thankful to God that her life was back in order.

The only gray area in her mind right now was her inability to reach Trudy. She hadn't spoken to her friend since she warned her about Aaron and Flex's possible involvement with a mass homicide. She felt like something wasn't right. If Sonya would just dig a bit deeper, she would find out the shit that she really didn't want to know. She figured that if she didn't hear any word by now, then she must be okay.

After shutting down her laptop, she heard the front door opening. She knew it was Mark and his cousin from Connecticut, but she really wasn't in any hurry to rush out there and meet the man that called her a bitch.

"This is quite a pad man. Is the rent high in these shits? Y'all got a balcony too?!" Claude looked around in awe in the spacious living quarters.

Fatima came out of the bedroom to finally be able to meet Claude. She had heard so much about him that she felt that she knew him.

"Hey baby," Fatima said, giving Mark a peck on the lips.

"Hi sweetheart? I want to finally introduce my cousin to you. This is my girl Fatima, Fatima, this is Claude."

"The infamous Claude. How are you? It is a pleasure to finally meet you," Fatima said civilly, giving him a hug.

"Likewise Fatima. Mark told me a thing or two about you," Claude said kindly.

"I hope it wasn't anything bad," Fatima said playfully.

"Nah, never that," Claude said, removing a rose from his bag.

"Is your sister here Fatima? I think I owe her a huge apology."

Fatima smiled when she saw the rose, knowing good and well that her sister will swallow her pride within moments.

"Yes she is. Sonya, come out here and meet Mark's cousin," Fatima yelled.

There were ruffling noises behind the door before she opened it. She stood in the doorway, looking at the man that verbally insulted her. She told herself that she would give him the cold shoulder until he apologized. However, the more she looked at Mark's cousin, the more her guard dropped. She hoped that he didn't discover her reckless eyeballing. She couldn't believe how handsome he was. Mark showed Sonya and Fatima some young pictures of Claude from back in the day, but to Sonya, he looked extremely different. The thin young boy she saw in the pictures turned into a hard body heartthrob.

"Hi Sonya," Claude said, his deep voice music to Sonya's ears. "I'm glad that I finally get to meet you, but I want to apologize for calling you a bitch. I was wrong for displacing my anger out on you."

Claude walked up to her and presented her with the rose. When she accepted it, he gave her a hug and a kiss on the cheek. Sonya beamed because she didn't expect any token of kindness by the so-called ruthless man that Mark described. His cologne scent made her want to stay attached to his person. She could just die in his arms.

"Apology accepted. It is nice to meet you, and I am sorry

about your friend's passing," Sonya said politely, her Texan accent turning Claude on. Sonya tossed her cold shoulder attempt out the window. Mark and Fatima smiled because they knew there was definitely instant chemistry between them.

"He is in a better place." Claude captured her beauty instantly. Her chinky eyes were mesmerizing. Enticing. His eyes were stranded on hers and vice versa. He couldn't believe that he called her a bitch. The unsettling silence bothered him. "Now that we got the air clear on that, I'm pretty sure your homeboy would come out this late for a few pounds."

"That's only if he got it like that," Mark said as he dialed the weed man's number.

"Got it like what baby?" Fatima asked Mark.

"Like havin' four pounds of weed."

"Four pounds of weed?" Fatima was excited.

"Yeah, if homeboy pick up the phone," Claude stated.

Sonya didn't know what kind of attraction she was developing for Claude, but she didn't want to seem noticeable. She knew what Claude was all about and wanted to stand clear of him to avoid looking like a hypocrite. She told herself that she didn't want to deal with anyone who was a felon, and most importantly, anyone who was currently in a life of crime. She found herself drawn to him and she had only been in his presence for three minutes.

"What up Billy? I think we need to gain about two pounds to make weight. Can you do that," Mark asked his supplier.

"Maybe," Billy said suspiciously because he never sold Mark anything above an ounce.

"I got your vibe and you should know me better than that dawg, but there is someone of interest that doesn't go below the weight limit, you know what I mean? The cost of livin' up north is higher down here."

Billy understood Mark loud and clear.

"Alright, but can you give me an hour 'cause I got to go get that from the promoter."

"We'll be here," Mark said before hanging up.

"We need to grab some Dutches…lots of them," Claude said.

"We'll be back," Mark said to the women.

"While we're out, I got to call…"

Claude's phone vibrated.

"Speakin' of the motherfuckin' devil," Claude said evenly before answering the phone.

"Yeah," Claude answered.

"C, what the hell happened with Ty and Link?" Sahara asked loudly.

"I heard, but I will see you tomorrow or in the near future," Claude said. He shifted his response on purpose because he knew where she was going with the conversation.

"What do you mean you'll see me tomorrow? You're not planning on comin' down here, do you? You are on parole. And why is Mark actin' like he don't know shit. He picked me up from the airport, dropped me off at Aunt Pearl's house, and played dumb ever since," Sahara said with growing agitation.

"Because he doesn't have any information to give you Sahara. And for your information, I am down here, but I'll talk…"

"You are on fucking parole Claude!"

Sahara said that so loud that Claude felt that all eyes were on him, but when he looked at everyone, they weren't paying him any mind accept for Sonya, who secretly wondered who he was talking to. She hoped that it wasn't his girlfriend or jump-off. Claude's eyes met hers, but he looked away.

"Sahara, I will tell you everything tomorrow. I can't talk right now," Claude said.

"Keeping me in the fucking dark! I am your damn sister!" Sahara blasted before hanging up on him.

"Damn," Claude said dejectedly, putting his phone in his pocket.

"I will bring you over there in the morning. She flipped on me yesterday. That's exactly why I told you to call her."

"You okay?" Fatima asked, being nosy. She knew Sonya was probably dying to know.

"Yeah, it was just my sister talking shit," Claude said. "It ain't nothin' new."

"Baby, can you bring back a Kit Kat?" Fatima asked.

"You want anything Sonya?" Mark asked.

"Yeah, bring me back some Skittles."

When Claude followed Mark outside the front door, Sonya kept her eyes on Claude's back. When he turned around, their eyes met again. Sonya smiled bashfully while Fatima witnessed the exchange. When Claude closed the door, Fatima looked at her sister and displayed every tooth she had.

"Girl, look at you. That man has not been here for no more than ten minutes and he already got you sprung," Fatima said humorously.

"You need to stop. I ain't paying him any mind. You called me out here to introduce myself and I did. That doesn't mean I'm digging him like that," Sonya fronted.

"You better tell that to someone who doesn't know any better," Fatima said with a smile as she stopped near the entrance to her bedroom. "By the way, you going to work in the morning?"

"Yeah, but I'm getting out early. You?"

"No. I'm about to call out. Two pounds of weed is on its way," Fatima said excitedly.

"I'm joining y'all, but not for very long. I want to get in some decent rest before goin' to work," Sonya said, walking back to her room.

"Maybe Claude could help you get some sleep," Fatima teased.

"Whatever Fatima," Sonya said with a huge smile on her face. She closed the door and walked to the mirror above her dresser and did some modifications to her face. As soon as she picked up some perfume, she set it down and thought about Aaron. Aaron approached her with good mannerisms, but turned out to be one of the most dangerous individuals she knew. Life was about taking chances, she thought as she continued to look into the mirror. *Lets see how Mr. Claude acts during the time he is down here,* she thought devilishly. She was curious about Claude and wanted to get to know him. She didn't find any wrong in that.

"Slow this goddamn shit down Ali! A nigga just got home and I don't want to see any boys in blue," Flip spat angrily.

Ali switched lanes on East 10 repeatedly, tailgated other drivers, and he almost smashed into the front passenger side of an eighteen wheeler rig. Wade sat in the back, happy that Flip spoke out about Ali's reckless driving. If it were Wade that told him to slow down, Ali would have blatantly ignored him and continue to drive dangerously.

"Flip, I haven't seen you years and you already talking shit. Why don't you smoke a joint and chill out," Ali said playfully. Ali didn't like anyone trying to control the way he drove, but he slowed down out of respect for his older relative.

"Your little ass is drivin' this big ass boat like it's a bike. If you slow down, I could relax," Flip said.

Ali had a feeling that he probably would clash with his cousin some time down the line. He had been gone for almost ten years and he was already talking his shit. He held his mouth tight as Flip ran his mouth.

"Whose these niggas we 'bout to see? I hope y'all motherfuckers didn't recruit no fake ass generals."

"Come on man, I ain't gonna put anybody behind a trigger if they were never behind it before. Trust me, these niggas is on point," Ali said convincingly.

Flip snarled his face and looked at Ali.

"Yeah, just like Earl and B-Bum. Them niggas was supposedly on point. They got lit up just like my brother. Don't kick that on point shit. Where the fuck were you at when that shit went down?"

Ali looked at his cousin evenly.

"Where the fuck were you?" Ali shot back.

Flip looked at Ali like he wanted to bash his face through the window. He didn't want to because Ali was driving, but if he would have said that on solid ground, he would have stomped Ali into the Earth.

As an outsider, Wade knew and felt that Ali hit a spot with his comment. Wade blew a sigh of relief when Flip stopped grilling Ali and continued to scan his environment. Ali didn't get hit because Flip knew he was right. He was all the way across the continent doing a bid. He couldn't blame Ali for what happened to Colin. Flip told Colin on numerous occasions to keep Ali close, but Colin didn't want to fuck with Ali like that, although it wasn't personal. Ali didn't complain because Colin kept a grip in his pocket for doing other shit. Flip thought that if Ali was around his brother, he wouldn't be underneath the Earth. Ali may be a liability, but he was a lot more street savvy than Colin. Ali would have detected some bullshit and drew first blood. It took Colin's death for Flip to understand how valuable Ali was.

Wade was surprised that Ali didn't move Flip with the comment. Wade figured it might have been a lot of truth to what Ali said. If Flip would have attacked him, Flip's guilt would have been confirmed.

"So you stepping on a nigga when he's down?" Flip asked.

"It ain't any different then what your doing to me. You can't put that shit on me just like I can't put that shit on you. I always told that motherfucker to watch the people he had around him. It was up to him to listen," Ali said truthfully.

"I hope these motherfuckers is as murderous as you say they are," Flip said, lighting a cigarette. He didn't feel there was a need to press the issue further.

"Trust my judgment Flip, but what the fuck took you so long? Got up this early in the fuckin' morning. I thought you would be here earlier," Ali said.

"I had to put some work in for my man. And boy, did a nigga make out!"

"What kind of work?"

"A few one eighty sevens."

"I guess you needed some target practice that would prepare you for this super nigga," Ali said, his words dripping with sarcasm.

"I taught you a lot of shit and you know that I wouldn't kick out instructions from across the country without a reasoning. Y'all niggas ain't ready for a nigga like that, now you trust me. He ain't just your average, typical thug," Flip said.

Ali started to get pissed. He hadn't seen his cousin in years and he was already telling him what he was or wasn't capable of handling. Ali also felt the fumes from the backseat. Wade just met Flip not even a half hour ago and he was already offended by what he said, but he wasn't going to sleep on Flip's statement.

"Lots of shit done changed Flip. Don't make assumptions that could blow up in your face," Ali said, getting off of exit 13 off of East 10.

"Don't be a loudmouth Ali. You know I hate loudmouths," Flip said, seeing where Ali's head was. He knew exactly what he was doing. A lot had changed, but he can still control Ali. He knew he hit a few switches with his cousin, but now Ali and Wade were in positions where they would have to prove their worth. Aaron was, in Flip's opinion, an expert at beef. He wouldn't keep his eyes closed on a cat like that. He never gave Ali the full details about him, but he will find out soon. *Maybe it's a good thing Aaron is out of town. Gives me time to add some finesse to the blueprint,* Flip thought.

. . .

Ali pounded on the apartment door like it was the police. Flip and Wade waited patiently behind him wondering when the motherfuckers were going to open the door. A moment later, someone was undoing the locks from the other side of the door before they finally opened it, exposing the mess-stricken apartment. Empty bottles of beer, weed, cocaine, trash, CDs, DVDs, and other types of shit were accumulated in big piles of clutter. Dishes were piled up in the sink that still had "days" old food on them. A combination of weed and cigarettes made the apartment smell like an after hours night club that blended in with the smell of shit. The three visitors turned their noses up because of the horrid smell.

"It smells like shit in here. Niggas been fartin' in an apartment with the motherfucking windows closed," Ali said.

"Fartin' my ass! This nigga took a shit two hours ago after I told him that the toilet didn't flush," Blast said, referring to Needles.

"You goddamn right. It took me damn near a half hour to

get over here and I'm still not granted with the privilege of takin' a shit in peace. Who the fuck has a toilet that doesn't flush?" Needles asked with sarcasm.

Everyone laughed except Flip, who stood stone-faced against the wall with a cigarette between his fingers.

Needles was born Jonathon Hawkins, but the street gave him the nickname "Needles" because of his malnourished appearance. He was a twenty two year old dusty and dirty looking dude that looked as if he hadn't showered since the summer. His nose always ran because of his coke habit.

"Hell yeah, fuck that," Needles continued, unintentionally changing the subject. "I'm praying for that Puerto Rican dude to be in there. I don't like him and wouldn't mind peeling his motherfucking cap back."

Flip looked at Dungeon and Needles like they crawled from beneath a rock.

"This is the shit I'm talking about. Y'all young niggas is taken this shit personal instead of looking at the big picture. I could see motherfuckers digging their own grave," Flip said dejectedly.

Needles gave Flip the screw face.

"Who the fuck asked you? We don't recall anybody talking to your bitch ass," Needles said belligerently.

Blast, who was sitting near the window, recognized Flip at first glance. He shook his head and knew Needles life was in possible danger for coming out of his face. Blast heard stories about Flip and hoped that Needles didn't voluntarily be the dummy out of a reenactment.

"Chill motherfucker. He's been putting in work since the days you couldn't leave your backyard," Ali said as he lit a cigarette.

"Those days are over. Niggas is goi…"

Flip jammed the pistol Ali just gave him into Needles's mouth. A few of his teeth were on the floor from the impact of the gun. Blast and Dungeon fell back because they knew better.

"Niggas is going to do what?!" Flip had a murderous look in his eyes. He had been in the air all night and wasn't in any kind of mood to take anyone's bullshit, especially by some young cats who had no respect for authority.

"Can't talk with a gun in your mouth, can you?! Look nigga, we gon' do this shit the way I want it to be done! Fucking with these marks, you'd be one dead ass nigga! If you ever disrespect me like that again, it ain't gonna be any warnings, now go sit the fuck down!" Flip took the gun out of Needle's mouth, grabbed him by the back of the neck, and forcefully shoved him onto the aged coffee table, snapping it in half. A gram of some broken up weed disappeared into the once-white, filthy carpet.

"Anybody else got a fucking problem?" Flip asked, looking squarely at Dungeon and Blast. The silence indicated their answer.

"You," Flip said to Blast. "You look familiar; you ain't Spyder's little brother, are you?" Blast was light skinned and of medium height. His dark hair was cut into a taper and he had a thin eyebrows. Blast was a spitting image of his brother.

"Yeah," Blast answered quietly.

"Don't be a loudmouth like your homeboy on the floor," Flip said, pointing at Needles. Flip used to put in work for Spyder years ago until he caught an eight forty eight charge (continuing criminal enterprise).

Dungeon watched the entire incident with a closed mouth because he didn't want any problems. Flip may have respect in the hood, but Dungeon didn't think Flip had the right to manhandle his homeboy. Although he kept his lips tight, he was far from being afraid of Flip, Ali, or Wade. The men could provide him a path to the money. That was the only thing that mattered. He heard Aaron stories, but no man or thing was going to stop him from getting paid. Even though Needles got roughed up by an older, wiser OG, Needles was heartless and desensitized. Dungeon knew it would be a while before he got over Flip mushing him to the floor, but he would have to take it on the chin and keep his eyes on the prize.

Dungeon wasn't anything different than Needles, but Dungeon had a little bit more sense. Only twenty years old, he had brown skin and only stood five seven. He had a series of razor bumps. He always wore shades, even when the days were gray. He had four bodies under his belt; Needles assisted him with two of them. He wasn't going to get far in life and he knew it. He just got home from Folson a month and a half ago. Dungeon and his two comrades were heartless and would run up in the White House with guns blazing if the price was right.

Since his meal ticket was on the hit list, Wade secretly embraced Flip's arrival. He had a feeling that being on Flip's team would only generate him more money. Even though Flip talked shit and criticized him and Ali, Flip can formulate more money making schemes then his simple mind could ever muster. Wade liked Flip's plan of getting at Aaron's people and not make any noise. His ear was opened from the time they picked Flip up from the airport until they reached the filthy apartment.

"I'm sure Ali told y'all about that nigga being out of town, which is good, 'cause we gon' make sure he come back and find himself alone 'cause we gon' wipe 'em out," Flip said coldly. "Timing is the key though. When do y'all link up and discuss business," he asked Ali.

"We just did two days ago, why?"

"Because there is gonna be some money missing out of a few stash spots, maybe a house could come up short two, three days in a row. Money shortage calls for a meeting. Once everybody is there, we holocaust them fools," Flip said sinisterly.

"No loud shots, just silencers. We gonna do 'em just like they did to my cousin and 'em," Ali finalized, summarizing what Flip told him on the way to the apartment.

Flip felt Needles digging a hole in his grill with his beady eyes.

"Is there still a problem? My gun would be the first to go off and the last one to smoke?"

"He straight," Dungeon shot.

"What the fuck? Is he your bitch or something cuz? This nigga could speak for himself," Flip said evenly.

"Ain't no problem," Needles said irately. Droplets of blood leaked out of his nose.

Ignoring him, Flip continued to scheme. He had everyone's undivided attention when he started talking about money and lavish living.

"All y'all gotta do is stick to the script and nothing could go wrong. Questions? Problems with me running shit? Niggas got other plans? What up?" Flip asked. He wanted to let them know who was in charge. No one said a word.

"Good. Let's go," Flip said to Ali and Wade.

. . .

Sonya couldn't believe the foul curse words coming from Claude's mouth as he tossed and turned while he talked in his sleep. She didn't know the reasoning of his arrival, but she could tell it was something major. Claude had been sleep since two thirty in the morning after the group circulated three blunts. Twelve hours later, Claude was snoring, grinding his teeth, and cursing someone out in his vivid nightmare.

Sonya just came home from work. In any normal circumstance, she would have come home around five, but she requested a half day to do some well-needed shopping. She planned on taking a shower, getting dressed, and hitting the mall. She wouldn't mind having some company, which was why she was pondering the idea of waking him up. Sonya had been thinking about Claude all day. She knew there was danger lurking around him, but there was something about him that seemed magnetic. When they all chilled last night, she expected him to drop war stories and talk a report about himself, but he proved her wrong, at least for last night. She thought that Claude was far removed from how Mark described him, but she remembered that he was in Texas for a reason.

She looked at Claude's resting body and fought with the decision of waking him, but she didn't want to seem too pushy or desperate. She didn't want to display the slight interest in him, but she knew she was going through symptoms of being wide open. As she debated, Claude's cell phone rang loudly on the glass table in the living room. After it rang six times, Claude popped up out of his sleep. Sonya figured he must have had one of those near death dreams because he was dripping with sweat. The phone stopped ringing, but Claude was wide awake. Sonya turned her attention to the mess in the kitchen to avoid looking like a stalker.

"Good morning," Claude said with a smile, despite

looking at the look Rocks had on his face when he was murdered. He had been dreaming about that incident since it happened.

"You mean good afternoon," Sonya corrected.

"Damn, what time is it?"

"Quarter to three. Mark and Fatima left two, maybe three hours ago to look at houses. I guess he didn't want to wake you."

"What time did you get in?" he asked.

"Like ten minutes ago. Do you always sleep this late?"

"Not at all. I haven't slept this late since I was locked up."

Claude turned the TV on and was relieved that he didn't have to find SportsCenter because Mark was watching it this morning while Claude snored.

"So," Sonya started. "Do you have any plans today?"

"I'm down for whatever. I'm a guest in your home state. What's poppin' wit' you? Have any plans?"

Claude marveled on how fine Sonya was. The more he looked at her, the more he wanted to get to know her. She was exactly his type. She was petite, light-skinned, and had it going on for herself. He needed a road dawg in his life, not just a simple "fuck." Mark gave Claude vague details about Sonya leaving her man out in California, but he vowed to find out how crazy a man was for leaving his treasure unattended for another man to discover. He knew he was nothing more than a criminal, but he would tell her everything she wanted to know about him, excluding the murders, in due time. He didn't want to tell her about the money he got stashed because he wanted her to like him for who he was. He would release that if she got situated with him and if there was a feeling of trust.

Last night, over a few hands of Spades, Mark and Fatima turned in to get some sleep. Sonya stayed out in the living room and kept Claude company. She introduced vague details about herself, and Claude did the same, including mentioning Big Chris and the reason for his incarceration. He would have never told her if she didn't ask. During the conversation, Sonya noticed he was drifting until he finally fell asleep. She had decided that it was time for her to go to bed. When she left

Claude alone, she went into her room and pulled out an extra blanket for him.

"I want to do a little shopping and have lunch. My mother is cooking gumbo tonight. Wanna come?" she asked.

Claude smiled.

"Your accent is sexy," Claude said, looking her straight in her eyes.

"Awe, thank you so much."

"Can you give me a little time to shower and get dressed? It won't take any longer than fifteen minutes," he said.

"Well, I was hoping you could roll something while I shower. I have all these germs on me from this hospital and I got to jump in there fast," she said.

"Sure, you do that," Claude said as he got up to check his phone. When he did, he had ten missed calls; one from Mark and the others came from Sahara.

"Oh, call Mark. He tried to call you when he left, I think your sister called also," she said before leaving the living room.

"Yeah, I'm gonna call him while you shower," Claude said, knowing exactly why Mark called. Mark was going to tell him the whereabouts of the large package in Fatima and Mark's walk-in closet. He wasn't in any hurry to talk to his pissed off sister, but he couldn't dodge her forever. *Damn, she even called the house phone.*

When Claude heard the shower running, he saw it as an opportunity to call his sister. He couldn't blame her for being heated, but it looked a lot better when there was life altering money involved, with an additional eighty four thousand dollars. He didn't like keeping her in the dark, but she had to be kept there until the dust settled.

"Sahara, what's up?" Claude said, expecting a tongue lashing.

"You tell me C," Sahara said evenly. "What is going on and I want to know now."

"Can't tell you anything over the phone, but everything is all good," he said.

"Is that right? Everything can't be all that good for you to suddenly change our lives," Sahara said sternly. She was fuming.

"It was only for the good," Claude said in a low-tone. He put on his slippers and jacket and stepped outside so Sonya wouldn't hear him. "I don't know why you so fidgety being that we sitting on some life-altering cheddar and that attitude of yours still didn't subside. What the fuck?! I sent y'all down here for a goddamn reason."

"Everything ain't about money Claude, so fuck you and that blood money 'cause it ain't all about that! It's about that little girl in the next room who doesn't have a fuckin' clue on what's going on. She's in school one day and absent the next five."

"Why didn't you enroll her?! I didn't give you all that money to make a living in Waterbury. You're the one that's always cryin' about Waterbury not having shit and how depressing the shit is. Why can't you take it for what it is?" Claude said, opening the front door to hear if Sonya was in the shower.

"Take it for what it is Claude? You got me and my daughter down here without a fuckin' reason and you're telling me to take it for what it is? Fuck you Claude," Sahara shot with venom.

"Fuck me? It would have been real fucked up if y'all was up here when niggas broke into the fuckin' house! If y'all was up there, those cocksuckers would have held y'all for ransom!"

Claude said that a little louder than he had to. He covered the phone, opened the front door again and still heard the shower running. There was a dead silence between them.

"You ain't got nothin' to say now, huh," Claude said harshly.

"Somebody broke into the house?"

"That's what I said," Claude answered. "Look, I don't mean to come at you like that, but there are a lot of things that I had to do that will leave permanent scars on my conscious, but I did what I had to do and I have no regrets. I know you want to know, but I can't talk over the phone. Can you have a little patience?"

"It's been like a week. How much patience do you want me to have?" Sahara said forcefully.

"Why don't you count your stack and come over today to count the stacks that I sent down here while you're waiting," Claude said sarcastically, hoping to decrease some of the tension between the both of them.

"Once again, this isn't about the money. Rocks got killed and somebody you associate yourself with is dead. Tommy is in jail and that heist y'all pulled off might be related. Now you're telling me the house got broken into. Why C? To kill you? I got Destiny over here scared to death because she thinks you're in danger. I swear to God, you better tell me something Claude because I know its more than that heist. I would never put you in a situation like this without providing some kind of explanation. You owe it to me and you owe it to her," Sahara said tearfully. Sahara was fearful for her brother's life, as well as his freedom. Destiny walked into the room, wondering who her mother was talking to and walked towards her. She hugged Sahara while she talked.

"Mommy, is that Uncle C?" Destiny asked.

"Yes, but he's busy…"

"I want to talk to Uncle C," she said loudly. Lately, Destiny's behavior took a turn for the worst. It was coming to a point where Sahara felt she was losing her.

"Sahara, put Destiny on the phone."

Sahara sighed and handed Destiny the cordless.

"Hi Uncle C! Are you coming over today? I miss you," Destiny said joyfully.

"I miss you too sweetheart, but I need you to be strong right now Des. I'm alive and well. I may see you sooner than you think. I know that attitude of yours better change or I ain't getting that bike you wanted."

"I'll promise I'll be good," she said excitedly.

"Nah, I don't think you deserve it," Claude said, using psychology. "You keep givin' your mother a hard time. What did I tell you about disrespecting her? If that shit doesn't stop, you won't get nothin' else from me, do you understand?"

"But I…"

"Do you understand?" Claude asked again.

"Yes Uncle C," Destiny said obediently.

"Now put your mother back on the phone, now you be good now, you hear?"

After Destiny complied tearfully, she handed her mother back on the phone.

"I gotta go," Claude said, trying to rush her off the phone before Sonya got out of the shower.

"Don't catch amnesia."

She hung up.

Claude went back inside. He heard Sonya in her bedroom and hoped that she didn't hear him raise his voice when he was talking to his sister. He grabbed his duffle bag and dug into it. He pulled out what he wanted to wear.

An hour later, they were ready to make moves to the mall. Claude wore brown khaki pants, a black Ralph Lauren sweater, and a pair of dressy low-cut black Timberlands. Sonya wore light blue, boot cut jeans that exposed the full length of her ass, a green scoop-neck knit sweater, and a pair of medium-cut black leather boots.

"I don't even know what to say. You look beautiful."

"So beautiful that you could just eat me," Sonya asked flirtatiously. She quickly regretted saying that. Since Aaron raped her, her desire to have sex dwindled, but just the mere sight of Claude made her get wet. She was allowing her guard to slip. Claude was mesmerized by her appearance and vice versa. Claude's smile was wide because the feelings were mutual. Sonya felt she gave him a little too much by saying that.

"I'm just playing, but thank you," she said softly. "You don't look too bad yourself."

"There is truth in every joke," Claude said slyly, smiling radiantly.

She believed that Claude was the sexiest man alive. She could see the outline of his chest through his sweater. His hair was shaped up, including his mustache and goatee. His hair was dark and his waves were spinning.

"Whatever," Sonya said, shaking her head playfully.

After she retrieved her pocketbook off the counter, they headed out.

. . .

After nearly two hours of shopping, Claude and Sonya got hungry and stopped at T.G.I. Fridays to have lunch in the North Park Experience mall. During their shopping, their conversation shifted from general things such as likes and dislikes to Sonya's reasoning on why she moved back to Dallas. Of course, Claude knew about her situation, but not in full detail. Mark put a bug or two in his ear about her, but nothing too revealing. Claude listened as she explained the beatings and rape in full detail, which caused her to have an emotional moment because of a past she was trying to keep behind her. Claude gave her a long, tight hug as she became teary-eyed. She felt a safe haven in his arms. She didn't want to let him go, but she did to avoid looking vulnerable.

"Thank you," Claude said politely to the waiter who sat them down at a booth.

"You know what you're ordering?"

"The spicy southern shrimp. I get the same thing every time I come here," he said. You?"

"I'm ordering the honey pecan salmon. I don't order the same thing, but I've been in the mood for some salmon," she said.

"What else are you in the mood for," Claude flirted.

Sonya smiled at him. Claude looked at her hands and would do anything to put one of her fingers in his mouth. He had dreamed about beautiful women with warm personalities on lonely days, months, and years of being in prison. His dream was directly in front of his face. He wondered how he could keep a woman like that around while trying to fight for his life and freedom. She was stunning and could have any man she wanted. Why would she settle for someone that didn't have the privilege of leaving his home state without repercussions? He didn't want to re-live that Darlene incident over again.

"Boy, you need to stop being fresh," she said good-naturedly, but loving every minute of it.

Sonya watched Claude look over the alcohol menu, wondering why she was so crazy about him. She gave him her story; it was time for Claude to drop his. When she opened her mouth to ask him, the waiter arrived at their table, pen and pad ready. They sealed their orders with alcohol. Claude ordered a Hennessy and Coke and Sonya requested the White Russian.

"So Mr. Porter, I'm still waiting to hear your story," she said.

"I was locked up for the last fifteen years, just got out this past summer. Don't have much of a work history other than that job I got fired from because I lied on my application, fell back into the game and now I'm down here."

The waiter came back and placed their drinks on the table.

"Why are you down here?" Sonya pressed.

He took a long swig of his beer and looked her right in her eyes. He prepared for the questions he knew she would want to know, but he didn't prepare for the one she just asked. He wanted to be honest with her, but not honest enough to tell her that he just murdered two people. If he told her about the heist, she would know that he had money. He figured he'd take more of a neutral approach.

"Things just got hectic, that's all. The only state that I have been to outside of Connecticut is New York. I just needed to see another side of life, you know what I mean? I haven't breathed this easy in a long time Sonya," Claude said, taking another sip.

He was holding back on something, Sonya figured as she tasted her White Russian. She decided not to press him. This was her second day of being in that man's presence and there was no need to place him under the red light. She did, however, knew that Claude shot someone. That was one of the stories Mark provided, but she never asked Mark why. His sister and his niece were down here for a reason. *He must have done something crazy for him to move his sister and his niece down here.*

"Ok, but I have to ask you one more thing and I promise I won't bug you anymore," she said.

"Ask away, but I can't promise you the answer that you want, but I'll try to be as honest as I can."

"Why did you shoot someone," she asked.

"Because I thought I could get away with it," he said evenly.

"Do you think it is possible to get away with murder?" She

thought about Aaron.

"It's very possible," Claude said, thinking about the moment he pulled the trigger on Twalique and Domino.

"When was the last time you went out on a date?" Claude purposely changed the subject.

"Since I was with my ex."

"So since you've been home, you haven't been out with anyone?"

"I gave you my story Claude. I'm trying to get my life back in order. A man wasn't on my mind during that time," she said truthfully. "So what's up with your love life? Any jump-offs? Potential?"

"I had a few jump-offs, but that's a wrap."

"She was just a jump-off to you? She didn't have any potential?"

He chuckled. "We had potential fifteen, sixteen years ago, but that was thrown out of the window when she came up to the prison and told me she was pregnant. Don't get me wrong though; we were young. I just couldn't get over the fact that it only took her a year to have someone else's baby while I'm locked up. For her to fuck someone, it's natural. But to get pregnant, nah, I couldn't have that. You would think that I was five years in, you feel me?"

More than you think. "I understand, but why rekindle if she crossed the line?"

"Truthfully," he smiled. "I was fresh home from jail after doing a dime; you do the math."

"So you used her."

"Just two consenting adults having sex. Keep in mind Sonya that she was willing to leave her child's father and her son to pursue something with me. If someone could leave their family for someone that doesn't love you the way you want to be loved, she could leave me for the next man. The same shit she did to me when I was on lockdown."

"So what happened next?" she asked, licking the creamy alcohol off the straw.

"I fell back because she was getting obsessed. To make shit worst, she told her baby father what we were doing and..."

"You knocked him out," she finished for him.

"So you mind as well ask Mark about me. I officially declare him my representative," Claude said jokingly.

"Nothing too invasive, just the outline of your life, but I'm not judging' you. Mark just told us his cousin knocked somebody out at the club, but that was it. No one is perfect Mr. Porter."

"You are the only one that can call me Mr. Porter and get away with it." Claude laughed because she sounded funny and sexy when she said Mr. Porter.

The waiter came back with their meals. Claude asked for refills on the drinks. They talked, laughed, and joked while they enjoyed their meals. At the conclusion of their lunch, Sonya excused herself from the table to go to the bathroom. While Claude waited for the waiter to come back to their table with the bill, Claude couldn't believe how much he'd missed while being locked away. He loved everything about Texas so far and would love to make the state his home, but he knew he had to find his piece of the pie by investing in something that could generate revenue. Why not? He had the money to do it. He could invest the money that he had in his bag at the house and make something happen, never mind the money he sent Mark, which was still packed and sealed in a box. Many possibilities crossed his mind about establishing himself in Dallas. Since he had a self-made security blanket, he figured he could go back to school since he'd already earned a few college credits in prison. If Sonya was who she was cracked up to be, a relationship with a woman of her knowledge, education, independence, and beauty made the plan remarkable.

After he paid the bill, he looked around for Sonya because he didn't know what direction she took to go to the bathroom. During his search, his eyes rested upon a black man that seemed as if he couldn't take his eyes off of him. He looked away for a moment and continued to look around for Sonya, but then his eyes shifted back to the man's person. The dark skinned, tall man looked at Claude like he stole something from him. Claude refused to take his eyes of the man because he took that as a challenge. Claude and the dark-skinned man locked eyes. Both of the men refused to back down. *Who is this motherfucker?* Claude couldn't understand what the dude's beef was. He decided to be the bigger man and ignore the guy.

Sonya came from behind Claude and sat down. She noticed a peculiar look on Claude's face.

"Are you ok?" she asked.

"Yeah, I'm good," he said, looking in the dude's direction, but he wasn't there. "Some cat that was standing over there was looking at me like I owed him some dough," Claude said in a low tone.

"Maybe he was feeling ya," Sonya said jokingly. She looked in the direction where Claude pointed and didn't see anyone. "Did the waiter come by the table?"

"Everything is already taken care of," he said, still looking around for the dude that grilled him.

"That was so sweet of you. I asked you to join me, but you end up paying for our meals," she said thankfully.

"Stop. Its nothing," he said, getting out of his seat.

After looking around another time without Sonya knowing, they picked up their bags and left the restaurant. They stopped by a few more stores before leaving the mall. Sonya drove around Dallas and Fort Worth, playing the role as a tour guide as she exposed him to sights such as the new Cowboy stadium. Later on during the evening, they stopped at a bar, drank, and continued to enjoy each others company, developing a flame to go with it.

. . .

"Hello," Flex answered.

"I just saw this bitch with another nigga," Aaron said like he just ran up a flight of stairs.

"Come on man, what do you expect? You haven't seen her since the summer and she left you. Just handle the business and come back."

Aaron opened his mouth to talk massive shit, but held his own tongue because he knew Flex was right. When he saw her leave the apartment this morning, he felt tempted to approach her, but it would have defeated the purpose of him being in Texas. He was there to kill her, not reconcile. Sonya knew something. If she didn't, Trudy would be alive.

"Who's this nigga anyway?" Flex asked without thinking.

"How the fuck should I know? Am I from down here? Goddamn you ask some dumb shit sometimes!" Aaron blasted, displacing his anger out on his cousin.

"Don't get mad at me because you just ran into some truth," Flex said nonchalantly.

"You asking me like I should know! Look, I didn't call to argue; imagine seeing you're old bitch with another nigga," Aaron said.

"I don't have to imagine," Flex said eerily, thinking about Trudy's betrayal.

"Is everything flowing right? Fuck ups?" Aaron asked, catching his cousin's drift. He knew he had no right bashing his cousin because of his predicament with Sonya.

"No."

"Good. Will call you tomorrow," Aaron said before ending the call.

Aaron sat in his parked car across the street from *The Old Monk* smoking a cigarette. *I can't believe I'm across the street from this bitch.* His evil mind touched upon some warped shit. As for the dude she was with, he could get it just as bad if he stayed around long enough to find out.

Aaron looked at the entrance of the door waiting for Sonya and that dude to come out. His cell phone rang about three times before he decided to acknowledge it. He looked at the screen and cursed because it was Jimmy calling. He was in no mood to decipher his stuttering, but if Jimmy was making an effort to call, which he normally didn't, something was wrong.

"What's the word Jim?" Aaron asked.

"Th...th...th...they...just...found...Pri...Pri...Prime and Linda's bodies out on G...Gr...Grape St," Jimmy said.

"What!?

"Hold on," Jimmy said. Marco just walked through the door. Jimmy passed him the phone.

"Jim told you right."

"Yeah, but Marc, I know exactly what you're thinking, but I don't know a damn thing about that," Aaron said truthfully.

"If that's the case, somebody is gonna know something."

"Fuck do you mean by that."

"Think about it. When the fuzz start askin' questions, names is gonna be brought up."

"Fuck!" Aaron said in disbelief. Aaron was starting to be fully receptive to the news of Prime being murdered. Although he was angry at Prime for transporting Sonya to the airport, Prime was one of his best friends. Aaron felt a heavy burden of guilt. He also felt a rug underneath him slipping.

"Something ain't right Marc. Prime and Linda is fucking dead man. Keep your ear pressed to the street real hard," Aaron stressed, not in any mood to hear any more real talk.

"Alright. Will call you once I get the drop on some more shit. Call you later," Marco said before he hung up.

Aaron took out another Newport and lit it. He thought wildly on what Marco said. He hoped that Prime and Linda's murder wasn't related to what he and Flex did to Colin and them over the summer, but he knew that was only a slim chance. His cell phone chimed, indicating he had an incoming text message. It was Raven letting him know that the trip to Freddie's house went smoothly. Once he texted her back, he focused his attention on the entrance where people polluted it with cigarette smoke and their shit talk. He called Flex and gave him the news and told him to go see Prime's mother to see if she was alright. If the cops were talking to her, she might indirectly put them in a path of interrogation. They didn't need any police presence asking them shit, but in this case, it was more than likely going to happen. He sighed as the news of Prime and Linda's death and the kind of repercussions that it could lead to sunk into his head.

Once Sonya and that dude walked out, he started the car and realized that he had to do what he came here to do and make moves back to California as soon as possible. He was going to go back to Los Angeles, collect everything he had worked hard for, and slide back out of state while the storm was calm. He drove cautiously back into traffic, following his target. He called Flex and told him of the news of Prime and Linda's murder, but changed his mind about asking him to get in contact with Prime's mother. Prime's mother would get suspicious.

55-Los Angeles

Detective Taft rubbed his temples smoothly at his desk as he tried to piece together all the information he had so far regarding the unsolved murders that happened last August. A few weeks ago, he was ready to turn in his badge, papers, pride, and dignity and call it the day. When Detective Jacobs approached him with some information from the case he was working on, a wave of determination overrode his decision to retire. His wife noticed the time he was spending in his office and knew he was on to something regarding the most complex case he had ever worked on.

The day was young and his thoughts were fresh. In front of him, he had Pittman and Anderson's autopsy photos. The autopsy photos of Colin, Earl, B-Bum, and Dennis Howard were in a manila folder to his right, wondering and hoping their murders were connected. He wanted to believe that Pittman was the guy Dennis Howard was last seen with, but he still couldn't get in touch with his sister. His sixth sense told him she knew something and he was determined to find out. When he decided to make a surprise visit to her home yesterday, he knew she was there and vice versa. She saw Detective Taft standing outside holding a cup of coffee, looking up at the blinds. Raven made sure she didn't move the blinds an inch. Unbeknownst to Detective Taft, Raven was only a hair away from calling him to disclose the location of Trudy's body. She still couldn't believe Ali and Wade helped Aaron and Flex ditch it, but her comrades were doing what they had to do.

Taft chain-smoked two Marlboro cigarettes and drank two cups of coffee and it was a little after three O'clock. The other homicide detectives paced and grumbled about their own fucked up, complex cases while Detective Taft was beaming with confidence. He told the captain about the possible connection between Pittman and Anderson and the mass homicide that happened this past summer. Once the captain gave them the nod, they have been working together, even though Detective Jacobs and Rinaldi didn't get along. It was business as usual.

Detective Taft saw Jacobs walking slowly towards his desk, looking like the pure asshole he was made out to be. An older black woman in her late fifties followed his rear. He cursed Jacobs because he felt that he should have given him some kind of warning if visitors were coming. He didn't know who the hell she was. She could have been somebody from internal affairs for all he knew. The closer the two got, the more he realized that it wasn't anyone with any rank in the department.

"Ms. Pittman, allow me to introduce Detective Taft, who I may say has taken a special interest in your son's case," Detective Jacobs said cordially.

"How do you do, Ms. Pittman?" Detective Taft asked gently.

Instead of responding to Detective Taft's greeting, Ms. Pittman's eyes scanned the area around Taft's desk. She ignored the cigarette smoke and the candle as her eyes rested on the autopsy photos that were in front of him. Without seeking permission, she picked up the photo that stood out; it was a photo of Prime on the slab at the coroner's office with the entry wound, created by the bullet, to the right hemisphere of his brain. She saw the other photo that contained the image of Prime slumped over, his chin touching his chest while his eyes were opened. She put the photos back where she found them.

"Who did this to my baby?" she asked, her voice broken with tragedy of losing her only child.

Detective Taft looked into Ms. Pittman's eyes and saw nothing but sorrow. The bags under her eyes signified insomnia. Ms. Pittman, a light skinned, fifty something heavy set woman, looked like she released every tear in her system. It didn't only come from Oscar's death, but his sudden departure. She remembered her son being fine one day and being withdrawn the next. He remained in that state of mind until the last day she saw him alive. Rapid thoughts racing a few hundred laps kept her up, wondering what her son did for him to leave. Oscar was all she had. She knew her son wasn't an angel, but she didn't think he would do something so horrendous that it would cost him his life.

"Mam, I want to first offer my condolences for your son. I

have children myself and can only imagine what you're going through," Taft said sincerely.

"Thank you," she said quietly.

"May I offer you anything? Water? Coffee?"

"No. The only thing I want from you is some answers or any kind of information pertaining to my son," she said seriously.

Detective Taft nodded. "Understood. I just want to be honest with you here," he started. "The information that I have is nothing in stone. The only information I can give you could only be a mere coincidence, but it's the only solid, possible lead that we have. And whatever information you can provide would be extremely beneficial for the case."

"A theory is better than having nothing at all," she said humbly.

"Ok. Now Ms. Pittman, as I stated earlier, these are just educated guesses."

"Please Detective," she said impatiently. Taft caught her drift.

"Do you recall the murders out on Monteith last August?"

"Yes," she said. "A friend of mine lives up the street from where it happened. She was vacationing during that time."

"We interviewed the sister of one of the victims a day or so after it happened and she said she seen a light-skinned black male with her brother the night he was killed. I told my partner that it could have been any light-skinned male. That was all the information that we could go off of. We've tried repeatedly to contact her, but we were always unsuccessful. It's now February. When your son and Ms. Anderson were found, Detective Jacobs made an interesting note. Ms. Anderson is the same individual that found her male friend or lover in her car with his throat slit."

"I'm aware of that," she said coldly.

"So you knew the other victim?"

"Yes. Oscar used to see her time to time, but I didn't think it was anything serious, but I always had a strange feeling about her. I would see her hooking up and down the street. Would even see her around the house I just moved into. I asked about my baby, she didn't know, but I knew she was lying. And now my only child was found dead with that whore."

"You see Ms. Pittman, the reason why I took an interest in this case is because of the information you gave to Detective Jacobs, but I wouldn't jump to conclusions regarding Ms. Anderson. Since she was Oscar's only contact, she may have been checking up on you. You told Detective Jacobs the last time you saw Oscar was Aug 7th"," Detective Taft asked for clarification.

"Yes, that's correct."

"The murders on Monteith happened on the fifth of Aug, two days after he disappeared."

Detective Taft gave her a little time to ponder the possibility of her son's involvement. Just when one would think Ms. Pittman couldn't shed anymore tears, they started to build up in her eyes.

"Ms. Pittman, we have a time match and your son's cell phone that we found on his person. The last call that he received was from the other victim. Now, we've developed another strong theory, but like I said previously, this is not a fact, but only a guess. There may be a possibility that someone may have coerced Ms. Anderson to lure your son back from wherever he came from. We don't know if that could be a subject of retaliation or a random hit, which we totally doubt, but one thing is for sure; whenever a situation like this happens where someone coerces an individual, that individual wouldn't live to see the next day. It's collateral damage. It's a common pattern in violence," Detective Taft said before continuing. "Now I need something from you. Did you think Oscar was capable of…"

"No, No!" she interrupted abruptly. "Oscar would never kill anyone. He was no angel, but he would never kill!"

"What about those around him? Any negative influences? People you thought were up to no good?"

"Oscar didn't have too many friends, but I couldn't stop him from being around them two boys he came up with. His cousin was a follower, just like Oscar. I just think Aaron is a pure demon. Don't get me wrong, I feel for that boy, I mean, his mother getting killed while he was in an apartment was something else," she admitted.

Detective Taft narrowed his eyes, wondering if he was hearing her correctly.

"You don't mean Aaron Banks, do you? That other boy you're referring to is Walter?"

"Yes," she replied coldly.

"Not to say Aaron, Walter, or your son had anything to do with it, but do you think they are capable of gunning down four people with guns of their own, disregarding your son," he asked. While Ms. Pittman was there at the station, he was determined to squeeze the most information out of her as he could.

"I don't know," she said. "But my baby didn't kill anyone, but Aaron and Walter, I wouldn't put nothin' pass them."

"Why wouldn't you put it pass them?"

"The apple doesn't fall far from the tree. I met Aaron's mother once. It was maybe twenty-seven, twenty-eight years ago, but I remember it like it was yesterday. Aaron came at the house at eleven o'clock at night, and he may have been five or six years old at the time, probably after he stabbed that little boy in school. When I brought him home that night, his mother was high out of her mind. She acted like she didn't know he was gone, but she had no idea that he walked damn near across town to see my son. That was the only time I met or seen her because she was killed two or three months later."

"So that's why you think Aaron was capable? Because his mother got high?"

"Detective, that's all I have. That boy grew up with no guidance. If his grandparents are alive, it would be a miracle that they didn't die worrying about them. From the time they were little, those boys put them folks through so much, including my baby. All the trouble Oscar has been into was because of that demon. Now that's a fact! I pray to God my baby didn't help make any families weep, but if I could get some answers, it would put my mind at ease."

"Ms. Pittman, we will do our best to find out the mystery of Oscar's murder. I only ask of you, Ms. Pittman, to be silent in this matter. It's important because hearsay could make or break a case. And remember, if you have any additional information, please contact me anytime," he said, giving her his card.

"Thank you Detective Taft. Please, find the monsters that did this to my baby," she said emotionally.

"We will try everything within our power to bring the suspects to justice. In the meantime, we have to try to reach Aaron and Walter. Do you know any locations that they may frequent?"

"I don't know Detective," she said while rising out of her chair.

After he walked her to her car, he came back inside the station and loaded Aaron and Walter's arrest records, which were longer than a pipe dream, and got their grandparent's address. After he wrote it down, he gathered his keys, gun, cigarettes, and coffee. He hoped the information Ms. Pittman gave him was concrete.

. . .

After ringing the door bell for the third time, Detective Taft realized that Aaron and Walter's grandparents weren't home. When he stepped inside his unmarked cruiser, he decided to call it a day because today was very productive. Although the information that Prime's mother provided wasn't anything set in stone, it was something. He reached over at the passenger seat and picked up the mug shots of Aaron, Walter, and Oscar, who also had a solid history of arrests. He sighed as he wondered if he was even going in the right direction because all the information was abstract for the time being. He called his partner.

"We can't go around and get blue balls on this case Taft, but goddamn, the shit does make sense," Rinaldi said.

"Yeah, I told Ms. Pittman that everything is all hearsay, but get this. About a month ago, my wife asked me about a little boy who witnessed his mother's death. During that time, the case caught a lot of buzz because the fucks that did it were never captured. That same boy my wife felt sorry for could be a possible suspect. Can you believe that shit?"

"I want to believe everything, but we need more," Detective Rinaldi said.

"We will, but it's hard to solve a case when there are no prints, evidence, witnesses, snitches, nothing. We need to get a hold of Howard's sister and try to apply some full-court pressure. Just like I said before, there is a reason why she's not cooperating with us," Detective Taft said as he pulled away from Aaron's grandparent's house.

"Personally, I think she's one of the three. She may be fearful, vindictive, or guilty," Rinaldi said.

"Yeah, I haven't ruled out knowledge of any retaliation and her possible hand in the murder, but I seriously don't think she's involved, but it's possible."

"You know just like I do that black people don't trust law enforcement," Detective Rinaldi said truthfully.

"She's gonna have to. Look, tomorrow we start from scratch. We will go by her apartment tomorrow with Pittman's mug shut, autopsy photo, and the flick from the actual crime scene. I will bring her brother's autopsy photo to remind her of what those assholes did to him. If that doesn't work, we could tell her our theory of her possible involvement. I don't want it to go there, but nothing drives me crazy when the victim's relatives or friends fail to cooperate, making our jobs a living fucking hell."

"Sounds good to me. Remember, the donuts and coffee are on you tomorrow," Detective Rinaldi reminded.

"I know asshole," Detective Taft said jokingly.

"So the grandparents aren't home, huh," Rinaldi asked.

"No, but another visit is on our agenda for tomorrow. Will call you in the morning, but in the meantime, get some rest because we're gonna have ourselves a long day."

"One more thing, this Pittman guy; his mother had no idea where he was all this time?"

"Not a fucking clue Rinaldi. Anderson was the only one with the number. That's what makes his case interesting. He probably didn't tell his mother or anyone else a goddamn thing so no one can say they know his whereabouts."

"Well, look at him now," Detective Rinaldi said

sarcastically.

"Every dog has his day. Hopefully we'll have ours so we could keep these political pricks off our asses. See you tomorrow Rinaldi."

. . .

In each of the stash houses Flex counted money, the cash was short. Ali stood next to him while he counted it, pleased that the plan was in full effect. Flex counted the money like he was going to come up with a different amount, but the total remained the same.

"See, you ain't focused. You got these young, nickel and dime motherfuckers all up in this shit and these motherfuckers are stealing money. Your boy Wade? He responsible for this house. Either he come out of his pocket and pay this shit back or he suffer the consequence. I don't got time for this shit. And you, I'm surprised nigga. You slipping cuz, you really are," Flex said heatedly.

"You act like Marco and Jimmy don't make moves up in these shits. You can't blame..."

"Nigga, did I ask you to speak?" Ali and Flex locked deadly eyes. Ali almost forgot that he had a plan to follow. Flex was on edge because of Linda and Prime's murders, wondering if someone was hip to the murders that happened last summer and if the hit on Prime and Linda was retaliatory. Aaron wondered the same thing.

"Look cuz, I got a lot of shit and running around to do. You got a week little nigga. On Friday, you gather up the cocksuckers and have 'em meet me here. Niggas need to know that death is a consequence for stealing. And another thing, I don't give a fuck how my cousin praise y'all niggas, but if I find out you and Wade stealing money, y'all gonna be some dead ass, ungrateful niggas."

Ali had his pistol on him. He was close to smoking Flex for coming at him like that, but he had to swallow his pride. Flex was feeling himself since Aaron left him in charge. He knew Flex never liked him or Wade from the jump, which made their plan on killing him and the rest of them easy.

"Alright. We'll get to the bottom of this," Ali said like

someone had to manually take the words out of his mouth.

Flex left Ali standing there pissed off, but happy that Flip's plan was working. He called his cousin to inform him of what went down.

"I almost blew it, I'm tellin' you," Ali said.

"Good. Meet me at the spot in an hour," Flip demanded.

56-Dallas

Claude sat alone on the couch, holding a small glass of Hennessy and Coke, watching Sonya, Fatima, and their mother, Julia, exchange stories while they gathered and prepared the food in the kitchen. As he watched Sonya interact with her sister and mother, it reminded him of how close knit his own family was. He and Sahara didn't have much growing up, but their mother gave them all she could. When Claude and Sahara's mother served meals such as bread and fried bologna, Claude and his sister never complained. They had many good times over those meals. They shared whole-hearted laughter while Delores made silly faces, tickling Claude at the table with Sahara joining in. He thought of the times when he was old enough to hold his own. Claude smiled radiantly when he thought of his mother yoking him up while play fighting. He never understood his mother's physical strength until he figured out how strong mentally she was.

When Sonya introduced Claude to her mother, Julia perceived him as the perfect gentleman. Sonya was thankful that her mother wasn't trying to dig any information on him, but out of nowhere, Julia asked him what he did for a living. The sisters looked at one another and wondered what would come out of his mouth. He told her he was a consultant. Oblivious to Julia, Fatima turned around and fought back a huge grin. Sonya had given Fatima an icy stare because she didn't think it was funny. Sonya saw the discomfort in his face, but was proud that Claude played it off coolly. She felt that her mother was out of line for invading Claude's privacy, but knew she was just being protective.

He didn't feel any guilt for telling Julia he was a consultant because technically he was one. He consulted with other criminals and henchmen to make a profit. He did, however, feel a little ashamed because he didn't have a legit occupation, but felt bad because Julia held him in high standards, despite Sonya telling her repeatedly that they were not an item. Their mother would smile in his face, thinking that he earned his way in life. What she didn't see was the money seeping blood out of his pockets. Most importantly, she didn't witness him pull the trigger on two foes last week.

He had only been in Texas for a week and he had already fallen in love with the atmosphere, environment, and Sonya. He didn't want to fall for her because he had to go back to Connecticut to finish out his parole, which could take six months. He didn't know if she was ready to wait for someone she just met a week ago. Although Claude never voiced the feelings he developed for her, he was sure she was feeling the same way. He recalled the staring. Two days ago, during a game of Spades, they locked eyes for so long that Mark and Fatima noticed. Yesterday, they fell asleep watching a movie, only to wake up in each other's arms. Even though nothing transpired, he saw the passion in her eyes.

Whenever they conversed, they were always patient with one another. The thing that Claude liked most about her was that she was not judgmental. Sonya knew he was hiding the real reason why he was down there, but she didn't make any attempt to drag it out of him. Out of respect, Claude never questioned her about her brutal past with Aaron. He knew she was haunted by it and it would be best not to unearth her past. A few hours ago, they almost shared a kiss in the car on their way over, but got interrupted by a honk of a horn and their goal of not trying to go in too deep with one another.

"Hello? Claude, are you with me?" she asked.

"You want me to be?" Claude asked, wishing that he didn't go there. Sonya smiled gently, gazing into his eyes as she recalled the incident a few hours ago. The more she looked at him, the more inappropriate her thoughts became. The doorbell unlocked their look of lust and desire. Sonya smiled one more time at Claude before she walked to the door.

"Hey," Patricia greeted, followed by Amy and her young daughter, Purity.

"What's up y'all? How were the directions?" Sonya asked.

"I think Mark explained it better," Amy admitted.

"I told y'all Fatima would have you drive to Austin just to get over here," Sonya said comically.

As Sonya, Fatima, and Julia engaged in more small talk,

Claude got a text from Mark stating that he'd be there in any minute.

"Sonya, I know I raised you with some better manners than that. Introduce your male friend over there," Julia said joyfully.

"I'm so sorry. Pat, Amy, this is Mark's cousin Claude. Claude, these are my co-workers slash friends, Patricia and Amy."

Claude stood up.

"How do you do?" Claude said civilly, extending his hand to Patricia.

"Hi. You could call me Pat. I heard a lot about you," she said.

"Hi, you could just call me Amy," Amy said jokingly.

"Hello Amy. The pleasure is all mine," Claude said. "And how do you do young lady?"

"Fine and you?" Purity asked cheerfully.

"She is so cute," Julia complimented. "How old is she?"

"Five going on twenty-five," Amy said.

"My niece is the same way. These kids these days are something else," Claude interjected.

"Yes they are, and speaking of kids, when are you and Mark giving me a grandchild?"

"Mama!"

"And where is that son in-law of mine?"

"He's on his way, Ms. Williams. He just texted me," Claude said.

"Mama, you had him stopping at like every store known to man," Fatima said.

"You want to eat, don't ya?"

"Y'all both need to stop. Claude, you want another drink?" Sonya asked, following her mother, sister, and peers into the kitchen.

"Please," Claude said, handing her his empty glass. Mark opened the front door with three bags, allowing Sahara and Destiny entry into the house.

"Uncle C!" Destiny ran over to Claude with opened arms.

"How's my favorite niece?!"

"I'm your only niece silly," Destiny joked back. She held onto her uncle with a firm grip, missing his presence. Claude felt the love she had for him and tears fell from his eyes, despite Sonya standing in front of them. She introduced herself to Sahara and Destiny and walked to the kitchen to give them their privacy. The image of Claude shedding tears made her smile. She had always thought that it was beautiful when a man cried.

"I'll see you in a few minutes C," Sahara said with an attitude that only Claude and Mark picked up. After Mark walked Sahara and Destiny to the kitchen, he came back out into the living room with a look of concern.

"What's good?" Claude asked suspiciously, sensing something was wrong.

"I looked you up on the computer. They got you as absconder," Mark said disappointedly.

"Word?"

"Word," Mark shot back. "I called Zane, but she didn't pick up.

Claude pulled out his cell phone out of his pocket and called Tank, but he didn't pick up. He called Zane's number, getting no answer. He called her at four different numbers before he finally got her.

"Zane, what up?"

"Nothing but the weather. What's good with you?"

"Damn, someone is calling me. Let me hit you right back," Claude said before clicking over.

"Hello?"

"C, this J-Rock man. I gotta pull your coat to some shit," he said urgently.

"Hold on," Claude said. "Mark, I'll be right back. If anyone ask, I'm on the jack out front."

"You good?" Mark asked with concern, thinking about Claude's troubles in Waterbury.

Claude nodded, grabbed his coat, and walked out the front door. Sonya saw him from the kitchen walk out the door. She secretly walked away from the women's chatter and walked out to the living room. Sahara saw Sonya slide out of the kitchen and followed suit.

"Mark is everything alright?" Sonya asked sincerely.

"That's a good question," Sahara interjected before Mark got a chance to answer. Ever since he picked her and Destiny up from their Aunt Pearl's house, she displayed a cold attitude. The ride over to Julia's house seemed long, even though it was only a fifteen minute ride. He conversed with Destiny while Sahara stared blankly out the window. Mark felt relieved that they were out of the car and around people. Claude and Mark were the only people at Julia's house that knew Sahara was putting on a front. On the outside, she was nice and personable, but internally, she was steamed and disgusted.

"He just went outside to use the phone," Mark said flatly, giving Sahara a blank stare. Sonya noticed the small tension.

"Ok, but if y'all need anything, just let me know. There is food and drinks everywhere in this house so dig in," Sonya said kindly.

"Thank you Sonya. I also want to say once again that I appreciate you inviting me and my daughter. We needed the fresh air," Sahara said cordially.

"Don't even mention it. We could use more people to help bring some of this food home."

When Sahara walked out the front door, leaving Mark in the living room by himself, she wondered what the hell was going on with Mark's family, particularly Claude.

"What's good J-Rock? What's the deal?"

"Them niggas is on to us. They found Roscoe's body in a basement out in Bridgeport. I just need to know one thing C. Did any of your peoples leak that shit?"

Claude knew J-Rock was trying to be civilized, but he could hear the fear and anger in his voice. He couldn't blame him for his reaction about Calvin finding out, but he knew he couldn't be up front with him because he didn't want anyone knowing about the biggest crime he had ever committed. Claude would make sure that God would judge him before a judge in court had a chance to nail him. He would protect his neck with tight defense before he gave up his freedom, foundation, and family. Since he would be charged with an escape, he may get up to an additional year for that, but that would be the only time he would give to the state of Connecticut or any other jurisdiction.

"No. We don't even talk about the shit amongst ourselves. So it's like that, huh? Niggas is all of a sudden findin' out shit," Claude said, flipping the script.

"I don't know C; I'm just sayin' though, that shit didn't come from my end. That tall nigga got murked, and your boy Rocks? He didn't get killed for nothing."

J-Rock broke the switch with that comment.

"Yo, you don't know what the fuck you're talking about! Rocks got nothin' to do with this shit, so don't come out your face wit' that bullshit J-Rock, for real," Claude said hotly. He looked around the suburban neighborhood to see if he disturbed any kind of peace people were having.

"It's funny that tall nigga got left out of some major shit and he all of a sudden plant food. You and those motherfuckers the only ones that knew about this shit, but Calvin knows everything," J-Rock said heatedly.

"So what are you trying to say J-Rock? You didn't say one word about that nigga Roscoe. You didn't think for one second that Roscoe probably let the goddamn cat out of the bag, but you're blaming my peoples? You put the shit together, now shit is crumbling, and now you blaming me because you running right now."

"You should be doing the same. Thanks to your bitch ass crew, we got a hundred thousand dollar price tags on our heads," J-Rock said icily while he packed a duffle bag of clothes, ready to haul ass.

"Thanks to my crew? Word?" Claude chuckled. "I don't see them running. Listen, you shook motherfucker, so what they found out?! What we did to them niggas ain't no different on what they do to everybody else so fuck 'em! Calvin bleeds, shit, breathes, and fart just like I do. He or anyone bring that shit over here is goin' to see the truth!"

Claude hung up on him. He was mad as hell by the way J-Rock came at him, but he had every right to be pissed. If Ty would have never ran his mouth like a bitch, no one would have known shit about the heist. He felt bad by not being honest with him, but he had his own freedom and foundation to protect.

"I want to hear some truth," Sahara said with her arms tucked. Claude didn't see her approach him from behind. She startled him.

"What's up?" Claude asked like he didn't know what was on her mind.

She stared blankly at her brother.

"What I'm about to tell you ain't pretty so brace yourself."

"C, I'm you're sister and you should be able to tell me anything. If it's hard for you to trust anyone, you should have not for one second think you can't trust me."

"Sahara, I hear you, but it's fucked up right now, but I'll drop it how you want it. Believe me, it would be shit that you wished I didn't tell you."

"What's going on C?" she asked, wanting Claude to get straight to the point.

Claude told her everything from start to finish, including the conversation he just had with J-Rock. When he told her what he did with the bodies, her mouth dropped, wondering what kind of man she was raised with. Although she didn't agree on how he handled things, she understood game and what needed to be done. At the end of Claude's confession, she gave him a huge hug, releasing all the tension that existed between them; however, she developed an aura of fear that won't go away any time soon. She didn't fear Claude getting caught and apprehended, but feared for his life.

The rest of the night consisted of music, liquor, and other cards. Destiny and Purity played themselves to sleep. Purity started to cry and pout once she was woken up by her mother. Once Patricia, Amy, and Purity left, Julia felt her age and couldn't hang with the youth. She fell asleep once she got comfortable on her bed. While Sonya, Fatima, and Sahara conversed, Claude and Mark were posted in the living room having a discussion of the conversation Claude had with J-Rock.

"Truth be told Mark, J-Rock got a right to be heated, but if I would have told him about Ty, I would have given him an opportunity to link me to the bodies. Not that he would have snitched, but it is just a chance I ain't willing to take."

"Yeah, I understand your point," Mark said, sipping his beer.

"But fuck that, I need you to do me a solid while I'm away. Remember, you the only nigga that I could trust with all my cash."

"Come on man, you don't even have to start off like that. You gave me ten g's and plus you family. Whatever you need C, I got you."

"I need you to stash my money as tight as you can and I need you to contact a lawyer in case they send the hounds on me."

"Already done C. What you need to do is invest in some property and flip it."

"That's phase two. I will let you know when the time comes. You know me Mark. I don't ditch out no plans unless it is thoroughly thought out, but I did plant a seed."

"So C, what's up with you and Sonya? You feeling her?"

"Hell yeah. I have never met anyone like her, but I'm scared Mark, I ain't even gonna front. I'm about to get locked up and I don't want another Darlene issue, you know what I mean? Don't want to set myself up like that. She's a good girl that went through some shit and I don't want to burden her by her waiting on a nigga to come home."

"I don't know C; I have a feeling that she may be feeling you more than you think. I think if you step to her about what you told me, she'll respect you even more, but that's just my opinion. Fatima won't tell me shit because she figured I would have told you, which I would," Mark said with a laugh. "But not to change the subject, but did you tell Sahara the whole truth or half of it? She's been getting on my nerves lately trying to dig some shit out of me."

"Who you telling? I gave her the entire story, but she cool with it. She scared to death though, but I'm telling you Mark, I would pop any nigga that's trying to lay hands on me and y'all."

"Better chance of that not happening if and when you move your black ass down here," Mark said.

Before Mark could say anything else, Sonya walked out into the living room with her leather jacket on, holding two plates of food.

"You ready," she asked.

"Yeah," Claude said.

"I'll see you later on at the house C," Mark said before getting up and joining Fatima in the kitchen. Mark wanted Claude to spend as much time with Sonya as possible because it would be a minute before they would see each other again.

57-Dallas/Los Angeles

Sonya's bedroom carried a sensual aura. Floetry's "Flo'Ology" seeped through the small speakers of the small radio. The raindrops falling from the sky tickled the window pane and an occasional bolt of lightening flashed in the night time sky. While the incense spread its rich aroma, Claude and Sonya sat on the bed with their backs against the wall since the bed was posted against it. They were smoking a blunt, comfortable in each other's company. They had finished a long discussion of the Da Vinci Code, both of them making strong, valid points surrounding the controversy. During their silence, Sonya tried to fight her sexual urges as hard as possible, but she was becoming weaker by each second as the silence grew lengthier.

When Sonya stepped out of the shower when they arrived from her mother's house, she prepared herself for relaxation and easy access in case Claude tried anything with her. She wore blue sweatpants and a baby phat tank top. She wanted Claude so badly that her nipples seemed they would poke a hole straight through the fabric. Claude pretended to be oblivious, but she knew he was staring at them. The thrill of him staring at her turned her on and it added more spice to her fantasy of making love to him.

They passed the blunt back and forth for the next five minutes and didn't say a word. Claude was so high that he started comparing Sonya to a woman that lived in the outskirt of his mind when he was locked up. For years, he dreamt of making love to a woman on an island in the middle of the Caribbean sea, but he used to wake up to the sounds of the guard's keys jingling when walking, cell doors opening and closing, and most importantly, he woke up without the woman he made love to on the island. Now, the woman sitting next to him was real. Her skin looked ethereal as the moonlight shone through the window. She looked like a goddess that was ready to indulge deep into her sexuality; to say she looked exotic was an understatement. He stole another quick glance at her and wondered if her thoughts were just as naughty as his. With each passing minute, the sparks that existed between them got hotter and hotter.

"Just when I was warming up to you, you're leaving to go back to old Waterbury. It must be something else up there," Sonya said, breaking the long-lived silence. She still wanted to know what went down with the phone call and the tension his sister brought over to her mother's house, but if he didn't want to tell it now, she wasn't going to stress it.

"So you're warming up to me, huh? I would have never figured that."

He knew Sonya was curious on why he was going back to Connecticut so soon, but he decided at Julia's house to keep her in the dark until he knew for sure she was trustworthy.

"You would have never guessed Claude? Ok, lets see, I believe I told you the reason why I left California. If that's not warming up, then I don't know what is," she said while she flicked what was left of the blunt.

As "Feelings" blared, a long silence surfaced again. There was nothing else to say between them. They knew what they wanted. They locked eyes, just like the episode in the car earlier when they almost shared a kiss. She wanted to move her eyes from Claude's vision, but she was too weak to do it. When Claude moved in on her, his natural odor got stronger. As he got closer, Sonya didn't bulge. She sat with her back pressed against the wall, her legs spread, inviting him to come to her with her half-shut eyes. He was poised and robust, but his hormones were raised to their peak. His heartbeat increased as he got closer. When their lips touched, she closed her eyes and kissed him back. She sucked softly on his bottom lip, moaning as they shared soft kisses and touches. Their kissing got deeper and their hands slowly expanded to more territory of their bodies. He traced her ear with his tongue and made her moan louder. He allowed his tongue to roam free across her neck. He felt her nails on his skin tighten as he added more impact to the pleasure he was giving her. They explored each other's bodies with the rhythm of Floetry's beat that blared out of the speakers. Sonya positioned herself to lay flat so she could feel more of the sensual jewels he was dropping on her. He reasoned that her mind and body gave him the signal to break all the boundaries of her flawless, petite body. He started to message her feet, temporally depriving her of the passion that she hadn't had in what seemed like eternity.

After a few moments of teasing her, he sucked on her toes. Her eyes rolled back in ecstasy, wanting to have that feeling of being cherished last forever. Once he stopped sucking on them, his hands wondered. His opened hand found her inner thigh. She slowly gyrated upward to his touch. Once he worked that traveling hand to her uncharted territory and rubbed it smoothly, her head fell back and she squeezed her thighs. She extended her pelvic area upwards. She invited each and every one of his advances. He gripped her sweatpants and slowly pulled them down, along with the thongs she wore. She kept her body arched so her sweatpants and thongs could glide off easily. Her lower body wear dangled from the brim of her toes before kicking them to the floor. When he got up to reposition himself, his manhood was on a verge of busting a hole in his windbreaker pants. She extended her arm, reaching for his dick. Once she got a hold of it, she massaged the tip of his shaft, feeling all of his pre-juices. Satisfied with the size of his penis, she stopped rubbing it and wrapped her legs around Claude's upper body, pulling him in. He went straight for her inner thigh and then traced his tongue to the tip of her clit. He used the tip of his tongue to lick her clitoris in a circular motion. She grabbed the back of his head, pushing his face farther into her sweet scented vagina. Squeezing her thighs, she made love to his mouth. She made fuck noises while he sucked and tongue fucked her pussy. A few moments later, Claude hit a spot. Her body jerked, squeezing off a thunderous orgasm.

He made his way to her naval and traced a circle around it as he caressed her body. Using his thumbs, he lifted her Baby Phat top over her breasts. Her dark brown nipples stood at attention as Claude licked and sucked them. He grabbed one breast while he toyed with her other nipple with the tip of his finger. He was on all fours over her body, sucking on her breasts. She pulled at Claude's windbreakers, indirectly telling him it was time for them to come off. He took a moment out of his foreplay to take off all his clothes. As he stood naked, Sonya took a second to take in Claude's muscular body. His body was everything what Sonya fantasized about since the day she laid eyes on him. She scooted over to the side to make room for her king in the making. Sonya moved slowly on top of him. She began to kiss and nibble on his ear lobe while she stroked his erect penis. She guided her tongue along his upper body and worked her way to his penis. She planted soft kisses on his shaft until she placed her entire mouth on it, using no teeth. Her hair covered the sight of her lips around his shaft, but when she moved her hair to the side, she looked at him compassionately as she took her time pleasing him. Claude felt like climaxing right at that moment, but he had to control himself. She heard him breathe heavily so she increased the pace of her head game. She eased off his manhood, leaving it to stand stiff, and she crawled her way up to him. She grabbed his penis and massaged it with her clit, teasing him. She laid down on him, her breasts touching his chests, and her rear elevated so she could grind his dick. She went slowly at first, but she didn't want to tease herself with his jewel any longer. She positioned the shaft of his dick at the entrance to her womb. They were both so sexually and mentally hypnotized by each other that neither one of them gave the use of condoms any thought. The had a feeling that they would belong to one another. She pressed on his manhood until the tip of his penis disappeared into her womb. He grabbed her waist and finished what she started.

She met his every stroke, even though it was painful since she hadn't had sex in so long. Claude knew her pussy was going to be tight so he had entered her with care and caution. Slowly, the mild pain she felt began to subside, replaced with pleasure. He long stroked her using moderate speed. Her pussy felt so warm that if he would have gone any faster, he would have climaxed prematurely. After an hour and four sex positions later, he was fucking her doggy style with perspiration dripping on the side of his face.

"Oh daddy, make love to me," she said passionately. "I... love...this...dick so much."

"You like this dick," Claude asked as he started stroking with rapid speed.

"Oh yes daddy…fuck me…I'm….gonna cum…ohhhh!!"

Sonya's body jerked wildly as she tightened her walls. Her vaginal secretions seeped from her womb and ran down her leg. After Claude witnessed her release, he placed his arm around her stomach, cupped one of her breasts, and pumped her wildly.

"Come inside me baby. I want to feel it," she said sensually.

Claude flipped her over on her back. Claude slid it in. She wrapped her legs around him tightly as he gave her a few more thrusts before he exploded inside of her.

"Ah shit, goddamn," Claude mumbled as his body went limp from his release.

Exhausted, Claude laid there on top of her. She planted soft kisses all over his face as she held on to him.

…

Sonya had her head on Claude's chest, listening to his heartbeat while one of her legs was wrapped around one of his. She toyed with his nipple as he stared at the ceiling. She wondered idly what he was thinking and vice versa. They had been making passionate love for the last two hours and they were exhausted.

"What are you thinking about?" she asked quietly as he ran his hand through her silky smooth hair, gently massaging her scalp.

"Not sure if you really want to know."

"And why wouldn't I want to know," she said, repositioning herself so she can look at him face to face.

"I don't know," he said, reaching for the roach in the ashtray.

"Is there something you want to tell me? If it's something I don't want to hear, its ok. All I ask of you is to be honest with me," she said, kissing him softly on his chin.

While she waited for his answer, he remembered that hurtful feeling of being kicked to the curb when he was only a year into his fifteen year bid. He spent many lonely nights thinking about Darlene and all the good and bad times they had. When she broke the news about her pregnancy during a visit, he was a millisecond away from flipping out in the visiting room, but he refused to give anyone the satisfaction of seeing him lose his cool over something that was destined to happen. Instead, he walked away quietly with bottled up anger, leaving her with a fifteen year guilt trip. He remembered that nasty, dreadful feeling like it happened five minutes ago. The more he gazed into her eyes, the more he realized how much he would miss her when he leaves to do the rest of his time.

Although he meant what he said to Mark about him not wanting to burden Sonya with his troubled life, that didn't stop him from wanting her. He was lonely and couldn't deny it. He was only fucking Darlene to fulfill a massive void. Since Zane's friend Diamond was a lesbian, she was of little use to him. When he knocked out Lloyd that night at the club, he had a few sessions with her at the hotel, but that was it. Every time he thought of home and the amount of pain he had to endure coming up, the more he thought about how badly he wanted to endure some happiness. It bothered the shit out of him that he met Sonya under fucked up circumstances. A sharp, nagging thought of the murders he executed turned his hopeful thinking into thoughts of him being tried and convicted for the people he turned to stiff bodies…and then into ashes. He worried more about doing life in prison then watching his back, as well as his front, from the invisible men sent by Calvin to murder him and his people. He would rather die than to spend the rest of his life in prison.

Claude finally knew what it was like to breathe and relax. It had been a long time since he did that. He could see why Mark moved to Dallas and never looked back. His life had been nothing but disaster. If he played his cards right, he'd have a chance of being happy. He figured a reasonable approach to that journey should be to simply keep it real.

"I'm going back to jail Sonya," he said dryly and without giving her any eye contact.

"Why"? She asked softly, giving him her full, undivided attention.

"Because I'm down here," he said, looking at her.

Since she didn't respond, he went into what drove him to skip parole. He told her everything, excluding the murders. He was ashamed when he told her how he forced his sister and his niece to come to Dallas because of the life threatening heist him and his people pulled off, but didn't regret his decision to fly them out of state, especially after Link and his goons broke into the house in hopes of finding his stash.

"Baby, why was it so hard for you to tell me?" Sonya asked.

Claude looked away.

"Because I got feelings for you Sonya, and that's real. I don't know, you seem like you are a breath of fresh air. Never felt that way about a woman. And the worst part about it, I have to leave. I really dig you, but I don't think it's fair for you to be left in a gray area. I told you how my ex came to visit and how she told me she was pregnant. I expected that, but not so soon in my bid. I rather not keep my hopes up while I'm locked up. Besides, I don't want to burden you by waiting for me to come out of jail."

Sonya had tears building up in her eyes as she recognized the sincerity in his words. She knew that she'd come to a point where she'd do anything for him. She appreciated his honesty because he didn't have to tell her half the things he told her. That alone told her he felt deeply for her. As far as she was concerned, she'd be more than willing to wait faithfully for him. She gazed at him longer than she had to before she said a word.

"What if I told you that I wouldn't mind waiting? I really like you Claude and it's too bad we had to meet under extremities like this, but I want you," she said romantically and with tears trickling down her cheeks. She climbed on top of him and kissed him passionately to verify the feelings she had for him.

Claude couldn't believe her response. The feeling he had at that moment couldn't be sold for a million dollars. He squeezed her tightly to make sure he wasn't dreaming.

"Sonya, are you sure…"

She placed her finger on her lip and silenced him.

"I want you, but out of curiosity, how long will it be before I have you in my arms again," she asked.

"To be honest sweetheart, I may have to do six months for skipping my parole. It may be a year," he said disappointedly.

"Baby, you just said six months," Sonya said.

"I know, but if I'm out of jail in six months, it will mean that I would have to stay in Connecticut for another six. I want to be done with parole and all that shit so I'm better off doing the rest of my time."

"Can't I just come to Connecticut and wait for you?" she asked, still trying to cut corners.

"That will be nice, but I need you to stay strong and put. You have it going on down here, and besides, I don't want to take any chances of me putting you in danger," he said logically. "I want to come back down here and start a new life with you."

Sonya allowed Claude's words to sink. Claude had no credentials, but she had a feeling of security being in his arms. She felt that Claude can protect her from all the dangers in the world.

"So what are you saying Claude? Is it official? Are we exclusive?"

"Is that what you want?" he asked her as he rubbed her back and buttocks.

"Yes, I do, and that means you are now officially mine and off limits," she said jokingly.

Claude and Sonya's love connection may have been quick, but they were at vulnerable stages in their lives and they have developed a flame that would not dwindle. They stayed up and talked until the sun rose from the horizon. They fell asleep in each other's arms, excited at the commitment they created together.

. . .

Raven and Octavia moved hastily throughout Raven's lavish condo packing things into black trash bags. She only had two pieces of luggage and couldn't shop for any at four o'clock in the morning. Raven led Octavia to believe that she was moving simply to get away from it all. Raven didn't think she was stupid enough to believe it; Raven knew she would take that for an answer.

Her conscious had been gradually waging a war against her because she couldn't get what Aaron did to her brother out of her head. When Ali told her about his discovery, she wanted Aaron to die, but she came to the conclusion that death would probably be too easy for him. She knew the girl in the picture she found as Sonya, one of the nurses that used to take care of her grandmother, and wanted to warn her of Aaron's incoming presence, but she had no contact information. She even called the hospital to see if they could provide her with information, but the receptionist wasn't allowed to release any kind of information. If Raven stuck around long enough, she'd also be in line to get lit up by a bullet. She was playing a dirty, violent game and she knew she wasn't built for it. In order for Ali and them to get at Aaron, the rest of his people would have to get cut down. Raven wanted no part of that, but she knew for a fact that Marco, Scoot, and Jimmy may know something about her brother's demise.

She wanted to figure out a way to protect Ali and Wade from law enforcement, alert Sonya, and point the law in the direction to get to Trudy's decomposing body. The way she received the information, Prime was involved with the scheme of setting up her brother, Colin, Earl, and B-Bum, although he denied having a hand in the murders. However, that made him just as guilty. A few hours ago, she came up with the right scheme that would keep her hands clean by using the process of elimination.

Prime and Linda's death was going to the grave with her, so that was out. Raven gritted her teeth with the thought of talking to the two detectives having the knowledge she had regarding everything that they were looking for. As far as Jimmy, Marco, and Scoot, she would have to live with it. They may have nothing to do with her brother's death, but she would bet money that they have some knowledge of it. Besides, she knew the blueprint. Ali or Wade was not even going to be there so that automatically ruled them out. That left two of the main prospects, Aaron and Flex. She didn't want to do it to her, but Octavia was her new and last resort.

Since childhood, Raven always had Octavia's back from the days when people called her ugly to her face and, in the present, when people called her ugly behind her back. For years, she had been nothing but loyal to her friend. Raven had never crossed her. She only stood beside her. Even the dirt Octavia did behind

Raven's back such as spreading STD, fuck, and slut rumors about her never forced her hand; however, the shit Octavia pulled yesterday pushed Raven to the edge.

Raven had left the shower running as she scrambled around looking for toiletries. She wasn't even half-way down the spiral, plush steps when she caught Octavia stealing money out of her Gucci bag. She had a stack of hundreds. She pinched a few of the greenbacks out, figuring Raven was going to miss it. Raven had a towel draped around her. She smiled and shook her head at Octavia's betrayal. She turned around in her heels and returned to the shower. That money in the Gucci bag wasn't shit. All Octavia had to do was ask for the money; that little bit of cheddar she stole sealed the deal on their friendship. It was too bad Octavia was oblivious to the trap she walked into when Raven called her over to help. If Raven would have watched her a little longer, she would have caught Octavia scrolling through her cell phone. Octavia was helping Raven pack the entire night. She hoped Raven would let her in, but so far, she hadn't said anything about Prime and Linda's murder.

While they stashed clothes in bags, Raven's cell phone rang three times before picking it up.

"Hello," she said into the receiver.

"What?! Girl, don't be calling me dropping names like that! What the fuck is wrong with you? I don't care for that reward shit!"

Raven ended the call abruptly.

"Bitch," Raven said under her breath.

"What's the matter with you?" Octavia asked, wondering who was on the phone. She wondered if she heard the word reward.

"It's nothing," Raven said, shoving more of her wardrobe into a hefty trash bag. "Just a young ass fool trying to make a profit off of someone else's misery."

"Rave, you got to get that money anyway you can. America ain't giving us shit."

Raven cut her eyes away from her when she said that. What she really wanted to do was cut her throat for that piracy shit she pulled yesterday, but that wouldn't be a good move on the chessboard. She was in a fucked up situation and gave Octavia the status of being a pawn. Raven just wanted to get through the game without getting her hands dirty.

"You talk a lot of shit Oct. I guarantee you wouldn't snitch anyone out for money, especially if you hate the nigga. Let's keep it real."

"Hell no, I don't trust them white folks and that anonymous shit. Fuck that, I ain't no snitch, but since you asking questions, why don't you tell me the latest. It's all quiet in here. What's up?" Octavia asked, sniffing around a mouse trap.

"What's up with what? I'm not speaking on no murder I'm not too sure about," Raven said nonchalantly as she poured the last of her cosmetics in a plastic bag.

"Murder? What murder you talking about?"

"I really don't feel comfortable having this conversation…"

"Come on Rave, you know me. I ain't going to say nothing. I just want to hear the latest word. You know how your bitch gets down, damn, you act like I ain't going to find out, acting all secretive an' shit." Octavia hoped Raven was going to reveal the information she saw in her phone about Prime and Linda.

"Don't say nothin' Oct, but this chick just told me who killed that girl Trudy and she knows where the body is, but I tell you one thing, that five thousand ain't worth it, fuck that," Raven emphasized. "But yeah, she said Flex choked her out. She said her body is buried in some woods along the highway rotting somewhere, but that's all hearsay. That money was probably mentioned to get people to talk." Raven put the last of her linens in a bag. She had just enough stuff to leave with. Raven would pay a million dollars to see the look Octavia had on her face when she mentioned the five thousand dollar reward that didn't exist. What was more fucked up was that her cell phone never rang. It was her alarm clock that was set as soon as she decided to give Octavia a little payback.

"What?! Flex did that? Why? Was he fuckin' with her or something?" Octavia asked, pretending not to be moved by Raven's mentioning of the cash.

"I don't know. First time I heard about it. Aaron never mentioned nothin' to me about it."

"Why would he? After all, that is his cousin. It probably wasn't attended for you to know," Octavia said.

"Well, it got nothing to do with me and neither does Aaron. My goal is to be out before he gets back. Once again, thank you for helping me," Raven said civilly.

"Girl, you don't got to thank me. I told you that nigga was corny and that you could do a lot better."

"I guess you were right," Raven said.

"Please Raven, I know I'm right. He must be one stupid motherfucker to be oblivious to you moving. And he calls himself going out of town to handle business. He can't even keep up on what's happening at home."

Octavia got up and put her jacket on. She had a seed planted in her head. She was dying to throw some water on it.

"Don't forget to call me when you settle Rave. I'm about to take my ass to bed. I didn't even know it's almost five o'clock in the morning."

"I won't. Thank you once again Oct. You will hear from me in the next day or so," Raven lied.

"Don't forget girl, you be safe. If there is anything you would like me to do, you know what to do," Octavia said coolly.

She gave Raven a tight hug and a kiss on the cheek before she walked out the door. A devious grin formed on Raven's face. As she watched Octavia pull away from the curb, she knew it would be just a matter of time before she talked to the police. In just a half hour, she would be out of that condo forever. She was headed straight to New York to join her mother. She packed what she needed. As far as the other stuff, such as her bed, furniture, and appliances, it was fair game for whoever found them.

58-Dallas

The gray skies outside the apartment promised heavy rain. The turbulent wind to go along with the weather made it easier for anyone to stay in the bed. The comforter Claude and Sonya were sleeping under was thick as they created their own body temperature by cuddling. They were deep into their sleep. It had been a great while since he rested comfortably, not since the day he came home from prison. They fell asleep after their many sexual exploits and conversation. During his sleep, Claude involuntary broke his hold from Sonya and moved from his side to his back. His mouth was wide opened, enjoying his much needed sleep. He should enjoy it because it would be a while before he could get old fashioned rest like that again. He fell asleep to the sound of Sonya's voice and the assurance that he finally had a woman who joined sides with him during a rough time. Since she stepped into the eye of the storm, he knew she had the potential of being his soul mate. He couldn't imagine a woman in the right state of mind to fall for an ex-con on his way back to prison. Sonya looked good and had the personality to get a celebrity's attention, but yet, Sonya threw all of her eggs in one basket and was willing to take a rain check for his return from prison.

During their sleep, they didn't hear any scuffling or voices in the living room because the mild commotion was loud enough to wake folks up if they were in the vicinity. Claude and Sonya were sleeping hard, but Sonya's sleeping exceeded heavy, which was why Claude heard someone in the room. Sonya remained asleep, snoring lightly and resting peacefully. When Claude opened his eyes, he saw a tall, dark figure with cornrows standing over him with a gun in his hands. The image of the man with the gun in his hand was the last thing he saw before his eyes closed again from the brute force of the gun's handle.

. . .

"What you know about them murders? And who the fuck you been talking to and don't lie, otherwise I'm gonna kill everybody up in this motherfucker! You better start talking," Aaron said coldly, shoving her bounded, half naked person on the kitchen chair. "The first lie that come out of your mouth, I'm starting off with your boy, and I'm gonna work my way around the room. And then I'm going to kill your moms. Yeah, I saw that green car in the driveway."

Sonya hadn't been so afraid in her life as the man who created her nightmares stood before her. She looked stunned and petrified, realizing that she wasn't dreaming and the man she ran away from had traveled thousands of miles to find her, and he did. She looked at her sister, Mark, and Claude bounded, bloodied, and unconscious through teary eyes while thinking that he had been following her. She remembered when she took Claude to the mall and he said someone was looking at him while she used the bathroom. She thought about her mother being all alone in her house and Aaron knowing where she lived. She wondered how Aaron knew where she rested. She didn't have time to think for now; instead, she had to be on point.

"Someone asked me about it, but I said I didn't know…"

"Ask you about what?" Aaron asked harshly.

She shook noticeably. Aaron didn't like the potential of killing four people, but he had to do what he had to do. The sight of Sonya lying naked next to another man enraged him and it only increased his motivation to kill. Since Sonya was still silent, Aaron raised his gun and pointed it at her sister, and then at Claude.

"Trudy," she said frantically.

"Trudy, huh? You sure that's all she asked you?" Aaron asked, now pointing the gun at her.

"I'm positive," she said through crying and flinching from the sight of Aaron's gun.

"So it's like that, huh? This is the reason why you moved back here?" Aaron asked with controlled aggression, pointing his .44 at Claude, who was unconscious with his hands tied behind the small of his back. He was next to Mark, who looked like a bloody mess from Aaron pouncing on him with the gun he knocked Claude out with. Fatima's nose dripped blood from Aaron punching her viciously in her face as Mark lie helplessly on the floor, wiped out from the stomping he received. Fatima wasn't regaining consciousness, but Claude's leg moved while Mark's eyes squinted.

"No Aaron," Sonya said with tears trickling down her face. She responded to Aaron like he was a ghost. She couldn't believe the man she feared was standing in her sister's living room, holding a gun, out in Dallas from Los Angeles with a murderous look in his eyes. Sonya's hands were tied with duct tape, along with Mark and Fatima. Claude's hands were tied with rope that had a thick texture. She feared for her and everyone's life because Aaron didn't travel thousands of miles for nothing. Aaron's presence in the apartment verified her answer on the killings that included Dennis Howard last year. Since the options seemed out of reach, she figured, in her fear stricken state, she had to be strong, no matter the outcome.

"I moved on Aaron. I got fed up with the beatings. I tried to hang in there, but you didn't let me. And you even raped me Aaron!" Sonya paused to gather herself as Aaron listened intently. He didn't have any remorse, but he would have gained it if he didn't find Sonya in the bed with another dude. She started to cry uncontrollably.

Aaron watched Sonya weep with hatred brewing in his mind. The visual of catching Sonya in bed with another man was forcing his hand to go with a homicidal route.

"That's 'cause you was fucking wit..."

"I wasn't fucking wit' nobody Aaron! That was only in your mind! You fucking accuse me, beat me, and raped me and I'm supposed to stay with you? I didn't need that shit so I rocked the fuck on! Look at you, coming all the way up here from the other side..."

That was as far as she got. He pistol whipped her hard. When she fell out of the chair after the blow, her head bounced off the floor. She was sprawled out on the kitchen floor. A small pool of blood formed next to her head.

"Coward ass motherfucker," Claude grunted, infuriated at what he just saw. His mind went into a zone where it never had gone before. He knew the chances of survival were slim, but he would use every strategy to increase their chances. If he was going to die in the process, so be it.

"What you say nigga?" Aaron gained a grip on his pistol.

"You heard me," Claude said, feeling a sharp pain on the bridge of his nose. He was tasting his own blood.

Aaron rushed over to where Claude was bounded and kicked him brutally in the stomach. Claude curled to a semi-fatal position, held his stomach to ease the pain, and laughed.

"You think this shit is a joke motherfucker," Aaron snarled, this time, kicking Claude on his head. He felt the pain, but he continued to laugh. Aaron was about to kick him again, but held his foot back. Aaron was somewhat taken back and inadvertently gained a little respect for the man. Aaron figured that the man Sonya was with may be just as fucked up as he was.

Instead of saying anything, he turned around to start doing what he had in mind. Mark and Fatima were up and fully alert. They knew for sure that Claude was a second away from dying with all of his taunting. Claude made eye contact with Mark and Fatima and winked at them. They hoped that he wouldn't taunt Aaron anymore because of their compromised situation, but Claude couldn't just fall back and be a hostage. He had other plans.

Aaron picked up Sonya's unconscious, limp body from the floor and started walking towards the bedroom.

"I would respect you more if you would have approached me last week in the mall homey like a man, but instead, you do this bitch ass shit by tying me up. I heard a lot about you Aaron, but Sonya never told me how much of a pussy you are," Claude spat with a smile on his face. Claude didn't have an ounce of fear, even with his hands tied up and the excruciating pain he was going through. On the surface, Claude displayed his machismo, but internally, he hurt like hell seeing everyone in their predicament. As he watched Sonya lie limp over his shoulder, the rage he accumulated at the moment exceeded fear and pain. He wanted to get at their captor for doing that to the handful of people he sought comfort with. Claude decided that he would do anything to come out of the hostage situation on top. He was holding on to the little hope he had left.

As expected, he put Sonya down, pulled out his burner, and charged at Claude, but stopped in his tracks as Claude sat there without flinching. He didn't bulge an inch.

"Alright tough boy, you going lose that stupid ass grin after I rape and kill this bitch. You heard her right. I raped her dry pussy and I'm about to do it again before I pop her."

Without warning, Aaron coughed up a wad of saliva and mucous and spit directly into Claude's face. Claude was beyond his boiling point, but he composed himself by smiling.

"Yeah, you are a pussy, cocksucking motherfucker," he said nonchalantly, reassuming his position on the wall as the saliva dripped from his chin.

Aaron smiled, picked up Sonya, took her into the room, and closed the door, confident that his hostages were secure in their restraints. He couldn't wait to put a bullet through the shit talker. He could honestly admit he was slightly thrown off by the man's balls, but he'd give the man respect after he killed him and everyone else out there in the living room.

. . .

If there was anything that Claude learned from one of the few male figures he had in his life, he learned it from Mookie, his mother's deceased boyfriend. He taught Claude how to free himself from thick rope, duct tape, and handcuffs. Claude's friends use to marvel at how he used to free himself effortlessly, but today, Claude and everyone's life depended on him to remember how he did it when he was being taught that Houdini type of shit.

Mark and Fatima looked on with desperation as they watched Claude make attempts to manipulate the knot tied over his wrists. Claude knew that he didn't have much time so he worked as speedily as possible. Since Claude's hands were behind him, he brought his knees to his chest and worked his wrists over his backside. He moved his bounded hands from under his legs and feet, and finally, over the top of his knees. He had his hands in front of him. He gnawed at the knot until it became loose. Once it became loose, he untied the knot. Once he was free of restraint, he quietly tiptoed to the kitchen and retrieved a steak knife. Moving cautiously, he undid the duct tape that kept Mark's hands together. Mark cut Fatima loose and told her not to panic. Fatima was so scared that she was barely receptive. Claude put the rope behind him just in case Aaron walked out the door; Mark did the same. Claude leaned in Mark's ear and tried to make his words as clear as possible because there was no time for mistakes.

"This nigga slipping. He should've done what he came here to do and bounced. He is just giving us more time to think. I'm going to be on the opposite side of the door while you stay right here. Leave your hands behind your back and don't make a sound. Is your pistol too far?"

Mark nodded affirmatively.

"Alright. Fatima, we need you to be calm so don't give that motherfucker no signal. We going surprise his ass. When I give you a peace sign, throw something at the door. Once he steps out of it, I will be on the other side of the door waiting."

Fatima was worried to death about Sonya, who was literally seconds away from reliving her past of being a rape victim and being murdered. Fatima had never seen any drama. Her shaking seemed uncontrollable.

"Fatima, we have to be on the same page. It's either we lay the fuck down or we cancel this nigga's plans. If we decide to lie down, none of us will make it out of here alive, you hear me," Claude asked with the lowest tone.

Fatima nodded her battered head. He didn't have to ask Mark if he was ready because Mark was waiting for an opportunity to get at Aaron for what he did to everyone in the room.

Claude tiptoed his way past Sonya's bedroom door. He prayed that the vantage point he selected would offer leverage. Claude quickly looked behind his back to see if everyone held their positions in which they did. Claude knew he was gambling with his own life, but he didn't care. He could hear Aaron taking off his pants, but he didn't know if he had his gun close by so he kept caution in his back pocket. He waited a few seconds before he settled himself against the wall. As soon as Claude held out the peace sign, Mark went into his pocket, retrieved a quarter, and threw it at the door, producing a noise. Claude heard him put back on his pants hurriedly. Aaron opened the door harshly, his sight only set on the hostages. Aaron saw Mark and Fatima and remembered exactly where he posted them up at. When he realized Claude was missing from his position and restraint, he became instantly alert and pulled out his gun, but Claude connected with a short, sharp right to his chin from his vantage point. Aaron lost his footing and dropped the gun, but swung wildly at Claude, missing him by not even an inch. Aaron regained his balance and stood straight, but that was short-lived as Mark attacked Aaron from behind, rushing him to the floor. The tables had turned dramatically because Aaron was now on his back. Aaron tried to rush the men from his position on the floor, but Claude snapped his head back with a right cross, followed by Mark's Timberland. The next few minutes, Aaron endured the most horrific pain his body had ever received. Claude and Mark stomped and punched Aaron from all angles. Aaron was powerful and could hold his own, but the men were giving him the ass whipping of his life. Their thudding blows were too much as Aaron began to weaken. His body was curled in a fetal position as he covered his face for protection. Fatima watched her man and his cousin in horror as they kicked through Aaron's guards. Claude took his belt off and used the buckle to whip all over Aaron's body.

During the spurt of violence, Fatima rushed into Sonya's room. There was blood on the sheets from Sonya's gaping wound and with her panties down. The rape didn't go down, but she was still unconscious. In the midst of tending to her sister, Mark opened the front door while Claude dragged Aaron from the hallway. Once they were outside, Claude tucked his fingers in the waistline of Aaron's pants, grabbed him by his shirt, and tossed him down the stairs. Before they had a chance to run after him, they saw Aaron sprawled out on the asphalt. Timothy, a thin biracial man in his late thirties, Mark and Fatima's neighbor, rushed out of his apartment and dropped a jewel on them.

"Y'all need to chill man. My wife just called the police. We didn't know what was goin' on," Timothy warned.

The word cop had just registered in Claude and Mark's head. They came to their senses quick. Aaron squirmed on the ground from his flight down the stairs. He took a horrid beating. Both of his eyes were black and puffy, and his body leaked blood all over the place.

Despite the thrashing, he got up and limped out of plain sight as he held on to his side. When he made it to the vehicle and sat inside it, he looked in the mirror and examined his face. He reasoned that he had no one to blame but himself. He should've killed them all right then and there when he had a chance. He started his vehicle and peeled off.

Fatima held Sonya tightly, despite blood being all over her sweatshirt. Timothy's wife ran in the room with a few wet towels and a medical kit. Fatima rarely knew or spoke to the Caucasian, slender woman but she didn't mind allowing her to take control of Sonya's desperate need of medical attention. The woman wasn't a nurse, but she understood the signs and symptoms of being in shock. Sonya was out of her unconsciousness, but she was sweating profusely and appeared confused and nauseated.

"Can you hear me talk to you?" the woman asked.

Sonya didn't respond. She just looked around as if she was confused. The woman asked her a few more questions and received no response. Although Sonya's bed had blood all over it, the woman said it was best to leave her in that position because repositioning her could be fatal.

The police and an ambulance were due on the scene at any moment. Claude wanted to be with Sonya and be in tuned on her well being. He didn't give a fuck about being sent up north with handcuffs and shackles. He had no choice but to look on while the woman prepped her before professional medical help arrived. He felt like shit physically and mentally because he couldn't do anything to help her. Claude told Mark that he wanted to be with Sonya at the hospital.

"C, I'm just as fucked up over this shit as you are, but you ain't thinking rationally. I know you want to be with her, but you on parole man. I think it looks better if you turn yourself in instead of taking a flight with handcuffs on."

Claude wasn't trying to hear it, but Mark was right. He knew he had to get the fuck out of there fast, but he didn't want to leave the lady of his life in a compromising situation. He knew, once he was on that plane, the visual of her getting hit with the handle of a gun will nag at his brain. The mere thought of seeing her in that predicament drove him insane.

"Alright, get me out of here," Claude said to no one in particular. He seemed as if he was on the verge of crying.

"Y'all don't need any medical assistance?" Timothy asked.

"Yeah, but I got to get my cousin to the airport. That's a priority," Mark emphasized.

Timothy knew something was odd, but he wasn't going to question it.

"Mark, get your ass to the hospital, for real. You too Fatima. I will take your cousin to the airport," Timothy said.

Mark nodded.

Without taking any of his belongings, Claude followed Timothy out the door. Time was so precious that he didn't have time to look back at the woman who accepted him for who he was.

. . .

"The only good thing about working this third shift shit for tonight is the time and a half, but besides that, it is a goddamn waste of time and money. We're only relying on hearsay at this moment. Everything is fucking abstract," Detective Rinaldi bitched.

Detectives Taft and Rinaldi drove around downtown Los Angeles in the early morning hours. It was the second shift in a row they worked and they were both exhausted and frustrated from trying to solve a six month old case.

"Everything abstract eventually leads to something concrete. And speaking of abstract, I dug into some cold case files today and came by Aaron Banks Sr. Did you know that son of a bitch was a suspect in six homicides at the time of his death? Maybe the apple doesn't fall too far from the tree," Taft said.

"Jack, this origin shit you're expressing is not enough to crack this case open. We need something more solid than a woman coming to the station pointing the finger at her deceased son's negative counterparts. For all we know, those fucks could have nothing to do with this shit."

"True indeed partner, but I have a feeling we're going to

bust this case open sooner than later. It's detective instinct. I can feel it," Taft said convincingly.

Rinaldi turned to face his partner. Detective Taft looked focused and determined as he drove the cruiser expertly through the light traffic.

"Then why can't I feel it?"

"I don't know, but the Banks, including Pittman, have a lot of petty shit on their arrest records. Those guys are low level runners who probably deal to get by."

"So?"

"Greed and self-interest can be a strong motivator for murder," Taft said.

"A come up," Rinaldi finalized.

"Exactly." Taft's phone vibrated on his hip.

"Yeah," Taft answered.

"Hey Jack, you might want to pack up some hiking gear," Detective Jacobs said evenly.

"Why is that?"

"Mill Creek Route. There are two search teams with cadaver dogs and more enforcement in tow, heading towards the trailhead," Jacobs said.

"Jesus, it's gonna be like looking for a needle in a haystack. There are fucking giant redwood, sycamore, and maple trees out there covering most of the sky. Fuck! Who is the vic anyway?" Taft was annoyed at the idea of being in the woods in the early morning hours.

"Trudy Douglas. And get this, an anonymous caller called in, dropped a dime, and expected a reward of some sort. She probably shitted in her pants when Helen told her a reward wasn't being issued. The woman hasn't been missing that long."

"So what the fuck does that have to do with us? We have our own shit going on?" Taft said, playing Jacob's game so he could get to the point.

"Walter Banks."

Taft looked at his partner like he heard there was a pot of gold at the end of the road. Rinaldi scrunched up his face with uncertainty, unaware of the news Taft just heard.

"You're shittin' me?"

"I shit you not, but just be prepared to wade through some water."

"Sweet," Taft said before Jacobs ended the call.

Detective Taft took a deep breath and looked out the driver window for an opening for a U-turn.

"Walter Banks supposedly killed that Trudy Douglas woman. We're going to Mill Creek to unearth, if there is even a body, and we're going to snatch that asshole from where ever the fuck he is at. Now you got your moneys worth," Taft said as he proceeded with a dangerous U-turn.

"A civilian would have gotten a ticket for that Jack," Rinaldi said jokingly, no longer feeling fatigued from working a double shift.

Taft didn't respond but kept his eyes on the road, spacing out pieces of a puzzle that was nowhere near piecing together.

. . .

Aaron was an hour outside of Los Angeles after driving for over twenty hours nonstop despite the pain he was going through. Flashbacks of the first ass whipping he received in his life taunted his normal thought track, making him grit his teeth. He couldn't get over on how stupid he was for leaving his guard at the door. He was supposed to go to Sonya's house, kill her, or anyone else that got in the way, and be gone. Instead, his dick held his mind hostage. The man who was talking shit despite being tied up and having a gun in his face was on the wall of his mind like a poster. As far as Sonya, he still wanted her dead, but he didn't think God or Satan would have her now. When he went as far as down the street after he got stomped out, he debated on whether or not he should stay and finish the task, but he would have ran the risk of getting snatched in the Dallas, Texas jurisdiction and that was what he didn't need.

As he began to wonder how the man broke free from the rope he tied him up with, the scene of Sonya lying naked next to the dude replayed repeatedly in his mind.

Another issue that bothered him was that Raven disconnected her phone, which left a huge question mark over his head. His first instinct told him that it was nothing and that she'd call him with the new number, but he had a feeling that something wasn't right. He spoke to Flex yesterday and he said everything wasn't going that well because someone was skimming cash from every stash house. As usual, Aaron went off on him, but he knew it wasn't entirely Flex's fault because he wasn't as respected as he was. Aaron concluded that once he found out who was responsible, he would deal with them accordingly.

When his phone rang, he looked at the called ID on it and decided to let it go to voicemail, but when his cell phone rang again, he decided to bypass his own rule of picking up blocked calls.

"Who's this?" he answered rudely into the phone.

"Octavia," she replied.

"What?" Aaron asked suspiciously. He knew something was strange because she never called him before. He wondered how she got his number.

"Raven left you, that's what. Now the next piece of information is gonna cost you."

"Fuck you mean Raven left me?"

"You heard me, but that should be the least of your worries. Are you back in town?"

Aaron didn't respond. His mind automatically went to rewind as he started noticing Raven's strange behavior, but he didn't give her change in attitude any thought besides the fact that she was still mourning her brother. Everything made perfect sense. The bitch knows I killed her brother!

"You hear me? Are you back in town?"

"Close. What are you tryin' to tell me Octavia? If you got something on your chest, get it the fuck off. I don't got time for games?"

There was no turning back. She fought her own conscious tooth and nail to have the nerve to shit on Raven, but the devil side of her mind kept telling Octavia that Raven played her. Her mind rewinded to New Years Eve when Raven blatantly disrespected her in front of everyone, which added emphasis to her betrayal. Octavia may be grimy, evil, ugly, and pompous, but she was smart enough to figure out what drove Raven to lie about the reward money. Octavia had a feeling that she knew about her petty theft, but she thought that Raven went overboard by tricking her into leaking information about a murder case. She knew she was lying about the reward money when the person that picked up the phone said she had no knowledge of any reward money regarding the woman's disappearance. Octavia felt stupid for falling for some old, juvenile trick. She was unclear on whether or not the phone call Raven received last night was a hoax, but she knew Raven ran a bout of trickery on her. On top of it all, she reflected on all the times when they would share the most secretive details about one another, but it took Octavia to invade Raven's privacy for her to find out about what happened to her brother. She saw everything from Prime's body to the coded conversation from reading the text messages between Raven and Ali. She deciphered the coded text messages and realized that Aaron and his people were living on borrowed time. She figured Raven ran a game on her. It was time for Octavia to run her game to Aaron.

Since it was a fact that Raven wanted to remain out of Los Angeles for good, fuck it, Octavia reasoned. It wasn't like Ali or Wade was her best friends. They never acknowledged her even if she was in their faces.

"I ain't talking over this phone. Meet me at Kitchen 24," Octavia said, wanting to meet some place public in case Aaron wanted to inflict bodily harm because of her knowledge of what happened.

"Give me about forty five minutes," he said, hanging up the phone. Since he thought about killing her, he figured a few thousand dollars would shut her up.

59-Los Angeles

The men went over the remaining details of the plan for the third time. Everyone knew what they had to do. The ride to the stash house was unusually quiet as each man mentally attacked the task that lay ahead of them. Dungeon drove with his lips tightly sealed while Blast rode shotgun. Needles sat in the backseat fixing up his weapon, making sure his gun didn't have any potential to jam. The plan was to slide in, hit them quick, and slide out with the goods. The plan was that simple. The men made the plan extra user friendly by telling Flex someone was coming up after the meeting to make a huge transaction. Ali and Wade knew how fucked up Flex was since he murdered his woman and that Ali could throw anything at him and Flex would just bite. Pussy and regret dominated his common sense. If Ali would have ran that shit to Aaron, he would not have let that pass because no one outside was supposed to know where any of the stash spots were located.

The only sound that could be heard in the car was the preparation of weaponry. Needles and Blast locked and loaded their weapons. Needles was having a hard time screwing on the silencer, but no one took notice. Needles disregarded it, placed his gun on safety, and pulled out a bag of wet. Blast heard Needles fumbling with the bag and turned around.

"Put that shit away," Blast demanded casually.

"What the fuck for? This is how I prepare for war," Needles said, still trying to dump the wet on the CD cover evenly.

"Needles, put that fuckin' shit away," Blast said, elevating his voice a little.

Needles started to say something, but he read the murderous look in Blast's eyes and did what he was told. The men remained quiet, calm, and murderous minded for the rest of the ride. Nothing else was needed to say because they all knew what they had to do.

...

Aaron stormed out of the diner in a rage. The few grand he dropped was worth it because she dropped the bomb on him. As soon as he got into his truck, he tried to call Flex, but his phone rang repeatedly until it went to voicemail. He tried to call everyone else, but he was unsuccessful. None of his people picked up their phones. He had to act fast. His tires screeched as he peeled away from the diner.

. . .

"Damn, where the fuck is this dude at? Been waiting damn near an hour and this fat motherfucker ain't even picking up the goddamn phone! Daylight didn't even break yet and this nigga fucking around," Scoot bitched.

"Ali and Wade ain't here yet and I'm starting to get the sense that somethin' ain't right," Marco said worriedly.

"Why you sa…say that?" Jimmy asked.

"Jim, we here to discuss missing cheddar, not hand to hand shit. I don't give a fuck about how much of a purchase it is. Since when do we make direct, major transactions from a stash house?" Marco asked. "Scoot, try Ali or Wade and ask them what the fuck is going on. After all, it's his man we dealing with. Them little motherfuckers need to be here. I don't know why Aaron left that hungry motherfucker in charge. Nigga making all that money and he stressing a bitch."

Marco didn't completely understand why Flex murdered his woman, but he had an idea, and he knew it had something to do with the murders. He figured Flex's girlfriend may have known something about the killings and he shut her up permanently. The same went for Sonya, he figured. She probably knew too much. Even though that may be the case, he hated to see men resort to that kind of shit. Marco had a gut feeling that Aaron drove all the way to Texas to kill Sonya. The thought of Aaron killing her bothered him, but he'd never express it because he could easily go on the hit list.

Scoot called Ali's number and let it ring. On the ninth one, Ali picked up the phone.

"We on our way man, relax. Everything is in motion," Ali said smoothly, telling a bold face lie. He and Flip were situated four blocks away with no intention of riding through.

"Relax? What the fuck you mean relax? Niggas is boosting cash and you telling me to relax? Just get here. Your man better show up correct," Scoot said sternly before hanging up.

"I go…go…got to go take a shit," Jimmy said before getting up.

"Yeah, you do that homey. Marco, I'm given niggas a half hour. If they ain't here by then, I'm gone," Scoot said irately.

The men engaged in silence. Jimmy was releasing a liquid shit, but no one paid him any mind. Scoot was thinking about what Marco said about making exchanges at a stash house. Marco, on the other hand, was battling his first instinct, which told him that it would be wise to leave because something wasn't right. Marco's cell phone chimed.

"It's about damn time…hello?" Marco asked.

"Marc, don't talk, just listen! Y'all niggas need to get the fuck out of there now! It's a set up!" Aaron said loud and clear.

While Marco listened to Aaron about Ali and Wade setting everything up, Scoot knew something was up by looking at Marco's body language. Marco looked shook while Aaron dropped it on him. When Aaron revealed Raven's betrayal and the reason why, Marco wanted to drop the phone. They were sitting ducks.

"What the fuck is you still doing on the phone?! Get out of there now!" Aaron hung up the phone.

"Aaron said it was a set up! I knew something wasn't right," Marco said, moving hastily to retrieve his belongings and all the greenbacks and product in the spot.

"Jim, get the fuck out of the bathroom…"

Three unrecognizable men ran up in the stash house, kicking the door off the hinges and all that shit. They were going to go in smoothly, but heard Marco warn the others about a set up. Marco and Scoot were caught out with no weapons in their hands. Before they could muster another thought, Needles squeezed a shot off, blowing a ghastly hole through Marco's face. Pieces of skull fragments and brain matter scattered all over the place, some getting on the assailants. Quick flashbacks of Scoot's criminal life flashed before his eyes as he stared at the open cannon. Dungeon unleashed the silent shells of death on his upper body, his body rattling wildly from the bullets. Once Scoot's body hit the floor, Blast looked at Needles like he grew a dick on his head because when he shot Marco, the noise was loud enough for anyone up early to hear it.

"What the fuck? You was supposed to use the silencer..."

Blast froze as he saw a hole appear on Needles head. His eyes shifted upward from the bullet hitting his forehead. He was dead on his feet. Jimmy squeezed off another shot, tearing up the side of Blast's torso. He fell to the floor, squirming like a fresh fish out of water. Dungeon didn't even acknowledge Blast's trip to the floor because he didn't have enough time. He fired two shots. The first one hit Jimmy in his chest. The bullet made his body hunch over, knocking empty Hennessy and beer bottles off the small kitchen table. The second bullet went straight through his throat and out the back of his neck. Jimmy's gun hit the floor, causing it to go off. Dungeon walked over to the body with his gun drawn, checking to see if busting off another shot was necessary. The repulsive look Jimmy had on his face verified his soul's departure from his body.

Dungeon walked slowly around the bodies, wondering why everything went wrong. The living room of the stash house looked like the aftermath of Gettysburg as his eyeballs went back and forth, looking at his fallen comrades and his adversaries. Being that he didn't have time to mourn the losses of his closest friends, he went straight for the goods, particularly the goods Marco had on him before he was cut down. When he was done gathering money and product, he started to leave, but he was held back by Blast's groans. Blood gurgled in his mouth as he used all the strength he had to use his arm to beckon Dungeon not to leave him, but Dungeon planned on leaving him right there. His entire side was covered with blood, he couldn't move, the chances of him surviving the gunshot wound was slim to little, and most importantly, he would have been a burden on Dungeon's journey to financial freedom. Instinctively, Dungeon frisked his ailing friend's pockets, taking everything he had. He did the same thing to Needles, who had around three hundred dollars on him. After he shoved the money back into his pocket, he saw the plea for help that Blast had in his eyes. Dungeon pointed his silencer at Blast's head and pulled the trigger. He stood over Blast's body, telling himself that he only did the man a favor by putting him out of his misery. After quickly checking the stash house one last time, he had to make moves because he had little to zero time to waste. He could hear the faint sound of police sirens. When he opened the door to leave, Aaron stood in the doorway with his heat drawn, the barrel of it inches away from Dungeon's nose. Dungeon had no idea who the man was that now had him hostage, but he would find out soon enough.

Aaron grabbed him by the collar, held his gun in the other hand, and forcefully made Dungeon walk backwards into the house. He knew his crew was gunned down so he didn't acknowledge the bodies as he backed Dungeon up against the wall.

"Look man, I don't know who you are, but I'm sure something could be worked out," Dungeon said, hearing the sirens getting closer.

"Who sent you?" Aaron asked calmly, taking the only gun Dungeon had on him. Aaron could hear the police sirens getting closer and knew he had to act fast.

"Ali, Wade, and some nigga named Flip gave me and my homies a lot of money to do them niggas," Dungeon said easily.

"Flip?" The mentioning of Flip's name caught him off guard, but he would have to acknowledge that later.

"Open your mouth."

"Come on man, this shit ain't nec…"

Aaron stuffed the gun in his mouth, cutting off his plea. Dungeon's clear, concise words turned to muffles. Dungeon stopped talking after Aaron pulled the trigger, blowing the back of Dungeon's head off.

Aaron looked at Blast and Needle's bodies and didn't recognize them, but swallowed hard when he saw Marco's body sprawled out, half of his face a few yards away from him. The sight of Jimmy's body was what really fucked him up. He saw the gun next to Jimmy's corpse and retrieved it. He knew Jimmy went down shooting because his gun was still hot.

On his way out the back door, he ran into Scoot's body, but didn't marvel at it. The police were closing in on the stash house. He quickly grabbed the money and drugs that Dungeon had on him and slid out the rear entrance. Aaron jumped a few fences and made a couple of dogs bark, but he made it to the truck in no time, even though the pain he experienced was excruciating. When he peeled off with Flip on his mind, the police began to surround the stash house and scream demands that no one couldn't hear.

. . .

Wade's thoughts were consumed with greed and fear while his vehicle was idling at a red light. When Ali broke down the amount of product Aaron had in the street and the stash houses, he almost lost his mind. The money and product in the stash houses was the jackpot though. Those trap boys out there in the streets could keep all that shit. As far as Freddy was concerned, he won't be a problem as long as someone was out in the streets moving his product. He didn't give a fuck either way.

He smiled, using all of his teeth as he thought of the abundance of rewards they'd receive once Aaron and his people were eliminated from the equation. As far as their corner men, they'd worry about them later, but for now, they had bigger fish to fry. His heavy smile faded when reality snuck up on him. Although it was confirmed that Aaron and Flex murdered Ali and Raven's people, he wasn't sure if he agreed on his partner's cast of characters. Wade told Ali continuously that Blast, Needles, and Dungeon may be too violent, dangerous, and unorganized to carry out the mission. Flip expressed this also, but it was too late in the game to make adjustments or replacements. If everything went down as planned, Aaron's main henchmen, especially Flex, should be memories by now.

Wade was so zoned out that when the light turned green, he didn't move, which made it easier for Aaron to establish a simple vantage point directly next to Wade on his left. When Wade snapped out of his funk, he saw the truck stationed next to him before he noticed the green light. Wade froze with fear as he watched Aaron aim a pistol at him. He didn't recognize Aaron at first because Aaron's face been through hell. Without saying a word, and by the time Wade recognized him, Aaron pulled the trigger three times and pulled off.

The second Aaron turned Wade into a corpse, Wade's whip drifted because it wasn't in gear. Wade's car ran into another car coming from the opposite direction. Both vehicles went up in flames.

...

Ali and Flip pulled up to the curb outside of Ali's pad to find out why Simone wasn't picking up the phone. He had spoken to her, and then suddenly, the line went dead. Ali tried to call her back at least ten times, but didn't get an answer. He called her mother so she could try calling her, but Simone's mother didn't get an answer either. He hung up on her quickly to avoid being bombarded with questions. As a precaution, he decided to stop at his crib to see what the deal was.

Ali was taken back when he noticed his apartment door left opened ajar. Flip noticed it too and they instinctively pulled out their guns as they filed in. The living room light was off, but the hallway light was on. The men could hear Ali's son crying from the bedroom. They looked at each other strangely before they made moves in that direction. Ali called out Simone's name, but she didn't answer. Ali's heart was beating rapidly, not knowing what to expect next. His hands shook visibly as he hesitated a few yards near the bedroom's entrance. The child cried loudly as if he was disturbed by something. Flip took the lead, sensing Ali really didn't want to know what was behind his bedroom door. When Flip turned on the light, his mouth opened wide and his eyes bulged from the eyesore he had in his line of vision. Ali saw his cousin's facial expression and wondered what the fuck was going on.

"Brace yourself," Flip said gravely.

Ali twisted his face at Flip's comment and stepped pass him. The second he saw the baby crying hysterically next to his mother's shot down, dead body on the bed, Ali ran in the room, not quite fully grasping and accepting on what was before his eyes.

"Oh shit," Ali said with despair as he ran over to his son and the body.

His son cried tremendously. Flip ran to Ali's side and removed the baby from the bloodied corpse. Simone lay flat on her bed with her eyes and mouth wide open, leaking blood everywhere on the bed. Ali planted himself next to her body and rocked her gently back and forth. He held her, blood getting all over his clothes, and cried heavily as the mother of his only son lay dead in his arms.

Flip empathized greatly with his cousin, but they didn't have time to mourn. Flip told Ali when he first touched down in Los Angeles that Aaron was nothing to fuck with, but it went in Ali's ear and out the other. Simone's brutal murder had Aaron written all over it. Aaron knew where to strike where it hurt the most. Flip's first instinct told him that Aaron was responsible..

"This shit is fucked up Ali and I know it hurts, but we got to go before this nigga do some other wild shit. Just tell me where them other guns is at. We gotta move," Flip said carefully, hoping that his cousin would cooperate.

Ali sat there on the blood infested bed holding Simone with tears heavy in his eyes, rocking her back and forth. When Flip called out to him again, he used his hand and closed her eyes. Finally coming to his senses, he pointed to the closet where he held his small arsenal of guns. Ali covered Simone's face with a blanket after kissing her on the forehead. The second he left her body, he saw a small piece of paper with some blood on it where the leg of the body rested. When he picked up the paper and read it, his saddened person turned into a killer with a deeply rooted vengeance. The note read: *Y'all don't know who y'all fucking with. Ali, you know who did this, so bring it!*

After Flip read the note and retrieved the guns, Ali snatched up his screaming son and they bounced. After they drop off Ali's son, the men would not rest until Aaron was dead.

"It's like fucking Hamburger Hill in here man," Detective Rinaldi remarked.

"Yeah, first we find the body and now this shit," Detective Taft responded. When Trudy's body was unearthed, placed into the coroner wagon, and taken to the medical examiner's office, the dispatcher sent the detectives to another crime scene that consisted of six bodies.

The detectives went around the crime scene one last time before the crime scene investigators started tagging, logging, and packaging all the potential evidence in the stash house. Detective Taft took multiple pictures of each body in various angles. The bodies weren't moved yet. They were all in the same position they fell into when they were cut down by bullets. In total, six bodies were in the stash house with a sign of forced entry. The fuzz didn't know if they were all together or if a seventh man cooperated in the mass homicide, but Detective Taft noted an excellent observation.

"Rinaldi, come over here for a second," Detective Taft said. He kneeled down next to Dungeon's body that looked unrecognizable because of a point-blank range shot in his mouth.

"Close range, but the rest of these men were shot from somewhat of a distance," Detective Taft said.

"Could have been a self-inflicted shot," Detective Jacobs said as he approached the men.

"It would be a great idea to arrive on time at the crime scene," Detective Rinaldi said nonchalantly.

"What the fuck is that supposed to mean?" Detective Jacobs asked, clearly offended.

"It means that it's a great idea to gather facts before you jump to conclusions. I believe they teach that in the academy," Detective Rinaldi said sarcastically.

Detective Jacob gathered a half smirk. "Oh yeah? Maybe it would be a good idea to get your little pecker checked for..."

"Enough you guys! We got some serious shit here in front of us so settle down. Jacobs, no, this man didn't pull the trigger on himself because there isn't a gun on him. There had to be a seventh man here."

The woman police dispatcher interrupted whatever opinion they had on Detective Taft's theory. They listened attentively as she described a homicide that ultimately led to someone innocent getting killed that was ten minutes away.

"It never fucking ends," Detective Rinaldi said as he followed Taft and Jacobs to the unmarked cruiser.

. . .

"I know you fucked up right now Ali, but you need to focus on your girl after we find out what the fuck is going on. The car they used is still there with them pigs draped all over it. Something went wrong," Flip said truthfully. Ali wasn't in any mood to deal with anything, not even his own life. He just wanted to think of Simone. Reality told him that if he wasn't playing a dirty game, she would still be alive. Instead of pondering the fact, Ali took Flip's words and ran with them. He knew he had to resume his focus. He continued to rock his child to sleep from the backseat of his own car while Flip handled the wheel. He had the same feeling Flip had about the others, but nothing really mattered to him. His only concern was getting his son to safety and killing Aaron.

. . .

Niomi was fading in and out of a sleep as the laughter from the Cosby show seeped through the television. When she woke up and was alert, she got up and looked inside her bedroom to see if Wade was home, but there wasn't any trace of him. She wasn't worried or surprised because it was typical of him. After her brief search for her man inside the apartment, she went into the bathroom to wash up.

While she waited for the sink water to warm up, she looked at herself in the mirror, wondering what she'd look like if she was five or six months pregnant while rubbing her stomach. She smiled as she anticipated herself getting bigger, having a child for the first time in her life. Her smile disappeared by someone banging on the door. She walked in the hallway en route to the living room to answer the door. She produced a look of confusion when she heard a baby crying, but she still walked to the door. When she looked in the peephole to see who it was, she became concerned because she never saw Ali alone with his child. She didn't recognize the dude behind him, but since it was Ali and his son at the door, she opened it.

"I need you to look after Khalif," Ali voiced with desperation.

"Why? Wade is not with you?" she asked, looking at the door behind the stranger, anticipating Wade's late entrance.

Ali was so traumatized by Simone's murder that he had no idea what she asked. Flip didn't know her so he thought it was best for him to keep quiet.

"Ali, I'm talking to you. Where is Wade and why do you have Khalif with you at this hour?" she asked worriedly, sensing something was wrong.

The sullen look Ali had on his face told her he had a valid reason to be there, accompanied by his son that was literary screaming and the stranger. Ali shot her a look that would stay with her for the rest of her life. Tears automatically started crawling down his face.

"Simone is dead."

Niomi put her hand over her mouth in shock as the news of Simone's death didn't take long to register; she nearly fainted. They cried in each other's arms while Flip looked on with impatience. He felt for Ali, but if Aaron could do that shit to Simone, the chances of him being on his way over to do the same to Niomi was even greater.

"How?" Niomi managed to ask through all of her crying.

Ali showed her the note, but she didn't understand what it meant. After he told her who wrote it, she reflected on a conversation she had with Simone about the fucked up vibe she felt from Aaron. Flip felt that Ali gave away too much information.

"Don't want to jump to any conclusions. We don't even know yet for sure," Flip remarked. He knew it was Aaron, but he didn't want Niomi to throw a wrench in their plans by calling the cops. Flip figured Aaron needed to be in the morgue, not county jail.

Before anyone said anything, the men looked at a familiar

scene because they just rode by it. The news reporter stood directly in front of the stash house, reporting six bodies shot dead inside of it. She said police have not identified any witnesses and the motives behind the murders were currently unknown. The men stood in front of the television set looking at the pictures of all of the deceased, wondering what the hell happened. Niomi recognized three out of the six men found dead. Marco, Jimmy, and Scoot were at the New Year's party Raven had at her condo last month. That was the first and only time she met them.

"Ali, where is Wade?" she asked desperately as soon as the segment went off the air.

"I don't know Niomi, we've been trying to call him, but keep getting his voicemail. Look, just calm down, pack some shit, and take my son and get out of here. It's not safe here. We're going to look for Wade."

Niomi had a horrible feeling that the bad news she received wasn't going to be the last. Ali and Flip left abruptly, right after he told her it wasn't safe. The baby cried his way into sleep. Without packing a single item, besides her pocketbook, she picked up Khalif while still in the car seat and left, not realizing that in a matter of minutes, she would receive another powerful dosage of bad news.

...

Flex woke up from his vivid nightmare about Trudy walking out of her shallow grave. His bed sheets were drenched with perspiration. He looked around his bedroom to be sure Trudy's remains weren't in there with him. Slowly, he came back to reality. He took a large, deep breath to get a hold of himself because the look she had on her face haunted him. He would swear to himself that he could hear her call his name. Flex was a mess and he knew it. Life was like that sometimes. Something that was supposed to be a one night stand turned into a heat of the moment homicide. His natural state of mind was so fucked up that the thought of suicide crossed his mind. His grandparents even noticed a change in his behavior and nagged him thoroughly about it. His appearance was now wild and unkempt and he spends most of his free time alone. He regretted what he did to Trudy.

He knew that he was mentally weak and that nothing else mattered, not even the obligations to his people. Flex didn't want anyone seeing him in a vulnerable state of mind, especially Marco because Marco would have used Flex inability to live with regrets as his own ammunition. When he sat up, he retrieved the last cigarette in his pack and lit it, even though smoking was prohibited in his grandparent's home. The cigarette burned slowly while he held the cigarette in the corner of his mouth. When he checked his cell phone, he had forty missed calls, half of them coming from Aaron. His phone vibrated while it was still in his hand. It was an incoming call from Aaron. He thought for a second to dodge him because he was the last person he wanted to talk to, but since he had been calling all night and into the early morning hours, something had to be on his mind. If it were anyone else, he would have sent their calls to voicemail, despite cash being lifted from the stash spots.

"Hello?" Flex asked with some of the sleep left in his voice.

"What the fuck is wrong wit' you Flex?! Been trying to get at you all night," Aaron flipped.

"Just been sleep all day, but what's up?"

"Po-po is onto you about that bitch," Aaron said carefully. Flex didn't know if Aaron was serious or joking so he sat there holding the phone looking stupid.

"Stop playing around; it's too early for that shit."

"Do it sound like I'm playing around?"

Aaron was rambling on the phone about the action currently pending, such as the bodies at the stash house, but Flex didn't hear one word Aaron said. Instead of taking heed to his cousin's warnings about Ali, Wade, and Flip, he trained his eyes to the unmarked cruiser outside his bedroom window.

"Aaron man, them motherfuckers is outside!" Flex ended the call and discarded the cigarette.

Flex threw on some sweats, a t-shirt, and some sneakers. He was just about to open his bedroom door until he heard a soft knock. Flex knew he was between a rock and a hard place because if he jumped out his window, he was sure to break something on his body. When he opened the door, two stone faced detectives stood at his door while his grandparents stood at their rear. If Thomas would have looked outside before opening the door, he wouldn't have opened it, but he did, and Flex had no time to buy. Beverly was disgusted at her husband, but it was an honest mistake. Beverly was never a criminal, but she loved her grandsons and would die willingly to protect them if need be. Beverly had an incredulous look on her face as she wondered what Flex did for the detectives to be in their presence.

"Mr. Banks, this is Detective Dobson," Detective Jacobs nodded toward the young burly gray-eyed detective who was staring at Flex with disdain. "And I'm Detective Jacobs…"

"What do y'all want?" Flex asked sharply. He knew exactly why the detectives were standing outside of his bedroom.

"Should we remind you here or at the station?" Detective Jacobs countered, shooting his grandparents subtle glances, playing Flex's game. Flex stood still and didn't say a word.

"Walter, what is going on?" his grandmother asked.

"Grandma, I'm wondering the same thing," Flex lied. He didn't want them knowing anything to save his grandparents the heartache. Flex recalled the day he choked Trudy to death at the moment. He could still see the horrid look she had on her face after he killed her. Flex realized that he was going to jail and won't see daylight again because he knew he left DNA on Trudy's body, especially the insides of her nails where she scratched him. He still had the markings. The cut marks on Flex's face was the first thing the detectives noticed. Mentally, Flex was tired, and the detectives could see the mental and physical fatigue on him. He looked unkempt and he stunk. Detective Jacobs knew that he didn't have to look for any chinks in Flex's armor because he had guilt written all over his face. Detectives Jacobs and Dobson escorted Flex to the cruiser with handcuffs on, and without incidence. Flex's grandparents kept probing the detectives until Detective Jacobs finally said that their grandson was a person of interest in a case. He promised to provide the Banks with more details once they find out more information. Before departing, Detective Jacob inquired about Aaron, didn't get the response that he wanted, handed the Banks a card, and drove away. Flex watched as much of his grandparents as he could as Detective Dobson rounded the corner.

At the end of the street, Aaron watched the outcome of Flex's downfall in horror. He had a bad feeling that the detectives asked about him. Instead of pondering his cousin's capture and wondering if his cousin was a rat candidate, he turned around and sped off. Since his entire set engaged in their demise, Aaron decided that it was now time to skip town, but he had to complete a little unfinished business first.

. . .

Niomi was at a rest stop off of I-10 trying desperately to get in touch with Raven. She feared for Raven's life. When she dialed the number the first time, she thought she'd dialed the number too fast on the payphone, but when she dialed it again, she realized that Raven either forgot to pay her bill or she voluntarily cut the service off.

A few minutes before she left the house with Khalif, Wade's picture was on every local station, describing how he was first shot three times in the face and when slumping over from the gunshots, he crashed into another vehicle, causing it to go up in flames. If Wade didn't have his ID on him, dental records would have revealed who he was. His entire body was burned. His driver's license number didn't fade from the flames and was the only recognizable item that made it out of the inferno. The police ran the number in and Wade's information popped up. Knowing that Aaron was still on the loose, she dialed 911 after attempting to reach Raven so a cop could stop by the house to check on her. She had a feeling that Ali and the man he was with was going after him so she hoped the police would capture Aaron before he gets killed. Good or bad, she didn't need anyone's murder on her conscious. That was the type of shit she didn't need in her life. After placing the call, she got back into the car. Niomi rested her head on the steering wheel and cried herself because of the horrid events of a day. She literally screamed in agony at the mere thought of her unborn child not having a father. She balled herself in the seat and cried, thinking about Wade's horrific death.

She dropped Khalif off at his grandmother's house. She told Simone's mother Ali dropped Khalif off, along with someone she never seen, and left. Niomi hugged and held on to Simone's mother. Aretha knew Ali's lifestyle had a lot to do with her daughter's death. She wondered what Ali did that was so twisted that he placed his family in danger. Khalif could have also been killed. The women had cried on each other's shoulder, longing for the strength that neither one of them had.

Once she stopped crying and took off on the highway, she made up her mind to drive as far away from Los Angeles as she could. She feared for her own life.

. . .

When Aaron twisted the doorknob and realized that Raven's condo was unlocked, he stormed in there menacingly, despite having a noticeable limp. He had a puzzled look on his battered face because he didn't know if Octavia was bullshitting because everything looked properly intact. He charged up the stairs, looking around anxiously, hoping to see the slightest sign of Raven. He made moves to the bedroom, hoping to see her in plain view so he could inflict wounds on her that would never heal. Although Octavia told Aaron that she found out Ali and Wade's motive for murder, he never knew how they became hip to the morbid shit they pulled last year. The answer was the chain he currently had on his neck, but that never crossed his mind.

Since it was clear to Aaron that Raven packed what she needed and bounced, he explored the other reason why he made the stop at her condo. He limped across Raven's large, lavish bedroom to get the other half of what he came there for. A month after Aaron and Raven met, Raven confided in Aaron and trusted him enough to expose her stash compartment, but Aaron created another compartment within it, unbeknownst to her. He had five birds stored in there and he planned on heading out of state, establish a network, set up and expand.

Aaron heard some shuffling noises downstairs. He stopped, listened, and heard nothing after that. He continued doing what he was doing. He continued stacking the tote bag that was already in there with the dope, cash, and a P89 to go with it. His grandmother used to always warn him as a child about his habit of leaving the door opened or unlocked. She said someone will follow him in one day. If he would have taken heed to her advice, Ali and Flip would not have followed him into the apartment five minutes after Aaron charged up the stairs. After Aaron got finished loading the small come-up in his bag, he secretly pulled out the P89 because he felt the presence of a few human beings standing in the entrance of the bedroom. He put the bag to the side and turned around slowly and froze in his tracks.

"Don't you even fucking think about it! Drop that shit! I see somebody got to you before we did," Flip said evenly. The men had their guns drawn. Ali was shaking miserably. It wasn't from fear. It was from his raw desire to send Aaron to hell. Aaron took note of it.

"If it ain't motherfucking Flip. Long time no see. I've always wondered how many bitches cringed at the sight from the beauty mark I created on your face," Aaron said with dripping sarcasm.

"You got a lot of nerve nigga," Flip said coldly. "I ain't going to ask you again, drop the fucking gun!"

Aaron knew he was fucked as he accessed the situation. He saw the hate and fire in the men's eyes and knew that they were going to kill him, but he saw Ali's hands trembling and was buying some time.

"Ali, just to let you know, you're girl got some dynamite pussy. That's just a case of some good pussy gone hard, you know what I mean? Too bad the bitch had to die. And Flip, you should have taught your brother better than that."

Aaron's words were cold and callous. A switch went off in Ali's head. Flip knew what Aaron was trying to do. He was trying to distract the men, using their own tragedies in life against them to buy even a fraction of a second so Aaron could fire his weapon. The men locked on each other's menacing eyes. Aaron knew he was in a compromised situation and wasn't afraid to be in it. Flashbacks quickly entered Ali's mind about the joyful times he spent with Simone on her short stint on Earth. The main thought he pondered was when Simone delivered their child in the delivery room. The bright smile she had on her face when the doctor placed their bundle of joy in her arms vanished as Aaron quickly raised his gun. If Flip wasn't quick on the draw, Aaron could have shot Ali and killed him. Flip fired a shot, hitting Aaron directly in the core of his heart. Aaron collapsed to the floor from the single, deadly shot. Unsatisfied, Ali walked up to Aaron's corpse and emptied the rest of the clip on him. Ali stood over Aaron's body with a crazed look on his face while Flip gathered the goods that belonged to Aaron.

"Fuck this nigga Ali. Let that nigga burn in peace," Flip said.

Moments after Ali and Flip left the vicinity, Detectives Taft and Rinaldi were back inside Raven's apartment for two reasons. A civilian called and wanted Raven to be checked upon. Ten minutes after that phone call, the radio dispatcher received a call from Raven's neighbor stating she heard gun shots. They split up once they were inside. Rinaldi checked around downstairs while Taft checked the upper level, both of the detectives using keen experience by enacting stealth, holding their guns, peeking around corners in the condo. After Rinaldi checked the entire perimeter in the lower level of the condo, he heard his partner calling from upstairs.

"Yeah," Rinaldi answered.

"We have ourselves a 187 up here."

Rinaldi walked up the stairs, sighing at the many bodies that turned up within the last few hours. When he entered Raven's bedroom, Taft was radioing the dispatcher, standing over the body.

Rinaldi joined his partner near the open eyed corpse, wondering why Taft was grilling the body as if he never seen one before. Taft rolled up the victim's sleeve. The tattoo on the African American man verified his identity, according to the mugshot and face sheet inside the cruiser.

"The suspects just fled," Taft said, scribbling in his notepad.

"You could say that again," Rinaldi said. It wasn't any

argument in that. Aaron's corpse was still smoking.

Taft shook his head in frustration. Things would have been a lot better if Aaron was alive. There was so much that needed some answering. Taft knew that Aaron was definitely involved in the killings, but he didn't know why he would be in the home of one of the victim's siblings. That alone left a big question mark over his head.

"What's on your mind?" Rinaldi asked.

Taft looked out the window and spotted more police, a coroner van, and crime scene investigators approaching the home. Taft's mind was spinning out of control, knowing that they still didn't have a break in the case.

"A lot of shit Rinaldi. That's why I never rule anything out. I have never once ruled out Raven Howard as a suspect. She knew something we didn't. Why the fuck is this bastard lying dead on her floor? I will tell you one thing, Aaron is dead and he can't tell a tale, but Walter, that's another story," Taft said, knowing all about Flex's confession at the station not too long along. "That kid is looking at life. A year under that mark would be a gift. The same rule not only applies to money, but it applies to deals. Right now, we don't have a fucking clue what's going on, but I'm pretty sure our boy Walter, or shall I say Flex, yeah, he knows what the fuck is going on. Jacobs said Walter isn't talking about the mass murders and Peter Sullivan, but he will when he finds out his cousin is on a slab," Taft said coldly, giving a vibe to Rinaldi that he had never seen before.

"What are you trying to say Jack?"

"The more years doing this shit, the more prone you are to meeting friends in high places. Politics is going to put that bastard back into the streets Rinaldi. Those fucks want that case busted open bad, and I know they will be more than willing to cooperate. Pay real close attention to how everything unfolds and watch your career soar. It's not about the dead drug dealers; it's about Peter Sullivan. That bastard at the station knows exactly what happened to him."

"What makes you think the kid will talk?" Rinaldi asked with greed all over his face.

"Because everybody around him are memories. What the

fuck does he have to lose? If he ever comes home, which I doubt and would be a miracle, he'd do us a favor. He'll kill the bastards that killed this son of a bitch," he pointed at Aaron's body. "Less killers off the street. To add more stink to shit, we find the alleged killer in the house of his victim's sister."

"You're not going to retire until this case is fully solved and you're going to use Walter to do it."

Taft looked at Rinaldi and smirked. "Watch and learn." Taft felt his cell phone vibrating and it was an incoming call from Detective Jacobs, who was waiting patiently for the coroner to pull Simone's body out the wall of cadavers at the morgue.

"Taft, I just spoke to the family of that dead girl we just found in the apartment. We have a huge break," Detective Jacobs said with an even tone.

"Feel me in."

"Ali fucking Ward."

"He killed the girl?" Taft asked, knowing exactly who Ali Ward was. He was a person of interest in the murder of Tyrone Peeler, a junkie who some say Ali killed over a twenty dollar debt a day after Colin was killed.

"The family doesn't think so, but they think his lifestyle played a vital role in their loved one's death. Simone's mom has no idea of his whereabouts."

"What makes you so sure Jacobs? Ali is a little fucking demon and it wouldn't surprise me. That is one dangerous sonofabitch."

"Taft, her sister told me Ali and Colin are first cousins. Dennis and Raven are brother and sister. Or is that just a coincidence?"

"Not a coincidence Jacobs, it's a fucking war out there underneath our noses. It's a goddamn war. Ali Ward and Wade Smith, known fucking crime partners. Wade is dead, Ali's girlfriend...dead. The bodies at the stash house, Grape Street." Detective Taft placed many of the pieces together and knew without a reasonable doubt that Ali, Wade, and Raven have choreographed the blueprint for retaliation because of their fallen loved ones.

"Jacobs, we'll see ya at the station. We have ourselves a case to solve," Taft said, containing all of his hidden excitement of solving a case that was getting cold.

"Yes, we do, and we start on Walter."

"He knows he's done Jacobs. May be pulling teeth."

"Two P's."

Taft caught on. "Peter Sullivan and politics. Just ran that shit to Rinaldi."

"See you in twenty five minutes," Jacobs said before ending the call.

While the other units, crime scene investigators, and many other staff from various agencies filed in, Taft looked at Aaron's body and thought of the night many years ago when he escorted a young, crying, screaming boy to the same home Detectives Jacobs and Dobson picked up Walter, after they brought Ruth Bank's body down to the morgue. He remembered that night like it happened yesterday. He started to wonder if the dead man in front of him was the answer to Muddy and Slim's demise.

...

Beverly screamed in agony in Thomas's arms after identifying Aaron's corpse in the morgue. When they got outside of the building, Beverly fainted into her husband's arms. While still on the ground, Thomas rocked her back and forth with a stone face, thinking of all the times he treated his eldest grandson like shit while Aaron was growing up. Many people on their way inside the building offered the elderly couple their help, but Thomas waved them off politely. A lone tear fell from his hostile face as he tried vigorously to stop the surge of regret running rampant in his mind. Thomas knew without a doubt that his wife would never be the same. Aaron and Flex may have been a terror to society, but Beverly loved her grandchildren unconditionally and equally. Beverly was in shock about the fate of her grandchildren because she was oblivious to the amoral roles they played in society, but Thomas wasn't surprised at all. He knew it would only be a matter of time before someone put Aaron out of his misery; it was inevitable.

...

"I'm afraid going home today is out of the question, young lady. You took a brutal hit and you're lucky you didn't slip into a coma or even killed from the blow you received. Some people endure a blunt injury to the head, fall asleep, and never wake up. We're keeping you overnight for observation to be on the safe side," Dr. Dominic Calhoun said warmly, his beefy hand moving the pen on his scribble pad as he noted Sonya's progress. He was a slightly overweight man with a receding hairline and blue eyes. Throughout his twenty years of being a doctor, he treated patients who endured similar blows and knew something drastic could happen if he allowed Sonya to discharge from the hospital. He was surprised at Sonya's strength and her willingness to get better, but there was still some caution he wanted to exercise for her.

Sonya rested on the elevated hospital bed with a gauze pad over the left side of her head. Both of her eyes were swollen shut, but she'd live. She didn't want to stay another night there, but she wasn't going to argue. She was thankful to be alive.

Yesterday, during the afternoon, Mark, Fatima, and Julia visited, as well as Patricia and Amy, but came and went at different times. Mark and Fatima had their share of scrapes, cuts, and bruises, but they were well enough to be treated and released on the same day. Since Sonya was recovering from the blow, she was unable to answer questions from the police, but Mark and Fatima were bombarded with a barrage of them. Mark coached Fatima to remain quiet. He said it was a random act of violence. There were four pounds of weed and the stacks of money Claude sent from Connecticut at the apartment. He wanted to stay as far away from law enforcement as possible.

Sonya wished that the blunt trauma she received from Aaron could erase the horrible memory of Claude, Mark, and Fatima bounded, beaten, and unconscious in the living room. The memory made her angry. Now that she heard about the murders from a horse's mouth, she wished evil on the man that made her life a nightmare. She never felt such hatred towards anyone, but Aaron was another story. He came all the way from California to put her on his death list, and he was almost successful. She cringed at the tormented look he had on his face before he inflicted massive bodily harm on her.

Her thoughts raced rapidly, starting from the look Prime gave her when she asked about the murders to the episode with Aaron yesterday. She was thankful that everyone escaped Aaron's wrath alive, thanks to Claude, but she felt depressed as she imagined Claude returning to prison. When Mark told Sonya in full detail what Claude did to get them out of their ordeal, the feelings she had for him escalated, but bashed him slightly for performing a suicidal maneuver. The man had placed a much needed spark in her life and now he was gone. She missed him badly and wanted to be in his presence, but for now, she had to focus on herself and recuperate from her mental and physical pain.

"Is there anything else I could do for you?" Dr. Calhoun asked.

"No thank you," she said.

As soon as the doctor left the room, a medium-sized, middle age detective knocked quietly on the door. Although he didn't flash a badge, Sonya read cop all over him. She remembered what Mark said about keeping quiet and she intended to do just that; however, flashbacks of the people she cared for lingered around in her head.

"Hi, Ms. Williams, allow me to introduce myself. I am Detective Willie Richardson and I promise you I won't take that much of your time. I understand that you may not be in any kind of mood or shape to answer any questions about yesterday, especially your brother in law and your sister, but there is information that requires your immediate attention," Detective Richardson said seriously. "There are more pressing issues at hand."

Sonya twisted her face, wondering what the hell he was talking about.

"What information?" she asked, giving him her undivided attention.

"What is your relationship with Trudy Douglas?"

The fog in Sonya's head disappeared as the anger she accumulated turned into chronic worry. She had a feeling that the detective came to deliver her bad news. When she didn't hear from Trudy since the last day she spoke to her, she swept any concern about Trudy underneath the rug. She tried calling Trudy back a few times, including her cell phone, but didn't get an answer. She didn't think anything of it. She figured Trudy was going through something and that she'd call when she was good and ready.

"She's my friend. What is going on?"

"To be frank with you, Trudy Douglas is dead. Her body was found earlier this morning in some wooded area in or around Los Angles," he said gravely.

Sonya had her mouth wide open with tears forming in her eyes, unable to fully grasp the words coming out of the detective's mouth. The detective gave her a chance to absorb the news he provided before moving on.

"An hour or two before her body was found, LAPD acted on a tip from an anonymous caller who identified the location of the body as well as a potential suspect."

Sonya just watched the detective's lips move as the news of Trudy's murder formed an adverse reaction on her mental being. She felt drugged because of the news she received from the detective.

"Ms. Williams, are you still with me?"

"Yes, I'm sorry," she said, wiping away a fresh set of tears.

"The reason why I am interviewing you is because you were the last person she spoke to before her disappearance, according to her phone records. Now, Ms. Williams, the suspect in Ms. Douglas's murder is Walter Banks. His deceased cousin is the one who attacked you."

"Deceased?"

"Yes, Ms. Williams, Aaron Banks was murdered earlier this morning. His cousin, Walter, was brought into police custody an hour or so prior and confessed to the killing. Do you have any idea on why Aaron would drive thousands of miles to murder you? Homicide detectives had been having a difficult time solving a mass murder case that's been ongoing since last August, a mass murder case that police think Aaron and Walter may have orchestrated. What was said during you and Ms. Douglas's last conversation? Did you warn her?" he asked carefully.

Sonya knew that Detective Richardson was trying to make her admit her knowledge of the murders, but she wasn't going to admit anything. She loved Trudy for aiding and abetting her out of Los Angeles, but she didn't want to involve herself in any legal proceedings surrounding Trudy's death. No one had a clue on what Sonya knew and she intended to keep it that way.

"Trudy told me she was dating a guy named Bill and dealing with her child's father at the same time. I didn't know Walter had a place in her life. Aaron and I used to date and I left him because he used to beat the shit out of me. Love would make anyone drive thousands of miles to rekindle. He drove up here and stalked me and used my sister and her fiancé to get at me. I don't know anything about any mass murder," she lied, leaving Claude out of the mix.

Detective Richardson eyed Sonya and knew she was lying, but couldn't blame her for not admitting anything. He knew many people who lost their lives for knowing too much. Like any homicide detective, he had his own bundle of cases to handle. He wasn't going to press her. From the looks of everything, Sonya already reached the outskirts of hell and made it back to talk about it. He wasn't getting anything out of solving a case from an entirely different jurisdiction.

"So you don't know anything about your ex-boyfriend and his cousin's possible involvement in that mass murder case?"

"Not at all," she answered.

"Thank you for sparing some of your time. Hope you get well, Ms. Williams," he said, rising up out of the chair.

"If you have any information pertaining to the case, please feel free to call me anytime," he said, handing her a card before walking out the room. He knew it was useless giving her that card, but he had to protect his own ass.

Sonya retreated back into her funk and wondered how she was going to get through the mental pain of Trudy's death, Aaron's attack, and Claude's imprisonment. The physical pain she was having wasn't comparable to the mental pain that was in store for her. If she would have admitted any knowledge of that mass murder last August, she would have had more mental strain to deal with. She had no regrets about lying to the detective. She didn't feel any pain for Aaron's death because her anger wouldn't allow her to shed any tears.

Epilogue

Jerry Bloomdale and George Hudson fished for hybrid, largemouth, and white bass in Fort Cobb Lake in Southwest Oklahoma. They were business associates and wanted to fish there for the lake's finest treasure since November. They had one more month until trout season was over and wanted to take full advantage of the little time they had before their work piled. They had moderate luck on their fishing trip and wasn't in any hurry to call it in.

"Maybe we can take a little more time to come out here again. I'll tell ya George, the scenery out here is simply gorgeous," Jerry said as he reached into the cooler for another Budweiser. Jerry was a late fifty, graying pudgy man with a thick salt and pepper mustache. Jerry was leaning back, holding the fishing rod, listening to the sounds of Mother Nature as George, a lanky man with curly brown hair, added more bait to his hook. They wore standard fishing gear completed with fatigue vests.

George responded. "I could vouch for that Jerry. It's good to just get away from it all and do absolutely nothing."

Jerry nodded his head. "The only thing we need to worry about up here is having enough cold ones."

"Hand me another one, will ya? Let's make a toast to our old good friend Sal, one of the best riflemen in Oklahoma."

They clicked cans.

"It's too bad George, the poor bastard had an itch to hunt for some quail and rabbit but accidentally got picked off by his partner. I know it was an accident and all, but experience prevents shit like that from happening. I'm even starting to wonder if it was an accident."

"Tell me about it," Jerry said, sipping his beer. "I've thought the same thing. That son of a bitch was in Africa sharp shooting exotic, rare animals but Sal gets in the middle of Paul's crosshairs? I just can't..."

Jerry stopped his own speech by something they noticed at the same time. A large, black object covered with weathered black bed linen floated slowly across the water. It was at least

445

five hundred yards away from them. A rope was tied at each end of the object. Jerry and George reeled in their fishing lines. Jerry started the engine of the boat and drove it in the direction of an object. They kept their eyes on it, wondering what the hell it was.

"What the hell is that?" George asked under his breath. Jerry shut the engine off and joined his friend near the edge of the boat, asking himself the same question. The men inspected the object without exchanging words. They had an idea what the object may be, but there was no telling what it was until they'd unraveled it. George extended his arm over the edge of the boat, yanking at the linen that covered the object until he pulled it all the way in. He used his knife to cut the rope. When he did, the men jumped back, taken by the sight of the gruesome, decomposing leg of a body.

"Holy Mother of Jesus!" Jerry yelped.

George cut the rest of the linen as Jerry looked on with a distorted look on his face. George spun the body around and continued to cut cloth until the head of the corpse was exposed. They didn't recognized it, but from the looks of it, he didn't put himself in the linen. He was murdered. The man's face was decaying slowly, but overall, the body was intact and moderately preserved.

The men called the police immediately. Their fishing trip ended abruptly because of their discovery of a body. The men will know the identity of the man once the medical examiner confirms that Russell Boyden died from a single gunshot wound to the back of his head. Julia would now realize that Russell's gambling addiction was deeper than she imagined.

. . .

Claude stood directly in front of Willard-Cybulski Correctional Institution waiting for Jupe to pick him up. The time went by smoothly for Claude because he did the bulk of his time with Tommy. He left a week ago, but Claude warned him to carry his burner because of the price tags they all had over their heads; moreover, the shit with Chester had to be monitored. During the year he was in prison, a few detectives came through to question Claude about Link and Domino's disappearance. They used some heavy tactics and everything from the book of detective trickery for Claude to be stupid enough to paint a picture. He didn't fall for any of that shit. He smiled during the three times they came and visited with him because he knew that the detectives didn't have a leg to stand on. If there were no weapons or bodies, then there was no case.

There had never been a day that went by that he didn't think about Sonya. He would sit on his bunk, reflecting on that awful near-death experience he and the others had when Aaron tried to keep them hostage. Visions of Aaron pistol whipping his sweetheart and harming his cousin and Fatima would destroy his mood in a fraction of a second. Thinking of that horrific day had kept him up for many nights.

When Sonya sent Claude that first kite two weeks after that dreadful event, he was ecstatic and thankful she was alright. When he read the last line in the first paragraph of the letter, it didn't surprise him that someone put Aaron to sleep, but some of the anger that he harbored gradually subsided because anyone that could do that kind of shit to a woman needed to die. Tommy told Claude when he first arrived to the cage that Darlene was completely strung out, courtesy of the late Link. Since Claude harbored anger at the time, he wrote Zane some instructions on what to do with the slut. It took some convincing, but Zane reluctantly agreed to sex Darlene. After their first and only fuck session, Zane left the cheap motel door open and split. Zane's mission was officially over when Darlene woke up a day and a half later with no clothes on. She had a strong case of amnesia. Darlene would never know that at least nine dudes ran up in her. Five of them didn't were rubbers. Zane knew exactly what she was doing when she left the hotel door unlocked. She knew the drug she placed in Darlene's drink was strong enough to knock a horse out for a few days. Zane felt guilty afterwards, but she did it in the name of Rocks. After running into Pam on a Saturday night, she told Zane that Darlene called Link and told him Claude was at the club with Rocks, which was the same night Rocks was killed. If Darlene would have never run her mouth, Rocks would still be alive.

After ten minutes of waiting, Claude sighed. He wanted to

get as far away from prison as possible. He didn't owe Connecticut any more time and he was anxious to step into the world. Mark did exactly what Claude asked him to do with the money he robbed for, so of course, money wasn't an issue. The only issue he had was that he was still waiting for Jupe to show up. He paced and cursed for fifteen more minutes. He seriously thought that Jupe got the days mixed up until he remembered that he spoke to Jupe not even two days ago. When he was about to step back into the prison to use the phone, someone driving a black Cadillac truck drove slowly in his direction. Claude couldn't make out the identity of the person that was driving the car, but he recognized the Texas license plate. The driver of the truck stopped directly in front of Claude and rolled down the tinted window.

"Don't get institutionalized on a nigga C," Mark said jokingly, wearing shades. Fatima was in the passenger seat smiling, showing all of her teeth. "When you get…"

Claude's jaw dropped. He was stunned when Sonya rushed out of the vehicle from the back and charged at him with tears dripping from her eyes with opened arms. The love birds wrote letters non-stop to one another and spoke once a week, but Claude couldn't believe Sonya was actually on Connecticut soil, participating in his release from prison. She told Claude she had a surprise for him. He figured she went out and bought a gift. He understood what her surprise was as soon as she stepped from the truck.

As soon as they touched for the first time in a year, Claude and Sonya exchanged wet, deep, and emotional kisses before they settled into a tight hug. Administration and a few guards walked by. One of the guards scrunched up his face at the sight of the newly released ex-convict hugging on a sexy ass woman, but Claude didn't give a shit.

"I still think Sonya should have waited for the nigga to get in the truck," Mark said good-naturedly.

"Baby, she missed him. Besides, we had our moment when you were gone for the week where I missed you badly," Fatima said romantically.

"Sweetheart, C was gone for a year, not a week, but damn,

she kept it tight with him," Mark said as he watched them make their way to the truck.

"Yes she did, and she yearned for this day to come. You think we should tell him that his sister didn't come because she is moving into her newly built condo that could have came out of a magazine?" Fatima asked excitedly. Little did Fatima and Sonya know, Claude bought the quadplex for all of them to occupy, his mother included when she was released. It was one of the few tasks that Claude asked Mark to do while he was away. Sonya still lived with Mark and Fatima, and all three of them desperately wanted to get out of the spot Aaron invaded last year. While Mark participated in Sonya and Fatima's misery of living in that apartment, Mark worked expeditiously around the clock so he could invest Claude's money the way he wanted it invested.

Besides the quadplex, Claude was going to be surprised when he finds out the medium-sized building he and Mark looked at last year was now one of the hottest barbershops in Dallas. Mark had to feed Claude the same "Its coming along" story for a year just to see the look on Claude's face after he found out that his investment, including Mark's share of the barbershop, was turning into a goldmine.

Mark and Fatima waited for them to have the moment that they both been longing for before stepping out of the truck to greet Claude for the first time in a year. When they finally broke their embrace, Claude gave Mark a brotherly hug. Fatima embraced Claude as well, especially after he risked his life so they could live to tell about it.

"You thought Jupe was gonna pick you up, huh?"

"You got me Mark because I didn't expect it. I thought he was gonna scoop me from this shit hole, but I guess Jupe had a hand in the scheme," Claude laughed. "Let's get the fuck up out of here though. I don't want to spend a minute longer up here."

"So we off to Dallas?" Claude asked. "And I know it took y'all a few days to get up here. So I'm stuck with y'all in this truck for another two?" Sonya playfully elbowed Claude at his side.

"Yeah you fucking gazelle face ass nigga," Mark joked,

throwing Claude two stacks of hundreds from the front seat. "We out again after that."

"We out again? Why, where we going?"

Everyone smiled in unison except Claude.

"Las Vegas." Claude buried his head in his hands and smiled with excitement.

After pulling away from the state correctional facility, Sonya held Claude as if he was going to intentionally jump out the vehicle while it was in motion.

"Baby, I love you," Sonya said quietly, pecking Claude softly on the lips.

"Love you too sweetheart. Good looking for doing my bid with me, for real," Claude said sincerely.

"C, you don't have to thank me for that. I wanted to wait for you. I wanted you since I first laid eyes on you. Now that I have you back, I'm going to love and cherish the ground you walk on, and that's real," Sonya said before burying her head in his chest to dry her tear ridden face. Claude cried and held Sonya tight. He did so much dirt in his life that he never believed that he deserved a woman like her. Mark quickly glanced in the rearview mirror and smiled because he had never seen Claude cry from a big spell of happiness.

"Let's get this party started dammit," Mark said loudly as Mark took a right onto the highway.

They were all a long way from Dallas, but in the meantime, the foursome will endure a lot of fun during their road trip. It was exactly what Claude needed; a chance to breathe.

. . .

J-Rock was living the life of a don. His beach house was fully insured, situated on ninety six cubic feet of white sand in Cancun, Mexico. In 2005, Hurricane Wilma came through and fucked up the place, but it didn't stop J-Rock from starting a new life a year after he ran from Connecticut. He would recall his last night in CT when he called Claude out, but the news of Link and Domino's sudden disappearance made his anger for Claude subside because he knew he was responsible for their disappearing act. He figured that was the reason why Claude didn't provide him with any information and took a brash way out when he asked about his peoples running their mouths. Claude was only protecting himself. Even if that wasn't the case, he was a long way from Bridgeport and he had money.

J-Rock relaxed in his beach long chair, taking in some sun with his two thousand dollar shades. He was lounging hard in his silk boxers. The consistent paradise-like weather had kept him from wearing clothes around the house, especially Melinda, an exotic dime he met last week at one of the clubs out there on the Gulf of Mexico.

If J-Rock wasn't in the midst of passing out from comfort, he would have barked at Melinda from being late with his drink. While his eyes were still closed, he heard his drink touch the table. A few moments later, a sensual touch to his shoulders took him out of his light snooze. J-Rock sat up and took a sip of his drink.

"I see you made my drink just the way I like it, huh? Daddy going to treat you good later on. Hit you wit' the drunk dick, just the way you like it," J-Rock said with his eyes still closed.

The sensual touch he received turned into a hard, painful rub. He didn't say anything at first, but when more pressure was applied, he lost it.

"Damn bitch, ease up off me with that aggressive shit. Fuckin' shit hurt like hell…"

The moment J-Rock opened his eyes, Bam stood over him looking evil as ever with a smirk on his face.

"Y'all niggas came away with all that cheddar and you couldn't hire yourself a bodyguard? Motherfuckers wanna just party and bullshit," Bam said nonchalantly before slicing J-Rocks throat.

Bam walked coolly through the living room. The moment he opened the front door, as expected, Melinda walked up on his rear.

"I don't work for free you know," she said with a heavy Latin accent.

"I know," Bam said.

Melinda's hands were shaking with greed and excitement

as she anticipated Bam pulling out a stack of the cold, hard cash. Instead, he pulled out a .38 with a silencer attached to it. Bam smiled and pulled the trigger. It looked like Melinda looked at the bullet as it made its entrance to the middle of her forehead before dropping to the floor. Bam tucked the gun away and went about his business. He walked out the front door and onto the beach as if nothing had happened. He blended in with all the pedestrians on the beach before walking into the comfort zone of Calvin's limo.

"It's done, including that beautiful pawn. It's too bad," Bam said.

Calvin lit up a Cuban Link and blew a smoke circle.

"Good, good, two down, four to go," Calvin said dryly, ignoring Bam's subtle complaint about killing the girl. The woman didn't mean shit to Calvin and could care less, but he needed to set something straight with Bam.

"You complaining?" Calvin asked, looking straight into Bam's beady eyes. Bam lowered his head and realized he had a lot to prove to Calvin. He was lucky to be alive after bringing in a crooked motherfucker that costed him a few million.

"No sir, not at all," Bam said humbly.

"That's what I figured," Calvin said, emphasizing his point.

Calvin instructed his driver to make moves to the open land where the pilot was waiting near Calvin's private plane. While the vehicle was in motion, he reached over in the seat and retrieved the manila envelope that contained the photos of the cats that invaded his home. Bam poured Calvin and himself a drink. Calvin took a sip of the gin and sighed as he gazed at the intake photo of Claude. He cracked a smile knowing that he was looking at a dead man. As for the others, they would get theirs too, even if it would take him years to do it.

When he saw Zane's intake photo, an idea flashed in his head like a light bulb. He slid the intake photos back into the manila envelope, along with Tommy and Tank's photos, and took another sip and started laughing at the terror he created in his own mind once he got a hold of those responsible for putting his family in danger.

96446350R00248

Made in the USA
Columbia, SC
28 May 2018